T0196801

DEMON'S MERCY

Also by Rebecca Zanetti

The Dark Protector series
Fated
Claimed
Tempted
Hunted
Consumed
Provoked
Twisted
Shadowed
Tamed
Marked
Talen
Vampire's Faith

The Realm Enforcers series
Wicked Ride
Wicked Edge
Wicked Burn
Wicked Kiss
Wicked Bite

The Scorpius Syndrome series
Mercury Striking
Shadow Falling
Justice Ascending

The Deep Ops series
Hidden
Fallen

DEMON'S MERCY

Rebecca Zanetti

LYRICAL PRESS
Kensington Publishing Corp.
www.kensingtonbooks.com

To the extent that the image or images on the cover of this book depict a person or persons, such person or persons are merely models, and are not intended to portray any character or characters featured in the book.

LYRICAL PRESS BOOKS are published by

Kensington Publishing Corp.
119 West 40th Street
New York, NY 10018

Copyright © 2019 by Rebecca Zanetti

All rights reserved. No part of this book may be reproduced in any form or by any means without the prior written consent of the Publisher, excepting brief quotes used in reviews.

All Kensington titles, imprints, and distributed lines are available at special quantity discounts for bulk purchases for sales promotion, premiums, fundraising, educational, or institutional use.

Special book excerpts or customized printings can also be created to fit specific needs. For details, write or phone the office of the Kensington Sales Manager: Kensington Publishing Corp., 119 West 40th Street, New York, NY 10018. Attn. Sales Department. Phone: 1-800-221-2647.

Lyrical Press and Lyrical Press logo Reg. U.S. Pat. & TM Off.

First Electronic Edition: January 2019
eISBN-13: 978-1-5161-0746-9
eISBN-10: 1-5161-0746-2

First Print Edition: January 2019
ISBN-13: 978-1-5161-0750-6
ISBN-10: 1-5161-0750-0

Printed in the United States of America

This one's for Minga, who works so hard and is such a wonderful friend. She's also Talen's favorite.

Acknowledgments

I'm so thrilled to be writing more Dark Protector books! I have many people to thank for getting this book to readers, and I sincerely apologize to anyone I've forgotten.

Thank you to Big Tone, Gabe, and Karlina: for their love, support, understanding, and willingness to bring me Panera on demand when I'm under a deadline.

Thank you to my hardworking editor, Alicia Condon, as well as the amazing group at Kensington Publishing: Alexandra Nicolajsen, Steven Zacharius, Adam Zacharius, Lynn Cully, Vida Engstrand, Jane Nutter, Lauren Jernigan, Kimberly Richardson, Arthur Maisel, Ross Plotkin, Sharon Mulvihill and Rebecca Cremonese.

Thank you to my wonderful agent, Caitlin Blasdell, and to Liza Dawson and the entire Liza Dawson Agency.

Thank you to Jillian Stein for the absolutely fantastic work and for being such an amazing friend.

Thanks to my fantastic street team, Rebecca's Rebels, and to their creative and hardworking leader, Minga Portillo.

Thanks to my author gal-pals who get that living the dream often means old coffee, all-nighters, and a victory lap when the right verb is found: Joanna Wylde, Lexi Blake, Asa Maria Bradley, Kristen Ashley, Boone Brux, and Augustina Van Hoven.

Thanks also to my constant support system: Gail and Jim English, Debbie and Travis Smith, Stephanie and Don West,

Jessica and Jonah Namson, Kathy and Herb Zanetti, and Liz and Steve Berry.

Finally, thank you to the readers who have kept the Dark Protectors alive all these years. It's because of you that we decided to return to the world of the Realm.

Chapter 1

Logan Kyllwood had never gone for the career type with the business skirt, buttoned shirt, and upswept hair. But this woman... she rocked it. Head to toe, high heels to hair clip, she owned the pencil skirt look.

He relaxed on his tall stool in the sports bar, behind a dented table, and watched her stride around other tables toward a booth in the back. Almost on an automatic swivel, men turned from chips, potato skins, and loud discussions about the Hearts and Hibernian football teams to watch her move. And hell, could she move. Tight ass swaying in the skirt, toned legs moving with the grace of a dancer. She was petite enough to be considered fragile...also not his type.

Her features were narrow to the point of being elfin, her lips full and lush, and her skin pale and smooth in contrast with her dark red hair. She wasn't so much beautiful as intriguing. Very.

She reached the booth where two of her friends sat drinking what looked like margaritas, stiffened, and did an about-face, turning to look directly at him.

Everything in him fell silent.

She stared at him for two seconds before gliding back into motion—*toward* him. Then, keeping his gaze, she drifted past tables to reach his.

A guy with narrow glasses and a designer flannel shirt grasped her arm from a tall table, halting her progress. Her eyes widened.

Logan straightened, his blood sparked, and he set his glass down with a loud thump.

The guy turned, his lip twisting. The second his gaze met Logan's, he released the woman. Immediately and based on what were probably pretty decent instincts.

Logan settled back down and grasped his chilled mug again, his concentration returning to the woman.

She glanced at the man turning quickly away from her, and a small smile played on her enticing mouth. Then she visibly gathered herself, lowered her chin, and continued uninterrupted toward Logan.

The second she arrived, he kicked out the stool across from him in a silent invitation, unable to look away from her. This close, her eyes were the dark green of a Scottish moor. The kind surrounded by enduring moss and ancient stones. He wasn't sure if he was impressed or surprised when she slid onto the stool. Maybe both.

"What do you want?" she asked, her voice intriguingly smooth and sultry for her petite frame.

Her scent washed over him, wild and free gardenias, heated in its intensity. In its effect on him. He sure as shit couldn't answer her question honestly because his entire system had just gone into overdrive. *If all else fails, deflect.* "Excuse me?" His hoarse voice hinted at his demon heritage, but she wouldn't know that.

She met his gaze levelly, unusual for a human. "You've been watching me the whole hour I've been here with my friends. And even though you tried to hide behind a pillar, I saw you at the coffee shop earlier this morning. Also watching me."

He hadn't been hiding. "You don't believe in coincidences?" he asked.

She rolled those stunning eyes. "No. Never have. I do, however, believe in stalkers and creeps."

A light and mellow energy cascaded from her, not nearly as strongly as he'd expected. Her enhancement—the ability that made her one of the three female Keys his people needed to find—was surprisingly subdued. He gave her his most charming smile. "Which am I? Stalker or creep?"

She craned her neck to the side, and her gaze ran from his head down his torso to his boots...and all the way back up.

His chest heated and his groin tightened. The woman had guts. Not many people, especially humans, faced him so fearlessly. Their instincts warned them away.

Did this woman not have instincts?

"Well?" he prompted. "Stalker or creep?"

"I really couldn't say." Her narrow nostrils flared. "If I had to guess...it'd be lost soul."

Wasn't that sweet? And disarmingly damn correct. His soul had been lost years ago.

She leaned in. "Are demons chasing you?"

The entire room disappeared around them, and his focus narrowed only to her. Adrenaline poured through his veins and his muscles clenched. "Excuse me?" he said for the second time.

She sighed, looking both put out and impatient. "You heard me." Those finely arched brows drew down.

He swallowed. Wait a minute. She'd meant the question figuratively. The woman was just flirting with him. It had been so long since he'd flirted with a female, he'd forgotten how. "Demons are always chasing me, sweetheart." His answer was more truth than banter, but she wouldn't know that. He smiled. "You gonna save me?"

"Sometimes it's too late to save a soul," she mused, as if talking to herself.

How much tequila had she enjoyed? He cocked his head to the side and studied her. What exactly was her enhancement? Sometimes humans surprised him. "Do you, ah, save souls?"

She grinned then, and it was like the sun appeared when he hadn't realized he was sitting lost and alone in the dark. "Sounds like an admirable calling, but no. Sorry," she said, folding her hands on the table. Her nails were long and unpainted. Strong with natural white tips.

He motioned for the blond waitress, and she hurried toward him, large breasts barely restrained by her tight shirt. "You want something?" she breathed.

He focused on the pixie. "Margarita?"

The woman nodded, her gaze remaining on his face. "Blended with salt."

The waitress pouted but turned and swayed back to the bar.

"Logan." He held out his hand.

"Mercy O'Malley." She slid her small palm against his, and the shock of her touch almost made him growl. Electricity and enough heat to burn a forest. "Nice to meet you." Her face registered no emotion.

Had she not just felt that jolt? That beyond-strange connection? He was never thrown off-balance, and he sure as shit didn't like it.

He reclaimed his hand. The dossier he had on her was way too light, but he'd already known her name. He'd spent the day debating whether to cajole her from safety or just kidnap her. For some reason, he didn't want to frighten somebody so delicate. "I did see you at the coffee shop, and I was definitely watching you tonight. But it's a coincidence to find you at both places." He tried to look harmless.

Both of her eyebrows now rose.

Harmless had never been his default setting. If she had half a brain, and it appeared that she did, she wouldn't fall for his bullshit. He tried again. "Okay. I may have noticed the Paddy's Bar logo on your coffee cup this morning."

She frowned and then relief filtered across her sharp features. "Of course. I won the travel mug here last week during a trivia game."

"I figured there'd be a chance to run into you here tonight and introduce myself. I haven't been following you all day," he said gently, lying his ass off.

"Oh, good." She chuckled and leaned toward him just a little. "I wasn't sure what to do if you had."

Not approaching him would've been the smart move, but why tell her that? She was obviously innocent and trusting, which unfortunately suited his purposes just fine. But he wouldn't let her get hurt. Ever. He felt attention and turned to see her two female friends looking their way. "You might want to let your friends know you're okay," he murmured.

"Oh." She started and then turned, giving them a wave.

They nodded and settled back down to their drinks. At least she had a small amount of protection by having friends around. Not enough, though.

The waitress delivered the lime-green margarita and waited, sparkling eyes focused on Logan. "Can I get you anything else? Anything?"

A very quiet snort came from the woman across from Logan. He bit back a grin. "We're good. Thanks." The waitress moved away.

Mercy took a sip of her drink. "For a stalker, you're cute."

Nobody had ever called him cute. Not once in his life. He'd been oversized from day one, and he'd learned to fight and kill shortly thereafter. "Tell me about yourself, Mercy O'Malley." Even her name was adorable. It was too bad he had to kidnap her. He took a drink of his beer.

She shrugged narrow shoulders. "Not much to tell. I'm the VP of Acquisitions for a private family trust. Pays the bills."

Smart and humble. The woman was checking more boxes than he'd realized he had. "What do you do for fun?" He tried to keep his voice light, but it was getting late, and he had a job to do.

"This." She swept her hand out to the still-boisterous patrons around the bar.

Her friends finished their drinks and stood, gesturing her toward the door. One female was a tall blonde and the other a shorter brunette, both wobbling a little.

Ah, shit. Now what?

Then she shook her head and motioned that she'd call them later. "We all live close, so they can walk home," she said, focusing back on him. The friends left as if nothing was amiss.

Okay. Way too trusting and innocent. He couldn't help but shake his head. While he didn't have sisters, he had a mom, sisters-in-law, and a niece he'd die for. He'd already killed for them—more than once. "You probably shouldn't remain by yourself in a bar with a guy you just met." Yeah, he should just keep his damn mouth shut.

Her eyes lit up. "Aren't you sweet? Don't worry. I can take care of myself." Her amusement filtered through the air between them.

Sometimes humans were so clueless, having no idea that predators walked right beside them. If he told her he was a vampire-demon hybrid, what would she do? Probably laugh it off and keep flirting with him. He sighed. "All right. Took a couple of self-defense classes, did you?"

She chuckled. "Not really. But I have excellent instincts about people."

That statement was so sad it pissed him off. He took a couple of drinks to cool his suddenly heated throat. The woman was about to learn different, so maybe this was a good thing. He'd keep her safe and also teach her not to be so careless. Why her trusting nature ticked him off, he'd figure out later. "It's a nice night. How about a walk outside?"

Her teeth played with her bottom lip for a moment.

His groin tightened again. Hard and fast. This effect she had on him was annoying. He finished his beer and pushed away from the table. Either she'd come with him, or he'd acquire her later that night from her apartment. "You coming?"

"Yes." She stood and faltered slightly. For the first time, doubt filtered across her expression. "But just for a walk."

His heart thumped and warmed. "I'm not going to let anything hurt you, Mercy." Truer words had never been spoken. Oh, she might hate him within hours, but she'd be safe.

She smiled, her face taking on a serene beauty. "That sounds like the truth." Walking around the table, she slid her soft hand into his.

His lungs seized, and he led her through tables to the door. Once outside, he finally took a deep breath of fresh spring air. Night had fallen, and the stars above Edinburgh sparkled high and bright in the darkened sky.

They fell into step easily, and he shortened his stride to accommodate her smaller stature. Her head barely reached his shoulder. He naturally switched their places to keep his body between traffic and her, taking her other hand instinctively. He might be a killer, but his mama had taught him manners. And it was easier to contain Mercy when she couldn't run across the street.

"You didn't tell me what you do, Logan," Mercy murmured, eyeing closed storefronts as they passed.

"Well, at the moment, I'm in acquisitions as well," he said, having no doubt she wouldn't appreciate his humor.

A woman's muffled scream shot his body into sharp awareness.

The blonde friend ran out of the nearest alley, one of her shoes gone. "Help," she cried, panic streaking across her face.

Logan reached her quickly and put Mercy behind him as they halted.

The blonde pointed into the alley. "He has Trina. Grabbed us both."

"Stay here." Logan released Mercy and shot into the darkened alley toward a black SUV.

Within a second, pain lanced into his neck, and electricity ripped through his body so rapidly he dropped to his knees. Water from a mud puddle washed up. What the hell? Another jolt, and his vision grayed. Stun-gunned? Not a normal jolt, either. This was meant either for vampires or, hell, a brontosaurus. He tried to turn, but a third jolt beneath his left ear bashed through his entire head. He swayed. Mercy. Where was she? He opened his mouth to yell for her to run, but only a croak emerged.

"Get him in the SUV." The blonde suddenly appeared and shot an arm beneath his shoulder.

Then Mercy was in front of him. "Hurry. He should be completely out, but his eyes are still open." Her voice was crisp, but those pretty eyes looked worried.

"M-Mercy?" he asked, his brain feeling like Jell-O.

She winced. "Sorry about this, sport." The brunette emerged from the side of a dumpster, a black box in her hand. Between the three of them, they managed to drag him to the rear of the SUV and shove him inside, where he landed on his back with a hard thump.

"He weighs a ton," the blonde muttered, disappearing around the side.

Mercy jumped in beside him and quickly shackled his wrists and ankles with iron. The good kind. The door slammed shut, and then the vehicle peeled out of the alley.

Anger finally spurted through the shock and pain of the electrical attack. Who the fuck were these females? More importantly, what were they? Witches? He growled.

Mercy's eyes widened and then she grimaced, sitting on the newish carpet and leaning against the side of the SUV. "I'm really sorry about this, Logan."

Sorry? Oh, the woman didn't understand the meaning of the word. Yet.

The brunette leaned over the back seat. "You can't kill him here. We'll have to take him to the warehouse."

Logan kept his focus on Mercy's angled face as the feeling started to return to his limbs. Kill?

Mercy sighed. "I know. That's where I left the sword, anyway. A demon has to be decapitated." She leaned in, her wild scent filling his head. "I truly am sorry about this, Logan Kyllwood. I wish I didn't have to kill you."

Chapter 2

"He doesn't look like a demon," Trina said, brushing her frizzing hair away from her face as she slowly backed away from the unconscious male chained to the steel-reinforced wall inside the warehouse. They'd had to zap him three more times in the vehicle, until finally he'd passed out. Then they'd had to just dump him out of the SUV, onto the cement, and roll him to the restraints. He really was heavy—and all muscle.

Mercy swallowed. Purebred demons were blond with black eyes, but Logan had dark hair and green eyes. "He's part vampire. Maybe that's the dominant force in his genes." Though his voice had been full demon. His family ran the demon nation, so she'd think of him as such. She forced away a shiver.

A gentle rain started pattering down and sprayed inside the open garage-style door. More water dripped somewhere in the recesses of the huge space. Mercy eyed the ancient sword leaning against the wall, several feet down from the demon.

Sandy shut the back of the SUV and read a text from her phone. "We're needed on the south side, Trina." She looked up, her dark eyes worried. "This is a terrible plan, Mercy." She frowned and studied the unconscious male. "He won't believe you're going to kill him. It'd take two of us to get a blade through that thick neck."

Logan's deep green eyes opened, already clear and focused.

Mercy's breath caught, and she took an unwilling step back. She was a heck of a poker player, and she could bluff with the best of them. "I've got this," she whispered, her voice shaking just a little.

Trina came to her side, staring at the male. She slipped the tricked-out stun gun into Mercy's hand. "We are in so much trouble," she said quietly.

Mercy nodded. "I know."

Sandy grabbed her arm. "The king doesn't make idle threats. Get this done and get home. No more mistakes, Mercy."

Icy fingers clutched Mercy's heart and squeezed. Damn anxiety. "I know." How she was going to succeed here without getting caught was beyond her at the moment. But she had to do it. "Get out of here. I'll be in contact."

Logan hadn't said a word. He casually tested one wrist restraint and then the other, not seeming concerned that the cuffs were shackled by chains to a wall. And his gaze hadn't left hers. Not even for a second.

Warning ticked through her. The kind a smart person would heed. A lump settled in her throat.

Trina and Sandy jumped into the SUV and sped out of the warehouse, hitting a button and shutting the garage door as they passed.

Quiet descended except for the drip, drip, drip in the distance.

Logan finally released her gaze, turned and studied the sword, then focused back on her. "Who the fuck are you?"

Whoa. So, he'd been masking the full hoarseness of his demon voice. Logan's tone, set free now, shot past rumbly to rough. Seriously rough. And way too sexy for any male.

Mercy sighed. "Mercy O'Malley. I already told you that." Yeah, she was stalling. She wouldn't let herself look away, though. The male had black hair to his shoulders, thick and wavy. Scruff covered what could only be described as a rock-hard jaw that matched his fierce features perfectly. His shoulders were broad, his chest muscled, and his body incredibly tight. Logan Kyllwood was a warrior among warriors, and she didn't stand a chance in hell of fighting him should he get free.

Good thing she'd used real iron cuffs.

His gaze raked her, leaving sensitivity and an odd tingling in its wake. "You're more than human."

"Aye," she said softly. There were several immortal species.

His gaze narrowed. "Not a shifter."

"No."

"Or demon," he mused, remaining so still it was kind of eerie. She shook her head.

"You're a fucking witch." He knocked his head back on the reinforced steel wall. "Another witch. Damn witches."

Her chest hitched and she straightened to her full, rather unimpressive, height. "I most certainly am not a witch." Did she look like a witch? Hell, no. Witches played with elements and threw fire. That's all. For Pete's sake. She was much more powerful than that. "A witch," she muttered, kicking off the way too high heels that had been killing her all day. Who wore those things, anyway?

His frown slashed down dark eyebrows. "What's left?"

How insulting. Seriously. Maybe he was a moron, and she'd given him too much credit earlier. "I'm Fae."

He blinked. Once, twice. Horror crossed his hard expression. "You're a *fairy*?"

Well. Her nostrils flared. "We prefer Fae. Have you ever even met one of us?"

"No." He studied her as he would a newly discovered creature. "But fairies are all…"

"Crazy," she finished for him, rolling her eyes. "So we've heard. Time and time again." Such a stupid rumor. "Let's see. What other rumors are out there? I know. Vampires are pale and need human blood to survive. They turn humans into vamps on a whim. Oh, and the sun kills them." None of that was true. Vampires loved the sun and were their own species. There was no turning of anybody. When a human mated a vampire, she remained human…but did gain immortality through a chromosomal change.

"Point made," Logan said. "But still."

"Still what? Demons? Oh yeah. They're hell beasts." She snorted. Maybe that was rather true. "We are not crazy." No more than any other species, anyway.

"Right," he muttered.

It was true that her people hadn't exactly been visible enough to counter the rumor—which was exactly how they liked it. Now, because of him and his people, she had no choice but to be visible again. For a time. "You have no idea what you're doing," she muttered, scrunching her toes over the rough concrete. Those stupid shoes had left red marks across the top of her feet.

"What I'm doing?" His chin lowered, giving him a predatory look even though he was sitting and shackled. "Oh, baby. You don't know what you've *done*."

The saliva in her mouth dried up. Completely. Her knees weakened, so she forced a hard expression onto her face. Hopefully. "You haven't left us much choice."

Dark amusement filled his ancient eyes. "So I heard. You picking up that sword anytime soon?"

Her mouth tightened. Shouldn't he look at least a little bit scared? "Don't let my size fool you, demon," she said.

"It's your eyes that got me," he rumbled. "Green and soft and sweet. Your power is there." He shifted his weight very casually.

Her power was in her brain, and she knew it. "These are contacts. Don't get used to them."

Interest sizzled across his chiseled features. "What color are your eyes?"

One of them was the actual green he'd seemed to like. "None of your business. By the way, we dropped your wallet and phone back in the alley, so you can stop looking for them." There wouldn't be any way to trace him to the warehouse. She narrowed her gaze. "My research on you shows you can't teleport. I figure that's true, since you haven't given it a try." Many demons, not all, had the ability to teleport through dimensions to a different place on Earth.

"Not yet," he said calmly. "I'm not even thirty yet, so there are centuries to develop the talent."

Odd. Sure, all immortals appeared to be around his age, regardless of their time on Earth. They looked centuries younger than their real years, but this male? He looked older. Early thirties with that tough, *I've seen shit* expression that wasn't an expression. It also gave him the *Don't worry, baby, I can protect you from all evil if I want* sexy look that some males just seemed to have. The wounded ones who also looked like they could kiss. For hours.

She cleared her throat. "I need some information from you before we continue."

"Sure," he murmured. "Name is Logan Kyllwood, and I've been sent to retrieve you since you're one of the three Keys. A fact you obviously know."

She rolled her eyes. "The only reason you know I'm a Key is because we put the information out there to draw you in."

"No shit," he drawled. "Even so, you have a gift, and you need to be protected."

Gift? "It's a curse, demon," she snapped. "And you're in no position to protect anybody." She knew the three female Keys were needed so their blood could be used in some stupid, ancient ritual that would do nothing but cause more problems for everybody.

One of his dark eyebrows rose. "Curse? How can you say that? You have the ability to rid the world of true evil with one little ritual."

Ha. That's what he thought. Idiot vampire-demon hybrids. Why didn't he look a little more worried? The guy obviously wasn't taking her seriously. "That ritual won't even dent the evil in this world," she said. "Regardless, it isn't going to happen."

"Sure, it is." Logan tilted his head. "Why are the fairies declaring war on the demon nation?"

She blinked. "We're not. You're not here because of the demons. You're here because of the Seven. Right now, your friends are only six strong, and we have to keep it that way until we take out a few more." The Seven were a group of hybrids who thought they were tasked with protecting the earth from the most evil of Kurjans, the one currently confined in a prison dimension. But they were wrong. They'd messed with physics in a way that was catastrophic, and they had to be stopped. "You can't be allowed to take part in your ritual and become one of the Seven." The Seven couldn't reach full force. It would be the complete package to doom.

"Mercy," he said, almost gently. "Even if I disappear, somebody else will step up and take my place."

They truly didn't understand, did they? Nobody should mess with the laws of the universe without freaking understanding them. Was it because they were hybrids or males that they were so arrogant? Probably both. "Not exactly true, demon." She shook her head. "There's a reason only ten percent of the males who've undergone your ritual survived. Only certain bloodlines can even attempt it."

He exhaled slowly. "Yeah. I figured." He looked way too casual just leaning against the wall, iron bands around his wrists. "What's the fairy nation's problem with the Seven?"

That would take much too long to explain to him. "Let's just say you've screwed things up for us, and now you have to disappear."

His lips twitched. "I've faced more than my share of killers, Mercy O'Malley. You're not one."

Oh yeah? She moved for the sword and lifted it. It was solid and pure, and the balance was perfect. She hadn't spent much time learning sword fighting, and cutting through a guy's throat would be difficult, especially for a novice. The blade was razor-sharp. She moved toward him and pressed the tip to his throat. "I'm stronger than I look."

He met her gaze evenly, his lids half lowered. "You think you have time to slide it in before I stop you?" The innuendo in his words wound between them, and she clenched. A trickle of blood dripped down his skin.

Her stomach dropped. Could she? The male didn't even look worried. More like slightly interested and possibly sleepy. "Yes," she bluffed. With the stun gun in one hand and the sword in the other, she should feel a lot more in control of the situation than she did. "Why aren't you attacking my mind?" Demons could mentally slash through brains like a crop reaper if they wanted.

He lifted one massive shoulder. "Meh."

"Meh?" she snapped. Seriously? The insult was just too much. Pressing the button on the stun gun, she let the charges attach to his chest with a powerful jolt. The smell of burned cotton filtered up.

His eyes darkened, flashing black and returning to that intriguing green. "Ouch," he said, his voice mild.

She took a step back, her hand trembling. "Your body has already figured out how to counteract the charge."

"Yep."

Okay. That was fast. Much quicker than her scientists had said it would happen. This was no ordinary demon, a fact she'd already figured out. "I don't want to kill you." She let the tip of the sword drop to the pavement.

"Yeah. I got that." The small nick on his neck healed and closed. "Am I your first job as an assassin?"

"I'm not exactly an assassin. We were just trying to get your attention with the threat."

"Oh, baby. You definitely have my attention."

She shivered from the rough tone and then started to calculate scenarios in her mind. "In fact, I'm going to get in some serious trouble for warning you to stop this nonsense with the Seven. My people don't want to work with you, and they're more powerful than you can believe. I don't suppose you'd lie low for the next couple of decades until I can figure this out?"

"I don't suppose I would," he said, too agreeably.

"Well." She bit her bottom lip. Why wasn't he buying her bluff? "If I let you live, my people won't stop coming for you. Ever."

His expression lost the lazy amusement. "Let them come, Mercy. Unlike you, I have no problem killing."

She shuddered before she could stop herself. "You're really not giving me a choice here."

His eyebrows rose. "You're going to try to kill me?"

"No," she sighed. "You're right about that. I don't want to kill anybody." She tossed the sword and stun gun across the cement and they clattered away. "There's only one logical conclusion, and it's risky, but you've left me no alternative." Moving toward him, she walked alongside his extended legs then dropped to straddle him, pressing her hands to the burn marks on his shirt. She couldn't afford the loss of energy this would cost her, but there was no choice.

His smile was more wolf than demon. "I like where this is going."

She rolled her eyes and tried to look calm, even though his thighs were warm and so damn hard. The guy had sleek, strong muscles everywhere. "Have you ever teleported? With somebody who could?"

Interest crossed his expression. "Can you teleport?"

"Yes." She closed her eyes and drew on the forces of time and space, the power in the universe. She'd take him somewhere he couldn't escape. Power trilled through her, and she concentrated. Something detonated in her solar plexus, and the power sputtered out and dissipated. She gasped and opened her eyes, still in the damn warehouse.

Green eyes drilled into hers. "You've got some gifts there."

Her mouth gaped open. She snapped it shut and lowered her chin. "How did you just stop me?" It was impossible.

He shrugged, nearly dislodging her. "I may not be able to teleport yet, but I can sure as shit stop anybody from teleporting me."

Huh. She hadn't realized demons could do that. Must be a state secret or something.

"Where did you think you were taking me?" he asked, his thighs tightening just enough to give warning.

"Somewhere you've never been," she said, not willing to reveal any more information than she already had.

"Hmm. Maybe next time." In a move that was as graceful as it was powerful, he threw both arms out and snapped the chains holding him to the wall.

Oh, God. She bunched to jump off him and he manacled her arms, the cuffs still around his wrists. He tugged her farther up his thighs until they sat groin to groin, his face only an inch from hers. Heat cascaded off him like a volcano.

She froze. Completely. Like a deer reaching a ravine. The power dynamic had shifted so quickly, she hadn't even had time to breathe. Control. She had to keep control somehow. "I don't want to hurt you, Logan," she breathed.

His chin lifted, and his lips twitched. "That's too bad, because I do want to hurt you right now."

Before she could so as much as struggle, the garage door exploded open, wood flying in every direction.

She screamed.

Chapter 3

The force of the blast knocked Logan's head back against the metal siding. Stars exploded behind his eyes. Even so, he rolled to the left and leapt to his feet before his brain could catalogue the threat, ripping the iron cuffs off his wrists and dropping them to the ground.

Burning slats of wood littered the cement. Haze, hot and filled with particles, obstructed his view of the dark night outside.

A force of four soldiers burst through the fog, dressed from head to toe in black, boots to face masks.

He sent out a piercing brain attack at the nearest threat while jumping close to where Mercy's sword had landed. The soldier shrieked and dropped to his knees. Kicking the handle up, Logan caught the sword and started swinging, slicing the second-closest attacker across the chest.

The guy's tac-vest didn't even rip.

Tossing the sword to his other hand, Logan went for the guy's upper arm, shoving hard. When he felt bone, he yanked the blade out.

The soldier continued on, reaching for a gun at his waist with his good hand.

The other two fanned out.

Mercy. Were they with her or looking for her?

His answer came sharply with a high kick out of the blue. She nailed a soldier beneath the chin, and he stumbled back several feet. Logan concentrated on the attackers.

The guy on the floor finally passed out. Two bullets pierced Logan's upper arm, and he stumbled back. Growling, he lowered his chin and ripped into the mind of the guy shooting him.

The nerve centers in the brain broadcasted horrific pain that felt just as real as a hot blade. The guy grabbed his ears and bent forward, fighting it hard.

"Get her," yelled the soldier Mercy had kicked.

Get her? They wanted Mercy? "Here I thought I was the prize," Logan muttered, pivoting and going for the legs, his sword flashing too fast to see. He caught the guy in the thigh.

"You are," the soldier countered, his voice muffled by the mask. "But our orders are to bring her back to the king, regardless of cost." He continued to fight, despite the damage to his thigh. They must've had some sort of protective clothing on. Impressive.

Mercy battled hand to hand with the fourth soldier, who had about a hundred pounds and at least eight inches on her. He methodically countered her moves, but she shot a surprisingly fast kick to his groin and knocked him back a step. The guy bent over with a pained yelp, his arm coming up to protect his face.

Logan concentrated harder on the brain attack. He needed that guy out cold. "Mercy," he bellowed. "Teleport the hell out of here." Even though he didn't have the skill, she could go anywhere, if she'd been telling the truth.

"They'll kill you," she gasped, blocking a punch that knocked her back about a yard.

She was staying to fight with him? Who the hell was this damn fairy? He threw a hard punch and nailed the soldier across from him right beneath the chin.

The guy growled and kicked the sword out of Logan's hand, and it clattered across the concrete into the haze.

Who were these people? Logan couldn't get a read on them. Not demons or vampires. More Fae? If so, why were they after

Mercy? She was holding her own, but the soldier was advancing on her. "Get out of here," Logan snapped.

"No," she snapped back.

Logan led with his good arm, punching rapidly into the soldier's face. The mask took too much of the impact.

Who commanded these soldiers? Their gear was better than the demon nation's.

The guy caught Logan with an uppercut, and his teeth slammed together. Damn it. The mind attack lessened, and the soldier on the floor began to get up. There was no choice. Logan lowered his head and sent out a blast hard enough to drop the guy cold to the pavement.

Pain blared through Logan's head from the strong attack. Blood dripped out of his nose. He couldn't strike that ferociously without repercussions. The vision in his left eye fuzzed. Now he was mentally spent—for at least an hour. Maybe more.

His ears rang, and his spine felt swollen.

Mercy cried out behind him.

Anger caught him, and he shoved emotion and sensation away. His role, one he was more than familiar with, settled him into place. Defend and kill. There was nothing else.

He jumped forward and clasped the soldier beneath the chin, manacling his hand around the guy's neck. Growling, he lifted up with all his strength and crashed the bastard to the ground—head first.

The mask took too much of the impact, and the guy struck upward, hard and fast.

Pain exploded in Logan's jaw and neck.

He altered his approach, methodically hitting and ducking until he felt the soldier's cheekbone finally give beneath the mask. Seven more punches in rapid succession, and the man passed out.

"No!" Mercy yelled.

Logan flipped to his feet, turning in time to see the soldier fighting her ignite a stun gun.

She tried to dodge to the side and out of the way. Her hair stood on end. The air sparked around her as it looked like she started to teleport away from the fight.

Logan jumped for the guy, but he'd already pressed the button. Several odd blue wires burst out, biting into Mercy's upper chest.

She screamed. Her body convulsed, and her eyelids fluttered shut. She fell to the cement, her small body curled into a ball, and her long hair floating around her head from the static electricity.

The remaining solder went for her, the air already sparking around him. Shit. If he got to her, he might be able to teleport her out of there. Wasn't happening.

Logan tackled him into the nearest wall and away from Mercy. Sparks flashed against his arms. Drawing on what little strength he had left, he stopped the bastard from teleporting him. The guy struggled, his power increasing. Logan groaned with the strain and brought his knee up, squarely in the guy's groin. The soldier made a sound like a strangled cat.

"Sorry about that," Logan wheezed, grabbing for the guy's neck with both hands. His left one was weakened from the bullets in his shoulder, but he made do.

The guy fought him, flopping like a fish. But Logan pressed harder, choking the air out of him. Finally, the soldier went limp.

Logan stumbled to his feet and looked at the carnage. Four down—five including Mercy. He reached down and ripped off the mask of the guy he'd just knocked out, shoving it into his pocket.

The soldier had dark hair and a very faint immortal signature.

Shaking his head, trying to clear his vision, Logan reached Mercy and lifted her. There had to be reinforcements coming.

He needed to get her away.

Fast.

* * * *

Mercy caught her breath and woke up, remaining perfectly still and keeping her eyes closed. Her nerves felt like a thousand-degree sun was beating directly on them—and they were exposed and misfiring. Something soft cushioned her, and traffic sounds filtered in from outside.

A scent caught her attention. Male and woodsy. Cedar and pine mixed together with a hint of something even wilder.

"Logan," she whispered, opening her eyes to find herself lying on a bed. She could see clearly. Oops. Her one colored contact had fallen out in the fight, revealing her two different colored eyes.

He sprawled in a chair across from her, his green eyes thoughtful. He overwhelmed the chair, his elbows on his knees, a gash slowly closing above his left eye. The male was a force even just sitting. "Why didn't you teleport?" His voice was even hoarser than usual after the fight—deep and rumbly. Almost gritty.

The tone washed over her, warming her where she'd been cold. "It was four against one."

By the tightening of his chiseled jaw, he didn't like that answer. "You're not adding up for me."

Aye, that made sense. She sat up and looked around. Cheap but clean hotel room where they probably couldn't be traced. "Are we still in Scotland?" she asked, her mind way too slow to process information.

"Yes," Logan said, peering closer. "What's up with your eyes?"

"One contact to make them match." She rubbed them. Like most Fae, her eyes were two different colors. She had one blue eye and one green.

"Hmm. I like these better than the matching set. They're pretty."

A warmth spread through her extremities to her abdomen. She cleared her throat. "Is this place safe?"

"Not for long. If you'd like to transport us out of here, I wouldn't mind."

She shoved her hair away from her face. "I wish."

Those dangerous eyes narrowed. "Explain."

The male had saved her, so he was entitled to some information. "The blaster. For lack of a better description, it fried my circuits." She ran a trembling hand down her scraped knee.

His chin lifted. "It destroys your ability to teleport?"

She nodded. "For about a week. It's one of our earliest weapons, actually. Since all of us can teleport." It was surprising that the demons or even other immortal species hadn't developed something similar through the years. Too busy concentrating on guns, probably. "So. This is a fine mess." She threw up her hands.

His eyebrows rose. "Isn't it, though?" He sat back and extended his long—very long—legs to cross those huge boots at the ankles. "We were just attacked by fairies."

"Fae," she corrected automatically. "We're pretty dangerous, you know."

"I noticed," he said dryly. "Want to explain why your own people tried to hurt you?"

How much should she reveal? He and she were most likely enemies, even though he'd fought like the warrior he was rumored to be to shield her. "Why did you protect me?" she asked.

He blinked. "We were attacked. I defended. It's that simple."

Nothing was ever that simple. The many dossiers she'd read on him showed he was driven by duty, but they hadn't revealed the intensity with which he performed. The pictures hadn't done his spectacular eyes justice, either. She cleared her throat. Concentrate. "Thank you for your assistance," she said, rather primly.

His expression didn't change. "It's time you started explaining."

That's what she was afraid of. Mustering a calm she didn't possess, she began to stand. "So. I should be going."

"You won't make it to the door." His gritty tone remained nicely casual.

Well, she had been hit with a blaster. But he'd been stun-gunned about seven times, shot twice, and taken numerous punches from trained assassins. "You sure about that?" she chirped.

"Yes."

She sat back down. Her fighting skills were about average, truth be told. His? His were more impressive than she'd ever seen. Fast and brutal with a chilling precision. "Surely, you must see that we should separate."

He smiled then, the sight both deadly and enchanting. How was that possible? "Start talking, Mercy."

She'd initially argued with her leaders that telling the Seven the truth would be their best path to success. She'd been shot down. "My people weren't trying to hurt me. They just wanted to take me, and since I'm pretty good at teleporting, they took that ability away."

"I thought you all could teleport."

She nodded. "We can, but some of us are stronger at it." She rubbed her nose. How did she explain this? "Okay. Demons jump through dimensions and always end up somewhere they've seen or been on Earth, right?"

He nodded.

"Some of us, about ten percent, can stop during the process."

His brows lifted. "Stop? In other dimensions?"

There were so many. Billions upon billions. "Yes."

His head lifted. Realization dawned. "That's why we've never met many of you. You don't actually live here."

"We didn't," she said, trying not to sound bitter. "When you morons started messing with dimensions, you caused problems with a very nice paradise we've been inhabiting for two centuries. We had to bring our entire civilization back here. Home."

"I thought you all were from Ireland," he mused.

"Scotland. The Highlands, to be specific," she said. The place actually did feel like home. "Until we get the Seven under control, we can't leave. So, the Seven has to be stopped."

"You know why we need the Seven," he said quietly.

"You don't know what you are doing," she snapped back. They had no clue. They were like children playing with matches and enjoying the pretty flames.

"Then show us," he said.

"Not a chance," she said softly. No way would the Fae leaders allow state secrets to fall into enemy hands.

His nostrils flared, and he studied her for several oddly calm moments. Finally, he spoke. "Why were your own people trying to kidnap you?"

She sighed and clasped her hands in her lap. "Because I disobeyed orders and came here to rescue you. My hope was to get you somewhere safe and warn you. But you've screwed that up, now."

Chapter 4

Logan studied the pretty pixie. In the muted light, her hair looked more auburn than red. She'd shown a lot of heart and courage with her fighting, but it was obvious her skills lay elsewhere. "I won't let them hurt you, Mercy."

She drew back, her eyes widening. "You don't seem to understand." Leaning forward again, she dropped her voice to a whisper. "We're enemies, Logan."

Damn, she was cute. His life was clear-cut with no fuzziness. There existed good, bad, friends, and enemies. A lot of enemies. No gray areas for any of those categories. And this female? She'd risked herself to keep him alive. It didn't matter that she'd had nearly zero chance of killing or kidnapping him. She didn't seem to know that fact. That made her an ally and somebody he'd protect in turn. "You didn't come here to kill me?"

"Of course not." Even her huff was endearing. "That was a bluff. Like I said, I was hoping to get your attention with the sword."

Oh, she'd gotten his attention all right. "Why?"

Her lips twisted and she shook her head. "Killing just seems wrong, and I thought I could reason with you." She rubbed a small bruise along her chin. "And killing is ineffective. Even if we took you out, at some point another hybrid would survive the ritual."

The female had risked her safety with her own people to give him a warning. This woman was all heart, and every protective instinct he had woke right up. He sent a few more healing cells to the remaining bullet hole in his shoulder. "Your people must have a plan to prevent anybody else from surviving the ritual." Something that they needed time to execute.

"Probably," she agreed.

"What exactly was your plan today?" he asked softly.

She straightened. "What do you mean?"

He didn't want to hurt her feelings, but as a kidnapper, she sucked. "You're not a killer, and I'm a nearly impossible target when it comes to kidnapping." It wasn't bragging if it was the truth.

"Yet I got you out of the bar and onto the street and unconscious," she argued, lifting her chin.

Good point. "Using beautiful women as bait is an old trick, sweetheart. Usually there's an actual assassin or fighting force waiting somewhere in the wings."

A very pretty crimson filled her pale face. "You think I'm beautiful?"

If she got any cuter, he'd just take her home to his mama and let Fate have her way with him. But his path was a different one, and he knew it. One that didn't include cuteness or anything sweet. "Yes. Hence...bait."

She pursed her lips. Then she cleared her throat. "I've been considering that. I think maybe they figured out I meant to rescue you, and they let me go, planning for the attack force to come in and finish the job." She kicked her feet out while mulling it over. "I guess no one realized how well you'd fight. I mean, we had some idea of your skills from our research but witnessing you in action is different."

Who would set her up to fail? Every time he got an answer from her, three more questions sprang up. Was she trying to drive him crazy? If so, it wouldn't work. His best skills were patience and reconnaissance. "Who allowed you to put yourself in danger like this?"

She pressed her lips together and shook her head.

More secrets. He'd heard that fairies, or rather, the Fae, were nuts. Turned out that was a special little nugget of truth. "We need to get out of here." Once he got her to safety, he'd question her until satisfied.

"Oh, no. You should go, but I need to report in," she said, straightening her white shirt, which was marred with soot and had lost two buttons. "Take my lumps, as they say."

If she thought he was saying good-bye at this juncture, she hadn't read him correctly. "No. You said you failed." He couldn't let her go get hurt now. Not until he figured out what the hell was going on.

"Yes, but I've failed before. I won't be harmed." Her odd eyes sparkled, giving her the look of an imp. "The attack force didn't know I *wasn't* going to succeed in either gaining your cooperation or squiring you somewhere you couldn't leave. When they arrived, a fight started, and they lost. You totally kicked butt, to use the vernacular of human teens. So, we all failed. I won't be punished for that."

His gut rolled at her words. "What kind of punishments do the Fae have?" he asked.

She shrugged. "I guess there's always banishment. But that won't happen with me."

"Why not?" Could he trust her assurances? So far, she'd been way too blasé with her own safety. Challenging an experienced demon soldier was pure folly for somebody with her level of training. Or non-training. "Why won't you be banished?" He didn't like repeating himself and let his displeasure show.

"Let's just say we all have a purpose, right?" The sides of her mouth creased just enough to show a slight dissatisfaction. Or was that fear? "Banishment isn't an option right now."

Interesting. "What's your purpose?"

"None of your business," she snapped, her fingers curling into the worn bedspread.

Fair enough. "Where do your people get banished?" he asked.

"Other dimensions usually," she said thoughtfully. "But since travel has been mostly suspended, I'm not sure. The rules are still being listed."

He was really starting to dislike the Fae. "Listen. I'm no diplomat. But my brother heads the demon nation, and we're tight with the King of the Realm, so maybe we should get them in touch with whoever rules your people." Though the secret of the Seven had to be kept—even from his brother. This was getting complicated.

"Niall Healey is our king, and Alyssa Dawn is our president," she said grimly. "Neither trusts diplomacy with the Realm or the demon nation, believe me."

"Why not?"

She blew hair out of her face. "You're all barbarians. More concerned with fighting than knowledge."

That was a tad harsh. "Says who?"

She blinked. "Says everyone. The mere fact that the Seven still exists shows that you're muscle-bound morons."

He wanted to be insulted, but she was so earnest, amusement took him again. "I'm the first demon or vampire you've met, right?"

She nodded.

"Then how do you know anything about us? About me?" Why the hell did he care what the little fairy thought about him? Proving her wrong shouldn't be at the top of his to-do list right now. Yet he waited for realization to dawn.

It didn't.

"I read every scrap of history about your nations. Both of them." She leaned in, her gaze more than direct. "And I know everything about you, Logan Kyllwood. Down to your interest in architecture and your odd fascination with the British royal family. You send flowers every time they procreate."

His eyebrows rose. The intel on him was a mite impressive. "The British royal family has been our ally for centuries. We're friends."

She leaned in, her eyes widening. "Is Kate Middleton as nice as she looks?"

He nodded. "She really is. Brilliant, too."

"I thought so." Satisfaction curved Mercy's smooth lips now. "Well, this has been entertaining, but I really must go, unless you'd reconsider my offer to send you to an out-of-the-way paradise to sit out the action for a while?"

"Not a chance," he said evenly.

She exhaled slowly as if counting. "Very well, then. You've left us no options."

"Your people won't survive a war with us," Logan said reasonably. "Your leaders will have no choice but to talk with us." While their tactical gear was impressive, he'd taken down four of the attackers rather easily, even after having been shocked seven times.

She winced. "Don't let one bad night fool you. We have powers you've never heard about."

Totally possible. That's what he was afraid of. It was time to learn more about the Fae. If he turned her over to his eldest brother and the demon nation, she'd be questioned—harshly if necessary. He wouldn't let that happen. Logan would have to go at this alone for a while. Until he understood all of the facts.

Keeping the existence of the Seven a secret from his brother and the demon nation was starting to take a toll on him. He had to find a better plan overall, without question.

But first, they needed to get the hell out of Scotland. The walls were closing in, and he could sense the enemy drawing near. The ability had saved his ass more than once during the last war, so he never ignored a warning itch between his shoulder blades.

He reached for the hotel phone and dialed a secure number, giving two of his codes and following up with, "Jim Beam had a bad weekend on the beach."

Mercy's eyebrows rose.

Two clicks came over the line, then, "Logan? What's up?"

"Sam." Logan relaxed at hearing his older brother's voice. Sam was the middle brother and definitely the most easygoing. Usually. Until something ticked him off enough and he went nuclear. Not a pretty sight. "I need an extraction. Here's the address."

He'd barely hung up the phone when Sam appeared in the room. Mercy yelped and fell back against the wall with her hand on her chest.

Logan grinned and stood to hug his brother, leaning back to take a good look. They both had their vampire father's size, standing well over six feet tall, and they had his dark hair and green eyes. But where Logan had been told—many times—that his hollow-eyed gaze showed his time in war, Sam's eyes were deeper and darker. As if he, and he alone, knew secrets not even Fate could reveal. "Thanks for coming."

"Always and every time," Sam said easily, clapping him on the shoulder. "I was just doing some research in Tibet. Found an old monastery—great place. None of the monks talk."

Logan grinned. He could see his brother loving the silence. "I was hoping you'd take a friend and me out of here sooner rather than later." At the narrowing of Sam's eyes, Logan guessed he wasn't falling for the casual act. Oh well. "This is Mercy." He gestured behind Sam.

Sam turned and studied the female for a moment. His head cocked to the side, and he held out a hand to shake. "Sam Kyllwood. It's a pleasure."

Her mouth gaped open. "Oh, God. You're Sam. *The* Sam."

Chapter 5

Holy jumping jellybeans melted twice into a gooey mess. She should so not have said that. So bad. Both Kyllwood men were staring at her with different degrees of surprise. Sam's look had a curious tinge, while Logan's seemed more…pissed.

"Care to explain that statement?" Logan asked mildly as Sam retracted his extended hand.

Not really. Nope. Not at all, in fact. Even though she wanted to crawl into a corner and hide until the next century, she couldn't help but study them. Two of the three Kyllwood males in one place. And man, were they something to look at.

Thick hair, spectacular eyes, hard-cut bodies. Even among immortals, they were something unique. And they were brothers. Sam had come the second Logan had called. The idea of a brother had always fascinated her. More than once in her childhood, she'd daydreamed that one would appear for her. Lost and somehow found.

The shape of their jawlines was a little different. Logan's was squarer, while Sam's angled. Both firm and too sexy for description, but she'd definitely give it a try later on with Sandy.

Still, there was no doubt they shared genes. Really good genes. She'd seen pictures of the eldest Kyllwood, and he was just as good-looking.

"Well?" Logan prompted, his tone hinting she'd better come up with something.

Sam studied her eyes and seemed to look around her head. His body stiffened. Geez. Did he see auras or something? "You're a fairy," he murmured.

Logan shot him a look.

"Fae," she corrected. When would the world understand how tough they were? It might help if the Fae remained in this dimension for a while, and it certainly would be beneficial if they actually won a fight. Logan had beaten her soldiers way too easily the night before. It wasn't a surprise to find him not taking her seriously. Yet.

"Why are you on Earth?" Sam asked, his tone more curious than anything else.

Logan leaned back in his chair, his expression clearing to nothing. Blank. Ah. The youngest Kyllwood didn't know everything about his older brother, now did he? That had to smart a bit.

"We didn't have much of a choice but to return here," Mercy said.

All of a sudden, the atmosphere in the room changed. Tension, dark and deep, poured off Sam. He slowly turned to face Logan. "Wait a minute. There's only one reason she'd be here. The Seven have *not* approached you."

Logan stood so suddenly, Mercy tensed from head to toe. He leaned toward his brother, chest first, eye to eye. Both overwhelming in size and power. "What the hell do you know about the Seven?"

Mercy cleared her throat. Thank the gods he wasn't glowering at her like that. Testosterone, a whole boatload of it, poured through the room with the force of an Atlantic storm gale. "Um, I should go."

The brothers ignored her.

"What do you know about them?" Sam asked, his teeth clenching so tight his head had to hurt.

Logan pressed his hands to his hips. His earlier anger now seemed like mild irritation compared to the raw fury vibrating along his skin. "I know that you shouldn't know a damn thing about them."

"Jesus." Sam wiped a hand across his broad forehead, and it was shaking just enough to be noticeable. "Is this where you and Garrett have been for the last month?" His eyes darkened. "Holy crap. Where is Garrett?"

Logan drew back. His expression smoothed out into a blank mask.

"No." Sam grabbed his brother by the upper arms, his fingers digging in. "Tell me he hasn't undergone the ritual of the Seven."

When Logan didn't answer, Mercy piped up. "Not only has Garrett Kayrs finished the ritual, he almost died during it. Got caught between dimensions and barely made it out." Her people didn't know how he'd survived, but they'd find out. Somehow. When both males looked at her, she calmed her expression. "Or so we heard."

Logan growled. Low and hard and deep. "How do you know about Garrett's ritual?"

Oops. Damn it. She just wasn't smooth like she wanted to be. If awkward had a picture next to it in the dictionary, it'd be her. She tried to flutter her eyelashes. "Gossip?"

"Try again," Logan snapped, shoving free of his brother.

Nope. Not a chance. The demons had no clue what the Fae could do, and she didn't have time to deal with a treason charge if she told them. She was in enough trouble at the moment. Way too much trouble. "The Seven can't be allowed to form completely. It just can't happen." The power that would unleash on the world, all the worlds, was unimaginable.

"It has to happen." Logan sighed. "You know we were created to protect the world from Ulric, right? We put him in a prison world, created two worlds to contain it, and sacrificed our own members, Ronan and Quade, to live in them to make sure Ulric's prison held."

"Yes," she said. The rituals the two must have undergone on a regular basis to keep the magnetic fields working properly awed her, even to this day. What kind of toll had that taken on the males?

It was amazing Ronan had survived and was now on Earth again. What about Quade? It didn't look good.

"You understand that Ulric is evil? The most evil Kurjan Cyst ever born." Logan's chest seemed to expand as he visibly struggled to keep his voice level in an attempt to reason with her. "He has the ability to kill every Enhanced female in this world—mated or unmated. We had to create the prison worlds."

Of course, she was well versed in the role of the Seven, as well as Enhanced human females—those who had special abilities and could survive a mating with an immortal. "One of your worlds failed. Ronan Kayrs is now in this realm." She shook her head. "The other two worlds can't be allowed to fail. If the Seven form completely, that's exactly what will happen. You just don't understand." And she couldn't tell him everything without permission from her president. Even she wouldn't break that law.

Logan's eyes widened. "We are not leaving Quade Kayrs behind in a bubble world way distant from this dimension. His world will fail, and he will be brought home."

Oh, if Logan had any idea what he was talking about, he'd stop talking. She shook her head.

Almost in slow motion, both Kyllwood males turned their heads toward the window, imperceptibly lifting their chins in a nearly identical movement.

"What?" Mercy asked, standing and turning, the hair on her arms rising. Faint signatures caught her attention. "Crap. They're here." A Fae force had found them. Probably the last force still standing after Logan had done his damage to the others last night.

She thought about calling out for help and then stopped. No way could a small Fae force take on two Kyllwood brothers. This time, Logan might not let them live, and Sam already seemed furious. Damn it. She ripped her destroyed shirt over her head and reached to unbutton her skirt.

"What in the hell are you doing?" Logan hissed.

She shucked out of her skirt. The pink bra and panties should be fine. "Get naked." Reaching him in two strides, she grasped the bottom of his shirt.

Sam took a step back. "Um, bro? What's happening right now?"

Logan manacled her hands, his eyes narrowing on her. "Explain."

Man, he was bossy. "Take off your clothes," she breathed, her heart beating too fast. "We have tracking dust. They probably coated us both in the warehouse during the fight."

"Tracking dust?" Logan glanced at his brother.

Sam shrugged, his body visibly on full alert. "Never heard of it."

The force outside drew nearer, their signatures strengthening.

Mercy tried harder. "It's minute, like glitter you can't see. Can track us anywhere. Great invention."

"Shit." Logan let her yank the shirt over his head and shoved his jeans to the ground. "If you're messing with us, Mercy—"

"I'm not," she gasped. Whoa. His bare chest was even better than she'd imagined. Muscled and strong—with a scar across his left pec. How badly did a demon have to be injured to be scarred for life? Usually they could heal all injuries. His wartime exploits hadn't been exaggerated. If anything, she suspected his records left out too much information.

Why in the heck had she allowed herself to be tased? She needed to teleport and right now. There was only one choice. Grabbing Logan's arm, she pulled him over to Sam, thankful he let her do so. "Dunk us. Any freshwater lake will do." An ocean would be fine, but she hated sharks. Damn things liked to bite.

Sam frowned but slid an arm around her waist and one over Logan's shoulder. "This is crazy, but what the hell. Dunking Logan is always fun."

Mercy kept a good hold on Logan's arm out of instinct, needing some sort of connection with him.

The Fae soldiers breached the hotel. The door exploded open just as the universe dropped away. Pressure and darkness moved in on her, and she closed her eyes, unable to do anything but remain on Sam's path. Her skin tingled, and sparks flitted behind her eyelids. It was like driving a high-powered machine on an old country road. She was so much better at teleporting.

An energy caught her, and she opened her eyes.

Only blackness.

She tried to yell, to give warning, but nothing came out. Helpless. At the moment, she was truly helpless. They'd been followed into the path by Fae soldiers. Did Sam even know that was possible?

Light cut into her eyes, and a second later, she plunged deep into cold water.

The shock stole her breath. She closed her mouth and started to struggle, fighting the depths. Logan's warm hands wrapped around her upper arms, and she moved into him, seeking safety. He kept a tight hold and kicked to the surface. The moment oxygen filled her nose, she started to cough and sputter.

"You're okay." Logan's voice softened, and he held her aloft, providing a shield against all danger. They floated in the calm water.

Sam appeared from the depths next to them, his dark hair plastered to his head. His wet clothing clung to a very ripped body. "Will this wash off the tracking dust on you two?"

Gulping, she nodded. They were in the middle of a bluish-green lake surrounded on all four sides by thick forest and wild mountains. Far away from Scotland. Snow covered the tall peaks in the distance. "But we have a problem," she sputtered.

"What?" Logan asked.

Two Fae soldiers plunged out of thin air into the lake. Coming up, they each grabbed one of Sam's arms.

Logan yelled and moved toward his brother.

Electricity crackled through the water, and then all three men disappeared. Waves whipped around wildly.

"Sam!" Logan yelled.

But he was gone.

Chapter 6

Surrounded by icy water, Logan Kyllwood went full hot. Fire roared through him. He splashed around, looking toward the shore, trying to find his brother. His lungs seized. Then he stilled, going calm. Deadly. "Where are they?"

"They're gone," Mercy said, quietly treading water.

He turned toward her, moving rapidly through the waves to reach her. Focus. He had to focus and not go ballistic. "Where did they go?"

"I don't know," she whispered, her dark red hair floating on the water. "They could be anywhere."

Why the hell hadn't Sam stopped the teleporting? Was he just taken by surprise, or had the dual energy from the two Fae stopped him? Damn it. Logan was about to lose his mind. "Can you trace them the same way they followed us?"

"Not without my ability to teleport," she sighed, her lips turning blue.

Anger tried to grab him, but he banished all emotion. The woman knew more than she was telling. "Let's get to shore." Without waiting for an answer, he grasped her arm and started swimming hard, not giving her a chance to hesitate. She had to either kick to keep up or go under.

She kicked.

He slowed down so she wouldn't have to exert herself too much. Then he pulled her along, making sure she kept her head above water. The smell of snow tinged the air, and the water was definitely glacier fed.

There was no question the Fae knew a hell of a lot more about the universe and dimensions than his people did, and it was time for a little physics lesson. He didn't want to scare her, but he'd do what he'd have to do to save his brother. The two soldiers who'd taken Sam hadn't hesitated. They'd wanted Sam, not Logan or Mercy. Right now, anyway.

How had they known Sam was even with them? The soldiers must've seen them when breaching the hotel, and in that short amount of time, they'd set their sights on Sam?

No. So there was an order in place for Sam, and the Fae had already known his face. They'd recognized him in a couple of seconds. What the freaking hell was going on with his brother? The chilly water sluiced over Logan as he swam, failing to cool him in the slightest.

Finally, he reached the rocky shore. He stood and lifted Mercy so he could maneuver over the downed branches and jagged rocks. They'd cut her bare feet to pieces. She felt small and cold against his chest, and he held her tighter. Demons let off a lot of heat; apparently fairies did not. She snuggled her tight, almost nude body closer, and his own went on full alert.

Desire caught him by surprise, and he squelched it. The delicate female was stubborn and oddly fierce, but she had knowledge about Sam, and Logan had to be careful with her.

Pain ripped into his heel, and he automatically sent healing cells to both feet until he reached a large downed spruce tree that had lost its branches. He set her down gently and took a step back. His voice remained quiet when all he wanted to do was scream. Where the hell was Sam? "Talk, Mercy."

She shivered in her pink bra and panties. Both had a cute rose in the center.

Why had he noticed that? Shaking his head, spraying water, he concentrated only on her face. Just her face. Not lower. Nope. Not an inch lower.

What the hell?

He peered closer.

Her eyes glowed a nearly translucent yellow. They were beautiful. "Your eyes."

She huffed out air and rolled those eyes. "I know. Like vampires, we have two colors. Three considering my normal eye colors are one blue and one green."

Those were pretty, but this soft yellow was so spectacular he was in awe. She truly looked like something…other. Even for an immortal. But if her secondary eye color was showing, she was having strong emotions. Or physical pain. He stiffened. "Are you hurt?"

"Just cold," she said, running her hands down her bare arms.

He looked around. Letting her get ill wasn't in the plan. Shit. He didn't have a plan and needed one right now. Urgency tensed every muscle in his body. "All right. Just tell me now. Does your taser device work against demons?"

Gulping in air, she nodded. "Of course. That's why we invented it in the first place."

Damn it. Sam wouldn't be able to teleport out. The bastards would definitely tase him. Logan wiped water off his face, not surprised when steam rose. His temper lurked, ready to blow. "Do your leaders plan to kill Sam?"

She shook her head. "Not until they know everything he does." She turned even paler. "Then, probably?"

Okay. He could deal with that. Good. Sam was as tough as they came. He wouldn't tell the soldiers a damn thing, which would give Logan time to get to him. "Why Sam? Why do your people want him?"

Her gaze dropped to his chest, which was drying rapidly. "I can't tell you."

Oh, that was going to change. A bird squawked in the distance. "We need to get the hell out of here before more of your soldiers turn up. As soon as we're safe, I'll build a fire and we can talk. A lot."

She sneezed.

His chest hitched. How vulnerable was she to the elements? She was small and shivering, and she brought out a side of him he rarely felt. He had to find warmth for her. They couldn't build a fire right here and now. It was too easy to spot.

She coughed. "Where are we?"

He looked around at the peaks in the distance. Spruce and hemlock trees covered the forest. "I have no idea," he lied. They definitely weren't in Scotland. Sam could've taken them anywhere, but they'd found refuge in the islands off Alaska more than once during their shitty childhoods, and it was as good a guess as any. "Since your people somehow tracked us here, they can find us again, right?"

She nodded.

"But the tracking dust, whatever the hell that is, is gone?" His feet finished healing and he stood straighter.

"Yes. The water will have washed it all off." Her lips were turning an even lighter blue.

He reached for her and she shrank back.

Damn it. He rubbed a hand through his wet hair, slightly combing it. "You're freezing, and demons are all heat. Let me carry you to safety and warm you up at the same time." He planned to move at a pace she couldn't match, anyway. While they wouldn't be able to talk on the way, if he got her warmed up and feeling better, it'd be easier to get answers from her once they reached safety. His motivation had nothing to do with making her feel better and safe. *Yeah, right.*

Her pointed chin lifted. "And if I say no?"

He didn't allow any expression to cross his face. His skin was already dry, and the need to run flexed his feet. Family was all that had ever or probably would ever matter to him. "Your people just took my brother, Mercy."

Her teeth chattered. "I guess that's my answer."

"I guess it is," he murmured. The woman was going to freeze to death if she didn't find some heat. And he had to get answers from her before he went after Sam. He needed to find out where they were right now. The air felt different—much cooler than before. The scent was different, too. Definitely one of the Alaskan islands.

She scrutinized the dense trees as if searching for an escape route.

There wasn't one, but he let her reach that conclusion on her own. His gaze caught on the perfect outline of a key on her left hip. Ah. There it was. His heart thumped. Hard. "Nice Key birthmark," he said.

She turned back toward him, her panties hiding nothing. "I'm not a Key and never will be."

Of course she was. Fate sometimes didn't give choices. He now knew the location of two Keys. Where was the third female? Time was drawing close...he could feel it.

She looked over his shoulder, obviously trying hard to find a way to escape him. He could've told her that she'd have to look forever, but the woman obviously had a quick mind and realized that fact within seconds. She sighed. "Fine. We'll do this your way for now. You'll need your arms free. Just in case."

True. He didn't sense any predators near, but apparently that didn't mean shit right now. Those damn Fae could come out of nowhere. So he grasped Mercy's arm and smoothly swung her around to his back. The female weighed nothing. "Can you hold on?"

"Yes." Her knees tightened against his waist, and her arms wrapped around his neck. Her feet were blocks of ice against his already dried boxer-briefs, and her nipples were sharp pebbles against his back. She shivered and settled closer to him, her chin dropping to where his neck met his shoulder and her long and very wet hair draping down his arm.

His body tightened. If he flipped her around... No. He couldn't think like that. Concentrate, damn it.

She sighed, settling in, her breath soft against his skin.

Jesus. This was torture.

Chapter 7

Mercy awoke with a start, her head spinning. Somehow, she was wrapped around a heater. Full warmth…. muscle. Her eyelids jerked open. Logan held her wrists together around his collarbones with one strong hand. Her ankles were clasped at his waist. Aches pounded in her thighs from being spread around his tight body for the longest piggyback ride in the history of ever.

Drool. Damn it. She'd drooled on his shoulder.

She rubbed her chin against his smooth skin, trying to wipe it away. How embarrassing. She'd been dreaming about a double cheeseburger from a place in Newark. Her stomach growled. When had she eaten last?

"There are some berries, and I can hunt game," he said quietly.

Wasn't he the hunter-gatherer of all time? She shook her head. "That's okay." Her voice came out slurred and sleepy.

Blinking, she looked around. They'd stopped. More trees surrounded them along a gently waving waterway that smelled of salt. They were close to a bay. Which bay? Where the heck were they? The scent of sulfur suddenly caught her.

"You fully awake yet?" he asked, facing the sea, his voice calm. Even though he'd obviously run for hours with her dead weight on his back, he didn't seem out of breath. Just what kind of shape was the demon in? Curiosity wandered through her, landing in inappropriate places. Sure, he was good-looking, with incredible strength, fighting skills, and stamina.

But they were enemies, right? Just how far would he go to get information about his brother? Would he hurt her?

"Mercy? You okay?" His gravelly voice dropped even deeper as he asked again.

"Um, yes." Her voice was still groggy. He was so damn warm, she didn't want to release him. His smell soothed her, and the feel of his skin intrigued her. Smooth over impossibly hard muscles. How long had she been on his back, pretty much passed out? "Where are we?"

"Not sure." He released her wrists.

Oh. She should probably get off the poor guy. The sun was dipping over the mountains, and night was coming soon. Hours had passed, and it'd be early morning in Scotland, so they were across the world. Wincing, she tried to remove herself from the demon's broad back. "How long have you been running?"

"Hours. We had to go in the wrong direction for quite a while, then I zigzagged, and finally we ended up here. They won't track us." He grasped her arm and gently swung her to the spongy ground with easy grace.

"What is that smell?" Her feet hit, and she grabbed his arm to regain her balance. Her leg muscles shook and protested. Had her thighs ever been this sore? Fogginess still filled her brain.

He grasped her shoulders and turned her toward a small pool surrounded by large, round rocks. "Hot springs. We both could use heat and some muscle relief. Do you need assistance?"

The male should be exhausted. She paused and limped around to face him. "You okay?"

His green eyes had lightened to the color of the deep embers in a dying fire—wild and mysterious. Scratches marred his forehead, chest, and upper arms—definitely from tree branches. As she watched, they slowly healed and closed. The demon had impressive healing skills. "I'm fine. There was a disturbance in the atmosphere about an hour after I started running, so I'm thinking your people are on the island."

Island? Made sense. They were on some sort of island surrounded by sea water but large enough to have that lake in the middle. Her breath caught. "Then they're coming." She couldn't let Logan take out the few remaining soldiers. How was she going to save them?

"No." He gestured toward the pool of rocks. "I led them in two different directions and up a mountain for a while. They won't track us."

Her people could track anybody—even without the powder. "They'll find us."

His grin flashed quick and slightly arrogant. "Not a chance. I scaled down a cliff and crossed another lake. Even if they conduct a grid search of this sprawling island, they won't find us before we're gone. Now get in the hot water, Mercy."

She wanted to protest his bossiness. Nobody ordered her around. But the idea of warm water over her aching body was too much to resist. She gingerly stepped over moss-covered rocks and slid into the pool. The soothing sensation and warmth were immediate and she groaned, moving across the small pool to sit on a ledge. Her thin bra and panties immediately turned almost translucent, so she ducked farther down in the water. It was bliss. Pure, heavenly bliss.

Logan remained in place, his head lifted, his eyes shut, and his senses obviously on full alert as he scouted the area.

In his boxers, he was the most masculine male she'd ever seen. Even his legs were powerful, although a scar marred the front of his right leg. His time in battle had been on the front lines, without a doubt. The roped muscles along his arms led to that impressive chest and down incredibly ripped abs. She tried not to look lower. She really did. She failed and took a peek.

Wow. Just wow.

Heat rushed into her face, and she turned to look at the quietly lapping waves in the bay. Where did this water go? Which ocean? "Do you have any idea where we are?" she asked, keeping her face turned to the freedom of the water that must lead to the open sea.

"Maybe." He entered the water quietly, sending ripples across her skin.

She couldn't breathe. He was just so much. She'd been wrapped around him, and her body still tingled from the contact. What would it be like to have the freedom to touch him completely? Head to toe? All of him? The female deep inside her, the one she tried to rule with logic and duty, itched to explore him in every way. "Where are we?" Her voice emerged way too breathy. God, she hoped he couldn't guess her thoughts. He didn't need one more advantage in this power struggle between them.

She didn't seem to be winning, either. Not even close.

"I'd just be guessing as to our location." His sigh as he sat lower feathered over her skin, even across the small pool.

She shivered and covered the motion by turning back toward him.

He sprawled in the water, which covered him almost to his chest. His head went back onto the rocks, and he visibly relaxed, that longish hair curling around his shoulders. Even at peace, he didn't seem very peaceful. That tension always surrounding him remained, permeating the soft steam rising all around them.

His stamina was impressive. He'd run all day while she'd slept, sprawled on his back. "Thank you for, well, today," she said. She could at least show decent manners before they started arguing again.

He barely nodded, his head still at rest. "Not a problem. Moving was faster with you on my back, and it helped you to warm up."

A wish caught her, one she didn't want, that she'd like to be his friend. His protectiveness, even though they were enemies, gave her a warm feeling she had never experienced. What would it be like to be on the inside of Logan Kyllwood's world? To feel safe and shielded by such power? His psychological profile proved he was loyal to the core.

What would that mean to a woman? One who could draw out that smile he'd only shown once? She could show him that life could be fun for the sake of fun only. From her research, it looked like he followed duty only. She could show him delights in other worlds he probably had never imagined.

But it could never happen. The Seven must be stopped, and her destiny was already charted. It had nothing to do with the Key birthmark that sometimes pulsed with its own energy. Period.

"You're thinking very loudly over there," he murmured.

She blinked. "Can you read my thoughts?"

"Dunno, but I'm not. What's on your mind, darlin'?"

She liked the endearment, even though they didn't know each other well enough for such intimacy. The Key on her hip flashed hot for a second, and she bit back a gasp. That had only happened a few times in her life. "I'm not your darlin'," she said. Dumb line. Real dumb line.

"Okay," he said, unmoving.

Enough daydreaming. But still, this was her only opportunity to know him. "In my research, I found you've taken many architecture classes through the years." It was odd for a soldier, such a distinguished one, to have time for a hobby.

"Um," he replied.

She cleared her throat. "I was just wondering why."

He sighed. "I like the design elements that go into creating the right space. Light and harmony and the environment. It's a nice break from hunting and killing." He shifted his weight, and the water rippled. "Plus, it's enjoyable to build structures that will last."

Interesting. She could spend all day delving into his head, but now she had to get back to work. The Fae would find them soon, and she needed a plan to protect them and get free of the demon. "Enough playing games, Logan. I'd like an idea of where I am."

His eyelids flashed open, revealing those predatory eyes.

She stopped breathing.

"Games? This isn't a game. You don't get to know where you are. What you do get to do is start answering my questions. Right now." Even lazily relaxed, his voice held the command of somebody accustomed to giving orders.

She swallowed over a slight lump in her throat. "And if I don't?" she whispered.

Chapter 8

Apparently, the woman wanted a clear answer before she decided whether or not to cooperate with him. In his experience, the less somebody knew, the more vulnerable they became. He didn't want her confident at the moment, but deep down, in a place mercy still lived, he didn't want to scare her too badly. She seemed to base all her decisions on facts.

It was cute, but he didn't have time for cute right now. The Fae might be torturing Sam this very second.

"You've read records about me, right?" Logan asked, enjoying the feeling of the warm water over his legs. He'd run for hours.

She nodded.

"Then do you really have to ask that question?" Truth be told, he didn't have an answer for her. During the war, he'd done things that still woke him up in a sweat. Things he'd never cleanse from his soul. But that was over. The war was over. It had to be, and he wouldn't allow another to start. Not so soon. "Mercy?"

She studied him with those spectacularly soft eyes. "Yes."

He sighed, the water mellowing him, despite the constant state of arousal he'd been in since he'd met her. He ignored the demands of his body. There had to be a way to reason with her. "Do you have family?"

She shook her head, her eyes sad, and he felt a pang in his heart for her. "No," she said. "Most of us don't have family."

His eyebrow rose of its own accord. "How is that possible?"

She licked her lips and studied him for a moment, obviously deciding what to say. Finally, she shrugged, and small ripples of water spread across the pool. "A long time ago, the Fae tried to move from one dimension to another, and there was a mistake. Nobody knows how, but we lost most of our people. Mainly adults. My parents were among them."

Logan drew in the information, his gut aching. Poor lost girl—poor lost kids. Why hadn't they turned to the Realm for help? Of course, that was during the last war, so perhaps going out on their own made more sense. Especially if they had a safe place. "That's terrible. You raised yourselves?" Sounded like something out of *Lord of the Flies*.

She nodded. "Um, kind of. There were a few adults left, but mostly, we just lived. Food was plentiful, and there were some elderly survivors who tried to guide us. Sandy, Trina, and I have always been close."

The two women from the other night. "They left you with me, thinking iron shackles would protect you," he said, not liking the thought. "Your people need to learn about predators, sweetheart."

"We are predators," she retorted. "While I don't have family, I consider them my sisters. We grew up together, and we had many manuals to learn from." Her eyes sparkled with challenge. "As well as advanced weapons and equipment. As you've already seen."

Ah. "So your soldiers are young, as well." Twenties and maybe thirties. No seasoned warriors had tried to fight him yet.

Her chin snapped up. "I didn't say that."

She didn't have to.

He eyed her. "How strong is your fighting force?" Whoever was in charge had let her head into danger too easily. The woman had an analytical mind, and he could almost see it spinning. She was also charming and seemed kind. So far, he'd seen not an ounce of the coldness needed to be an operative in this world. For any species. Instead, she seemed to think things through, make a decision, then jump in with both feet. Spies proceeded with deliberation. "How hard was it for you to create this ridiculous op by yourself?"

Her already stubborn chin seemed to firm even more. "I really can't tell you that."

This was getting tedious. The female had been set up to distract him as a decoy for the soldiers, and he didn't like how well the plan had worked. More importantly, he didn't appreciate that either she'd been used as a sacrificial lamb, or alternatively, that the Fae were so clueless they didn't realize how dangerous a demon soldier could be. He continued his train of logic with her. "You said that Trina and Sandy are like your sisters. What would you do to save them?"

"Anything," she said softly. "I get it, Logan. I really do. You'll have to do what you need to for Sam."

What exactly did she get? As far as he could tell, she'd been raised in some safe dimension with a bunch of friends. Had she seen war? Death? There was a naïveté, almost an innocence to her that he hadn't seen in way too long. In almost anybody. "Do what I need? You think I'll torture you?"

Her nose wrinkled. "Not really. You did just carry me across an entire island while I slept."

The female had a point. But how was she not seeing the big picture here? "Do you even understand that somebody is allowing you to be harmed? That you have an enemy close to you?" he asked, shaking his head.

She blinked. Her lip twisted. "You're trying to manipulate me. That's it."

Man, she was clueless. And he was losing patience. "You're not a killer, and yet your leaders allowed you to challenge another immortal here on Earth?" The idea was ridiculous. He could protect her, but he needed to get Sam to safety first. It'd also be damn nice to figure out how Sam suddenly seemed to know so much about the Fae and the Seven and the universe as a whole.

"Allow is a silly word. I manage my own fate." She shrugged, lifting a pale shoulder out of the warm water. There was still enough light to notice her see-through bra in the water. Her scent whispered across the small pool.

"If you were mine, you'd learn the restrictions of that word very quickly." Why the hell had he said that? Logan shifted his weight, trying to ease the pressure on his balls. The female was just too much. Sweet, stubborn, and sexy. An irresistible combination.

"Hah." Her lashes flickered, and she gave him a look that was all challenge.

One the demon inside him lunged to meet. Or maybe it was the vampire. Either way, the male inside him didn't like that look. Or rather, liked that look way too much. It was like a siren's call on a level neither one of them could be prepared for right now. He dug deep to keep from reaching for her. "You came to warn me or kidnap me. The kidnapping plan is over. So warn me."

She breathed out slowly as if counting the seconds. Finally, she spoke. "We will not allow the Seven to form completely. Find another path for your destiny, Logan Kyllwood."

Geez. The woman didn't even realize that her warning came with a threat. He shook his head. "Or what?" How was it possible he'd had to ask that question?

"Or the next attack force will aim to kill." She actually sounded sorry about that. Maybe worried. Was she concerned for him… or for her attack force? She'd gone back to looking at the sea and not at him, so he couldn't read her expression. The water reached her neck but was clear enough to show that her undergarments didn't hide a thing. "I really should be going now, Logan. It probably isn't proper for me to be here with an unattached male." Melancholy. The sound kissed right over his skin.

"Why not?" he asked.

"I'm promised to another." Her bottom lip quivered, then flattened into a line.

Promised? What the hell? "Who's this dictator leading your people?" Sounded like an asshole teenager.

"Well, we have a president who was president before the rift." She sighed. "There was enough genetic material left to create ten of us—five males and five females. We're the hope of the future." Oh, this sounded nuts. Crazier than nuts. "What else?" he prompted. Might as well get all of it.

"We now have a king, Niall." She rubbed water off her chin. "The queen died at the event, that's what we called it, so he's always been thought of as one of our leaders. He's recently written a bunch of new laws. Since our numbers are low, we need to rebuild with the ten of us. Our geneticists, a few of them a couple centuries old, came up with the best chances of success by building a chart."

A chart? Seriously? So the dickhead had a breeding plan? Rumors were true. Fairies were fucking crazy. Then an idea struck him, and his body instinctively settled into predatory mode. "Who are you promised to, Mercy?" His voice had gone demon hoarse.

Her head jerked up in response to his tone. She cleared her throat. "I don't see that as being any of your business."

Boy, did she have that wrong. He wasn't going to take a second to examine his reaction to her words, either. Contemplation would have to wait. "Who?" Somehow, he already knew. He really did.

She blew out air. "Fine. Niall and I have the strongest lineage. It makes sense to combine them."

"How fucking romantic," Logan snarled. While he had no intention of settling down ever, he didn't like anybody being forced to do so by a king. It was just wrong. Fate played a part. Had to. Not idiots with charts. He calmed himself. "I don't understand. Why would your...fiancé...allow you to go off into danger and almost certain failure?"

"Stop saying that word. There's no *allow*. I decided to head into danger, and I may just do it again." Her head snapped up, and waves cascaded across the small pool. "Who said that I have failed? I'm actually quite accomplished, Logan. In fact, my IQ is *so* much higher than yours, I should probably dumb down my vocabulary here." Her eyes flashed hot and yellow in the dim light. "And I've seen your files—all of them. I *know* your IQ."

He barked out a laugh, the humor catching him out of nowhere. If she'd had access to even half of what he'd done in the name of war, she'd be terrified of him.

Thunder rolled harsh and angry in the distance. Just great. He turned his head to see dark clouds blowing in way too fast. The storm was going to be impressive. They needed shelter. But first, he wanted answers, and his muscles could use a few more minutes of the water's healing warmth.

The woman should be terrified, but instead, she was barely irritated. "Why aren't you frightened. Of me?" he asked.

She bit her lip. "I know you're dangerous and exceptionally well trained. But you have a protective streak a mile wide—especially for petite females like your mother."

Well, shit. Maybe she had a point. And those bastards really did have a file or two on him. "My mother's biggest hobby is robbing banks, and she could take both of us out while painting the nails on her left hand." Obviously, the Fae didn't have a file on his mom or her mate, Coven Enforcer Daire Dunne. There was one witch the Fae should show respect.

"Right. But that doesn't change you or your vulnerabilities," Mercy said quietly. "You've sacrificed yourself for your mother, you've killed for your brothers, and you've been prepared to die for your niece since the day she was born seven years ago. That's why you're willing to risk your life to become one of the Seven protectors on Earth."

His chest settled. His blood slowed. The storm gathering force around him was nothing compared to the one that wanted to get free inside him. "What do you know about my niece?" The girl was a prophet, chosen by Fate, and that wasn't the half of it. Not even close.

Mercy broke free of his gaze, looking beyond him to the sea. "Don't you get it? Everything is about Hope Kayrs-Kyllwood. The first step was taking Sam. The next?" She shook her head. "It's inevitable."

Logan growled. Hurting this half size female was something he'd never get over. But with her last statement, everything changed. He'd do what he had to in order to get answers. "Get out of the hot spring, Mercy. Now."

Chapter 9

The slight rain splashed down from the trees, washing over Hope Kayrs-Kyllwood's new, bright pink bike. It was a normal spring in Idaho. Lots and lots of rain. She and Libby had spent hours putting unicorn stickers all over the bars, and Paxton had woven pretty ribbons through the spokes. It was perfect.

Paxton frowned, looking over the downed tree across the trail, his silvery-blue eyes nearly glowing. A series of branches made a cool ramp almost to the top of the bark. "This is a bad idea." At seven years old, the vampire-demon was shorter than most other males, but his hands and feet were so big he tripped a lot. "Let's go play music. I have a new song on the guitar."

She shook her head. "No more piano for today. I don't love making music like you do." It was time to play outside. Plus, Pax was getting so good on the guitar that it was hard to keep up, even though he only practiced when his daddy wasn't around. For some reason, his dad didn't like music much.

Pax looked around, his shoulders slumped. He rubbed his round belly. "It's getting dark, and we should go inside."

Hope wiped rain off her forehead. Libby was already on the other side of the jump, having successfully sped over it on her bike, her blond pigtails springing up. "Libby did it," Hope said, her arms tingling and her heart battering against her ribs.

Pax shook his shaggy dark hair, spraying water. "Libby is a feline shifter. They jump things for a living."

"Not at seven years old," Hope retorted. If Libby could do it, she could, too. "I'm a vampire, Pax." The only living female vampire ever. Vampires were just as tough as shifters. She swallowed. She was half-human, too. Kind of. In male vampires, the human part seemed to just go away. But in her...not so much. She'd just gotten over a bad cold. Finally. "I can do this."

"If you get hurt, I'd just die." Pax wiped rain off his round face. His cheeks were so full, it was kind of fun to squeeze them, but only once in a while.

She loved her best friends. "If I get hurt, I'll tell your dad you weren't here," she promised. Pax's daddy was a vampire who never smiled. Ever. His mama had been a really nice demon, but she'd died in the last war. So Pax tried to stay with Hope a lot—which was really cool.

Pax kicked a pebble. "I don't care about my dad knowing. I just don't want you to get hurt."

She straddled the bike. "Just 'cause I'm different from other vampires, I won't stop doing stuff." Though she didn't understand how she got colds or injuries, she couldn't let the fear of her being part human stop her. Someday she was going to hafta be a prophet, and she already knew it wouldn't mean just talking to people. Her path was different, and she had to be strong enough to run down it. This might be a first step. "No fear, Pax."

Pax looked scared.

Sometimes when she was with him, her stomach hurt. Like she should be doing something, but she didn't know what. Like she wasn't being a good friend, but she tried really hard anyway. Sometimes she could see the future or just know stuff that was gonna happen. But never with Libby, Pax, or her friend Drake. She couldn't see anything with them—or herself. "Trust me."

"I do." He looked away and then back. "But I think you're just doing dumb stuff so you won't go to sleep. I know you've been having bad dreams again." Pax often slept over.

Her shoulders felt heavy. "They're only bad because I don't understand them." Something was happening with her uncles Logan and Sam. Just when she'd got Uncle Garrett figured out, there were more problems. "I called Logan this morning and he didn't answer." That wasn't good, but she couldn't tell her daddy. Not yet, anyway. There was nothin' to tell.

Pax checked her back tire. "Please don't do this."

"I'm off!" She settled her weight on the seat and caught her balance. Letting out a yip of excitement, she started pedaling as fast as she could.

The rain dripped harder, and she blinked to clear her eyes.

Libby waited on the other side, out of the way.

Hope got closer to the jump. Her front tire wobbled in the mud and she corrected, sliding a little. The mud caught the back tire.

She yelped and hit the jump too far to the side. Screaming, she flew into the air, turning sideways.

Pax bellowed her name from behind her, sounding way older than normal. Libby shrieked and started running toward her.

Then everything happened in slow motion.

She jerked to the side, holding her handles as hard as she could. Her shoulder hit a tree branch. Something cracked. Her head knocked against a tree, and she heard the echo between her ears. Then she was falling, and the entire world went dark.

She didn't feel herself hitting the ground.

* * * *

Her head hurt. Hope opened her eyes to find herself on her favorite dream beach, the one with pink sand. A bright bluish-green ocean rolled waves gently toward her, while pretty white birds floated in the clear blue sky.

She sat up. Why was she in the dreamworld? She hadn't gone to bed yet.

Rocks led up to bright purple trees. A hidden bird squawked, and then her friend Drake ran out of the forest, straight toward her.

She squinted her eyes against the pain.

Drake was wearing dark jeans and a green shirt that brought out the color in his eyes, even at a distance. He ran faster, slid on his knees, and reached her. "Are you okay? Who hurt you?" He reached up and touched the pain at her cheekbone.

She blinked. Tears filled her eyes, and the flash of the bike hitting the tree moved through her brain. "I crashed my bike." She looked around frantically, but the dreamworld didn't go away.

"Okay." Drake helped her sit all the way up and patted her shoulder. "Take a deep breath."

Why was she here? It didn't make sense. "But—but I'm not asleep." She rubbed her aching cheekbone.

Drake settled on his knees in the pink sand, looking her over. "You must've knocked yourself out." As a Kurjan, he had pale skin and dark straight hair that reached his shoulders. But unlike most Kurjans, he could pass for human with his greenish eyes. He was very tall for a boy of seven, and Hope didn't think she'd ever reach him in height.

But they were friends.

He took her hand. "You're all right. I'm sure of it."

Her heart warmed. "You can't be sure."

His grin made her smile back, even though her head still hurt. "You wouldn't be in our dreamworld if you weren't okay. Just unconscious. Don't worry. You'll wake up soon."

Our dreamworld. It was the first time he'd called it that, and the idea made her smile. Her mama and daddy had met in a dreamworld that had blown up, but they'd been friends for a long time before getting mated. Now Hope and Drake were meeting in a world nobody else knew about. Well, almost nobody. She told Pax and Libby, of course. "How did you know I was here?" she asked.

Drake shrugged. "I'm not sure. It's like when you call me when you're sleeping. I heard you, then I lay down and got here somehow." He snorted. "I lay down in the middle of the training field. Hopefully nobody is kicking me."

She giggled. *"Nobody would kick you."* He was too tough. Even at their age, Drake was already learning to be a leader. She liked that about him.

Of course, the Realm and demon nations hated the Kurjan nation. But she and Drake were gonna change that.

He looked at the quiet sea. *"Who let you get hurt?"*

She dusted sand off her jeans. *"Nobody. Just me. I tried to jump a fallen tree."* Maybe she should've listened to her friends. *"Paxton told me not to, but I didn't listen. Libby jumped over it, and I thought I could, too. But the rain and mud kind of got in my way."*

Drake's hand felt cool around hers. *"Paxton is the vampire-demon you told me about?"*

She nodded. Someday, all of them were gonna be super good friends. *"Yeah. You'll meet him and Libby once I figure out how to bring them here. You'll like them."*

Drake twisted his face. *"Probably not."*

"You will," Hope insisted, holding his hand tighter. *"We can make things better. The four of us."* If they all became friends, then maybe the grown-ups would, too. *"Trust me."*

"I do," Drake said. *"But Pax and Libby are probably training to fight me right now, just like I'm training to fight them. The past won't just go away because we want it to. You understand that, right?"*

No. Not at all. She was training, too. But not to hurt him. *"You don't understand. You and me, Drake. We're supposed to fix everything."* The dark, winding prophecy mark down the back of her neck proved that. If she wasn't meant to stop the next war, then she and Drake wouldn't be meeting in a world so far away from their own. *"Fate is on our side."*

"Why does everyone always think Fate is on their side?" he asked quietly. *"Maybe Fate wants something different. Maybe Fate likes war."*

Hope coughed. What a bad thought. Fate had to be good, right? *"I don't think so."*

"Okay." Drake lifted his head and stared down the beach. "I think you're waking up."

Cold rain splashed into her face, and she lifted her head, coughing, next to a big tree. Her bike was beside her, covered in pine cones and mud.

"Hope. Oh, God. You're not dead." Tears streaked down Paxton's face as he held her. His knees were under her head, and his hands were against her cheeks. "I was so scared."

She swallowed and tried to sit up. A thought struck her. "Where's Libby?"

"Hope!" her daddy yelled, roaring toward her down the trail.

Oops. Paxton turned pale. "Libby went to get your mom," he whispered.

"Hope." Her daddy dropped to his knees, his big hands already running over her arms and legs. Rain splattered his thick black hair to his head. "How badly are you hurt? Where were you hit?" His green eyes were darker than usual, and his voice had gone demon hoarse.

"I hit my head." She let her daddy help her up.

Paxton let go of her and shuffled to his feet, his head down. "I'm sorry, King Kyllwood. It's my fault. It's all my fault."

Her daddy lifted her against his wide chest and held her close. Strength and really hard muscles surrounded her. His forest scent covered her, and she snuggled into safety. "It wasn't Pax's fault, Daddy," she whispered. "He told me not to jump, but I didn't listen. Don't blame Pax." It seemed like Pax was always in trouble, and this was her fault. Not his. It took her a second to realize her daddy was shaking a little.

She blinked, looking up into his hard face. "I'm okay," she whispered.

He nodded, and his huge chest shuddered. "I know. I can see." He turned and ruffled Pax's hair, even while holding Hope up so high. "Stop taking blame you don't deserve," he said gently.

Pax looked up at her. "I didn't want you to be mad at Hope."

"I'm not mad at either one of you. And you can call me Zane. You know that." Her daddy started down the trail, where Libby was waiting, wringing her hands. "Janie Belle is in town at a movie with her mom, so I'm making grilled cheese sandwiches for dinner. Pax and Libby, why don't you come keep Hope company and eat with us."

Pax's smile was a little wobbly, but he nodded.

Her daddy kept walking. "And then we'll have a little talk about biking and safety."

Hope sighed. She figured there would be a talk. There was always a talk. Too many talks. That's why she couldn't tell her daddy about the new dreamworld.

For now, it had to be her secret. But maybe she could find out if he'd talked to his brothers, Sam and Logan.

Her stomach hurt again and she closed her eyes.

Where were her uncles?

Chapter 10

The male kept her gaze after ordering her from the pool. Lightning flashed across the sea, temporarily turning the sky purple.

Something had just shifted in Logan. Mercy eyed him from beneath her lashes, trying to gauge his mood. Mentioning his niece had probably been a bad idea, but honestly, she'd wanted to warn him from the very start. Kids should be left out of wars. But this wasn't a war, was it? This was the survival of pretty much everybody. "I like it here in the hot springs," she said, a chill wandering down her back, even with the warm water.

Pressure instantly throbbed in her temples. She gasped. Then more, like a thumb pushing past her skull to slide along her brain. She gaped at him.

He kept her gaze, and her brain started to itch.

"Stop it," she snapped. At the moment, he was just tickling her mind.

Irritation darkened his eyes. "You have no shields. No defenses whatsoever against a demon mind attack."

Why did that make him angry? He should be glad it'd be so easy to fry her brain. "Then go ahead and do your worst." She'd known taking on Logan Kyllwood might end like this. Supposedly when a demon attacked minds, they came out of their bodies a little, so perhaps she could somehow knock him out the second he attacked.

He laughed.

She blinked. "What's so funny?"

"Come attack me. Please." His amusement combined with the rise in atmospheric pressure around them as the wind kicked in and started battering the surrounding trees. Branches waved and several cracked.

Her stomach dropped. "Wh-what do you mean?" He couldn't have read her mind. That was impossible.

"No, it isn't." His amusement deepened. "Guess your dossiers on demons didn't tell you everything, now did they?"

She shook her head, still feeling as if he had his hands inside her skull. "That's crazy."

He nodded. "It's a rare skill, I'll admit."

She narrowed her gaze, ignoring the storm gathering around them. "What am I thinking right now?"

"That the color green is your favorite," he murmured.

Damn it! Did he know how sexy she found him? How she'd dreamed of him from the first moment she'd seen his picture in a research dossier? "Can you read everyone's mind?" How freaking awful would that be?

He slowly shook his head. "No. In fact, it's unusual. When I attack a brain, sometimes I can get a thought or two, but normally I can't read minds at all. Most people, even humans, have shields that protect their thoughts. You don't."

Well, crap. She hadn't realized that was a skill she needed to develop. No Fae still alive knew how to do that. She couldn't let him know the full truth about her people. But she was a quick learner. She imagined a big iron shield slapping around her brain.

His smile deepened. "Nicely done. You could learn to do it." Slight pain pierced into her temporal lobe. "Not tonight, unfortunately."

This really wasn't fair. Not at all. Of course, neither was kidnapping him or his brother. She sighed. Tears swam in her eyes from frustration. He wasn't hurting her, not really, but he could. She couldn't stop him. A tear rolled down her cheek.

"Damn it," he muttered.

Suddenly, the pain receded, as did the pressure.

Her mouth gaped open. Were they done? Did he know everything? He fixed his dark eyes on her, and his face went tight. But his voice softened. "Here's the deal. I ask, you answer, and I'll stay out of your brain." He held up a hand when she started to protest. "If you don't answer, I'll wander through there as gently as I can, but I will know every thought you've ever had. The choice is yours."

How was that even a choice? The man had gotten his way without lifting a finger to harm her. She'd been sure he wouldn't hit or torture her, but this was different. He hadn't even hurt her when getting her thoughts. Still, this sucked.

"Come on, Mercy. You know you want to tell me everything, anyway." His gritty voice was almost a low croon.

She hated that he knew that. Of course, she hadn't hidden much from him even at the beginning—except the full truth about the Fae nation. If she had a brother, she'd want to save him. If Trina or Sandy were taken, she'd do whatever she had to do to rescue them. She couldn't really blame Logan for insisting she help find Sam, and the last thing she wanted was for him to see her thoughts about his hard body. How embarrassing. "Fine," she muttered.

The air shimmered behind Logan.

"Hell," he bellowed, planting one hand on a rock and leaping over to land on the swirling leaves.

Frank and Jocko appeared, disappeared, and reappeared behind him. Both were bleeding from head wounds, and their uniforms were torn and ragged. Man. Sam Kyllwood must've put up an incredible fight while they transported him.

Logan leaped at the Fae, taking both wounded soldiers down hard. The air sparked.

"He can stop you," Mercy yelled, splashing across the hot springs and reaching the rock Logan had bounded over. The soldiers didn't know Logan could halt a teleporting. She climbed over the rocks, and the cold air instantly puckered her skin.

Logan punched Frank in the face so hard that the bones audibly cracked. Frank's head bounced twice on the ground, and his eyelids fluttered shut.

Jocko hit Logan in the mouth and kicked up, trying to get the demon off him.

Logan backflipped, stood, and brought his foot down on Jocko's neck. The younger Fae slumped, instantly out cold.

The fight was over before Mercy even found her footing on the chilly ground. She couldn't let him kill them. They were friends, and the Fae were few. Way too few.

Logan turned around, his eyes so dark they were almost black. "They must've been teleporting all over the island to find us. How many times can your people do that without resting?"

She looked at the prone soldiers as the clouds opened up and rain started pummeling the ground. "Four, maybe five or six times. But if Sam fought them, they were weakened anyway." Only a highly trained and gifted demon could fight during a teleport. Or stop one, for that matter. "Don't kill them."

Logan gave her a look of disgust. "They're young and untrained. Don't worry."

She tried not to wince. They were her age, and they were among the best trained of the Fae. Only a couple of older soldiers still lived, and they worked tirelessly to train the younger ones. All ten of them, including her. "They got your brother," she reminded him.

His gaze hardened so quickly it made the moisture dry up in her mouth. "Looks like he gave them some trouble."

She nodded.

Lightning flashed again, and the sea started to churn. She shivered, the cold air brushing across her wet body. "You should go, Logan."

His snort just pissed her off. "I'm not afraid of these two. There's a forestry cabin at the north end of this island—it'll take me about two hours to get there. We can ride out the storm and then take a floatplane to the mainland tomorrow morning."

What? "Where do you plan to get a floatplane?" she snapped, blinking through the rain.

"There are two not far from here. I scouted as I ran," he said. "People camp and fish here, and it won't be a problem."

She swallowed and toughened her stance. While he'd had no problem knocking out the two soldiers, he wouldn't hit her. "I'm staying here."

"It's like you want me to put my hands on you," he murmured.

Her shiver this time had nothing to do with the cold. Why did her body have a mind of its own with him? The guy was just too sexy. Though he'd been nice by carrying her across the island and all, they still had far different goals. "I don't want to fight you, but I will." She was better trained than he knew. But then what? The soldiers were out for the duration, and she couldn't teleport. But if she could knock him out, she could get to a boat or plane or something and escape. So the plan was fight, win, and run.

Good plan.

No, crappy plan. But she had a chance—a slim one—and she had to take it.

He sighed. "I'm getting tired of your nonsense. Once again, I'm happy to carry you. Either piggyback like before, or over my shoulder, which I doubt would be comfortable."

Irritation clawed her. He was just so arrogant. So lazily sure of himself. "I think I'd rather fight," she said, bracing her legs.

"Fine." Any patience he'd shown seemed to be completely gone as the wind whipped into a frantic show of force. "Let's get this over with."

She held up a hand. "No brain attacks. This is a fair fight."

"Oh, darlin'. This ain't anywhere near a fair fight," he drawled, his eyes flaring. "But I promise to keep it physical, per your request."

Physical. Him and her. She swallowed over a lump in her throat. He wasn't trying to be sexy, but there it was. She really needed to get away from him to reclaim some sense of control over herself. "Fine." She motioned him forward.

He snorted. "You attack."

This was a one-shot chance. If she gave him any sense that she could fight, he'd lose that arrogance and watch her. Okay. She could do this.

She shook out her arms. He'd be expecting a kick to the groin. "Mercy, are you going to attack any time soon?" he asked casually.

What a dick. She nodded. "Yes."

Lightning zapped, hitting a tree near the soldiers. She jumped back and yelped. The tree cracked, and several branches dropped to the ground. The smell of ozone burned through the air.

Electricity caught her, and adrenaline flooded her entire system. She feinted a kick to his groin.

He twisted to the side, his hand already swiping down to strike her leg.

God, her balance had to work this time. She kicked up as hard as she could, catching Logan beneath the chin and completely by surprise.

His head snapped back with an audible crack.

Dropping and rolling, she came up with one of the blazing branches, swinging with all her might for his temple. The heavy wood hit him hard enough that blood spurted, and he dropped to one knee with a grunt.

Panicking, the blood roaring through her ears, she swung again at the same temple. Then again.

Logan pitched forward, landing on his face in the fresh mud. His legs flopped behind him.

She froze in place. Completely.

Rain slashed down, blown about by the furious wind. Three immortal males lay prone on the ground, out cold.

Had that really just happened? Seriously?

She gulped in air. Her fierce hold on the branch had the bark cutting into her palms, and she dropped it. Holy marshmallows on a spreadsheet of fire. She'd knocked out Logan Kyllwood. Gingerly, she nudged him with her bare foot.

Nothing.

She bit her lip. Victory tinged with a sharp warning rippled through her. That would teach him to underestimate her. Man, she had to get out of there, and now. She looked at the soldiers and then at Logan. Could she just desert them all? Logan probably wouldn't kill the soldiers, but what if they killed him?

Why did anybody have to die?

The rain punished them all, soaking them. The wind added debris, piling up against their hard bodies.

She blinked, trying to see.

Logan grunted. Then stirred.

Bloody hell. She turned and ran into the forest, dodging between trees. The demon would be safe from the soldiers.

She ran faster, rocks cutting into her freezing feet. Would she be safe from him?

Chapter 11

Pain flashed hot and bright through Logan's head. He tried to move past it, but it caught him and pulled him into a storm so wild he could smell the fury of the gods.

All of a sudden, he was barely ten years old again.

His mama was crying in the other room while he faced his brothers, Zane and Sam, in the game room that had been filled with fun just one month ago. Their eyes, green like his, were serious and sad. Their vampire dad had died fighting against the Kurjans, and now they had to go and live with their demon relatives. His stomach hurt.

No matter how long he lived, his heart would always have a hole in it. His dad had been the strongest vampire ever, and now he was gone. It wasn't right. Nothing made sense. Everything ached.

Zane was the oldest, and somehow, he looked older than he had a week ago as he sat on the pool table. "Uncle doesn't like us, but our one goal is to keep Mom safe. He hates her, but he rules the demons."

"Then why are we going there?" Logan asked, kicking away a tennis ball that had rolled out from under the sofa where he sat next to Sam. "Let's stay here."

"We can't," Sam said softly, rubbing his dark hair. "We're half demon, and the demons and vampires are going to war."

"Let's be with the vampires, then." None of this made sense. Logan wouldn't cry, though. He wouldn't.

Zane scratched his chin. "Most of our group was taken out, Logan. We aren't aligned with the Realm and never have been." Most vampires were with the Realm, which was at war with the demons. "We don't know any of them, and we'd probably be used against our demon family. So we go to our uncle."

Sam sighed. "We'll have to fight."

"I'll fight," Zane said. "I'll do everything I can to keep you guys out of it until we're old enough to find safety on our own."

Logan wanted to run, but there was nowhere to go. Sometimes Fate sucked. "We'll all have to fight, and you know it." He'd had some training, but not nearly enough. But he'd soon be trained by demons, which didn't sound like much fun. Still, if this was the only way to keep his family safe, he'd do it.

Zane hopped off the pool table, his black hair tied at his nape, his dark green eyes somber. Then he moved toward them, dropping to his knees. "I can't explain it, but I know we have to do this. Someday, no matter what I have to do, I'm going to take the nation from our uncle."

That was crazy. Nobody could beat their uncle. He was the toughest and meanest immortal alive on Earth. Fear caught Logan around the throat. "Zane—"

"Trust me," Zane said.

The only way Uncle would step down would be with his head cut off. Zane didn't really think he could kill the leader of the demon nation, did he?

Zane nodded as if Logan had spoken out loud. "I'll do what needs to be done. We're brothers. That's all that matters." The fear in his eyes was painful to see. Logan could almost feel it in his gut.

He lifted his chin. Faking a smile, he tried to keep his lips from trembling. "We're tough—the toughest. We're Kyllwoods." His voice cracked, but he kept the smile in place. "It'll be okay, Zane. I promise that we'll be fine and Mom will, too." He wasn't sure how he'd make that happen, but he fought better than any demon

*or vampire his age, and that had to mean something. He'd use
that gift and get even better. Stronger. Until he was unbeatable.
Zane's chin lifted, and he held out both hands.*

*Logan grasped his hand and then grabbed Sam's in his other
one. They were brothers. No matter what happened, no matter
what he had to do, he'd be what they needed him to be. If Zane
needed him to be a good soldier, then he'd do it. Anything to
protect his brothers and their mom.*

*Sam dropped his chin. "This is going to get bad for a while.
Really bad."*

*Logan shivered. Sometimes Sam knew stuff he shouldn't. The
future couldn't be already set...they had to be able to build their
own lives. Yet he'd learned to listen to Sam. "Will we live?"*

*Sam nodded. "For a while, anyway. We just have to remember
why we're doing this."*

Zane looked at them both. "Brothers."

*Logan straightened his back, his senses settled. That was that,
then. "Brothers," he vowed. Forever.*

Logan jerked awake and coughed out mud. He hadn't thought
of that day in years. Turning his head, he spit out more mud.
What in the world? Rolling over, he blinked as rain pummeled
his face. Memory returned, and he jumped to his feet, swaying
as dizziness rolled through him.

He reached out blindly and pressed his hand against a spruce
tree. The smell of the storm, wild and tamarack-scented, grounded
him. Straightening, he wiped mud off his face and stared at the
two soldiers still on the ground. Surprise and then anger scraped
down his back.

Mercy had knocked him out.

He'd just gotten his ass handed to him by a fairy small enough
to put in his pocket and carry around.

He shook his head and stars flashed behind his eyes, cutting
deep. Blood flowed down the side of his face, warming his skin
despite the icy rain. It had been so long since he'd lost a fight that
the shock of it kept him immobile for several moments.

Then fury roared in.

The woman had hit him with a branch and left him with two soldiers who wanted him dead. If they'd come to first, they might've cut off his head. His anger strengthened, mostly at himself. He hadn't taken her seriously, and she'd kicked his ass.

Looking around, he found her footprints in the mud. He lifted his head and caught her scent. Wild gardenias.

Shaking off the pain, he turned to track her. The woman knew where Sam was, and she knew what the deal with his niece was. Protecting his family was all that mattered to him. Nobody in this lifetime or the next would hurt Hope Kyllwood.

He'd do anything and everything to ensure that—which meant capturing Mercy. Again.

Never again would he underestimate her. When he caught up to her, and he definitely would, he'd show her that one simple fact.

* * * *

Pain rammed into Mercy's feet with each new rock, while the wind beat at her as if it was on Logan's side. Her hair whipped around in the rain, which had become so dense visibility was almost nil. She tried to keep to the rocky shoreline as much as possible. There had to be a cabin or two somewhere around there. Logan had said people fished from the island.

Of course, he hadn't said where the island was located.

The lake that Sam had dropped them into had been freezing—snow pack, or maybe glacier?

Lightning crashed through the darkness. Something brown caught her eye two trees ahead. With her heart racing in her freezing body, she shoved her way past them and almost started crying in relief.

A hand-hewn cabin nestled amid a large outcropping of rocks. It was dark and deserted, its boards hanging precariously in several places.

But it was shelter from this stormy night.

She stumbled over more rocks and reached the front door. No porch. No steps. The door was about a foot up, and she easily swung it inward. No lock, either. Shaking almost violently, her panties and bra soaked through, she crossed into the silent, dark cabin.

She sensed him before she saw him. Turning out of pure instinct, she caught sight of Logan charging through the doorway behind her. Her shoulders slumped. She had finally found shelter after hours of running, and here he was. Her victory was so short-lived.

And she was not even the slightest bit pleased that the soldiers hadn't killed him. Nope. Not at all.

Rain matted his dark hair to his head, and water slid over the incredibly hard planes of his body. He looked her over, head to toe, then glanced around.

She gulped in air and did the same.

Logs were stacked neatly next to a fireplace to the left of a counter with a cookstove and a couple of cupboards. Two bunk beds were shoved against a far wall. One scarred and ripped sofa faced the fireplace. Old fly rods and water skis had been mounted on the walls in various places. It was probably some guy's getaway in the middle of nowhere.

She shivered, her teeth chattering. Why wasn't Logan saying anything?

He strode toward the fireplace, a large shadow moving with grace. Lightning lit up the night outside, and with the door open, illuminated his wet footprints across the uneven boards.

She wiped rain off her face and edged toward the doorway.

"Don't make me stop you," he growled, bending to shove kindling into the empty fireplace and striking a match. "You don't want my hands on you right now."

The dark tone propelled her into motion out of pure instinct. She leaped for the exit, seeking freedom like any wild animal trapped in a snare.

He caught her before she cleared the doorway, one arm hooked around her waist. The air whooshed out of her lungs and she bent over, her hair flying around her head. He lifted her and swung them both around, kicking the door closed with one bare foot.

Then he pressed her against it, up high, his tight body holding her in place, his nearly glowing green eyes an inch from hers. "I'm done with the bullshit, Mercy." His chest was a hard plate against hers, his legs solid steel, and his...oh God. Only wet and very thin underwear separated them.

She could feel him. Hard and long and hot.

That quickly, she flushed head to toe with her own warmth. Her cheeks burned, but hopefully he couldn't see her clearly with the small fire behind him. He completely blocked her from seeing it, but the crackle as it ignited filled the night.

It took every ounce of control she had not to rub against him. Just a little.

What was wrong with her? She was trapped against a doorway by a very pissed off demon-vampire hybrid whom she'd knocked out hours before, and her body had a life of its own. "Let me down," she ordered, her voice breathy.

"No." He held her aloft with minimal effort. "We need to get a couple of things straight, and now."

The imagery that shot through her head made her groan. She was losing her mind. Completely. Squinting, she tried to see his temple. It was smooth and wet from the rain. Demons really did heal quickly. "This is my refuge from the storm. You need to leave. Now." He was crazy if he thought she couldn't knock him out again.

"You want to be tied to the bed?" he rumbled.

She jerked back. More images. Him, her, ties on the bed, his hard body. She shook her head rapidly, her hair catching in the jagged wood of the door.

"Good. I'm planting your ass on that sofa, and you're going to face the fire and warm up. Then, you're going to tell me what I want to know. All of it." He waited a second, and when she didn't argue, he easily carried her across the room to the sofa. "Move,

Mercy, and you'll regret it. I promise." He turned back to add logs to the fire.

The couch was soft and surprisingly comfortable. And the fire was already working to warm the room. She involuntarily leaned toward it.

He stood, crossed to the bunks and returned, unzipping a big plastic bag. Sitting at the far end of the couch, he pulled out a thick wedding-ring quilt.

She almost reached for it.

He held it back. "Question number one. Answer it, and you get the quilt. Don't answer it, and you lose an article of clothing."

Her breath caught. The bra and panties weren't hiding anything, but the idea of being naked with him filled her with vulnerability. And an odd breathlessness she could *not* examine right now. Even so, she met his gaze fully. The male thought he could intimidate her with thoughts of her own nudity? With fear? Not a chance. She couldn't let him win this. No matter what, she wouldn't give in. "Fine." Reaching behind her back, she unhooked the bra, drew it down her arms, and tossed it at his head.

Chapter 12

Logan stopped breathing. Her breasts were pert with sweet pink nipples, and they bounced when she threw the bra at him. He hooked one finger through the strap to catch it. Her defiance was an aphrodisiac to a demon like him.

But that spirit. He couldn't help but be impressed. And aroused, which he did nothing to hide. "Next question?" he dared. Would she take off the panties? Truth be told, he had planned to make her take off both wet garments after he'd given her the quilt to cover herself. She was certainly making this easy.

She faltered, but her eyes flared hot. One blue and one green. Fucking intriguing as hell.

"Sure." Standing, her legs shaking and her teeth still chattering, she gracefully slid the panties to her ankles and then stepped out of them.

His dick got so hard his entire abdomen began to ache. Bad.

She twirled the minuscule pink scrap around on her hand.

He kept his face stoic and his body relaxed, but what the hell was he supposed to do now? He wanted to look—badly—but that seemed ungentlemanly. Sure, she'd taken off her clothes, but even so. He'd dared her. She'd surprised him with the bra, and he'd looked before he could stop himself. But not now. Keeping his gaze on her face might kill him.

Then she'd be able to escape.

If that was her plan, it was shockingly good. If his cock got any harder, he'd have a stroke. Maybe there was an aneurism in his head about to go. The pressure attacking him made it seem possible.

If he threatened to tie her to the bed, she'd probably hold out her wrists. The woman was a rebel. If he threatened to spank her, something he'd truly enjoy at the moment since he'd had to run through a storm to find her, she'd probably bounce right at him and plant herself over his knee.

He winced. It was possible one of his balls had just exploded.

"What now?" she asked, her voice throaty.

His chuckle was pained, and he couldn't mask it. Well. If she was being direct, he could do the same. "How about we forget we're enemies and spend the next several hours on one of those beds? A détente of sorts." Then he held his breath.

Her chin went back and her eyebrows rose.

Good. He'd finally surprised her.

She bit her lip, looked at the bed, then back at him. "Then what?"

Holy fuck, she was considering it. "Then we go back to... this." Wait a minute. What the hell was he doing? Sam was in danger—and who knew where. Before Logan could take back the offer, she was sizing him up.

"Well, I would like to give it a shot," she said, licking her bottom lip.

His dick jerked. He tilted his head to the side. "Sex with me?"

"Yes. Sex. Always wanted to try that." She tossed the panties over by the fireplace. "All right. Do you know what you're doing?"

His mouth went dry. Wait a minute. She hadn't just said what he thought she'd said, had she? He shook his head. "You—you haven't, I mean..."

Amusement curved her pretty lips. "No. One of the laws of our people."

"And it's *enforced*?" he coughed out, his ears burning.

She lifted a shoulder. "We follow the laws. I mean, there has been talk of a revolution, but then the dimensions started to disintegrate because of the Seven and we've had to concentrate on other issues."

The female was a virgin. "Man, sweetheart." He tossed the bra over with the panties to dry. "You don't want to waste that on me." His body cooled fractionally. "I wouldn't waste it on Niall the asshole, either. You want that to be special." He'd wanted to fuck her hard and fast until neither of them could think. That wouldn't do now.

She rolled her eyes, her body illuminated by the fire. "It's not a spiritual thing, Logan. It's a law, one most of us don't like and had planned to change anyway. You made an offer, and I accept." She shoved her wet hair away from her face. "But I would like a few moments to myself if you don't mind. Where's the bathroom?"

"Outside," he said automatically. "Around the side to the left. It's just an outhouse with a mirror." He'd scouted the entire place before coming inside.

She held out a hand for the quilt, and he gave it to her, his mind spinning.

"I'll be right back," she whispered, heading to the door, wrapping herself tight.

He watched the door close. No. They couldn't do this. Not a chance. The second she returned, he'd let her down gently. Yeah. That was it. Man. His head hurt all of a sudden. He stoked the fire, making warmth spread through the entire room. Then he checked the bunks to be sure they were sturdy enough for the two of them to get some sleep during the storm.

Then he looked at the door. The woman was probably scared to death.

Sighing, he headed for the door and walked through the damn storm. Rain slapped him, mildly cooling his desire. The wind pierced his wet underwear and pissed him off. He'd nicely explain that she needn't worry and that it wasn't going to happen. Then he'd figure out how to get her to reveal Sam's location. Finally, he reached the outhouse.

It was empty.

* * * *

The quilt protected her from the wind and rain, but it hampered her movements. Mercy pulled it up higher on her legs to give herself more freedom to run. Logan would expect her to head back to the soldiers so she could teleport away if one of them was conscious. Heck. If one of them was still there.

So the smart thing to do would be to run in the opposite direction. Except...he'd tracked her to the cabin. Through the wild storm and crazy wind, he'd found her fairly easily. Apparently, it didn't matter where she ran. He'd follow.

The Fae soldiers were her only chance.

She figured she had a ten-minute head start while he gave her privacy in the outhouse. Part of her wanted to feel bad about fooling him, but the other part wanted to laugh like a hyena over the look on his face when she'd said she had never had sex. She sobered, dropping her chin and running faster. He had been awfully sweet about it, though.

The demon had also been fairly patient with her. So far she'd kidnapped him, knocked him out, and now had fooled him.

A chill clacked down her spine. Everyone had a breaking point, and surely she'd hit his by now. Even though they were on opposite sides of the situation, it hadn't really felt like he was her enemy.

She jumped over a downed tree, and the blanket caught. Swearing, she tugged the material free and loped back into a jog. The wind fought her, slowing her pace even more.

Had she pushed Logan too far this time?

As an enemy, a real one, she knew he was merciless. Cold and deadly. But she hadn't seen that side of him, and hopefully it was in the past. Left back in the war that was now over, relegated to manila folders and computer files that no longer mattered. She shivered at what she'd read.

Faster. She had to run faster.

He came out of nowhere, somehow ahead of her, a solid form in a swirling storm. His legs were braced, his chest broad and bare and scarred, his eyes black with green rims around the irises. He looked like the hybrid predator he was rumored to be.

She shrieked and tried to stop, but momentum threw her right into him.

He used it against her and swung her up, lifting her against a tree so they were eye to eye. His free hand wrapped around her throat, pressing in, and he leaned toward her, his nose nearly touching hers.

She couldn't move. Even if she could move, the look in his eyes would have stopped her in place. Stopped the entire world.

"I'm done," he said, the words barely discernible for the grittiness of his voice.

Her nostrils flared and her chest heaved as she tried to take in more oxygen. As she panicked. She struck out and struggled, but the comforter trapped her in place against his body. He let her fight it out until she gave in with a sob, her eyes wide on his. Her mouth opened, but no words came out. The vulnerability of her position shook her.

"Got it?" he asked, squeezing just enough to threaten the flow of air to her lungs.

She slowly nodded. There wasn't anything else she could do. He was so warm and she was so cold. So tired of being alone. For a brief moment, they'd almost been on the same side. Together. Her heart wanted that with a physical pang, but her head knew better. Soon they'd probably hate each other. That thought sliced through her chest.

So she kissed him.

She closed her eyes and went all in, trying to soften the impossibly hard line of his mouth. He went rigid against her. Murmuring, she licked along his bottom lip. He tasted of something unique—all Logan. Spicy and somehow sweet. She pressed closer, her arms finally freed of the quilt.

He released her neck and manacled his fingers in her hair, jerking her head back so suddenly she cried out and opened her eyes.

His eyes had lost the green. All of it. He breathed hard, dropped his gaze to her mouth, and then swooped.

It wasn't a kiss. She didn't have a word for what it was. His lips took hers with a fierceness that surpassed the storm whipping around them. Deep and hard and pissed, he took her over. Absolutely. There was a rawness to his kiss, a sheer fury, that should've frightened her. But the deeper he went, the more she wanted. She kissed him back, trying to follow, finally letting him take what he wanted.

And he wanted everything.

The wind shook loose the comforter, and it dropped to the ground to be swept away. Logan moved in closer against her, the hard length of him trapping her in place. She wrapped her arms around his neck, feeling the strength in every inch.

He pressed against the apex of her legs, a male demand with no subtlety. She moaned into his mouth, her thighs lifting to bracket his. Never in her life had she felt like this. Whatever this was. It was beyond comprehension or description.

She just knew she wanted more.

He released her mouth to let her breathe, his hold stronger than ever. Fangs slid down in his mouth, glinting in the darkened night.

She gasped, fascinated.

He tugged her head to the side, firm and relentless. Her hands plastered themselves against his chest, and she tilted even more. Curiosity and a burning need throbbed through her so quickly it hurt to keep her eyes open. But she had to watch.

His strike was faster than even she could track. The sharp points slashed into her neck, going deeper than she would've imagined possible. He pierced nerves, muscle, and struck bone, claiming a place in her she hadn't realized existed. Desire flooded her with a sharp intensity that cut deep. Her head rolled back, and her eyelids fluttered closed.

Sparks flashed through her body, zinging around like a thousand fireflies. He growled against her neck and pressed against her raging clit. She exploded into particles of light, crying out his name, holding on to keep to this earth. His hold was absolute, from his hands to his body to his fangs inside her flesh.

There was no pain.

Only the sharp edge of ecstasy coupled with a need for more. She wanted more.

He took her blood—her very life force. She was now inside him, and a part of her would always belong to him. He retracted his fangs and licked the wound closed, his rough tongue flaring her nerves wide awake.

She panted out breath, her body relaxing against his, her eyelids lazily opening. The intensity in his gaze shot her body into full awareness again.

"You're not a virgin," he rumbled, his hold tightening even more, his cock pressing insistently against her sex.

"No," she whispered, fully aware of her nudity. They were so close.

His eyelids dropped to half-mast, giving him a deadly quality that seemed right at home on his face. She shivered. Wait. This was too much. He'd only kissed her and she'd all but lost her mind. She'd orgasmed from his fangs alone.

Fear grabbed her, but she couldn't speak. Couldn't move.

His gaze narrowed on hers. His chin lifted, and realization dawned across his expression. His shoulders went back and, keeping her gaze captive, he leaned down and swiped the comforter off the ground. Then he gently, way too gently for what had just happened, wrapped it around her and provided cover.

She blinked. Her body was on fire. She wanted this. Mostly. "Logan," she whispered.

"No," he said softly. "Not if you're scared. No."

That quickly, after all the subterfuge and strategy, her heart slammed hard against her rib cage.

For him.

Chapter 13

Logan lifted Mercy into his arms, turning back toward the cabin. The storm was increasing in force, and they needed to find shelter to ride it out until morning. His body was still on fire and having her in his arms was a torture too raw to contain. He'd been less than a whisper from entering her, from going hard and deep into that wet heat.

Until he saw the fear in her eyes.

Oh, there had been desire and need, too.

But with the fear, he'd had no choice but to stop. Even if it killed him. Which fucking frankly, it might.

The anger still rode him, just under the surface. She was cute and sweet and spunky, and she'd done nothing but make a complete fool of him. A part of him he didn't much appreciate was impressed and intrigued by that fact. The other part wanted to lay her down and spend days showing her the true meaning of submission. Every time she dared him, the demon deep down inside, the demon he controlled ruthlessly, roared wide awake.

What was it with this female?

Why did he want to protect her—even from his own true nature? No stranger in the world could've gotten away with kicking him in the head and knocking him out. Maybe his mom or niece. Possibly his sister-in-law. But that was it. And not one of them would've done those things in the first place.

So why was he giving her a pass?

If he had half a brain, he'd turn her over to Zane to deal with. But no matter how much he wanted to find Sam, he didn't want her scared. Zane would never truly hurt a female, but he'd probe her brain until there wasn't a secret compartment left. Logan should do the same. Plus, he'd been the one to lose Sam. It was his damn job to find his brother.

"If they're hurting Sam, I'm going to burn your nation down," Logan said, ducking his head over her to protect her from the rain. "You might find it hard to believe, in light of the last twenty-four hours, but I could take out most of your soldiers in an hour—and not by knocking them out. I'm talking heads rolling away from bodies. And I would."

"I know," she whispered. She snuggled her cold nose into his neck like a satisfied kitten.

His chest warmed. What in the world was he going to do with her? He'd bitten her, for Pete's sake. While he'd been with more females than he could count, he'd never once bitten one. Not even the shifters he and Garrett had dated for a while.

Speaking of Garrett, Logan had to get back to the Seven. Garrett was still dealing with the aftereffects of the Seven ritual, and Logan was his best friend. More like brother. As soon as he saved Sam, he had to get back to Garrett.

But there was Mercy.

He looked down, mildly surprised to see her completely asleep. The scent of blood perked up his senses, and he leaned down to check her neck. His bite mark remained, but he'd sealed it. Where was the blood?

Her unpredictability should annoy the shit out of him. He'd scared her, and she'd kissed him. Who did that?

Holding her tight, he continued at a fast pace through the swaying trees. If she was bleeding, he had to find the wound. Couldn't she heal herself like most immortals? Everything he knew about fairies could be kept in a toothpaste lid.

They reached the crappy cabin in record time. He kicked open the door and moved to deposit her on the sofa, rapidly removing the wet comforter and grabbing the last remaining blanket from the bed to wrap around her. Feeling like an asshole, he crouched in front of her and placed his hands on her knees.

She opened her eyes, the pupils cloudy. She yawned and looked around. "The fire is still going."

"We weren't gone long," he said. Although a shit-ton had happened, now hadn't it? "I'm sorry to awaken you."

She blinked sleep away and swayed. "Shouldn't we sleep the storm away?"

Wrapped in the blanket, her hair a wild mess around her lovely face, she looked like an angel. Which she definitely was not. He actually had to take a moment and remind himself of that fact. "We have to talk, Mercy. Then we'll sleep."

She sighed, blowing hair out of her face. "Fine. Just fine."

Exhaustion often helped with interrogation, and he had to take advantage of the opportunity. But he'd learned a lot about her. She was sexy and passionate, kind and sweet. Smart, too. So he went with the truth. "I feel like it's my fault that Sam was taken, and the idea of him being hurt is like a kick to the gut. For so long, my brothers and mom were all I had. She was constantly in danger, and we did our best to be good soldiers to protect her from my uncle. Now one of my brothers is in danger." It was the most words he'd spoken at one time in eons. "Please help me, Mercy."

The sleep partially cleared from her expression. "And if I don't?"

Why the hell was she always asking that damn question? He dropped his chin and his wet hair fell forward. "Then I'll probe your brain. I don't want to, but I can do it without causing damage." Most demons could not. "I'd try to stay out of personal areas that don't deal with Sam or Fae plans against my people, but I can't guarantee it."

Curiosity burned in her eyes, lightening the blue one. "Can you control my brain?"

He grinned. "No. I can't do mind control or make you actually do anything that you don't want to do." His gaze lowered to the smooth skin of her neck. "We can manipulate the fear and pain sections of your brain so you get frightened or think you're in agony." He cleared his throat. "And I can massage the pleasure points."

Pink flooded into her face. "Is that what you did back at the tree?"

He blinked. "No. That was just you and me." Her orgasm had nearly thrown him into his own.

Her eyes dropped. "I liked it. A lot."

He leaned back. Was she manipulating him? He frowned, trying to read her.

She sighed and met his gaze again. "I know I lied to you about the no-sex law. But come on, Logan. We're a people that pretty much raised ourselves. Did you really think there would be no sex?"

Hell if he knew. Fairies were almost mythical these days. "It was a smart move for you to escape," he allowed. "I feel like I should threaten you with something if you try to escape again."

Her eyes lit. "I've never been spanked."

His cock jerked wide awake. "It's not a punishment if you like it."

"Oh." She pursed her lips. "I'm not afraid of much." Her gaze shot away again.

So that was something. She was a mite afraid of him, which showed intelligence if nothing else. "You ever been bitten?" he asked.

"No," she whispered. "That was something new and rather unexpected. Shockingly so. Would that, um, happen if anybody bit me? The orgasm, I mean."

Heat slid beneath his skin. Anybody else biting her? That idea did not fucking sit well. "No. It wouldn't." Which was more than likely the truth.

"That's what I figured." She eyed him, the firelight dancing across her smooth face. "I don't know where your brother is. Our headquarters are in Edinburgh, but they wouldn't have taken Sam there since I'm with you. You know. In case you tortured me for information and I gave it up."

Anger snapped through him. "Your people, your fucking fiancé, is just fine leaving you with a demon who could easily torture you?" He'd need to take this Niall out just on principle. If Mercy was Logan's, there was no way in any hell dimension ever created that he'd leave her in the clutches of the enemy for one second. Ever.

"I'm pretty good at getting out of scrapes."

Because she was an unpredictable pain in the ass. "Even so, why isn't there a full-out blanketing of this island right now? If you were my intended and an enemy had you, there would be a thousand soldiers here right now looking for you." Logan was done with this shit.

She reared back. "Stop talking about me being yours. It'll never happen. I'm promised and that's that." Was that anger or sadness in her voice? Maybe both. "Plus, who says I need help? I did knock you out."

His hands tightened on her knees. "You've done a lot, sweetheart. But you're right back here alone in a cabin with me. I could pretty much do anything I want with you, physically or mentally. And where the fuck is Niall or all your soldiers?"

She sighed, and her shoulders drooped. "I can handle this on my own."

Ha. It was unthinkable. As soon as he got Sam back, he'd have to take out Niall. Sometimes life was too simple. "You must have some idea of where they've taken Sam?"

She winced. "Somewhere in Scotland, but again, I don't know where the cells are. Where they take people for questioning."

"Can you find out?" Logan asked.

She started to finger-comb her drying hair. "Maybe. But I'd have to ask Niall."

That wouldn't do.

"And I can't help you anyway. It'd be treason, and I agree with what we're doing. The Seven are truly clueless."

"Then explain it to us," he snapped, losing patience again.

She threw out her hands. "I wanted to. I really did. But our elders said you males wouldn't listen. This is our only hope to fix what you've done. We can't sacrifice the universe for you guys. Just can't do it."

None of this made a damn lick of sense. "What do you want with my niece?" he asked, switching topics on purpose to throw her.

Mercy shook her head, and the firelight caught the wild red hues in the dark mass of her hair. "Can't tell you. I'm so sorry."

"So am I." Holding her knees, he gently probed into her skull.

"Stop it," she snapped, her voice weakening.

He kept the movement to a gentle glide. There was no choice. "Tell me about Hope."

She's the lock. The words came from Mercy's head as clearly as if she'd spoken them.

"How do you know that?" He pressed harder.

Mercy's eyelids fluttered closed. "The prophesy is all about her. The ritual of the Keys can't be completed without her."

He already knew that. The ritual would take down the most dangerous, evil bastard in the entire world. A being so bad he had the means to end all enhanced females, probably including fairies. He was being held in a prison world, another dimension, one that was about to fail. "Why don't you want the ritual to be completed?"

She swayed. "You don't understand. Messing with the laws of physics was a huge mistake. You created three prison worlds, then bound them together to keep Ulric in the middle one. You can't do that, you arrogant asses."

"Why not?" he asked softly. The three worlds had been created eons ago, trapping the biggest threat to his people in the middle. Two members of the Seven occupied the protective outer bubbles, keeping evil secured inside. One bubble had burst recently, leading to the conclusion that the other two would soon fail as well. "Why was it a bad idea to create the bubbles?"

She snorted. "You can't combine dimensions, dumbass."

The name-calling while he was in her head was interesting. She had defenses he hadn't come across before. "Watch the name-calling."

"Spineless, easy to knock out, vampire-demon dumbass," she returned, not opening her eyes.

All right. Enough. He slid against the pleasure zones in her brain. She gasped, leaning forward at the waist. "What are you doing?"

"I told you not to call names. The only repercussions available to me are pain or pleasure. You're lucky I was amused enough to choose pleasure." He was getting tired of her dicking him around.

She sighed and threw her head back on the sofa, relaxing. "I'm getting really tired of being turned on here. It seems like we should take the edge off and then negotiate. What do you think?"

He thought she was going to fucking kill him. "I scared you out by the tree."

"Nope. My reaction to you scared me. You haven't scared me yet." She opened her eyes. "Listen. I have no clue where Sam is, and I won't even have a chance to find him until we're off this island. We can't leave here until morning when the storm dies down. I won't tell you about Hope, and I know you can go through my brain, but truth be told, I don't understand her role in the ritual. I'm more of a community planner and moneymaker." She shrugged. "I'm just here until I escape. Nobody is worried about info I don't possess."

In other words, even if Logan tortured her, he wouldn't learn much. "Your betrothed is an asshole."

She nodded, her eyes widening. "He's not so bad." She reached out and rubbed a hand down his bare arm, leaving sparks in her wake that shot right down to his balls. "I'm not trying to manipulate you. It's just that we started something out there, and I'm having trouble thinking until we finish it."

No fear. Not an ounce showed in her eyes.

"You get that we're on opposite sides of this thing? That we might end up being enemies, and I could hurt people you care about?" he asked, his mind fighting his body over what to do.

She reached out and cupped his chin. "One night, Logan. Just one."

Chapter 14

Logan looked at her like he wanted to eat her alive. One bite at a time. She swallowed, feeling small and somehow powerful at the same time.

"You don't understand me," he said softly, lust and desire crossing his expression.

Mercy tried to make her smile saucy, but her lips still felt a little blue from the cold. "I've read everything about you."

"Your innocence is both adorable and fucking irritating," he growled. "You and me? We're different. One night with you wouldn't be enough."

Now that was beyond sweet. Her smile widened while his jaw hardened even more.

He leaned closer. "I've tasted your blood and heard you cry my name in pleasure, and I want more."

"Then take more." Good line. Yes. She hadn't seen many movies, but that was decent dialogue.

His eyebrows edged down. "I'm a demon. A vampire. A hybrid." He gave a sharp nod as if that explained everything.

"So?" Her nose wrinkled.

He shook his head. "Your people made a mistake in leaving this world." Then he straightened and frowned, his nostrils flaring. "Are you hurt?"

Her eyes widened. "Not really."

He made a sound lower than a growl and reached for the blanket. She slapped his hands. "It's just my feet."

"Damn it." He leaned back and lifted her feet to his powerful thighs, his hold infinitely gentle. "Shit." Wincing, he turned them over, examining them from toes to ankles. The rocks and rough ground had sliced them to raw hamburger. "Can't you heal these?"

She nodded. "Sure. We heal really fast."

He lifted his head to meet her gaze. "Nobody has taught you to send healing cells to injuries." Again, he shook his head. "Your people need help, Mercy. You need to seek shelter with the Realm."

The Realm was their enemy. She'd been taught that since she was five years old. "You're a demon, Logan."

"We're aligned with the Realm," he said absently, wiping blood off the pad of her left foot. "Close your eyes. Let's see if we can do this. If not, I'll give you some blood, but I don't know how a fairy will react to demon blood."

"Fae," she said. "And you drank *my* blood."

"That's different. Close your eyes and do what I tell you to do."

Sometimes he was too bossy. But the cuts on her feet hurt, so what the heck. She closed her eyes. "All right."

"Imagine cells in your body that have one function only—to heal injuries." His voice was a low, gritty croon now.

"Okay." She imagined them a fluorescent blue. With the crackle of the fire and Logan's soft touch, she was getting more aroused than before. "I can see them."

"Send them to your feet and tell them to heal the cuts," he said.

She felt a little silly, but she did as he'd suggested. She tried really hard. "Is it working?"

"No," he sighed. "It should've worked, even if just a little."

She opened her eyes. "Maybe we can't heal ourselves."

His newest frown was somehow thoughtful. "You're an immortal species." His fangs dropped, sharp and deadly.

She almost climaxed again—just from the sight of them.

He cut into his wrist and held it to her mouth. "Take just a little until we see how you react."

She'd never tasted anybody else's blood before. So she licked him like a cat. He growled again—this time deeper. Energy sparked on her tongue and down her throat. He tasted like fine spiced wine. She took more, and her body finally warmed. Completely. Her feet began to throb.

She looked down and watched as the wounds slowly closed. The stitching hurt, softened, and then went numb. "Wow."

He eyed her carefully. "Feeling okay?"

She nodded. "Yes. Really warm."

Satisfaction tilted his lips. "Good." Then he pulled back, a wince stealing his almost-smile. "What the fuck?" He looked down at the palm of his right hand, his eyes wide. Then his head fell back and he glared at the damaged ceiling. "I knew it. Why? I mean just why the fuck?"

She drew her feet away, eyeing the door and then focusing again on the ticked-off immortal. "What's going on?"

His hand closed into a fist. "Nothing. Not a damn thing."

Um, okay. She kept still out of instinct. When he did nothing but look at her, pure irritation in his eyes, she sought some sort of neutral topic. "Can we go back to flirting? Talking about sex? You were explaining that a vampire-demon hybrid shouldn't have sex."

An angry red splashed across his angled cheekbones. "We can have sex. A lot of it."

She rolled her eyes. "You know what I meant."

He exhaled slowly as if trying to regain control of his temper. "Okay. You push every button I have, Mercy. The good ones, the bad ones, even the hidden ones."

What the heck did that mean? "Okay. So that means no sex?" Which was becoming fine with her. Sure, he kissed like a god, and he had a body women dreamed of, but come on. She didn't need to talk a guy into sex. "So you don't want me." She *so* knew that wasn't true. But whatever.

"All right." His tone seriously lacked patience. "There's no having sex and then going our opposite ways as enemies. If we have sex, if you let me inside you, I'm taking over. There will be no more of you pretending to be a kidnapper or being sent off to fail and possibly get tortured or killed. You'll be put somewhere safe until I can deal with the threat against you. Hell. The threats. All of them."

Her mouth gaped open. "That's ridiculous."

"Is it?" He shook his head. "Maybe. But it's also fact. I am *not* looking for a mate right now because there's a good chance that I won't survive the Seven ritual. Garrett barely made it, and he had help. So it wouldn't be fair."

Her heart did a little dance even as her temper all but exploded. "I'm not asking to mate you, damn it. Give me a break, Logan." She'd heard the expression on a television show once, and she liked it. It fit. "Sex can be casual, just a way to release frustration and tension." Though as she said the words, they didn't work. There wasn't anything casual about Logan Kyllwood.

He nodded. "It can, and that'd be great. But I'd never allow a female I'd bedded to be put into danger—especially danger that came from me or my people. You're different, and I think you know it. There's more to us, and it's a fucking tragedy that we can't explore further what we could have. But it's impossible."

Yeah, he was right about that. She had to stop the Seven at almost any cost, and he was part of the Seven. And the Realm was his ally, which was another problem. And, of course, she couldn't let down her entire nation by refusing to mate Niall.

But she did deserve one good night. Branches clashed against the siding, and thunder bellowed even louder outside. She leaned forward and cupped Logan's hard jaw. Stubble scratched her palm. "You're one of a kind, Kyllwood." Most males would've hopped in bed with her and then gone on their way the next day. She wasn't all that experienced, but saying no had to have cost him. His honesty was genuine, and her heart thumped even harder. It kept doing that around him. "You're sweet."

"Baby, I ain't sweet. Not a bit. I'm giving you fair warning."

She drew back, alarm ticking down her torso. "I don't understand."

"I know," he said softly. "But take my words seriously and literally. I already feel responsible for you, and letting you go is gonna hurt when this is all over. But if I claim you, I won't let you go if there's danger involved. Right now, you have all the control and can call the shots."

Was that even true? "If I tell you everything I know about where Sam might be and what the plan for Hope is, you'll just let me go?"

A muscle ticked in his jaw. The raging storm outside and the crackling fire inside were the only sounds for several seconds. Finally, he nodded. "Yes. If you can come up with a good-enough story that you won't be harmed upon returning to your people, I'll make sure you get there safely."

What would it be like to belong with Logan Kyllwood? To be his one and only? The prospect of safety was alluring, but they'd definitely have power struggles. Most couples, especially immortal ones, probably went through the same thing. Logan didn't seem like a male accustomed to losing. Ever.

"I'm not a sit-on-the-sidelines type of girl." Her hands itched to touch him again, so she clasped them in her lap.

"Aren't you?" One eyebrow lifted.

She pressed her lips together. Just because she preferred working corporate strategy and battle plans near a computer, didn't mean she *had* to do that. She could do what she wanted. "No." Her voice lacked conviction. Darn it.

"Tell me you get me. That you understand what I've tried to explain." His voice held an urgency that demanded her full attention.

"I heard you and understand," she said. If they got together, maybe in a couple of centuries, after the Seven had disbanded and moved on, then she'd be better equipped to deal with power struggles. Right now, she was way out of her depth and self-aware enough to know it. "We're good."

He didn't move, but his eyes slid to the side and toward the door. His body visibly went on full alert.

"What?" she whispered, looking wildly around.

He tilted his head more. "There's something—"

The back wall, the *entire back wall*, blew open.

Logan roared, scooped her up, and threw her across the room to land on the top bunk. She bounced and scrambled to grab the edge of the mattress to keep from falling.

Then he leaped at two soldiers, taking them both down.

Her eyes widened. The two on the ground weren't Fae. They wore full tack gear and had long white hair, just down the middle of their heads, braided tight.

Oh God. They were Cyst. She'd read about them, but she'd never actually seen one of the Kurjan's special-force soldiers. They were rumored to be spiritual leaders, but their fighting skills were legendary. She struggled to free herself from the blanket so she could drop to the ground.

Logan backflipped to his feet, powerful and dangerous even in his underwear.

The soldiers did the same in an odd dance that was as elegant as it was frightening. Their eyes were translucent purple and their skin so white that the blue veins beneath stood out. The first drew a gun, but Logan kicked it out of his hand before punching the other soldier in the face.

Mercy shoved the blanket away and jumped to the ground. There had to be some sort of weapon she could use.

The first soldier smiled, revealing sharp, yellowed teeth. He drew a knife from the back of his waist, just as the second guy moved in.

Logan kicked the second guy in the balls and he hunched over with a cried "oof." Then Logan pivoted, grabbed the knife, and shot an elbow into the whimpering soldier's gut before ducking his shoulder and tossing him over his head to land near the fireplace with a hard thump.

Before Mercy could move, Logan spun around and whipped the knife across the still standing Cyst's neck. Blood spurted in a wild arc. They went down, Logan still slashing.

The first guy on the floor rolled and spoke into his wrist. "We've found him. Cabin on the southeast side of the island. Send backup. Now." He bunched his knees to leap.

"No!" Mercy yelled, running toward him full bore. She cleared the sofa and hit him midcenter, aiming them toward the fire.

It was like colliding with a solid brick wall. He caught her and barely took a step back.

She brought her knee up, nailing him in the groin. His hold tightened on her arms, and pain engulfed her biceps. She cried out, struggling wildly, going for his eyes. This close, his eyes were nearly see-through. No mercy, no emotion lived in them. He shook her, and she cried out again.

A roar of pure fury filled the cabin.

The guy holding her turned just as Logan rushed them, his fangs out, his eyes the black of midnight. The Cyst soldier tossed her to the couch as if she were nothing and braced for Logan.

Logan smashed into him, sending them both careening through the wall next to the fireplace. They kept going into the barraging storm, hitting a tree and cracking it right down the middle.

Mercy shoved to her feet, looking wildly around. The other soldier lay on his back, his body half inside the cabin. He didn't look right. Her breath panted out of her chest, and her arms tingled with adrenaline as she scrutinized him. His head was gone.

Nausea rolled up her throat and she coughed. A bone protruded from where his neck should be. She didn't look for the head.

Almost in slow motion, going into shock, she turned to see Logan fiercely beating the other Cyst with just his fists. The pale soldier bled from pretty much everywhere, his body starting to sag, his eyelids closing.

Logan was merciless. No emotion, no anger, no humanity.

He beat the Cyst soldier until his head started to separate from his neck.

Mercy took an involuntary step back. The wind blew through the demolished cabin, picking up her discarded blanket and twirling it through the air to be carried away.

Logan slashed hard with a knife into the Cyst's throat, following the body to the ground and wrenching off the head.

Mercy gagged, her bare feet glued to the floor, her body totally nude.

Without pausing for even a second, Logan ripped off the Cyst's tac-vest and shirt, standing and kicking the head across the rocks. He turned. "Come here," he yelled through the wind.

Her stomach dropped. She could only stare.

Blood covered his face and his torso, mixing with the rain and pine needles. He was more powerful than any storm and more dangerous than any enemy. If death had a face, right now it would be Logan's. "Now."

Her legs trembled. She couldn't move.

"Mercy," he snapped. "Get your ass over here."

Before she could stop herself, her legs moved to obey him out of pure instinct. When she reached him, he pulled the Cyst soldier's huge shirt over her head and grabbed her hand. "We have to find the plane they came in. Now."

Chapter 15

The plane hadn't been serviced in a while. Logan kept a tight hold on the controls, but the wings still pitched wildly in the storm. Taking off through the waves had been insane, but there hadn't been any choice. Mercy huddled on the seat next to him, her knees drawn up beneath the long shirt he'd forced on her.

She was pale. Way too pale.

"You're going into shock," he said grimly, jerking the stick to keep them level. "Try to take deep breaths."

Her breathing was too shallow. He kept his chin down and focused on the nearly black clouds. So now she'd seen the real him. It was probably for the best.

The plane pitched and she gasped.

He righted it. "It's okay. I've got this." Probably. Plane and helicopter crashes kind of ran in the family, but he didn't need to tell her that sad fact. He did, however, require information. "I'm so sorry about this. They're after me. Not you." He'd figure out how they'd found him later. They were, after all, hunting the Seven, and their tracking abilities were legendary.

Her teeth chattered. "I've never seen them. I've heard and read about the Cyst, but in reality, they're so…"

Yeah. Scary as hell. Without question. Here he'd been pissed that her people had thrown her into danger, and just being in his vicinity had almost gotten her killed. "Mercy? I won't let anything or anybody harm you. Ever." It was the best he could do, and he meant every word.

She turned and looked out at the darkness. "I can fight, Logan."

Right. She was smart, but her fighting skills were barely better than a trained human's. The fact that she'd knocked him out had more to do with his attraction to her then her abilities. "I know, sweetheart," he murmured. Did the Cyst know she was a Key? Probably not. He had to lock her down.

He didn't like unanswered questions, and right now, there were way too many.

They reached the edge of the storm and broke free of the clouds. Dawn was beginning to peek over the horizon, and he finally let his chest relax. Okay. They were off the island. He'd find a place on the mainland to land, and then he'd find a phone.

The female was way too quiet.

"I need you to talk to me," he said, putting just a bite of order into his words. "Keep yourself out of shock."

Her sigh was irritated enough to give him hope. "I don't know where Sam is. Probably in Scotland somewhere. I can show you our land acquisitions when I have a computer, and you can search for him from there."

Well, that was agreeable. Apparently, she'd decided to stop fighting him. Or maybe she was just exhausted. "Thank you."

"Whatever." She waved her hand in the air. "Chances are Sam won't be at any of those places because I know about them, and Niall and the president know I'm with you. But you can have access to all of my records."

Shit. That was a good point. Logan glanced at her. She still looked too small and vulnerable—and frightened. She'd seen him kill brutally and efficiently. So much for their casual relationship that wouldn't have been casual. His heart hurt for a moment, and he banished the pain. There wasn't time for regrets. "Tell me something else. Tell me about those two friends of yours. The ones who helped to kidnap me."

She blinked and huddled more into herself.

"Start talking," he said softly.

She sighed. "Fine. We've been close since birth." Her voice saddened. "I don't know a thing about my genetic donors that I haven't learned by seeing photographs or reading dossiers. I don't know what they smelled like, laughed like, felt like. But Sandy and Trina, I know everything about them."

He kept an eye on the gauges and made a quick course correction. "I lost my dad when I was young, too. Sometimes it still hurts when I least expect it."

She turned toward him, her gaze running across his face. Then she nodded. "Yeah. But at least you had your brothers."

True. He never would've made it without his brothers. "You said genetic donors? What's the deal?"

She sighed. "I guess my people were knowingly doing risky science in trying to combine a couple of dimensions to create paradise, and the strongest left behind genetic material just in case. In a safe dimension."

"Enough to make ten babies?" He remembered her words from earlier.

"Yep. The rest of our remaining people are thousands of years old. Too old to procreate."

That was truly insane. He cleared his throat, trying to keep her engaged. "Trina and Sandy became your family?"

For the first time in too long, Mercy smiled. "Yes. Trina is kind of the wild one, while Sandy is the voice of reason. I'm the organized one. We banded together, tried to find happiness where we could."

"When you're not heading out on futile missions, what do you do?" He wanted to know more about her before they had to separate.

She shrugged. "Even when we lived off-world, I'd come here to manage our investments. We knew that we'd need capital and land if we ever had to return, so I manage all of our portfolios. Playing the stock markets and moving real estate is a little like gambling for me. I love it." She sniffed. "That's probably seriously boring for you."

Sounded interesting. He'd always liked intelligent women.

She perked up. "Right before I left for this mission, I took the precaution of neutralizing our stock portfolio by matching our holdings to the SMP100." Her frown was beyond cute. "Even though that has the disadvantage of increasing my turnover ratio and generating capital gains on which we'll have to pay taxes in the USA, it does give me peace of mind."

Never in his life would he have considered taxes to be sexy. Until now. "Sounds like a good plan." It was truly enjoyable to watch her mind at work.

"I've also started planning operations like the one where we took you. We sent out the info that I was a Key in a way that you guys would be sure to respond to."

True. He lost his amusement. They'd done a good job of suckering him in. "That was your plan?"

She nodded vigorously, her wild, wet hair flying around her slim shoulders. "Yes. Then I sent Trina to acquire some of our hidden assets, and I sent Sandy as backup. She's the best shot among us. She's really good."

"Your people have overestimated your fighting skills," he said mildly. "You're a Key, and apparently your people value you. Putting yourself in danger like you did shows an alarming lack of knowledge when it comes to my species."

She opened her mouth and then closed it again. The color slid away from her cheeks. "You're right. We had no idea." She shivered.

He wanted to kick himself in the head. She'd just calmed down, and he'd reminded her of his two most recent kills. Damn it. When he'd heard her cry out after the second Cyst grabbed her, he'd gone into fight mode without a thought to her sensibilities. "I'm sorry you had to see that fight."

She turned back to the now calm sky.

His temples began to ache. Then another thought occurred to him. "Wait a minute. If you're involved in planning ops, you must know about any to take my niece. Is there a plan to kidnap Hope?"

Mercy turned toward him, her different-colored eyes soft. "There will be. We haven't come up with it yet." His shoulders straightened and his spine stiffened. "I won't let that happen. You know that, right?" She turned away from him again, her voice muffled. "I know."

* * * *

Hope Kyllwood watched from the sofa as her mama finished doing yoga poses on the living room floor. "Can't I do some?" she asked. Again.

Her mama looked up, blue eyes sparkling. "No. Little girls with possible concussions need to take it easy. Finish your ice cream."

Hope rolled her eyes, looking down into her empty bowl. She'd already finished. The prophesy mark on her neck started to itch a little, so she scratched it casually.

Her mama sat down, her legs crossed. Her light brown hair was piled on top of her head. The TV went silent behind her as she relaxed, stretching her arm muscles and then her neck. There was a coffee table between them covered with crayons and coloring books. She looked over them at Hope. "What's going on, sweetheart?"

Hope licked the rest of the ice cream off her lips. Her mama had always been special, and she sometimes saw things that hadn't happened yet. But she was still a mama, and they worried, and sometimes Hope just didn't know what to say or do. "Nothin'."

"Ah. Nothin'." Her mama smiled. "I used to say that a lot so I didn't worry my mama or daddy."

Hope snorted. "Nothing worries Talen." He was her grandpa, but since he looked as young as Daddy and always would, it was easier to call him by name. And besides. His name was her favorite ever.

"All daddies worry," Mama said.

The sliding glass door opened, and Hope's dad walked inside. He wore dark pants and shirt with a gun strapped to his thigh.

His black hair fell to his shoulders, and his green eyes twinkled. He was the strongest warrior in the entire world, and he had the bestest smile ever. While eyeing first Hope and then her mama, he placed the gun on the top of the bookshelf before picking Hope up for a kiss and then setting her gently down. "How are my girls?"

Hope giggled. Mama wasn't a girl.

Her dad walked around the table and dropped to the carpet, setting Mama in his lap. "Am I interrupting girl talk?"

Hope scratched her mark again.

Her daddy's eyes flared, but he didn't say anything. Just snuggled Mama closer to him. "Paxton joined training again today. He's getting good. Make sure you tell him I said that, okay?"

Hope nodded.

Mama frowned. "What's up with Pax?"

"I don't know yet, Janie Belle," Daddy said. "The kid seems skittish to me, but physically he appears fine. Maybe nothing is wrong. We'll see."

Her mama cleared her throat. "Zane? I think Hope wants to tell us something but can't figure out how to do it."

That might be true. Except some things they couldn't know. If they knew, then they'd do something, and sometimes they were supposed to do nothing for a while. The mark started itching more. Why did she have to be a prophet? The other two prophets were super old, although they looked young. It wasn't fair.

The door opened again, and Paxton pushed his head in. His messy hair fell to his shoulders. He grinned, showing a gap in his teeth. "Can I come in?"

"Of course," Daddy said. "Want ice cream?"

Pax walked in, paused, then shook his head. "No, thank you. Um, Zane."

That was cute. Calling Daddy by his first name. "You can have a little," Hope said.

Pax looked at Daddy and rubbed his round belly. "No. I have to get in shape. My dad is right. I'm roly-poly." He moved over to sit next to Hope. "I'm not hungry, anyway."

Mama's eyes darkened.

Hope bit her lip. What was going on?

Pax looked from her to her parents. "Did you tell them you can't find your uncles?"

Hope's eyes widened. "Paxton."

His face turned red. "I didn't know it was a secret."

Daddy cleared his throat and leaned down, twisting his head to see Mama's face. "Have you talked to Garrett?"

She shook her head. "Not in a week or so."

"What about Logan or Sam?" Daddy asked.

Mama's eyebrows rose. "No. Not them, either."

Her parents both looked at Hope. She bit her lip harder. She didn't know everything about the Seven, but Fate had whispered a little to her. And she knew the Seven had to be secret right now. She was so kicking Pax in the ankle later. How could he just open his big mouth like that?

He squirmed on the sofa next to her as if he knew he was in big trouble with her.

Drake would never tell her secrets, and he was a Kurjan. They were supposed to hate each other. She sighed. Pax was her best friend, though. And he really liked her daddy, so maybe she'd have to be careful what to tell him sometimes. If Paxton told about Drake and the dreamworld, her mama would go crazy.

Her daddy cleared her throat. "What do you know about your uncles, babycakes?"

Not much, actually. Uncle Garrett had survived the ritual, because she'd helped him through the dreamworlds to get home. He was safe now. But Logan and Sam? She couldn't see them at all. Didn't know where they were. "I think Sam and Logan might be lost. But I don't know where."

"Are they together?" Daddy asked, already standing after kissing Mama on the top of the head.

Hope shrugged. "That's all I know." Pretty much.

Her daddy nodded and headed for the door. "I'll gather more intel and report back."

Hope eyed her mama. "Can Pax stay the night?" She could tell he didn't want to go home. He never did.

Mama nodded. "Of course. And I'll make us a nice dinner later with lots of protein for growing soldiers." Her eyes sparkled and her lips curved.

Pax smiled back. "Protein. Yeah, that's good."

It was important to help Pax feel better about himself and the whole world, and Hope wished she could think of a way to help him. She'd keep working on it.

For now, she had other boys to worry about. Sam and Logan were lost.

Even to her.

Chapter 16

As the plane leveled out and her heart broke a little, Mercy allowed herself to fall asleep. Her body was done, her head was spinning, and her emotions were dropping quickly.

She needed to be alert with the demon next to her, but her body had decided to shut down. What she'd seen—what he'd done. It was so much different from reading about a fight to the death on a computer screen. Logan dealt death, and he did it with an ease she wasn't sure she could describe in her next report.

How could she still want him?

Her people valued peace over all else, which was why they'd left this world. For the first time, she wondered if the Fae nation could survive here. There were only fifty of them still living, and only ten were young enough to reproduce. Created just for that purpose, actually. Even with their breeding plans, they wouldn't build their numbers for centuries. That's if the breeding plans worked. All immortal species had trouble procreating. Sometimes it could take centuries for a female to conceive.

Logan would make cute babies. Black hair, deep green eyes, stubborn little jaws. Vampires only had males, but demons could have females. What about hybrids? She didn't know of any hybrid females.

At that odd thought, she dropped into sleep.

She was five years old, sitting in one of the big chairs of the main hall. They often watched plays there. But today, they were there for a lesson.

Sandy sat on her left and Trina sat on her right, both holding her hands. The president sat up on the stage, staring down. Supposedly there used to be a council and a queen, but they were gone long before Mercy was created. President Alyssa Dawn stood up, her opal and blue eyes sad and her hands shaking. She had been their president before the event, the only one of their original leaders to survive.

"It's time you all understood your place," the president said, sounding tired.

Their place was in super soft beds and pure silk clothing. Mercy scratched her nose.

"Because we misused our knowledge of physics, we lost most of our nation, leaving only forty adults. I was visiting the retirement paradise at the time of the event, or I would've been dead, too."

This was a lot. Why couldn't they just go play outside? Mercy sighed.

"Our elders took a chance five years ago and used genetic samples and an abandoned research facility to create you. It's your job to save our nation," the president said. "Ten of you. Five males and five females."

Cool. She could definitely save the nation.

The president pushed away her pretty hair. "We're going to stay here as long as we can, but our scientist says we'll have to leave in about fifteen or so years." She stopped to wipe her face. "Our numbers are dismal. But we will survive. I promise."

Mercy's stomach hurt, and she squeezed her friends' hands. "We're sisters, and we'll be okay." She didn't know how, but they were Fae, and everyone knew that the Fae were the most dangerous of people.

Niall Healey walked onto the stage. He was only five years old, and his mama had been the queen. Or so the president said. He took a seat next to President Dawn.

The president nodded. "I have requested that Niall begin preparing himself to be king. His mother would've wanted that." Niall had one brown eye and one blue eye, and he was bigger than most of the other boys. Right now, he just looked sad and maybe angry. His blond hair was defiantly short for a Fae. Mercy nodded. She was mad, too. None of this made sense. He stood, even though the president hadn't asked him to. He cleared his throat, and his chin wobbled. "I'll be a good king. I promise."

Mercy let go of her friends' hands so she could clap along with everyone else.

Finally. Something good was going to happen.

She came to with a jerk as silence replaced the drone of the plane's engine. They'd landed. She straightened and looked for the threat, turning to find Logan watching her. She pushed the hair away from her face and wiped her eyes. Had she broadcast while sleeping? She couldn't let him know how dismal their numbers were. Worse yet, had she been snoring?

"You all right?" he asked, somehow looking perfectly comfortable sitting in the pilot's seat in his tattered, dirt-covered boxer-briefs. The soft light kissed the very angled and sleek muscles in his chest, abdomen, and arms. Heck. Even his legs had muscles.

"Yes," she whispered, straightening up to look around as the plane bobbed gently in the soft waves. The sun had risen, warming the area only slightly. They were floating by a deserted dock in front of a darkened cabin. "Not another cabin," she sighed.

Logan chuckled and pointed to some wires. "There's a landline. I already broke in and called for help while you were sleeping. Didn't want to awaken you."

Help. She could finally get back to her people. At this point, she wasn't sure if she was in trouble or not. But if so, she couldn't leave Trina and Sandy to take the blame for her. "I told you everything I know," she said quietly.

"I said I'd let you go free," he muttered, his right hand clenching into a fist, watching as his knuckles turned white.

Why was he doing that again? She reached out and took his hand. "Did you hurt yourself?"

"No." Then he allowed her to uncurl his fingers.

She turned his hand over, stopping cold at the sight of his palm. A gorgeous *K*, jagged and masculine, was surrounded by harsh and somehow beautiful lines. *K* for his family name of Kyllwood. All black, slightly raised, a part of his palm. Her heart jumped into her throat and started pounding so hard it was difficult to speak. "Your marking," she whispered.

"Yes." He looked down, no expression on his immortal face.

Oh. She blinked. "You've found your mate." What an asshole. He'd brought her to orgasm while soon to be mated to someone else. Obviously he hadn't transferred the marking to the other female yet, or he wouldn't have been able to kiss Mercy without succumbing to the mating allergy. The fact that she'd done the same was irrelevant. "You're such a dick."

He jerked and turned toward her. "Excuse me?"

A mating mark only appeared when a demon met his or her mate, and then it was transferred to the mate during sex. She'd read all about it, fascinated. "You've met your mate, and here is the mark to prove it. Yet you kissed *me*." Man, she'd read him wrong. No honor. What a jackass. His poor mate. How incredibly sad. "I should tell her the truth."

"You are her," he drawled, dark amusement glittering in his eyes.

She drew back, releasing him. The world stopped spinning for a second. "Wh-what?"

"Yeah," he said, staring at the brand again. "It appeared when you took my blood."

"Uh, no." She shook her head, pressing back against the door of the plane. "I'm only twenty-five, and I can't mate a demon." Panic grabbed her along with a pleasing and intriguing warmth she didn't have time to deal with. Mated with Logan. Holy Greek yogurt. Branded by him. Her breasts tightened, and her sex softened. A lot. "A marking can disappear if it hasn't been transferred, right?"

He looked at her as if she'd lost her mind. "Yeah, they can disappear. Not often, but it has happened."

So maybe there was more than one possible mate for a demon. So much for having sex with him, though that had pretty much been taken out of the realm of possibility, anyway. "This changes everything."

His massive chest moved as he exhaled. "Agreed."

Two men suddenly appeared on the dock next to the plane.

Mercy yelped and pushed even harder against the door.

Logan sighed. "Perfect timing, as usual." He pushed open the door and held out a hand, the one with the marking, to help her out.

She frowned and shook her head.

"Fine." He stepped out onto the dock, leaving her to scramble across the seat and out while clutching the overlarge shirt around her naked body. She inched closer to him, staring up at the two males, who were both as tall as Logan. At least six and a half feet. That's where their similarities ended.

They were familiar to her from her studies of the Seven. These were two of the living Seven members, in the same place at the same time. Her people would go crazy if she could get them home with her somehow. "Ivar Kjeidsen and Adare O'Cearbhaill," she whispered.

Ivar's eyebrows rose. "Interesting." He was a Viking from years past, also a demon-vampire hybrid. His eyes were bluer than the surrounding sea, and his long dark-blond hair was tied at the nape. "And who are you?"

"Mercy O'Malley," Logan answered for her. "Stock-strategist, money launderer, part-time kidnapper, pain in the ass, fairy."

She cut him a glare.

"A fairy? No shit?" Adare said, his Scottish accent in full force. He'd been a Highlander, probably still was, and had black hair and the shockingly black eyes of a purebred demon, which he was not. His dark hair gave him away as part vampire. Purebred demons had blond, almost white, hair. "You look like a fairy."

She blushed. "Fae. We're the Fae. Get it right."

"You nuts?" Adare asked.

Logan rolled his eyes. "She's damn close."

Enough of this. She drew away from Logan. "Which one of you teleports?" They'd appeared out of nowhere, but she hadn't been able to track their signatures.

"We both do," Ivar said easily. "Why? You need a ride, pretty thing?"

Okay. So hybrid members of the Seven were a little flirty. She could use that. The second she tried to flutter her eyelashes, Logan growled and hauled her close to his bare side. "Knock it off. Everyone," he snapped.

Ivar's blue eyes sparkled. "You have got to find some clothing."

Logan rubbed a hand across his eyes as if the world's worst headache had just attacked him from the inside. "Why are you here, anyway? I thought you were on a mission dealing with human physicists and trying to figure out the prison worlds, dimensions, and teleporting."

Ivar grinned. "I'm multitasking. Why are you nearly nude?"

"Long story. I would very much like to find clothes." Logan dropped his hand. "We need a ride to Scotland. Who wants to take us?"

"No," Mercy breathed, planting a hand on his bare chest. "You can't come. My whole mission was to make you disappear, remember?"

Ivar lost the amusement. "Excuse me?"

Logan planted his hand over hers, so she could feel the even beating of his heart. "Yeah. Apparently the Fae nation wants to stop the Seven from forming completely. Since I'm the only one who still needs to undergo the ritual, they want to take me out."

It sounded so cold when put like that. "It's nothing personal," Mercy assured them.

Neither male looked reassured. In fact, their eyes had gone granite-hard. She shivered and moved closer to Logan's heat. "I wasn't really going to hurt him," she muttered, her feet freezing on the wooden dock.

"What's going on, Kyllwood?" Ivar asked quietly, his gaze remaining on Mercy.

"A lot," Logan said. "I'll explain later. For now, we need to get Mercy back to her people and make sure they don't want to harm her before I undergo the ritual." They needed to get going on that.

Adare nodded. "I'm thinkin' you shouldn't go to Scotland if they want you gone. Why don't you bring the girl with us, undergo the ritual, then take her back to her people?"

"You can't do the ritual," Mercy snapped, her temper finally overcoming her fear of these massive, overgrown males.

Logan looked down at her. Way down. "Would you care to explain why not?"

At least he was listening to her. Warmth surrounded her heart, and she smiled at him. He blinked.

Ivar cleared his throat. "I take it the fairy, er *Fae* nation doesn't want the Seven at full strength?"

Logan nodded.

"Why not?" Adare snarled.

Her legs wobbled. "You're messing with forces you barely understand," Mercy said quietly. "The arrogance that prompted you to move dimensions from their natural locations is beyond comprehension. The science involved is way beyond the physics we understand."

"Bullshit," Adare muttered.

Ivar studied her. "There is a lot about the physics of the ritual we've never figured out. Are you telling me the Fae know more than we do?"

"Definitely," Logan said easily. "Apparently they all can teleport...some even to other dimensions. They can actually stop and stay in those places." His heated body was warming her right through the shirt. "They have tracking dust that can coat a person. In fact, their tactical equipment is damn impressive."

Mercy kept the wind from blowing up her shirt and tried to tug her other hand free, to no avail. The marking on his palm heated her knuckles and zinged up her arm, through her chest, and down her entire torso. "Those are secrets," she muttered.

"Not anymore," he returned. "You try to kidnap a guy, and all bets are off in the secrets department."

Well, that did seem fair. She sighed. "Would you be willing to talk to my people about the Seven and your rituals?" For the first time in too long, hope took hold in her. What if they all just worked together?

"I will," Ivar said soberly, looking for the moment like one of those pillaging Vikings she'd read about so long ago.

Logan shook his head. "I'm going."

"No," Ivar said, firming his jaw with its five-o'clock shadow. "You're not one of the Seven yet, so if this gets dicey, they might just try to take you out. I have the best grasp of the physics involved, and I've been teleporting for nearly a thousand years, so I should go."

Logan released Mercy's hand and held up his palm. "This says that I go."

"Ah, shit," Adare muttered. "Not another one."

What did that mean?

Ivar dropped his chin. "I swear to God, I've had enough with complications. Why doesn't the world go as I plan?" He jerked his head. "Adare?"

"On it." Adare lunged for Logan in a full-on tackle, hitting hard, with the sound of two trees colliding. Then they disappeared.

Ivar smiled at Mercy. "So. Anything I should know before I take you back to Scotland?"

Chapter 17

Logan was already swinging when Adare dropped his ass at the edge of a familiar lake in Washington state.

Adare jumped back and out of range. "You might want to put on some clothes before you fight me," he said mildly, his brogue as rough as any purebred demon's voice.

"She can't go back by herself," Logan snapped, setting his stance in the sand.

"What's going on?" Garrett Kayrs jogged up on a stone path, sweat pooling across his bare chest and soaking his dark shorts. His thick hair was wet around his head, and his face was red. Too red.

Logan studied his best friend. "Are you supposed to be out jogging?"

Garrett came to a stop, bending over to breathe heavily. "Sure. Why not?"

"Because you survived the ritual just a week ago. Barely," Logan said as the change in Garrett's back caught his eye. The ritual fused impenetrable steel with the ribs and torso of each member of the Seven, and their backs showed the dark fusing, looking like a weird shield with ribs. Garrett's screams during the ritual still echoed in Logan's nightmares. "Take it easy."

"I'm a vampire." Garrett straightened up, his sizzling gray eyes somber. "There's no time to take it easy when the Kurjans are making a move on single Enhanced women across the globe."

Fucking Kurjans. "Are we on mission?" Logan asked, feeling torn in two. He couldn't let Garrett go alone, but he had to get back and make sure Mercy was safe, and he had to find his brother.

Adare sighed heavily. "We are on mission and stop worrying about your lady. The Viking is a fierce fighter, and if there's danger, he'll bring her here. Trust your new brothers, Logan. If you don't, you'll never survive the Seven ritual."

Garrett lifted one eyebrow. "Your lady? How did it go with the Key?"

Logan winced. "Not as smoothly as I would've hoped." In fact, he needed to call Zane and get the demon nation involved. "She's a fairy, her people hate the Seven enough to want us dead, and they've taken Sam. I have to let Zane know."

Garrett's jaw snapped shut. "A fairy?"

Logan sighed. "Yeah. They like to be called Fae. Maybe it sounds tougher?" He showed his palm.

Garrett shook his head like a dog with a face full of water. "Whoa. Dude. That's a marking." He looked at him like he'd grown three heads. "Congratulations?"

"No. It's temporary." But the damn thing didn't feel temporary. It was burned through his flesh. He cleared his throat and turned toward Adare, urgency tightening his chest until his ribs protested. "Here's the deal. Either take me to Scotland, or I'm calling Zane and letting him know all about the Seven, then requesting a ride to Scotland." The Seven were a secret and for good reason. "I have to find Sam." And protect Mercy, damn it.

Adare rolled his eyes. "I'm not dumb enough to keep you from your mate. I've had Ronan researching Edinburgh, land, and fairies while I came to get you. Get clothes on, and we'll go."

Logan's shoulders went down. Finally. He nodded.

"Did I hear my name?" Ronan Kayrs loped out of the woods, firewood in his hands. He had the dark hair of most Kayrs vampires but odd aqua eyes that seemed to see everything. He'd recently mated their doctor, and his gait had a looseness it had lacked before. He was no less a badass, though. "Where the hell have you been?"

Logan sighed. "I'll catch you up soon. For now, you need to know that the Fae nation is better at teleporting than we are, and get this. Metal can go with them."

Garrett's eyes widened. "They can bring weapons while teleporting?"

Ronan coughed. "You met a fairy?"

"Yes. They prefer Fae." Logan nodded grimly. No metal could be teleported by demons—weapons, phones, nothing. It gave the Fae yet another advantage. "But their training doesn't compare to ours. Yet."

A whisper sounded on the path, and a petite brunette edged across the stepping stones and out of the trees. "Garrett? The bossy doctor wants you back inside for a heart rate check."

Ronan snorted. "My mate is a mite bossy." Even though he was much more relaxed than when he'd first arrived in this century, his worry over his brother still being on a prison world kept him up at night. When was the last time he'd slept?

Logan partially turned toward the human. "Grace. You're up." The last time he'd seen the small human, she'd been in bed still recovering from a coma. Her hazel eyes were clear now, but her skin was still pale. Obviously she was healing, finally moving around. "Feeling better?"

She nodded, her gaze staying away from Adare. "Definitely."

"You should be resting," Adare growled, his tone one usually only purebred demons could reach.

She ignored him. "How was your trip, Logan?" Her voice was soft and tentative. Unused for two years.

Adare pivoted toward her. "I said to go back and rest."

Logan tensed. He didn't want to interfere with the two, but the woman was fragile.

Grace huffed out air. "Listen, buddy. I appreciate your mating me while I was in a coma and saving my life, but you've made it very clear that you were just doing a favor for your friend. So stop telling me what to do."

Logan grimaced. Adare didn't like humans and never would. But he'd done a solid because Grace's sister, the bossy doctor, was mated to Ronan, another member of the Seven. It was a miracle that Adare had been able to mate the woman with just a bite and brand—no sex. Of course, Grace was one of the three Keys. That had to mean something. "We've found another Key, Grace," he said. It'd be interesting to put Mercy and Grace in the same room. Would there be a noticeable energy?

Adare set his feet. "Get back inside, Grace."

Finally, the woman looked at him. "Bite me, Adare."

Logan bit back a grin, and Garrett snorted.

Adare moved. Fast. He whipped Grace up and was down the trail and out of sight before Logan could blink.

Garrett sighed. "They should just get a room and get it over with."

"Has there ever been a mating without sex?" Logan asked, already moving down the pathway.

"Nope," Garrett said, wincing as he fell into step. "I might've overdone it."

Logan kept an eye on his best friend as Ronan followed with the firewood. He wasn't doing a very good job of protecting the people he cared about. "They have Sam. I'm calling in the demon nation." A full-out assault was necessary. Adrenaline lit his blood. He had to find his brother.

Garrett exhaled. "Not a good idea."

Logan shook his head and loped into a jog. "I don't care about the secrecy of the Seven. If they broke laws years ago, they can face the consequences." Oh, they'd definitely broken laws, and he wasn't sure they shouldn't pay for them. They'd done the unthinkable to create their shields.

"I'm one of the Seven now," Garrett reminded him grimly.

"You weren't there when the laws were broken." Logan shoved past a pine tree. He had to hurry, damn it.

"Doesn't matter. I'm one of them now," Garrett said quietly.

Logan stumbled and righted himself. Caution rippled through him. He sighed. If he survived the ritual, he'd be held accountable as well. "Then I can't bring the demon nation into a war right now." Not unless he had to. Damn it.

"Yep," Garrett said, grunting.

The weight of the universe settled on Logan's shoulders. He had to save Sam, and he couldn't ask Garrett to go. It looked like he was going to have to trust the Seven, whether he wanted to or not.

He had to remain on the inside to protect his niece. No matter what.

* * * *

The breeze slid cold over the ocean and froze her toes on the rough dock. Mercy stared at the huge Viking as Logan disappeared. "He is going to be so furious about that," she said.

Ivar nodded. "Yep." He looked around them. "You can teleport?"

She nodded. "Yes. I was tased and have lost the ability for a short time. Could you take me home, now?" While she really didn't want to go through the darkness of a teleport she couldn't control, there was no more time to waste. She had to get to Niall and the president to talk some sense into them.

"Sure." The Viking slipped an arm around her waist, and the world dropped away.

They landed in a small apartment with slight traffic sounds outside. The ride was fairly smooth. It was dark again in Scotland. She kept chasing the night and missing entire days. She stepped away from him. "Where are we?"

"Safe house." The small living room sat adjacent to a compact kitchen. He pointed to the one bedroom with its door open. "There should be some clothing in the closet that might fit you. Take a quick shower, get dressed, and we'll come up with a game plan."

Her game plan was to get the hell out of there as soon as possible.

His smile, although charming, held a world of threat. "We're on the fourth floor, and I've never been considered a patient male. I understand you're Logan's mate, but—"

"I am not Logan's mate," she said through clenched teeth. "That marking will disappear." Her stomach went all floppy, and her face filled with heat. She turned and stomped through the door to the bedroom, clutching the ragged shirt around her with as much dignity as she could find.

"Right," Ivar said softly.

What a jerk. So far, demon-vampire hybrids were not her favorite people. Logan's *mate*. Just because some marking had appeared on his hand. Sure, she was attracted to him. A statue would be attracted to Logan Kyllwood. The guy was all hard planes, tough muscle, and sweet talk. But he was also a killer.

A chilling one.

If her people and the demons went to war, he'd be a formidable enemy. She couldn't forget that fact. Ever.

Maybe she should've tried harder to convince him to stay away from the Seven. He wasn't a member yet. Perhaps if the science was explained to him, by somebody who actually understood it all, then he'd be reasonable.

She walked into a tidy bathroom and within seconds stood under a steaming-hot shower. She moaned into the steam, and she didn't care. Finally, warmth. The pure bliss of the moment couldn't be denied. For five minutes, she washed her hair and body, forgetting about the world.

It was heavenly.

Regretfully, she exited the shower, dried off, and found new toiletries in the cupboard. After taking care of business and even swiping lip gloss across her mouth, she studied the twin bite marks on her neck. They'd already faded, but not enough. There wasn't any concealer in the bag. Biting her lip, she moved into the bedroom and scoured the maple dresser for clothing. There was a jumble of different colors and sizes of female clothing and even sexy lingerie sets still in the wrapping. How many women did the Viking date, anyway?

Shrugging, she chose a mint-green bra and panty set before dragging jeans and a T-shirt over them. The jeans were a mite tight in the butt, so she dropped into a couple of squats to loosen them. Male voices from the other room caught her up short.

She glanced at the window.

A knock sounded on the door. Damn it. She wouldn't have time to figure out a good escape. "I'm coming," she sighed.

The door opened and her heart stopped. "Logan?" What the heck was he doing in her home country?

He stepped inside, overwhelming the small room with his presence. He'd obviously showered and shaved. His wet black hair curled beneath his ears, and a muscle visibly ticked in his sharp jawline. A dark T-shirt stretched across his broad chest, and faded jeans covered his very long legs to black boots.

Warmth pooled in her abdomen, and she tried to calm her breathing. This reaction to him had to stop, and now. "Why are you here?" Her legs froze in place.

He held up his hand, showing the mating mark.

She swallowed. Once and then twice. "That doesn't mean anything." He'd said it could disappear. So long as he didn't transfer the brand to her, it wasn't her problem. "You can't be here right now, Logan."

His gaze raked her from head to toe. Her nipples tightened automatically. What was he thinking?

"We've found some holdings we think belong to your people," he said, not moving from the doorway. "Would you take a look at the computer?"

She'd do anything to get out of the bedroom. The bed was huge and way too inviting, as was Logan. Just being this close to him again was sending her entire system into overdrive. She knew she should run, but everything inside her wanted to jump into his arms and take him to the floor for a mind-numbing kiss. One that lasted for hours. "I can look."

"Thanks." Logan held out a hand, his gaze inscrutable.

She took it, and the brand burned against her palm.

"What do your people know about interrogation and torture?" he asked, pulling her from the room.

She stumbled and then righted herself. He had to be terribly worried about his brother. Why couldn't they all just talk and reach an agreement without the subterfuge? "Not much, to be honest. Just what we've learned from television shows here." Her need to soothe him was bothersome, but she tried anyway.

He led her into the living room, and she stopped short. The entire north wall across from the plush sofa was wide open, revealing weapons and tactical gear. She shook her head. "No. You won't need those."

Ivar looked over from strapping a gun to his muscled thigh. "Right." He tossed a knife toward Adare, who was tugging a tactical vest with pockets for explosives over his chest.

Logan tightened his hold on her hand. "Look at the holdings we've found and let us know where Sam might be. Then contact your people and arrange a meeting." He led her to the kitchen counter, where a laptop was already open with an impressive list.

She cleared her throat, reading it over. There were too many places Sam could be, and surely the Seven hadn't found all of the Fae safe houses, anyway. "The only way I can find him is to go back in. You're going to have to trust me." She looked up.

Logan's face was implacable. "Not a chance."

Chapter 18

Logan stood to the side as Mercy rapidly worked through a series of encryptions and secure sites on the laptop before the screen cleared, went black, and she focused on a face: a male in his midtwenties with short, dark-blond hair, one blue and one brown eye, and rough features. A bruise was barely discernible beneath the scruff on his jaw.

She straightened. "Hi Niall."

Logan kept surprise off his face. He'd expected the guy to look like an accountant, not a brawler. Interesting.

"Mercy." The male stepped closer to the camera. "Are you all right? I've had soldiers scouring the world for you. Tell me you're okay." His voice rose imperceptibly.

"She's not all right." Logan edged into camera range, giving Mercy no choice but to move to the side. "Which, I suspect, is what you wanted."

The male's eyes narrowed. His chin lifted and hardened. "You suspect wrong."

Logan let his teeth show. "You allowed a kitten to go after a wolf, asshole." The more he thought about it, the more pissed off he became. If Mercy had gone after any other soldier, she'd be dead. Very much so.

Niall leaned in. "You're no wolf, Kyllwood."

Logan clenched his back teeth to keep from snarling. "If you know what I am, then you know she could've died."

"I told you no," Niall exploded, facing Mercy again. "I *knew* this was a mistake, which was why I denied your request. But you didn't listen. As usual."

Mercy shuffled her feet.

Logan's shoulders went back. Wait a minute. "You've committed treason?" he said softly.

She shivered and cleared her throat. "I had everything under control. Why did you send those soldiers in?" she asked.

Niall frowned. "You obviously do not have it under control. You needed backup, and even they didn't help. Where are you?"

"No," Logan said, holding up a hand. "Don't say a word." If she gave their location, the Fae would be able to jump right into their space. "One hint, and I shut this conversation down."

Niall focused on Logan. "What do you want?"

That was a good question. "I want to know where my brother is."

Niall just looked at him. "Your brother is safe."

"Not good enough. Also, tell me why you sent forces to kill me. Then I want to understand why you're so afraid of the Seven. Finally, I want to know how you created your tracking dust and tactile gear."

"No," Niall said.

Mercy sighed. "Listen, Niall. They're well trained, and it makes a lot more sense to work with them than against them. To at least try to reason with them."

Logan looked past the computer to where Ivar and Adare were, out of range. Ivar read a handheld scanner, and he shook his head. No trace so far. Apparently the Fae had decent cyber defenses as well. It was impressive, considering they'd abandoned this universe for another. They must've been advanced even before they left. "I haven't called in the Realm yet, but I will if you don't turn Sam over," Logan said.

Niall shook his head. "The Realm doesn't concern me."

"Then you're a moron," Logan drawled. "Your fifty members can't take on even a fraction of the Realm. Don't be stupid."

Niall cut Mercy a look. "Apparently my mate has been talking. If you've hurt her in any way, I'll rip your guts up your throat and eat them for breakfast."

Logan could appreciate the sentiment—if the guy hadn't been clueless enough to let her plunge headfirst into danger. "She's fine. For now."

Niall growled almost as low as any demon. "Was that a threat?"

"Yes," Logan said easily, wrapping his hand around Mercy's bicep while ignoring the odd flare of pure irritation cutting into him from Niall's claim of mate-hood. "If you know anything about me, you know I don't bluff." Not true. Not even slightly true.

Mercy tried to jerk free, but he held her tight. She rolled her eyes. "We could just have you both whip them out and compare right now, or we could try to reach a compromise," she snapped.

The Viking snorted in the living room, his lips twitching in almost a smile. He read the scanner and again shook his head.

Logan looked down at the defiant pixie. "The only one getting whipped is you, if you don't quiet yourself."

She stared up at him and her lips parted slightly. Then she snorted. A soft chuckle tumbled from her chest. "You are so full of it."

Anger caught him so quickly his breath heated until his throat burned. "Fine." Grasping her other arm, he lifted her easily off her feet and carried her into the bedroom, slamming the door shut hard enough to crack the frame. Niall yelled her name as they went, his voice coming through the walls.

Logan set her down.

Her dark red hair settled around her slim shoulders. She shoved him with both hands in the gut, her eyes flashing yellow and back to blue and green. "What in the hell are you doing?"

He shook his head and reached for his belt, unbuckling it and ripping it free.

She blinked. Her head jerked back. Then she retreated several steps, her hands going up to ward him off. "Whoa. Wait a minute." Every muscle in her body visibly clenched.

"You are not getting me," he muttered.

"Um, okay." Panic had her looking like a doe about to bolt. "Keep your clothes on," she said.

He gathered the heavy belt in his hands, his gaze on her. Did the woman really think he'd use a belt on her? Good.

"Your pants might fall off," she croaked. "Put that back on."

"I'll risk it." He grasped her wrists and jerked her toward him. She struggled furiously, but he ignored her, securing her hands together quickly. "My brother is in danger. You're all the leverage I have, and your open defiance in front of that jackass isn't helping anything." He had to drag her over to the iron headboard to finish securing her.

Her relief was palpable for a moment. Before she decided to fight. She kicked out at him, and he swiped her leg back down.

Then he leaned in, grasping the nape of her neck until she settled, her gaze furious as she glared. "If you make one sound, I swear to God I will gag you," he said through clenched teeth. "I'm not bluffing. Read my face."

She did, and if anything, her glare got hotter.

The need to kiss her, to subdue that defiance, was a physical burn. Instead, he released her and stomped out of the room, shutting the door just as loudly this time. Finally, he faced Niall again. "My brother for your…mate. You have two seconds to make up your mind."

* * * *

Mercy fought against the restraints, using all her strength and finally her teeth. How had he secured her so easily with just one belt? Once she got free, she was going to kick Logan Kyllwood so hard in the balls that he'd never procreate. Which was a good thing. One of him in this world was too many.

How dare he.

And she'd get even for the fright he'd given her, too. As he'd stood there with the thick belt in his hands, it had seemed he'd been contemplating using it on her. He'd let her think that for several seconds. Payback was going to hurt him.

She was almost free from the leather when he walked calmly back into the room and shut the door.

He leaned back against it and crossed his strong arms. "You're almost free," he said, his voice way too mild.

His tone caught her, and she stilled like any prey sensing danger. "You're a dick." So much for caution.

"Whose idea was it for you to seduce me to my death?" he asked, his eyes a dangerous hue of green. One she hadn't seen before.

She swallowed over a sudden lump in her throat. "I'm not answering you until this belt is off me."

"The belt is either on your wrists or across your ass. It's up to you." His jaw hardened.

She blinked so rapidly her eyes started to itch. Then she stilled. Was he bluffing? It was getting harder to tell. Had she finally pushed him too far? Wait a minute. She hadn't done anything. Not really. Well, not in the last few hours. "Did you find your brother?" Maybe a change of topic was wise.

"No." The muscles in Logan's arms flexed.

Oh. Well. Hmm. "I'm sure he's okay." But she wasn't sure—not at all. "If you'd let me talk to Niall again, maybe I can get him to cooperate."

"He has already agreed to trade you for Sam," Logan said.

Why did that hurt? She and Logan couldn't be together, and she knew that, so why did her chest suddenly ache?

"But I'm not trading you," he finished.

Her heart leapt. Then she shook her head. "That makes no sense. You have to trade me." Her own people wouldn't hurt her. She was one of the special ten.

"No." Logan's frown would've scared even the most seasoned of warriors. "Are you in danger from Niall or your leaders?"

She shook her head. "Not really. It was my idea to kidnap you because I wanted to help you get somewhere safe. Niall won't be too mad, I don't think."

"Do you care about him?" Logan asked.

Her eyebrows rose even as the question registered. "Why?"

"Answer me."

She tugged again on the belt, and it got a little looser. "My personal life is none of your business. We've already established that fact." She had her whole nation counting on her to mate Niall. It was a shame that the guy was way too rigid and bound to the rules. But at least she felt somewhat in control when around him— unlike her feelings with Logan. He defined *control*. "Let me free."

He moved closer then, his scent of cedar and pine and wildness filling her senses. His hands gentle, he removed the belt and slowly wrapped it around his waist, buckling it with a loud clack.

She jumped.

Challenge filled his otherworldly eyes. He cupped the side of her face, the mark on his palm rough against her skin. He leaned in, and she stopped breathing. "Does he make you feel like this?" Logan's mouth brushed hers.

She breathed him in, her nerves jumping.

"Or this?" He licked the sides of her mouth.

Her legs weakened, and her eyelids fluttered shut.

"Who will you dream about tonight?" Logan dove deep, his hand holding her face, keeping her where he wanted her. His mouth devoured her, stealing her thoughts.

Her mind shut down and she leaned into him. Heat flushed hard and fast through her, while her head spun, and her lips sparked from the energy of his—from the demand in his. The roughness of his kiss spurred her even higher. He dictated her feelings, her reactions, with no more than his mouth.

Any control she had he stole away, his easy domination creating a yearning she'd never experienced, much less imagined. Fire licked through her, whirling in a storm too powerful to tame.

She was a careful and thoughtful female—but the lure of the fire, of going to the edge—had always tempted her.

Like *he* tempted her.

Too much and too fast and too overwhelming.

But she kissed him back. Moving into his hard body, she slid her hands over the rigid strength in his chest to tangle in his hair. His body was a hard plate against her breasts, and she rubbed against him, her entire body fully alive for the first time in her life.

A sharp rap on the door had her jerking away.

Logan stared down at her, his mouth reddened, his eyes glittering with dark desire and intent.

She tried to breathe. She tried really hard, but her lungs shut down. Her body ached with a need to be filled, and she curled her nails into his chest.

"Kyllwood? We've got to go. Now," Ivar ordered, his voice low through the door.

She blinked and released Logan, her body in an uncomfortable state of arousal. "Go?"

"We traced the call and think we've found Sam," Logan said, his voice rougher than mixed gravel. Taking zip ties out of his back pocket, he grasped her wrists again. "I'm sorry."

Chapter 19

The tac-vest was as familiar as his own skin. Logan stretched his arms out, his arousal finally dying down as they reached the grounds of the stone mansion overlooking the cliffs above the ocean. Electric energy signatures filled the misty night, making his nerves hum.

He took a deep breath and settled into fight mode. Fuck, he was tired. They'd gone from time zone to time zone too often, and he needed sleep. At least Mercy had caught some z's a few times.

But he hadn't. Sure, he'd been trained to go without sleep for long durations. But still. A couple of hours wouldn't hurt.

After this mission. Damn, this mission. It didn't feel right. He didn't feel right. Without one of his brothers or Garrett at his back, he was off. Adare went to his left and Ivar around to the rear of the mansion. He wanted to trust them, but it wasn't the same. Would it be after the ritual?

Or would he always feel alone in this new role?

Two guards covered the front entrance, their legs relaxed and their hands full of automatic weapons. Light green guns that no doubt harmed immortals. These two were his to take care of while his friends covered the back and side. Were they his friends?

God, he had to get out of his own fucking head. Images of Mercy after he'd kissed her kept crossing his vision. Her eyes had glowed a soft yellow, while her lips were a vibrant pink. Everything inside him wanted to return to her and finish what they'd started. The mark on his hand pounded in agreement.

But after he'd tied her—again—she'd promised to eviscerate him, in a voice so full of anger that it shook. He couldn't blame her. Much. But she had kidnapped him, so turnabout seemed to be fair. She hadn't agreed.

He shook his head and shoved his thoughts away. *Fight, kill, move, survive.* He repeated the mantra in his head, moving silently through the mist past a series of bushes, his knife already in his hand.

These guys were the enemy, and they had his brother.

The litany played through his head as it had a thousand times during the last war. *Fight, kill, move, survive.* Zane had taught him the words during training that he thought he wouldn't live through. But it had been necessary, and without it, he wouldn't be alive today.

He crouched behind a prickly bush and waited for the signal.

"Hold positions," Ivar said through the ear comms. "There's an alarm, and it'll take me a few minutes to disengage."

Logan hunkered lower, the scent of wild gardenias still filling his head. What the hell was he going to do with her? He couldn't take a mate right now, but he couldn't just turn her over to the enemy, either. Even if they were her people. Right?

Man, he wished he could talk to Zane. Keeping perfectly still, he let his mind wander to keep himself from feeling the burn in his legs from holding his position.

He was young and on the field training when Zane walked out holding their uncle's severed head in his hand. Logan immediately moved to flank him while Sam did the same. His heart had almost burst in two, and his head rang, but he followed his instinct to protect family.

In that moment, Zane had become the ruler of the demon nation.

At war with the Realm. With the shifters. With other demons. With the witches, too.

*Logan glanced at Sam, across Zane's bruised body. Sam had
nodded. All right. Whatever the future held, they'd stick together.
No matter what.*

*Zane looked over at him. "It's going to get worse. I need you
on the front line tomorrow."*

Logan lifted his chin. "I'll go where you need me."

*Zane's jaw tightened. "I'm sorry, Lo. It's gonna be bad. There's
no other way."*

*That had been the understatement of the centuries. Sometimes,
in the darkness of night when nobody was around, he wondered
who he would've been if his father had lived. If he hadn't become
a soldier in his teens, and if he hadn't become the killer still
whispered about as a warning to others to avoid the demon nation.*

Ivar's voice jerked him back to the present. "Alarm disengaged.
Breach in ten seconds."

Logan counted to three and started moving. *Fight, kill, move,
survive.* He jumped out of the darkness, his knife already cutting
across the throat of the first soldier before he tackled the second
to the ground. Three hard punches, and the guy fell unconscious
while his buddy choked on his own blood.

Logan flipped him over and zip-tied him. Then he moved to
the first guy, pressing a hand to the sliced throat. "Stop fighting
it." The male's eyes widened, and his bloody hands clutched at
Logan's. Logan shoved harder, and the soldier fought him but
couldn't escape unconsciousness.

Logan whipped the guy's shirt off and pressed it to the wound.
The blood made it stick, and he zip-tied the soldier's hands. "You'll
live," he muttered, dragging both bodies to the other side of the
bushes. He'd never gone for an easy kill, and he wouldn't start
now. These guys weren't well-enough trained to be covering the
door. Something was off, but he couldn't figure out what.

Then he edged to the door and turned the knob. It swung in
easily.

The Fae needed some serious training. He stepped inside, and a burst of sharp air hit him so hard and fast he flew backward to land on his ass, a prickly bush tearing into his forearm.

How could air be sharp? He shook his head and bounded to his feet, his ears ringing. Well. The Fae sure as shit didn't need any help in the gadget or defense department. He tapped his ear bud. "Warning. They have some sort of air defense that's shockingly good."

Ivar groaned into the comms. "No shit. I was nearly blown off the fucking cliff."

Adare came on. "It's one fast burst. I grabbed on to the doorframe and ducked, and then I infiltrated. We're on go, men."

Logan shook his head to gain his bearings and approached the door from an angle. Taking a deep breath, he crossed inside, grasping the doorframe and plastering himself to it. The air hit him hard, but he persevered.

Then calmness.

He moved fast before more air could attack him. Going left, he shut the door and marched into a darkened and silent gathering room complete with the biggest stone fireplace he'd ever seen. "I'm in," he whispered.

The place was too quiet. Why weren't there guards inside the perimeter? Did they really think a couple of air blasts would keep an enemy out for long?

The lights snapped on, and a male walked in from what appeared to be a kitchen. Ivar followed him, holding a gun to the back of his neck. "So you're Kyllwood." Niall finished eating what appeared to be a sandwich, his gaze curious and his shoulders back. In person, the Fae leader was taller than he'd seemed on the computer screen. At least a couple of inches over six foot. He didn't seem concerned about the gun.

Logan tensed. "Where's my brother?"

"He's been moved," Niall said, rubbing the bruise on his jaw. "Stubborn, isn't he?"

No blood. There was only the bruise and no blood on Niall. So either he'd washed it off, had somebody else torture Sam, or hadn't bothered. "Where is he?"

Niall shrugged. "He's elsewhere. Where's my mate?"

Logan kept his expression nearly bored while the beast inside him yanked against its chains. Adare strode silently through another doorway. "Scouted the basement. One room, chair, restraints, and some blood."

Logan's head lifted. "If you hurt my brother, I'll take off your head."

"I already hurt your brother," Niall said, his dual-colored eyes flashing. "He's a stubborn bastard, he is."

Logan studied the leader. The Fae people weren't good fighters, but their technology was superior. If Sam had been tortured, if they'd gotten close enough to draw blood, he could've still probably overpowered whoever was hurting him. Yet he hadn't. What exactly was he doing? "You'll never break my brother," Logan said, trying to sound angry.

Triumph filled Niall's smile. "Oh, I'm close. He was gasping for breath when we decided to teleport him."

Jesus. Sam could've stopped a teleport as easily as Logan. Probably even easier, because Sam actually could teleport. Had he been tased? "Where is he?" Logan let his voice crack.

Niall sighed. "That doesn't matter. He did send you a message, though."

"Right. You're full of shit."

"He said to kiss your mom for him. Tell her he loved her." Niall gave a mock shudder. "I think he's given up."

Ivar glared at Logan. "Want me to rip off his head?"

"No. We'll have to torture him," Logan said, his chest easing with the coded message from Sam. The word 'kiss' meant undercover and that he'd be in touch. Sam was working things from the inside. Of course. "I have the perfect knife."

"I have several," Niall said easily. "Some still coated with Sam's blood. Demon blood is darker than ours. Did you know that?"

How the hell would he have known that? Mercy's feet had bled, but they'd been so cut up, he hadn't really noticed. "Mercy's blood tastes like honey and spice," he murmured.

Red infused Niall's cheeks. "You have not bitten my woman."

Woman? She wasn't human. "You've been watching too much television here in this dimension," Logan drawled. "You don't have a woman."

"There isn't television in any other dimension," Niall shot back. "And you're wrong. She's committed to me—there's no alternative. She wouldn't even consider being disloyal to her people or her purpose." His grin held menace. "Of course, she's a hell of an actress. Has she convinced you otherwise?"

"Sorry. My mama taught me to be a gentleman. We don't kiss and tell." Logan kept still as Adare and Ivar both started to move in. "Although you should probably know that we were mainly naked for the first two days, or nights, of our acquaintance." They'd kept moving through time zones into darkness, so it was a pain to figure out the actual time they'd spent together.

Niall's chest puffed out—muscled and tight. "You're lying."

"Am I?" Logan said softly, trying to keep the guy's attention. "That Key birthmark she has on her hip is lovely." He'd been waiting for Fae reinforcements, but no sounds or signatures came from the house. Obviously Niall was counting on his teleporting skills. He nodded for Adare to move in before the asshole could zip away.

Adare shot into action, head down, in tackle mode. And bounced off the air next to Niall to crash into the stone fireplace. He landed on his feet, his chin up, blood flowing from a cut above his ear.

Fuck. The weird air bubbles could be employed around people? Logan squinted to see the weapon, but there wasn't even a disturbance in the air.

Niall chuckled. "You don't think I'm just standing here defenseless, do you?"

"No. You just send in defenseless females to do your job," Logan said. What the hell was it with the Fae and the air? Witches could create fire out of air. Maybe the Fae could create shields and even weapons. If so, why hadn't Mercy tried that? Or had the skill been inhibited when she'd been tased by a Fae weapon?

Niall grinned. "I didn't send her in, and you know it. She often has her own agendas."

Logan set his feet. "She is intriguing."

"Isn't she, though?" Niall strode around a thick oak table toward Logan. "I've heard that most demons can stop others from teleporting."

Logan's breath settled. "Actually, not many of us can do that." It was a lie, but if Sam had purposely refrained from stopping a teleport, Logan wasn't going to give him away. What the hell was Sam up to, anyway? Logan's stance widened. "Though why don't you try me? I think I can stop you."

"You've never encountered anything like me, Kyllwood," Niall said softly, moving with the arrogant grace of a pure shifter. "I'm going to take you to a hell dimension you can't even imagine. It's time you actually saw the devastation the Seven is inviting into this world." He drew nearer.

Oh, Logan wanted this. If he could get past the bubble of defense, he could take down this jackass.

"I'm going to transport you somewhere you'll never escape." Niall drew even nearer. "You won't survive a day, and the Seven will never be completely formed. Thank you for making this so easy for me."

"You bet." Logan braced for the attack.

A wave of air, a weird bubble, brushed his skin with a slight burn. He pushed against it, and the damn thing pushed back.

Niall spread out his arms.

Logan dropped into a fighting stance. "Let's do this."

"Good-bye, Logan Kyllwood." Niall rushed him, ducking his head and moving fast.

"No!" Ivar leaped from the side, energy cascading from him, already in mid-teleport. He crashed through the bubble and tackled Niall.

The air crackled, and they both disappeared.

Silence fell on the night. "Viking!" Adare yelled, rushing to the now-empty spot.

Fury filled Logan as his gaze caught on the burn mark on the perfect wood floor. "What the fuck did Ivar just do?" he growled.

Adare shot a hand through his thick black hair. "Damn it. Since he was teleporting, he could infiltrate that weird defensive bubble."

Logan couldn't teleport. He really needed to get that skill. "But why?"

Adare sighed, his eyes darkening. "You're not a member of the Seven yet. We need you here and in one piece, Logan."

Ivar had just possibly sacrificed himself for Logan.

"I guess I do have brothers," Logan muttered, the idea pissing him off beyond belief. How dare the Viking sacrifice himself? That was Logan's job. "All right. How do we find him?"

Adare looked toward the door. "We only have access to one person with knowledge."

Mercy. Logan nodded. "Yeah. It's time she told us everything." Whether she liked it or not.

Chapter 20

Mercy was really getting tired of being tied up, and she needed some daylight, damn it. They couldn't keep traveling from night to night across the globe. She sat on the bed, her hands tied to the iron headboard. These zip ties were even tighter than the belt had been. But she had to get free. She struggled until her wrist bled, but nothing.

Damn Logan.

Her head dropped. God, she was exhausted. When had she last slept? She drifted between sleep and wakefulness, finally landing on a dream of a memory she often had.

At fifteen years old, she and Sandy were already experts at using computers. They'd teleported back to the homeland, where they had several safe houses with the newest equipment. The walls of the basement were covered with large screens, while several tables holding computers were arranged across the floor. She looked over at her best friend. "I think if we move funds into this area of technology, we'll see a better increase." If they ever had to come back for good, they'd need money.

Sandy nodded, her fingers poking at the keyboard.

Mercy snorted. "I don't like how the hedge funds are warping the stock market by doing all their buying and selling at the end of the month."

Sandy grimaced. "Why would they do that?"

To drive Mercy crazy? She sighed. "*That's when they report to their investors, so they're cleaning things up and hiding mistakes in those last few days of the month. It can screw up prices.*"

Sandy groaned. "*Who cares?*"

"*I do,*" *Mercy said.* "*We'll need financial freedom when we come back here permanently.*" *She loved playing the markets.* "*Many technology stocks have high prices and they aren't profitable. But so many people are buying...*"

Sandy leaned back in her chair and planted her hands over her eyes.

Mercy grinned. "*Fine. Go back outside and work with the weapons. I can do this.*" *Sandy was the best at tweaking weapons to make them even stronger. She hated computer time.*

Sandy's eyes lit up. "*Really?*"

Mercy nodded. This was her thing. She had value, and she had use. Otherwise there was no reason to exist. "*Go.*"

The president moved toward her, bending over to read the screen, two white-haired ladies behind her. "*Moving funds?*" *she asked.*

Mercy's heart beat faster, but she kept her typing even and quick. "*Yes. I studied the worldwide forecast, and this will be beneficial to us in about five years.*"

Grandmama Geri clasped her wrinkled hands together. She was at least four thousand years old—maybe more. Fairies aged slowly, but after millennia, they started to look like elderly humans. "*You're a good girl, Mercy.*"

Mercy sat up straighter in her chair.

President Dawn patted her shoulder. "*You're doing a good job for our people, Mercy. We all must contribute.*"

Mercy nodded dutifully. They were few in number, so everyone counted. If one didn't contribute, one didn't matter. She wanted to matter. "*I'll keep studying. I promise.*"

"*I know.*" *The president took Sandy's vacated seat, her eyes serious. One was a light blue and the other a stunning opal color.* "*You have to work harder than the rest.*"

Mercy swallowed over a lump in her throat. "Because of the birthmark." The oddly shaped key on her hip. The one the president told her to hide from anybody not a Fae, especially when she was in the Earth dimension. "I still don't understand what the key means."

The president reached out to grasp her arm. "There are three Keys in the universe, and they must never meet. Never be in the same place at the same time. It would be catastrophic."

Chills spread down Mercy's back. "I'm bad?"

"No." The president smiled, but her eyes didn't crinkle. "You're good and useful. You have skills to help your people, and you'll mate someday and increase our forces. But with the Key, you must be careful. Don't take chances."

Which was why Mercy only rarely explored other dimensions with her friends. Did it somehow make her special? "You want me unharmed?"

"Yes. If you die, another Key will be born somewhere in your place. And we won't be able to control, I mean protect, that Key. I would like you to start an internet search for the other Keys. They're probably well hidden." The president looked up as Niall Healey strode into the room, one of the new guns they'd developed at his waist.

Although also only fifteen, he'd grown tall for a Fae and already managed the weapons research department. He nodded at Mercy and then focused on their leader. "President? We've altered some of the weapons after going through research left by our ancestors. Would you like to take a look?"

The president nodded and stood. "Keep working, Mercy."

Niall cleared his throat. "I'll pick you up for the movie later. We might as well enjoy the benefits here." He left without waiting for a reply.

Mercy turned back to the computer, her stomach hurting. Niall was nice and all, but she didn't get those tingles from him that the women in the books she'd found did. But at least he didn't seem to be bothered by her birthmark, which all of her friends had seen at one point or another. Nobody would tell her what the Key meant, but sometimes fear filled their eyes when they looked at her.

She hunched over the keyboard, working furiously. Her meaning and value should never be questioned. She'd prove it by working harder than anybody else. Always.

The roll of thunder pulled Mercy back into the present. Wonderful. Another storm in another night. Apparently Alaska and Scotland were experiencing a similarly stormy spring. Once she could teleport again, she would find a nice warm island in the Pacific somewhere and drink margaritas and eat coconut shrimp. All day.

Her head ached. She glared at the ties around her wrists.

She was Mercy O'Malley, damn it. Nobody tied her to a bed. Not even the sexiest demon ever born. Or vampire. Or demon-vampire hybrid. Whatever Logan was, he didn't get to secure her like this.

She studied the iron headboard with its design of a Celtic knot surrounded by intricate lines. The work was beautiful.

Swinging her legs around so her butt became a fulcrum on the bed, she kicked right below her bound hands. The iron clanged against the wall, vibrating wildly. Her skin prickled as adrenaline flowed. She could do this. Aiming even more carefully, she kicked in the same place. The bottom of the rod holding her seemed to give a little. She kicked harder, and pain ricocheted up her leg.

She bit her lip. That really hurt. Between her bleeding wrists and aching legs, she could use some more of that demon blood. Warmth flooded her at the memory.

No. Enough of that. She had to get free. So she kicked three times in rapid succession. The rod pulled almost all the way away from the bottom of the headboard, looking cracked.

Her lungs filled. Aiming carefully, she kicked right at the crack. It split all the way in half. She jerked her hands free with so much force, she rolled across the bed and nearly fell. Regaining her balance, she looked at her damaged wrists. The ties still held them together, but at least she was free of the bed.

Scissors. There had to be some in the kitchen.

Ignoring her shaking legs, she ran out of the bedroom and to the kitchen, where she yanked open drawer after drawer. No scissors. Who didn't keep scissors in the kitchen, damn it? She grabbed a knife and tried to twist it to cut the ties. The blade cut into the flesh of her palm, and she squeaked.

Ouch.

Okay. Dropping to her butt on the cold tile, she lifted her knees and clamped the knife handle between them. Lightning zinged outside. Great. More lightning. Enough already.

Holding her breath, she pulled her hands apart as far as the ties would allow and then gingerly rubbed the plastic material up and down on the ultrasharp blade. Slowly, it cut through. Finally, her hands were free. She relaxed, and the knife dropped to the floor.

Throwing the offending plastic across the room, she grasped the knife handle and stood. Phone. She needed a phone.

Scrambling through drawers again, she found more weapons, spices, and a couple of bottles of Scotch. No phone. What kind of a safe house didn't have a box of disposable phones? She slammed her hand on the counter and pain flowed through her bloody wrist.

She was really starting to dislike the Seven.

Grabbing a kitchen dishcloth, she wrapped it around her left wrist. The right one would just have to bleed. It wasn't cut as badly, anyway.

Urgency shook her. She had to get out of there before they returned. Rushing back into the bedroom, she pulled socks from a drawer and rushed to the closet. Several pairs of high heels, all in different sizes, were tossed haphazardly around.

A bunch of lingerie and high heels in different sizes. Ivar the Viking was a player. Definitely a player.

She dropped to her knees and shoved shoes out of the way. Come on. There had to be a decent pair in there somewhere. She couldn't run through the cobblestone streets of Edinburgh in high heels. Not with Logan no doubt on her tail soon.

At the very back of the closet, she hit pay dirt. A pair of tennis shoes, well worn. Thank goodness. She yanked them on. While they were about two sizes too big, they'd work for now.

All she had to do was find a phone.

Her heart thundering, she ran out of the apartment and down the stairs, bursting into the rainy night. It was a punishing rain, hard and brutal.

That island in the sun seemed so far away.

Gulping, she looked frantically around. The apartment building was in a quiet, older part of the city, and the street was silent at this hour. All of the apartments around her appeared dark.

Should she knock on one? What if there were more demons around? The sound of traffic filtered lightly through the night from blocks away. She had to get to a bar or store or something and just borrow a phone. If she could call Niall, he could teleport her home. It was time to talk some sense into her people, and it was time she fully understood the physics of the prison world. Burying her head in figures and strategy wasn't working for her any longer. She was a Key, and while she understood some of what that meant, she was missing information.

Turning, she loped into a jog through the puddles already collecting on the stones.

Lightning flared, illuminating the entire world. She yelped and jumped closer to the stone building.

"Mercy!" came a bellow from down the street.

Panic grabbed her around the throat and squeezed. Holy hell. Logan was back, and he'd seen her. All by himself. Where were his friends? Her timing totally sucked. No question about it.

She turned and moved as fast as she could around the building toward what looked like a park. Dodging between stone pillars, she ran full bore across a grassy knoll and around several benches, heading for the other side.

The thunder and pelting rain urged her on.

She had to get free. The too-large shoes and wet grass slowed her, but she tucked in her arms and fought the wind as best she could. A lone cab was driving down the road on the other side of the park. She yelled as loud as she could, hurrying, bursting out of the carved exit gate.

His brake lights flashed red in the storm.

Gulping in air, her wet hair flapping against her cheeks, she wrenched open the door and jumped inside. "Go. Go fast. Please go." She slammed the door shut.

The driver, a gray-haired gentleman with round eighties-style glasses, turned and looked over his shoulder. "Where to, miss?" His brogue was thick.

"Anywhere," she yelled. "Just go. North or south or wherever. Take me to a pub."

Muttering about women who couldn't handle their drink, he turned back to the steering wheel and pressed the gas pedal, driving leisurely down the quaint street.

Mercy turned in the seat to look out the back window.

Logan burst out of the park. Rain plastered his T-shirt to his chest and his jeans to his legs, giving him a predatory look that stole her breath completely away—maybe forever.

Even through the night, his eyes glowed a dangerous green. Hot and bright and full of fury.

"Hurry up," she whispered, her voice gone. "Please. Drive faster."

Logan's hands clenched into fists and he lowered his head like a ram about to attack. Then he launched himself into a run, his arms and legs moving too fast to track.

Mercy swung around and pounded on the glass divider. "Go faster, damn it. Hit the petrol. I'll pay you anything."

"There's a speed limit, miss," the driver said, his voice indulgent.

She pounded harder. "Look behind you."

The driver glanced up into the rearview mirror. His shoulders went back and hit the seat. Hard. "What in the world?"

Humans. She didn't have time to deal with them or their nonsense. "He's coming. You do not want him to reach us." Turning, she let out a squawk. Logan was gaining and fast. "For the love of God, hurry the hell up," she screamed.

The driver scrambled and pressed harder on the pedal. The vehicle jerked forward, its tires gaining traction.

But it was too late.

Logan caught the bumper, pulled back, and swung the cab into a fire hydrant. The clank of metal on metal filled the night. He yanked open her door, grabbed her arm, and had her out in the rain before she could blink.

The driver scrambled toward the passenger door. "Wait a minute."

Logan lowered his head and focused on the man.

The driver's eyes widened and he shrank back. Then his eyelids closed, and he slumped against the dash.

Mercy's stomach quivered. "Did you—"

"No," Logan snarled, his anger a force around them both. "He's unconscious and won't remember anything except hitting the hydrant." In one smooth motion, he hefted her over his shoulder, his arm hooking across her legs to keep her in place.

Her head smacked the small of his back, and she winced.

This sucked.

He paused, the raining slapping them hard. "Before I move, I have to know. Niall took the Viking somewhere he called hell. Can you get there or tell me how to find him?"

She blinked rain out of her face. Oh no. There were an infinite number of possibilities. "Yes. You let me go back to my people, and I'll track him." Not a chance. Not unless Niall told her where.

"No." With that, Logan started to run again. "Adare went to meet with contacts, and you and I are getting some sleep. I can go three days without, but I'm done. Then you're going to tell me everything—every single thing you know about how I can find Ivar and Sam."

That was the problem. She didn't know a damn thing.

Sleep? With him? She was exhausted, but suddenly her body perked right up, as if she'd been resting for days.

Chapter 21

By the time Ivar Kjeidsen started to fight the teleport, he was dropping through the air to land on jagged rocks. One pierced his rib cage and he cried out, bounding to his feet anyway.

Lava boiled up all around him between rocks, sending up impossible heat and the stench of burning sulfur.

Niall sat down a few feet away on a solid rock and swept out a hand. "This is what you're exposing your people to. The second you fucked with the laws of physics, the moment the Seven did the impossible, you made this a reality for everyone you love."

A creature howled in the distance, the sound soul-chilling.

Ivar breathed in and his lungs burned. The sky was a bruised purple, the atmosphere heavy with an unreal gravity. "Where are we?"

Niall lowered his chin, fury lighting his dual-colored eyes. "You might live long enough to figure that out." He lifted a shoulder, sweat rolling down his face. He pulled a silver weapon out from behind his waist. A type of gun Ivar had never seen before. "Or not."

Ivar bunched to teleport out, but Niall fired first.

Electricity edged with sharp blades crashed over Ivar's entire body. He cried out, his nervous system misfiring in every direction.

Then it stopped. Residual pain echoed through him, and his legs barely kept him upright. He gathered his strength to teleport and a fizzle popped the air around him. His eyes widened. He couldn't leave.

Niall nodded. "Yeah. Our weapons are far superior to yours. Portals will open for you, but you won't be able to direct your path for a while. If ever. Good luck with this." Then he was gone.

"Fucker!" Ivar yelled.

The creature screeched again, this time sounding closer.

Oh, this was so bad. How long would his ability be gone? He had to get out of there. The bottoms of his boots started to burn away from the heated rocks. Lava swelled and poured over the nearest stones. Was there some sort of tide? Bunching his weakened legs, he jumped for the rock Niall had stood on, landing and then sliding wildly.

Rocks surrounded by lava lay in every direction, too far to see anything else except to his left. Past a jumble of rocks, there appeared to be a forest. Sure, the trees were monstrous and a burnt-gold color, but at least the ground appeared solid.

He had to get away from the lava, which was rising. The bubbling mass now covered the jagged rock on which he'd landed.

To the forest it was.

His ribs weren't healing. Not a good sign. Gathering his strength, he tried to send healing cells to the wound and jumped again. His feet landed hard and jarred his ribs. He sucked in boiling air as pain lashed him. One or two might be broken.

Ignoring the agony, he started jumping, barely allowing his feet to touch down before he was in the air again. Even so, the bottom of his boots burned completely away.

A figure suddenly appeared at the edge of the trees.

He stopped short, only a couple of jumps away. What the hell?

It was a male. About his size, wearing some sort of yellow hide with more hide around his feet. Scars marred his chest and the side of his neck. He was filthy, and his leg was bleeding, but he looked at Ivar as if he was seeing a ghost. "Viking?" he snarled, his voice barely recognizable.

Ivar sucked in air. Pain burned into his feet. He jumped to the next rock and then the final one, landing on prickly grass. His mind spun, and his chest felt like a Buick had landed on it. "How do you know me?" he asked.

The male lowered his scruff-covered chin. "You're not Igor."

Igor. Igor Kjeidsen. Ivar's older brother, who'd been lost in battle long ago. Ivar had taken his place with the Seven. He looked more closely. Beneath the dirt, blood, and scars, the bone structure was hard and familiar. Ivar's back, the scorched tattoo on his ribs, began to hum. He'd just found one of his Seven brothers. "Kayrs. You're Quade Kayrs."

Quade looked around and then focused. "What the fuck?"

Now that was a hell of a question. A crack zipped across the sky, revealing silver on the other side. It quickly closed.

Quade didn't move. "Explain?"

Something large crashed through the trees.

"Follow." Quade turned and ran.

Chills rippling through him despite the unreal heat, Ivar followed. The pain in his feet competed with the agony of his busted ribs and burning lungs, but he kept pace as something chased them. They ran over another lava field to a forest made of burnt trees with orange branches covered in razor-sharp bark. Narrow trails went in several directions, and Quade took one. Ivar protected his head the best he could, but soon his arms and chest bled freely.

Finally, they reached a series of tall rocks.

Quade ran behind one and started climbing, hand over hand.

Ah, shit. Gasping for air, Ivar did the same, taking the shallowest breaths he could. His legs scraped against sharp edges that soon tore away the knees of his jeans and flayed his skin. Finally, he reached a cliff.

Quade pulled him up and yanked him inside a cave.

The instant coolness washed over Ivar's skin. He gasped, trying to fill his chest. Then he coughed, and blood dribbled from his mouth. He licked it away. Must've punctured a lung.

Quade pointed for him to sit. "Cool air, less gravity. Can heal."

Apparently the Kayrs' ancestor had forgotten how to speak in complete sentences.

Ivar sat and put his head back against the smooth stone, closing his eyes. Concentrating on healing cells, he forced them through his body to repair the damage. They were sluggish and slower than usual, but within a few minutes, he could breathe without puking blood.

He opened his eyes to see Quade sitting across the small cavern, back to the wall. The missing Kayrs was huge and scarred, with darker aqua eyes than his brother and matted black hair. Burn scars covered the side of his neck, disappearing beneath the animal hide he wore.

Ivar coughed and winced as his ribs rattled. "You're Quade."

Quick nod. "How long have I been gone?" Quade asked.

"About a thousand years," Ivar grunted.

Quade sighed. "That's all?"

It probably did seem like a lot longer. "Yes."

"Time is different." Quade took a knife from behind his waist, grabbed the nearest rock, and started to sharpen the blade. "Igor?"

"He died in the last war," Ivar said, the words a punch to the gut. He missed his brother every day. "I took his place with the Seven."

Quade tilted his head but kept his gaze on the knife blade. It appeared to be made out of some sort of silvery rock.

Ivar tried to mend his ribs. "Jacer Kayrs and Zylo Kyllwood both died as well." Three of the original Seven had passed on from this life.

Quade showed no reaction, but tension rolled through the cavern. "Ronan?" he rumbled.

"Alive. His bubble exploded, and he's back home." Ivar's feet began to heal over the burns.

Quade looked up, his eyes darkening. "Alive? Home?"

"Yes," Ivar said quietly. "The bubble burst, though. Yours is probably next, then, finally, Ulric will be set free."

Quade set down the weapon and rubbed the ruined skin on his neck. "Almost over."

Rebecca Zanetti

Ivar swept his arm out. "What's almost over? I kind of understand what Ronan did in his bubble to keep the prison world intact. But what do you do in this horrific hell?"

Quade stared at him as if the words had no meaning.

Ivar just looked back, his chest aching for this brother he'd finally met. "I can take your place."

Quade's eyes cleared. "No. I feed the dragon."

"There's a dragon?" Ivar tensed.

Quade snorted. "Figuratively. The magnetic fields of this world bind the prison world to it. Let the magnets fall…"

What the hell was he talking about? Did he even know? "There must be a ritual, just like Ronan had. Tell me what to do, and I'll take it over."

"You can't. It's too much, and it took centuries to develop." Quade looked around. "Didn't start like this." He wiped at a bloody cut across his upper arm, almost absently. "But it's gonna end like this. Soon."

Ivar studied him, his mind snapping. "You'll be free, Quade. Ronan survived the end of his world, and so will you. You can heal and find a life."

Quade's lids dropped to half-mast. "Already dead…Viking."

Ivar's stomach hurt. What hell the hybrid must've gone through. Ronan had no clue how different his brother's prison had been from his own. Ronan's had been calm and boring. Not so deadly. "You're alive."

Quade snorted. "I die every night."

What the hell did that mean?

A gust of wind swept into the cave, followed by a scattering of salt rocks.

Quade sighed. "You go now." He stood and moved to haul Ivar up by the arm.

Ivar shook his head. "I can't teleport yet. There's a weapon—"

"You have to go." Quade dragged him out of the cave to the edge. Three swirling portals were visible in the empty air. "Only way to get home." He clapped Ivar on the back. Hard. "You probably won't make it."

Ivar turned suddenly. "I'm not leaving you." The guy had been alone for far too long.

Quade's eyes, for the first time, showed a glimmer of emotion. Raw sadness. "Two die, only one come back. Can't guarantee it'll be you." He pointed to the portals. "Only way."

Well, Garrett Kayrs had gone through a series of portals when he'd survived the ritual. Maybe Ivar would do the same. He looked at the three swirling masses of electricity. They all looked like certain death with a whole lot of pain mixed in. Yet somehow, they drew him. His body began to lean toward them. "Which one?"

Quade turned toward him. "The Viking was strong—strongest I've ever met. You have his blood, and you have his strength." Urgency darkened his face.

"Come with me," Ivar said, his heart racing.

"Can't. If I go, Ulric gets free." Quade grabbed him by both arms. "Time is different. It might take you a thousand years to get back, but it'll be moments after you left. The portals—all lead to hell."

Ivar's back straightened. "I can handle it." Should he drag Quade with him? Ulric be damned. Ivar couldn't leave a brother, one of the Seven, in this hell any longer.

Quade shook his head. "No. You must go. Do you have a mate?"

"No." But an image flashed through his head. A pretty physicist he'd been following—one of many in the last month. Dr. Promise Williams. He hadn't even approached her yet.

"Good. You'll want to die a thousand times, but keep going." The wind picked up, throwing salt the size of tangerines at them. "Your name?"

"Ivar," he reminded Quade.

"Goodbye to Ivar," Quade said, his tone guttural. "Say it. Humanity is gone. Say it." His eyes flashed hot and dark.

The male had lost it. Completely. Ivar nodded, sliding his arm down to grasp Quade's wrist. They were doing this together. "Goodbye to Ivar."

Quade relaxed. "Viking. You're a Viking. The only. You can beat every monster out there. You're Vike."

He surely was. Ivar tightened his hold.

"Remember a good place. At some point, if you survive, you'll teleport there. If you're lucky." Quade tried to pull back.

Ivar stopped him. Then he turned to jump.

At the last second, Quade twisted and kicked out, sending Ivar flying into the abyss. "No!" Ivar yelled, reaching back for his brother.

Quade's grim face was the last thing Ivar saw before the portal swallowed him whole. Pain etched through his body to his soul, and he screamed, the sound silenced in the roaring void. Then he landed in pure ice.

It was the first of a million landings that held unimaginable pain.

Time became nothing.

He became even less.

Portals opened, and he jumped through them, at first hoping. Then wondering. Finally not caring.

Boiling water, monsters beyond comprehension, worlds filled with blades. He survived them all, his memories fading into nothingness. A face, a pretty face and intelligent eyes, filled his dreams sometimes. Promise. All he could think about was a promise.

But soon even that had no meaning.

He lost a leg and it slowly regenerated. More and more worlds— all hellish. No people, no vampires, no demons. Plenty of hell beasts.

Ivar was forgotten. Had to be. Had to die or he couldn't survive like the animal he became. Viking. He was Vike. As a mantra, trying to survive, that's who he became.

His hair changed color, streaked with black. As did his beard. He let it grow, trying to tell the passage of time, but then it stopped, too.

The ability to heal himself slowed finally. Death was near.
He didn't care.
Another portal, maybe this one led to his death.
So be it.

Chapter 22

Logan was so exhausted he could barely think straight, but he kept the fairy over his shoulder for the entire jog back to the safe house. Adare was working every contact he had to find Ivar, and Logan had to get some sleep before he continued. It had been too long. Even for him.

They reached the apartment, and he dumped Mercy on the bed. "Tell me where Ivar is."

Her face lost some of the fury. "I really don't know. There are zillions of dimensions, and Niall could've taken him anywhere."

Damn it. Hopefully the Viking could teleport home. Logan eyed the dark circles beneath Mercy's eyes. "Here's the deal. Get in bed, be quiet, and go to sleep. One peep out of you, and I'll tie you to the bed." The idea perked his cock right up, but he shoved arousal away. If he didn't get some sleep, he'd be no use finding either Ivar or Sam.

Mercy glared at him but dropped her wet clothing on the floor before sliding into bed, wearing only her bra and panties. "There have to be pajamas here."

He paused. "You require silk, Your Majesty?"

She snorted. "Well, I am accustomed to such. We take only the best back with us."

So his little fairy was a mite spoiled. Good to know. "Go to sleep."

She sat up partway, and the covers slid down her bare skin. "Bossy."

His balls drew up tight. She was trying to kill him. Were fairies part witch? He'd believe it right now. He kept her gaze while drawing his shirt over his head and then shucking his boots and jeans.

She licked her lips, settling back into the bed.

The mark on his palm heated as if even Fate was against him. How the hell could the mark appear for a crazy Fae who did nothing but drive him insane? He yanked up the covers and slid in, stretching out to his full length.

She rolled onto her side toward him, her face cushioned on her hand. "Should we talk about the mark?"

Right now, he wanted to plant it on her ass. Hard. When he'd seen her running through the rain and jumping in the taxi, he'd nearly lost his mind. He sighed and watched her from his peripheral vision. "Sure. You go first."

"It'll go away if not used, so you should stop worrying about it." She yawned, looking like a small kitten.

Well. "You know, in some circles, I'm considered a catch." He let his amusement show as his body finally relaxed one muscle at a time.

She chuckled. "I'm sure you are. But we're in an untenable position, and if we don't figure a way out, our people will go to war."

He was no longer amused. "Baby? Your people would lose."

"Maybe." She snuggled closer, and gardenias filled his senses. "Maybe not. We have pretty good weapons and defenses. And we can teleport anywhere, while you can't."

She made a good argument. But he had the entire Realm—so the Fae couldn't win. And he certainly couldn't let her get hurt, so he had to figure out a way to fix this situation. Once he got some sleep. Then his brain might kick in again.

She trailed her nails across his pecs, and he woke right up. "You have the most amazing chest," she murmured, drawing nearer to rest her head on his shoulder. "You're the largest male I've ever seen."

He partially turned his head on the pillow. "Are you teasing me?"

"No." Even her pout was sexy. "I liked kissing you the other day, but then you're the one who tied me to the bed. Of course I tried to escape and get back to my people. You can't be mad about that."

She had a point. Then she started drawing circles on his chest, and he forgot all about being fair or points. His dick ached, heavy and full. He hadn't slept in too long, he was worried about his brother, and he wasn't thinking straight. But his body didn't care.

"I liked kissing you, too," he murmured. Hell. He'd almost devoured her.

She scrunched up her face. "It's just, I mean, I've read a lot about you. You kind of get around."

What was she getting at? "So?"

"So..." Her gaze faltered. She shifted slightly away from him, her head ducking.

His heart turned over. "You're beautiful and sexy and smart, Mercy O'Malley. Of course I want you."

She shrugged, revealing a very smooth shoulder with only a small bra strap over it. "Okay. I just haven't been around demons, and I just, well, you know."

The most beautiful woman he'd ever seen was feeling insecure? Sometimes life was fucking crazy. He grasped her arm, rolled onto his back, and tugged her on top of him before settling back down. His cock jumped to life between her legs, where it was wet and warm.

Yep. This was going to kill him.

"Oh," she breathed, a lovely pink flushing across her face.

He grinned, putting his arm beneath his head so he wouldn't grab her ass and press her down on him. "Does that answer your question?"

Her lips twitched, and her gaze dropped to his mouth. "Kind of?"

Okay. Just one touch. He caressed her spine with his free hand, enjoying the feeling of her smooth skin. Part of the problem, one he wasn't sure how to explain, was how adorable she was. "I like you, Mercy," he murmured. "You're spirited and sweet and kind of a pain in the ass. Intriguing as hell."

"So?"

"So?" He wasn't sure he wanted to face the reality of them. "I warned you, remember? You're not a casual fling." The mark on his hand was proof of that. "The males in my family lose their minds over their mates, and I'm trying real hard to remain sane with you."

"We're not mates," she said, her lips moving even closer to his.

Her sense of risk and search for adventure was so at odds with her love for numbers and investments that it just drew him. But she didn't know demons or vampires, and she had no clue about the fire she was stoking. "I've never had anything in this life that was just mine, darlin'."

She tilted her head to the side, her nose lightly brushing his. "I'm not yours."

But she could be. "All right. It's like this." He rolled them over, pressing her to the bed. Her body cushioned his perfectly. The woman was soft everywhere he was hard, and he wanted nothing more than to explore every inch of her. But she really wasn't getting him.

Her hands slid over his shoulders and then into his hair. Her smile was all satisfied cat with cream. "Logan," she breathed. "We're finally playing."

Exactly the problem. "Spread your legs, Mercy," he said quietly.

She paused, tilting her head. Mischief danced across her face, and she opened her mouth to question him.

"Now." He pressed his cock directly above her clit. Hard.

* * * *

Mercy gasped as mini-explosions rocked through her lower body. She blinked, searching Logan's eyes for the lazy amusement always lurking there.

No amusement. Nothing lazy. Just a dark intent that sent shivers over her skin.

Swallowing, her heart rate speeding up, she widened her legs.

"Good," he whispered, a massive shadow over her. "Now take your hands out of my hair."

She frowned but released his silky hair and curled her fingers over the tight skin of his shoulders. While she wanted to protest, the deep command in his gritty voice compelled her to obey. "You're—" she started.

"No. No words." He ground against her again, and she bucked closer, wanting more. "Put your hands above your head, Mercy."

She didn't want her hands above her head. She wanted them on his phenomenal body. "No." The word came out more as a question than a statement. So she scratched her nails into his flesh.

"No?" he asked softly, his head lowering a fraction.

Her lungs constricted. Confusion and arousal battled through her, and she tried to concentrate when every urge she had prompted her to put her arms up. But she kept in place. Waiting. Questioning. Needing.

His movements controlled and deliberate, he grasped first one wrist and then the other, pulling them above her head. He stretched her enough that her back bowed, scraping her hard-as-rock nipples against his bare chest. She gasped, her eyes wide on him.

This was so out of her experience.

Her panties grew even wetter.

He smiled as if he knew exactly what he was doing to her. It hit her then, like a tennis racket to the head. He *did* know.

Keeping his hold firm, he rolled to the side, letting cool air brush across her heated body. She gave an experimental tug of her arms. Nope. They stayed right in place, easily secured with one of his strong hands. A whimper tried to escape her.

She moved to close her legs, to ease some of the pressure.

"No. I didn't tell you to move." He leaned in and bit her earlobe.

The small pain nearly sent her into orbit. She swallowed rapidly, freezing in place.

"Good girl." He licked her lobe and then up the shell of her ear.

Desire ripped through her with sharp speed. The vulnerability of her position gave her pause, and she turned her head to look at him.

He watched her carefully, his gaze hot. "You understanding?"

"Not really," she admitted, not sure what to do next.

"All right." His free hand cupped her jaw, his fingers sweeping gently across her cheekbone. He traced down her neck and over her collarbone before edging along the top of her bra.

Her nipples somehow hardened even more. She tried to push toward his hand, but he just explored where the bra met her skin. A frustrated groan escaped her.

"What's wrong?" he asked, amusement in his tone.

She bit her lip.

"I'll keep playing until you ask," he murmured.

She didn't play this way. Apparently, he did. "I want you to touch me," she whispered. There. She'd said it.

"Ask me."

Her gaze slashed back up to his. Stubbornness filled her, but the need was greater. Damn it. "Touch me."

"That's not asking." He leaned in and nipped her ear again.

She jumped.

"You're lucky we're just on ears," he whispered, his breath hot.

She shivered. What else would he bite? "Fine. Would you pretty please, with a cherry on top, touch me, Prince Kyllwood?"

His lids lowered to half-mast. "Sure." His hand swept inside her bra, and he pinched a nipple.

Shock took her, and she gasped. Electricity zipped straight to her clit. Her hips rolled.

"Is that what you meant?" he murmured.

Not exactly, but it was a turn-on. "Sure," she said, her chin firming.

"All right." He moved to the other nipple and flicked it.

Pain edged to pleasure in a heartbeat. This was too much. "Logan," she whispered.

He shoved her bra up, and then his mouth was on her. Wet and warm and insistent. He played with her breasts, nipping and biting, hinting at pain that flooded into pleasure. With her hands bound, she couldn't touch him. She could only feel, and soon she was a desperate bundle of nerves. She needed more. So much more.

As if he knew, he moved off her again, and his large hand flattened across her abdomen. "You want to come, Mercy?"

God yes. Definitely. She nodded.

"Ask me." His palm swept over her panties, and she pushed against him.

She didn't even think of using sarcasm this time. "Please, Logan."

He pushed his hand into her panties, his thumb scraping across her clit. She arched, the feeling too much and yet not enough.

Her sex clenched. His fingers dipped down farther, gliding through her folds and into her. His fingertips were rough but his penetration gentle. She caught her breath. He added another finger inside her, twisting and hitting a spot she hadn't known she had.

She arched, her eyes closing.

He paused.

Her eyes opened.

He nodded. "Keep your eyes on me. This is mine."

She shook her head out of instinct, her arms up and her body spread open for him.

"Yes." He hit that spot again and planted his thumb directly on her clit. "Do. Not. Move."

She bit her lip as tremors started in her thighs.

"Understand now?" he asked.

She blinked.

He stared at her for a moment as if thinking and then gave a short nod. Apparently he'd reached a conclusion.

"I want it all, Mercy. Understand that. Not playing, not casual, not temporary." He leaned in and kissed her. Hard. "Right now you're going to give me this. All of it. Then we're sleeping. Tomorrow, you can decide if you want to give me everything. But if you do, I'm keeping it."

He stroked her again, and she arched, her eyelids fluttering shut. She opened them quickly to concentrate on the burning green of his eyes. This was so much, but she couldn't move. If he stopped, she'd die.

His fingers increased their pace, and he fucked her with them, his thumb working her clit.

The orgasm hit her so hard she stopped breathing. The waves pummeled her, and she had to close her eyes, heat flushing hard and fast beneath her skin.

He worked her until she softened to the bed with a garbled murmur, her mind and body shutting down with pure relief.

"Tomorrow, then," he whispered against her forehead, pulling the covers over them both. Then warmth and safety surrounded her for the first time in her life, and she settled right into it, even as a warning ticked in the back of her mind.

She'd worry about that tomorrow.

Chapter 23

Mercy awoke, her body satiated, her mind rested, and her heart totally out of whack. The sheets were so warm from the immortal slumbering next to her that she had to snuggle in and enjoy the moment. Turning on her side, she studied him.

Logan slept on his stomach, one arm above his head, his face turned toward her. In sleep, he looked every bit as fierce as he did awake—maybe more so. His lashes were long against his bronze skin, and black scruff covered his firm jawline. He should have the look of a pirate, but he didn't.

Predator. While resting, when he should be vulnerable, his primal nature was even more evident.

The bedclothes had been pushed to his waist, and she fought the temptation to run her hand over the rugged planes of his back. Even the blades of his shoulders looked strong.

The previous night with him had been something new. She wanted to simultaneously run for safety and jump his body. He hadn't been bluffing about taking everything. Could she allow herself to be that vulnerable with anyone? Ever? He wouldn't allow for any other way, and she had a duty to uphold. An important one that did not include the sexy hybrid.

That thought alone should have her making a break for it.

Instead, she let herself enjoy the morning, drifting off to a place between dreams and reality, a vault where memories lived.

Smoke filled the kitchen, and she opened the window, using a towel to blow it outside.

At the cheery yellow table, Sandy laughed hysterically, holding her stomach, being of no use whatsoever. Her thick hair was piled high on her head, and she'd tried a new sparkly silver eyeshadow that was the rage in Scotland. "Stop trying to cook."

Mercy sighed and tossed the towel aside. She peered at the black contents in the pan. "Eggs Benedict looked so easy."

Sandy snorted. "It is easy. You're twenty years old. How can you not cook eggs?"

Mercy rescued several binders from the end of the counter and placed them on the island, away from anything that could burn them. She and Sandy were back in Scotland for a week so she could tweak her people's investments. It looked like they might have to return for good soon because of the dimensional disturbances rippling through time and space. "Don't you have work to do today?"

Sandy sighed, her eyes sparkling. "Yeah, but I'm hungry."

Mercy rolled her eyes and took a bacon and cheese quiche out of the fridge to microwave. "I bought it yesterday at a deli down the street. Just in case."

Sandy hopped happily in place. "Excellent. The humans have some new automatic weapons I'm checking out today. I don't think they're as good as ours, but I might as well double-check. Sometimes humans are innovative."

Meh. Maybe.

A knock sounded on the door.

"Enter," Mercy called, taking the quiche from the microwave. Now there was a decent human invention.

Niall entered the room, having obviously just purchased new dark jeans and a button-down white shirt. As he'd gotten older, he'd taken on more responsibility as king, and it showed in the way he moved. "Morning."

Sandy jumped up, glancing at her watch. "Morning, Niall. I was just heading to the local police station." She winked at Mercy and zipped out of the room before Mercy could protest.

Mercy slipped the quiche onto the counter and cleared her throat. She'd dated a few of the Fae and several humans while on Earth, but Niall always seemed to throw her a little bit. He watched her carefully, and while that should interest her, it was more annoying than not. It was as if he was waiting for her to screw up. Or perhaps that was just her imagination working overtime whenever she was around the Fae king. "I have a report ready for you and the president about some new investments I think we should make. Green energy might be the wave of the future on Earth," she said.

"All right." His blond hair was ruffled, and his brown eye was a little darker than usual. "The geneticists we've been consulting with have finalized the best plan for strengthening our people."

Her heart started to thrum. She had found a diary belonging to her mother, who'd been mated to her father, which is why and probably how Mercy's creation had been a success. They'd been in love. The real kind. There had been no chart for them. Fate had brought them together. "Human geneticists don't know everything."

"We've met with witches, too," Niall said, drawing a folded piece of paper from his back pocket. "A few that we trust."

Witches were brilliant with science, able to create fire at will and manipulate the laws of physics. Gut instinct told her what the paper would show, but she held out her hand anyway. Yep. There she was.

"They confirm what we've already been told. Want to be queen?" Niall asked, his grin charming.

Not really. She wanted to hop dimensions, play the stock market like a gambling addict, and fall completely and hopelessly in love with her direct opposite. "Why us?" she asked instead.

"Your ability to teleport and my ability to fight." He eyed her in a new way. One that seemed to see all of her.

He was good-looking, ambitious, and kind of dark. Those were his good qualities. "I'll think about it," she said.

"You've got five years," he said easily.

Ah. The magical age of twenty-five. "What about Sandy?"

Niall glanced down at the paper. "Bud Denvee."

Humor slapped Mercy hard. "Bud? Man, they hate each other." No way was that ever going to happen. Those two had been competing since they'd popped out of their test tubes.

Niall shrugged. "Then they'll burn up the sheets. But they will be mated."

Probably. Both would follow duty, as would she. But still. What about Fate? "There has to be some choice here, Niall."

His eyes hardened. "There is none. We ten were specifically created for this. We're few in number, and if we have to return to this plane permanently, we have to make ourselves as strong as possible. This is the first step."

A chill took her, and she forced a smile. Her entire life she'd been taught that her duty was to the Fae as a whole. Maybe this was part of that duty. No matter how wrong it felt. "We'll see."

A knock on the door had her jolting upright in bed in the present.

Logan leaped free and was at the door in less than a heartbeat. "What?" he growled, his body one long line of ticked-off male.

"Brought you a present, buddy. Get your ass out here," Adare said cheerfully.

Logan turned to look at her, his hair mussed, his face in a frown. "Get dressed."

Well. Bossy in the morning, wasn't he? She used the attached bathroom, brushed her hair, and borrowed the same toothbrush and lip gloss. Then she waited for Logan, and they entered the living room together.

She halted. "Sandy?"

Her best friend sat on the sofa by the fireplace, her hands bound with rope, her hair a wild mess. While her eyes were both blue, they were very different shades. One was aqua, while the other was the deep hue of the bottom of the ocean. "Hey, Mercy. How's it hanging?" Sandy eyed Logan from head to toe, and her eyebrows rose. "Sorry to interrupt." Her smile flashed twin dimples.

Until mating, it was fine for the Fae to have dalliances. But she didn't have to look so delighted, did she?

Mercy moved farther into the room, her head spinning. Her back teeth ground together, and her palms dampened. She glared at Adare. "What did you do?"

He rubbed his hands, which were covered in red welts. They went up his arms and were visible on his neck to his ears. "She was following me, and I stopped her. Then she started yelling about you, admitted she was a fucking fairy, and I brought her here. It's that simple."

"Well, I did try to teleport him to Iceland, but he stopped me." Sandy's eyes lit up, the intelligence there obvious. "Did you know they could do that? Stop a teleport?"

Mercy nodded. "I don't think all of them can. But yes. Kind of sucks, right?" She cocked her head in question.

Sandy winked at her, catching her question easily. "Wanted to make sure you were okay." Excellent. Sandy was the best. She could still teleport.

Logan stepped closer to Adare. "Jesus. Does that hurt?"

"Yes, and it fucking itches like you wouldn't believe." Adare scratched the back of his neck. "Damn mating allergy. This is what happens when you do a favor for your brother and mate a human. A human," he growled, his fangs glistening.

So it was true. Mercy believed the lore, but she'd never actually witnessed a mated immortal's reaction to prolonged proximity to a member of the opposite sex who wasn't their mate. The hives looked horribly painful. "How long will that last?" she whispered.

"Dunno," Adare muttered. "It's different for each male, and this is the first time I've experienced it."

"Your mate is a lucky female. Yes, she is," Sandy chirped.

Amusement took Mercy, and she covered a laugh with a cough. If she could get close enough to Sandy, she could get out of there. Her heart hitched at the thought of leaving Logan right now, but if she was going to find Ivar and Sam, she had to meet with Niall. She also needed the president's permission to try to negotiate with the Seven. It was time they all worked together. "I'm sorry they caught you." There was a bit of truth in that statement because now she had no choice but to go. "Are you all right?"

Sandy grinned. "I'm great. Talked Bud into a big wedding. He's so not happy about it."

It was nice to see her friend happy. Talk about opposites attract and enemies to lovers. They *were* a romance trope.

Logan cleared his throat. "Glad you're both so cheerful. Contact your leaders and let them know we have you. I want Sam and Ivar back. Now."

"He's kinda bossy," Sandy said, craning her neck to check Logan out. "Cute, though. You kiss him yet?"

Mercy nodded. "Yes. Good kisser. Very."

Logan growled. Low and deep.

Sandy jerked her head toward Adare. "I really am sorry about the allergy." She leaned to the side. "But I told you to leave me alone. You should've just listened. Why don't they ever listen, Mercy?"

Mercy shrugged. "It's a mystery. It truly is." She inched closer to her friend.

Adare ignored them, shoving his hands in the pockets of his faded jeans. With a gun strapped to his thigh and a pissed off expression, the Highlander looked even more dangerous than he had before, and that was saying something. "I've had it with pixie dust, unicorns, and rainbows. Let's go find somebody to fight," he said.

"Rainbows?" Sandy snorted.

"Fairies are nuts," Adare muttered, reaching for a phone in his back pocket. "Who do we call to get this over with?"

Mercy faltered. She would've liked a few minutes with Logan after last night, but she was having trouble meeting his gaze. And she couldn't talk to him in front of the others. Her timing always sucked with males. She sighed. "Go ahead and call the president." It didn't matter.

"Number?" Adare asked.

Logan was watching her carefully as she recited the digits of the local number. Then she smiled at Sandy. "It's dumb that he tied your hands. Let me help you." As casually as possible, she crossed around the table and headed for the sofa. The second she reached Sandy, she grasped her forearm. "Now," she whispered.

Sandy gathered the forces around them, the air shimmered, and the world started to drop away.

A steel band around Mercy's waist jerked her away from Sandy and fully back to this dimension. She yelped and struggled, fighting Logan's hold. Crap, he moved fast. Way too fast.

Damn it.

He whirled her around and set her down on her feet—not so gently. Anger flushed high on his cheeks.

She gulped as Sandy disappeared from the room with a shimmer. "You can't blame me?"

Adare moved for them. "What the hell? I stopped her from teleporting."

"You have to be touching them," Logan said grimly. "She let you bring her here so she could get Mercy."

Adare winced. "One should never underestimate a fairy. Good lesson."

Logan ducked his shoulder and tossed Mercy over it. Her stomach hit first, and then her head against his damn back. "Fae reinforcements will be coming. Get us out of here, Adare," he ordered.

Chapter 24

Amusement creased the Highlander's cheeks, but Adare wisely remained silent, wrapping his arms around Logan and Mercy and spiriting them away.

They landed at his lake with the afternoon sky dropping rain on the water. Enough with the rain, damn it.

Logan's temper frayed. Although he'd finally slept, he had a serious case of blue balls. And the woman responsible for them wanted to disappear on him again. The effort it took to hold back fury made his muscles vibrate and his temples pound. So far this week he'd kept secrets from Zane, had lost both Sam and Ivar, and had failed to help Garrett heal from the Seven ritual.

And he was damn tired of being carted through time and space like a damn toddler. He set Mercy on her feet.

He grasped her arm and forced her up the walkway toward the cabin. "First, you're going to explain to me what the fuck the problem is between your people and the Seven." Shoving a branch out of the way, he waited until she passed before letting it drop back. "Next, you're finding out where Sam and Ivar are being held." When she tried to slow down, he increased his pace so she had to keep up. "Finally, you're going to explain teleporting to me so I can figure out how the hell to do it."

She jerked her arm free. "I do not take orders from you."

He pivoted so suddenly into her, she would've fallen on her butt if he hadn't caught her. "Wrong."

"Last night doesn't count." She blinked and defiance filled her face.

Last night counted a whole hell of a lot. He growled. Low and dark and hard.

She gulped. "I would love to tell you about the Seven." The dark red of her hair blazed, even in the muted light of the cloudy day. Raindrops dotted her pretty face, and his knuckles itched with the need to brush the water away. "But I need permission to do so."

"From Niall?" he snapped.

"No. The president." Mercy turned on her own and finished the trail, breaking free of the trees and heading to Adare's cabin. It was not supposed to be their headquarters, but they'd already blown up two mountain strongholds and were out of options at the moment.

"Fine." Logan marched next to her, pausing when he spotted Ronan and his mate, Faith Cooper, snuggled on a porch swing on the covered deck, blankets and laptops on their legs. Both were typing rapidly and somehow in perfect sync. It would've been gag-worthy if they didn't look so right together. "Ronan?"

The vampire looked up. "We're going through traffic cams in Scotland, trying to find any sort of clue to Sam or Ivar's whereabouts."

Teleporting usually happened outside of camera range, but what the hell. There was nothing else they could do. Logan nodded. "Ronan and Faith, this is Mercy."

Faith smiled, her eyes sparkling. "Hi."

Ronan lifted an eyebrow. "So you're a fairy."

"Fae," Mercy said quietly.

Logan took her hand. "Do we have a secure line she can use to reach her people? One that can't be hacked?" The last thing he needed was Fae soldiers popping up out of nowhere.

Ronan nodded. "Yeah. Adare has a computer in the office that's clean. She can use that with no risk."

"Good." Logan pulled her across the deck, through the great room, to Adare's office in the back. The leather-filled room smelled of Scotch, fine cigars, and pine. Oil paintings of the Highlands adorned the wall, and the desk was large enough to hold several computers. He led Mercy around to sit in a high-backed chair about six sizes too big for her in front of a desktop computer. "Dial out. Now."

She rolled her eyes but did so, going through passwords and encryptions, until finally a stunning blonde woman with two different colored eyes appeared on the screen.

Mercy looked up. "I require privacy."

"No." Logan moved to her side so the woman could see him as well. "If you give one hint of our location, I'll shut this down."

The woman looked at him. "Logan Kyllwood. Hello, Prince."

Prince? Not his thing. "You must be the president of the Fae," he replied.

She nodded, appearing calm and collected. Wisdom and experience showed in her eyes, but her skin was as smooth and young as a twenty-year-old's. "Yes. Return Mercy, or I'll go public with every record I have on the Seven." Her voice was throaty, almost hoarse.

Mercy sucked in air.

Logan grinned. It was nice to finally deal with somebody who laid it on the line. "I'm not quite ready to let her go. However, if you return both Sam and Ivar to us, I'll certainly think about it."

The president paled. "I assure you that Sam is safe. Unfortunately, Niall lost his temper, and I can't tell you where Ivar Kjeidsen ended up. I'm sure he'll teleport home at some point."

Well, that didn't sound good. Logan leaned in and gritted his teeth. "My brother."

The president looked to the side. "All right. But you're not going to like it." The sound of clacking keys came over the line, and another browser opened to reveal Sam bound to a chair, bruises across his face. Stone walls surrounded him, and blood pooled on the dirt floor.

Logan's body temperature rose. He snarled. "Sam? You okay?"

Sam looked up, his green eyes darker than usual. "Hey, brother. How's it going?"

Logan dropped his chin, fury lancing him. "You okay?"

"Fine. Keep telling these bastards to kiss off."

Damn it to hell. The code phrase to do nothing? Sam wanted to stay there? Just what did he think he'd discover? "Sam—"

The screen disappeared.

Logan kept his face furious. His brother knew what he was doing. Now Logan had a part to play. "You have one hour to release my brother or you'll face the demon nation, and it won't be pretty. For now, give Mercy permission to explain your problem with the Seven to us directly."

"That's an empty threat. I know you won't reveal the existence of the Seven to the demon nation." The president sighed. "Mercy, you have permission to educate these animals. But it won't change anything." She clicked off.

What the hell did that mean?

Mercy looked up at him. "I require a whiteboard."

The absolute cuteness of her very serious request warmed the chill always in his chest. The world, his world, had gone to shit, and yet...he wanted to smile. So he frowned instead. "I'll see what I can do."

It took two minutes to yell for everyone to gather around the hand-carved oak kitchen table, and another three to find a legal pad and black marker. Then he sat closest to where Mercy stood at the head of the table. Garrett, Adare, and Ronan sat next to him with Faith and Grace on the other side. Ronan held hands with his mate, while Adare ignored his. Grace looked at Mercy with curiosity glimmering in her eyes.

"We have two of the three Keys right here," Logan said. Interesting. If they could only find the third.

Mercy shook her head. "I won't be a Key."

Adare's dark eyebrow rose. "I don't think you have a choice in that."

"Yes, I do." Mercy took her marker. "Before I start, please make a mental note not to be insulted by anything I say." She worried her bottom lip with her teeth, looking like an incredibly sexy librarian. "You just don't have the knowledge we do."

No. That wasn't insulting at all. Logan bit back another grin.

The back door slammed open, and Benjamin Reese, the final member of the Seven, stomped inside wearing his size eighteen combat boots. "I was fucking on a nice weekend with my nephews, trying to beat some sense into them, and you call me back here?" He came around the corner, looked at the group, then dragged out the remaining chair next to Grace. At six feet eight, with brown hair and blackish-green eyes, Benny looked every bit as dangerous as he was. He smiled, all charm, his frown disappearing. "Well, hello. I'm Benjamin."

Mercy blushed. "Mercy O'Malley."

"It's so very nice to meet you." Benny's voice dropped to pure gentleness.

Logan cut the vampire a look. "Mercy was just going to explain why we can't complete the final ritual."

"Well now. That's just silly." Benny's eyes twinkled.

Logan rolled his eyes. "Go ahead, Mercy." He'd deal with the pain-in-the-ass later.

She cleared her throat. "Have any of you studied bubble theory? It's the human theory that universes are like bubbles that collide, creating black matter."

Logan nodded.

"Humans, of course, are way off, but the bubble theory is an easy way to explain dimensions. Demons teleport through space and time—different dimensions—landing somewhere here on Earth that they've been or at least know about. We travel the same way, but we can stop at different dimensions."

"Like dreamworlds," Logan said, giving Garrett a look.

Garrett nodded, his sizzling gray eyes finally clear. Their siblings had met in dreamworlds during childhood. Was it possible they had been in different dimensions?

Ronan leaned forward. "When we created the prison world for Ulric with the two securing worlds outside it, we moved dimensions out of place?"

"Exactly." Mercy slammed down the marker. "You can't move dimensions without serious repercussions."

Ronan nodded. "All right. That explains the ritual I undertook that kept my place stable."

Well, that made some sense. "Ronan's bubble broke," Logan said. "We've assumed the other two will as well."

"No." Mercy's eyes turned yellow and then back to blue and green. "That's what you have wrong. The dimensions are finally stabilizing, and you have to leave them alone. Those two worlds won't burst. They're going to remain right where they are."

Adare held up a hand. The welts were already fading. "You're wrong. We've researched this extensively, and Ivar had new intel before he was taken. These dimensions, or bubbles, are going to fail. They're lopsided now that Ronan's has blown."

"Not true. Our science says otherwise," Mercy said, her hair tumbling with her agitated movements.

Logan frowned. "You really believe the bubbles won't burst?"

Her slim shoulders finally relaxed. "Not if you remain unmarked."

"Unmarked?" Logan asked.

Garrett kicked back. "She means the Seven. The marking on our backs and the fusing of our torsos."

Mercy nodded emphatically. "Thank you. Yes. If you leave the Seven incomplete, then the prison world will never blow."

That made no sense. Logan looked around the table at the various expressions of disbelief. "Why?" he finally asked.

She shook her head as if they were all morons. "As the Seven, you have power. True, real, physics-defying power. You know that. You perverted, and I mean *perverted*, the laws of physics to create your bond in the first place. This is all about gravity."

"So?" Adare growled.

She turned her glowing eyes to him. "The seven of you have a pull. Like magnets."

It was obvious she was dumbing down the explanation, but at this point, Logan didn't care. "Why have the Fae decided to intervene now? You weren't worried about the Seven before."

She blew out air. "We obviously didn't know when you first created the Seven. Then, you accidentally created the perfect counterbalance of two of the members in other dimensions and five members here; symmetry and safety existed with that balance."

"Oh." Logan glanced at Ronan. "But now Ronan is here, and only Quade is out there."

"Yes." She nodded again. "With six of you here, the pull would be too great. Way too powerful. Quade's world would burst, and then Ulric's. By completing the Seven, you'll draw Quade whether you want to or not. He's stronger than his dimension, or he wouldn't have survived it so long."

Garrett wiped both hands down his face. "Okay. It's time we took Ulric out for good. We know the combined blood of the three Keys will kill him, and we have two of you."

She threw her head back as if in disbelief. Then, taking a deep breath, she reclaimed the marker and the notepad, drawing circles on it. "You've attached three dimensions you shouldn't have bound together—and you've moved them away from where they should be. Now one is gone." She crossed out Ronan's old world. "You've left a void, but so far that seems to be okay. If these two go... what's going to fill their places? You're fucking playing checkers with dimensions."

Logan winced. Had he heard her swear before? "You don't know it'd be catastrophic."

Her eyes softened with a glimmering sadness. "Unfortunately, we do."

Ah, shit. "Your people. The ones you lost?" Including her family?

She nodded. "Yes. We were experimenting with creating a paradise where we could all live, and we caused a rift that split time and space. It was our fault, and we paid the price." Her voice rose in conviction. "You can't do the same thing. Learn from our mistake."

His heart hurt for her. "Honey, you have to realize that the Kurjans are working tirelessly to free Ulric. At some point, they'll burst his prison world to get him out."

She blinked. "One problem at a time."

The Fae really had no clue about the Kurjans. Logan shook his head. "All right. So you take me out. Somebody else will just step up and take my place. Your plan doesn't make sense."

Her mouth tightened until her smooth lips looked white. "Logan. Only warriors with certain bloodlines can survive the ritual of the Seven. Surely you've realized that fact."

Well, sure.

Wait a minute. Tension gathered around the table.

Logan's breath caught. "Tell me your people aren't planning what I fear."

She set the paper down. "Adare and Ivar don't have any other family. Their bloodlines die with them. The plan was to take Logan out just to buy time and then…"

"Take out Ivar and me so we can't reproduce," Adare said thoughtfully. "Of course, the Kayrs and Kyllwoods seem to procreate like rabbits, but there are only so many members of one family that can be sacrificed. It's not a bad plan."

She blanched. "It's a horrible plan, and one I wanted to avoid. That's why I tried to kidnap you." She faced Logan directly. "I hoped that once I explained the situation, you would decide not to complete the ritual. I just needed some time."

Benny planted his huge hands on the table. "The story is a good one, but it's irrelevant. At some point, Ulric will be free, and only the Seven can fight him. We need to be *the Seven*—forged in blood and bone—when that happens, or every single Enhanced female, mated or unmated, dies. Ulric has the power to do it."

"The original purpose of the Seven was to keep Ulric in prison," Mercy burst out. "If he's out of prison, you have no function."

Benny cocked his head. "So the fairies don't have all the facts. Good to know. You're wrong. That's all I'm gonna say. We need Logan in the Seven."

Logan's chest constricted. Benny was crude but correct—the role of the Seven played out until the very end. Looked like they were damned no matter what they did. In that situation, you went with legend and Fate. Always.

Benny cleared his throat. "Let's order pizza. I'm starving."

Mercy looked at Logan.

He met her gaze evenly. "I agree with Ben about joining the Seven, but I'm willing to discuss this further. Your people have much more experience with other dimensions than we do. Maybe we could work together to figure out a solution."

Her frown was more sad than angry. "My people won't work with you. And you won't listen to us. It's war, then."

Chapter 25

After a supper of salad and pizza, Mercy paced the guest bedroom, her mind spinning. War. Could the Fae really go to war with the Realm? The very idea seemed ridiculous, but the president and King Niall had never seemed worried about that possibility.

Were their defenses that good? Until recently, none of them had even seen Realm soldiers in action.

What about Logan? Those crazy-looking Cyst soldiers were after him, and they looked deadly. What if they caught up to him?

She scrubbed her hands through her hair, pulling it away from her scalp. Why hadn't the Seven listened to her? Why were vampires and demons so damn stubborn? Failure felt like a solid rock in her stomach.

Rain continued to patter outside as yet another night began to fall. She'd been in so many time zones, back and forth, she wasn't sure whether to sleep or not.

Exhaustion pulled at her. She missed her figures and the stock market. Missed watching the real estate transfers. Missed trying to learn how to cook. She was a disaster in the kitchen. Yet she'd never stop trying.

Would life ever get back to normal?

She sat on the bed with its plush floral comforter and tried to take several deep breaths. Logan had to listen to her. If she had a phone, she'd call Sandy. Sandy was so much better with males.

Crossing her legs, she dropped her chin and began a set of breathing exercises that were supposed to make her body relax. Instead, her mind wandered back to the past.

She sat in a spacious office with a view of New York City and several computers, buying and selling stocks with the speed of a rodeo bronc. She liked this world—the opportunities available to her, to her people, to build a portfolio that would sustain and protect them for centuries.

Money and land led to safety. It was that easy. The thrill of the hunt rushed through her.

Her door opened, and Niall sauntered inside. He wore a gray suit, bright green tie, and shiny loafers. He'd cut his hair and was clean-shaven, his jaw chiseled. That explained the sound of female chattering going on outside the office. Like the rest of them, he enjoyed his time with humans while in this world. How many girlfriends did he have, anyway? Not that she cared.

She partially stood. "King."

He motioned her back to her seat and shut the door, crossing to a leather guest chair. "I told you about our match nearly five years ago. Don't you think it's time you called me Niall?"

They'd been busy for the intervening five years, only seeing each other during official meetings. But lately, he'd been looking at her differently. Like he had a right to look at her. She breathed out, her mind spinning. Her duty was to her people. Being their queen would allow her to be of great use. He was good-looking and cared about the Fae as much as she did.

But still. Where were the tingles?

He studied her. "Is that a bruise on your forehead?"

She reached up and rubbed the purple bump. Ouch. "Yes. I was training yesterday. It's time I learned how to fight."

He laughed. "You're going to be queen. Learning to fight is a waste of your valuable time."

Oh yeah? Maybe she should show him the high kick she'd learned just last week. "I have plenty of time," she said.

He shrugged. *"How's the research coming? Into the Seven?"* he asked, glancing at his gold wristwatch.

Oh. There went the tingles. *"I agree that Logan Kyllwood is the most likely final candidate to join the Seven."* Her legs trembled, and she crossed them. What in the world was wrong with her? *"I've been studying him, and he isn't going to be easy to kill."* She'd only seen pictures, but his green eyes were burned into her mind. The more she learned about him, the more intrigued she became.

"I'm not concerned. Our soldiers will be able to handle him."

Hah. They only had six soldiers under the age of a zillion. *"I've come up with a plan, a way to lure him to us."* Her voice cracked, and she cleared it. She had to meet Logan Kyllwood in person. Just once. Just to see if he was as incredible as she'd read. As she dreamed. Then she'd follow duty.

"Your strategic mind always captivates me." Niall's smile was both charming and sincere.

Guilt cut through her. This male was her intended. And she was creating a scenario to save a demon who most likely would want her dead. *"I'd like for Sandy and Trina to work with me."*

He studied the snow globes scattered across her desk. One of her many collections. *"Sort of a final mission?"* His brown eye sparkled more than his blue one. *"The equivalent to a human bachelorette party?"*

She forced a smile. *"Only the Fae would consider tricking a demon to be a party."*

He chuckled, the sound low and smooth. *"That's a good point. But I'm sorry, there will be no mission. Not a chance. In fact, pack your bags, because we're going to Malta for our mating."*

She blinked. *"I haven't actually said yes, King."*

He smirked, arrogance in his expression. *"Playing hard to get is for humans, Mercy. You're above that."* He stood, smoothing down his pressed pants. *"As your mate, I'll have little patience for nonsense."* With that last mild threat, he exited the office.

She tried to like him, she really did. He was smart and extremely good-looking. Confident and assured. But where was the excitement? The sizzle? They had a common goal, and they were passionate about it. But where was her passion for him? She just couldn't find it.

Mercy reached in her bottom drawer and pulled out a manila file. She opened the top, and dark green eyes bored into hers. Just one time, she wanted to meet Logan Kyllwood. To put the dreams to rest. If that meant committing treason, then so be it. She had to take the chance to reason with Logan.

And she wanted to meet him more than she understood.

A barely there knock sounded at the door, and she snapped her head up and into the present. "Come in," she said.

Grace Cooper poked her head inside, her hazel eyes somber. "Have a minute?"

Mercy sighed and motioned her in.

Slight vibrations came from the human, revealing her enhancement. Enhanced humans, those with psychic, empathic or telekinetic abilities, could mate with immortals. And this one had become Adare's mate, despite the fact that she'd been in a coma at the time, at death's door. Mercy looked her over, suddenly curious. "You're the only female I've ever heard about who mated without intercourse."

Grace blushed crimson. "Yay. Lucky me." She flopped onto the bed, bouncing twice on her butt.

Mercy winced. "Sorry."

Grace shrugged, her narrow shoulders covered by a light-pink sweater. "I was in a coma, almost dying, but Adare bit me and saved my life. We think I was able to survive because I'm one of the Keys."

Yeah. Mercy figured that'd be the topic. "Don't worry, the ritual will never happen."

Grace looked at her, hazel eyes wise. "The fact that there's a ritual says something, don't you think?" She sighed and kicked out her feet. "Two years in a coma, and I get philosophical." The woman was pale and too thin, but there was no doubt she wasn't a typical coma victim. Being a Key had definitely kept her as healthy as possible. "I understand all of this immortal shit is about blood and bones and Fate, but what the hell, right?"

Mercy snorted. "Exactly."

"How is my blood supposed to stop the most dangerous evil asshat ever created?" Grace frowned at the closed door. "Besides my so-called mate."

Mercy chuckled. "Adare does seem a little cranky."

Grace sighed. "That's the understatement of all time. He doesn't like humans." Her lip twisted. "At all."

It must stink to be mated to somebody who didn't like you. Although, after everything that had happened, no doubt Niall wasn't liking Mercy much right now. Duty pulled her in one direction, while Logan Kyllwood yanked her in another. She shook her head and focused on Grace's problem. "Supposedly there's a virus, a new one, that negates the mating bond."

Grace grinned. "Already on it, sister. As soon as I get my health back, I'm seeking out that virus. For sure."

Of course, as far as Mercy knew, it had never been attempted on a mate with a still-living partner. Only widows and widowers. "Good luck."

"Thanks." They shared a grin.

Mercy wondered what Grace's enhancement was, but that was kind of like asking a woman her weight. "You understand the legend of the Keys, right?"

Grace shook her head. "I don't understand any of this. It's crazy. Completely nuts."

It truly must seem bizarre to a human. "All immortals can be killed by beheading," Mercy said quietly. "Ulric slaughtered a hundred Enhanced women, taking their blood and bones into his essence so he could become truly immortal. His entire body is impenetrable, much like the torsos of the Seven."

Grace tied her long brunette hair up on her head. "I've heard that part, but it was watered down a mite. I understand that he's impossible to kill from the outside."

"Exactly." Mercy swallowed. "But one of the women he sacrificed was a prophet. A powerful one who saw what might become of her. She poisoned her own blood, and when Ulric drank her in, he took in the poison."

"But he didn't die?" Grace asked.

"No. The poison is contained within him, shielded by the essence of the other victims." Mercy swallowed, her head starting to thrum. "The prophet had first infused the blood of her triplet girls—three Keys—with catalysts, so that if blood from the three is combined, the poison will be activated within Ulric. The only way to kill him is from the inside. Over the years, as soon as one Key dies, another one, another descendant of the prophet, is born. She ensured it would be thus."

Grace clasped her hands in her lap. Her fingers were long and graceful. "My blood doesn't seem different from anyone else's. And I don't feel anything sitting next to you. Do you?"

"Yes," Mercy whispered. "I sense a vibration or energy. Close your eyes and concentrate."

Grace shut her eyes, and a slight smile curved her lips. "All right. There's a warmth. An energy that's…familiar." Her eyes opened.

Logan suddenly filled the doorway. "I'd like to talk about your declaration of war."

Grace hopped off the bed. "That's a cue if I've ever heard one." She kept a wide berth around the demon, disappearing quickly.

Mercy's body went from relaxed to full-on aware. "You're the one declaring war," she said softly.

He stepped fully inside and shut the door. "I'm trying to work with you and your people."

He didn't believe her about the ritual. She'd had one job to complete, and she'd failed. What use was she to the Fae now? Her shoulders slumped. "You're not listening," she muttered.

"I'm listening but not agreeing." He overwhelmed the space in the quaint bedroom, a wave of tension rolling off him. "The conclusion our research and experts have reached is different from yours. It's that simple." His gaze traveled beyond her to the big bed, his lips slightly parted.

Her nerves perked up. "I've been of no use here."

His gaze warmed. "Baby, you are of incredible use just being you."

Well. That was sweet. She tried not to warm all over, but it happened anyway.

His head lifted. "You matter, Mercy. It's you. Not deeds."

How did he see so much? Even though his words reassured her, an odd vulnerability washed through her. She shifted her weight on the bed. A bed. A big bed. Did he want to sleep with her again? Heat poured into her face, and she ducked her chin, hoping her hair covered the blush.

"Where did Niall take the Viking?" Logan asked quietly.

Wonderful. She was thinking about the bed and his spectacular body, and he wanted to talk business. Irritation clamped down on her, giving her a reprieve from thoughts of his last kiss. "I really don't know."

"Look at me, Mercy." His tone was all command.

She looked up, unable to stop herself. "What?"

"Would Niall have killed Ivar?" A vein visibly ticked in Logan's thick neck.

She blinked. Niall had teleported Ivar right out of the room. And she knew taking out Ivar and Adare was part of his plan. "It's possible Niall left him somewhere dangerous. But Ivar is strong," she hastened to add. Then she shrugged. "I've never been to a bad place, Logan. I'm not a scout or a soldier. My usefulness to the Fae lies elsewhere."

His frown lowered both brows. "Your usefulness?"

She nodded.

"I thought we just shifted your mind-set there," he sighed. "You being you is enough. Say it."

She rolled her eyes. "Fine. I'm enough." Yet as she said the words, they hit her hard in the heart. Tears welled, and she ignored them. "All right. I'm useful just being me."

He grinned. "Good. Glad we dealt with that. However, my usefulness is protecting family. So far I've lost both Sam and Ivar."

Her heart hurt for him. "Ah. You defend and protect, right? But there's more to you than that." If he got to delve deep, so did she.

He frowned. "Not really."

"Yes." Everything inside her wanted to touch him, but she remained in place. "You matter too, Logan. Just you. All of you." She was revealing too much to him, but she couldn't stop.

His chest hitched and then settled. "All right." It was as if he accepted that she saw inside him—he accepted her.

She'd never felt special like this, and she had to help him somehow. Ease his mind. "I can find out where Sam and Ivar are. But first you have to let me go home." It was the only way she'd be able to get information.

He studied her for a moment.

Then an explosion rocked the house so powerfully the windows blew out. She screamed and ducked as glass flew.

Logan tackled her to the floor, already yanking a gun from the back of his waist.

Chapter 26

Logan had Mercy up and running in the next instant. They burst through the door to find the living room demolished. The roof had been blown away, and stones from the fireplace were strewn in every direction. Water spouted high from the kitchen sink. He was getting fucking tired of being attacked.

Adare rushed into the room, carrying a terrified-looking Grace. "Follow me," he bellowed.

Logan kept Mercy between him and Adare, catching sight of an attack helicopter turning around in the distance. Cyst soldiers appeared from the north and south, running out of the forest with automatic weapons. "Hurry," he yelled.

How the hell had the Cyst found them?

They followed Adare into a small pantry, and he hit a button near a box of granola. A wall opened with stairs leading down. Of course the Highlander would have an escape route.

The rest of the group fell into step behind Logan, and he turned to make sure everyone was there. Garrett was bleeding freely from a wound on his chin, but his eyes were clear, and he was running with the grace of a panther. They rushed down and reached a tunnel flooded with about a foot of water. The cabin's lakeside location made escape routes difficult.

Logan waited until they'd run for about a mile before he spoke. He tried to keep anger out of his voice, but he didn't succeed. This wasn't making a lick of sense. "Mercy? Did you give some sort of signal to your president about your location?"

The look she threw him could've melted concrete.

Okay, so no. How the hell had the Cyst found them? He thought through the last day. Wait a minute. The Cyst had found him on the island, and he'd figured it was via satellite. What if it wasn't? Ah, shit. "Adare? When you mentioned fairy dust, you weren't just being sarcastic, were you?"

"No," Adare snapped back. "That Sandy threw dust on me. I thought she was trying to blind me."

"Fuck," Logan muttered. "It's tracking dust. They can track you anywhere." But that meant the Fae were working with the Cyst. There was no other explanation.

Mercy stumbled, and he helped her regain her footing.

"I can carry you," he said, much preferring to leave his hands free to fight if the Cyst breached the escape tunnel.

"I've got it." She slogged through the water, her body hunched.

Yep, he liked her spirit. Something crashed far behind them.

"Adare, you're going to have to strip," Logan commanded, increasing his pace.

"Damn it." Adare set Grace on her feet and starting ripping off his clothing while running with Grace at his side. The human splashed up water, her eyes wide, her panic filling the air.

Mercy jumped over a rock. "He'll need to dunk his head in water, too. She would've aimed for his hair, since he has so much of it."

Apparently she didn't want to face the Cyst soldiers either. Had she put it together that her people were aligned with them? That was the only possible explanation. Sandy had covered Adare with tracking dust, and now the Cyst were here. Logan had to keep Mercy away from those bastards.

Adare ducked into a side tunnel where water poured from the ceiling and soaked himself, rubbing his long hair vigorously. The shield marking on his back danced oddly in the darkened tunnel, as if it had a life of its own. "Tell me I can keep the boxer-briefs."

Mercy brushed against Logan. "Those should be fine."

The group paused. Logan studied the design on Adare's back, unable to look away. Did it look like a tattoo to humans? Were they that dense? Adare's entire torso had been bonded together— forged in blood and bone—to create an impenetrable shield. No blade or bullet could ever pierce it.

Fuck, it was going to hurt to acquire his own shield.

Adare dodged back into the main tunnel, lifting Grace in one smooth motion and launching himself down the path.

She slapped his chest. "I can run."

"Quiet, woman," Adare said, increasing his speed.

Grace gave a very impressive tug on his hair, but the Highlander just growled.

The water rose, and the wet rocks grew slippery. Logan had to concentrate to keep his balance. Mercy tripped next to him, crying out. He ducked his shoulder and lifted her against his chest without losing his stride.

An explosion rocketed far behind him, and dirt dropped from the ceiling of the tunnel.

"The Cyst are coming," Garrett warned, covering his back. "Everyone step on it."

They increased their speed.

Mercy wrapped an arm around Logan's neck and leaned into him, holding on but letting her body go loose and easy to carry. She rested her head against his upper chest, her skin soft and her wet hair flowing down his arm.

Something shifted inside him at her complete trust. Oh, it was temporary, he had no doubt. But for this moment in time, they had the same goal, and she trusted him to protect her. It was all he'd wanted to do since the first second he'd laid eyes on her.

Finally, they burst out of the earth inside a crumbling barn housing two battered trucks.

Logan looked around. They'd need to go separate directions for now. Let the Cyst run in circles. This was a coordinated attack on the Seven, the Realm, and their allies.

Adare stopped, panting as he set Grace down. He studied the group. "I can't teleport everyone."

Logan set Mercy on her feet and held her arm until she'd gained her balance. Adare was the only one there who could teleport. Ronan had lost the ability after being in another dimension for a thousand years. "Adare, can you take Grace, Faith, and Ronan?"

Adare nodded. "I can, but it'll weaken me for a day or so."

"We can go to my weekend cabin," Faith said, sliding her arm around Grace's shoulders. "It's off the grid and not even in my name."

Benny clapped Garrett on the back. "Garrett and I will take one truck, and he can heal his head on the way. I'll drive—have family one state over. They'd love to see us, I'm sure. Everyone get somewhere safe, and we'll regroup later. We need a new headquarters. Surely Ivar had one already started."

The group went silent. Where the hell was Ivar? He was the planner—the organizer. Hell, the guy had been in charge of safety since before Logan had met the group. They had to find him. "Mercy and I will seek shelter, and then I'll focus on finding Ivar," Logan said. He might also contact Zane and organize an assault to rescue Sam, whether or not Sam wanted to be found. "Everyone call in tomorrow morning."

He lifted Mercy into the nearest truck, and for once, she didn't protest. He hugged Garrett and crossed to the driver's side, jumping in and slamming the door. Mercy's scent filled the cab, and the gardenia smell calmed him a little. They had to get out of there before the Cyst found the end of the tunnel.

Another headquarters lost. He shook his head, igniting the truck engine.

They were out of the barn and on the road within seconds. While the truck was nondescript and rather old looking, whatever Adare had under the hood was top-of-the-line. Logan drove for several miles before his shoulders finally lost some of the tension that was giving him a headache. Reaching across Mercy, he opened the glove box. Two guns, three knives, a disposable phone, and a stack of cash were waiting for him. Nice.

"Maybe Adare was a Boy Scout," Mercy said, squeezing out her wet hair.

"Put on your seat belt," Logan said, taking the phone and shutting the box.

She scoffed but did as he ordered. "Where are we going?" Her voice was sleepy, and dark circles showed beneath her eyes.

"Safe house." He only had two that the rest of the world didn't know about. All immortals, especially soldiers, kept at least one place that no other living being knew about. He and Garrett shared most of their safe houses, but just in case one of them was captured, they had to have a couple of secrets. Logan had never brought anybody to the one he had in mind. He'd designed it himself with a knowledge of architecture he'd never get to use.

"Where is it?" Mercy asked, putting her feet on the dash and wrapping her arms around her legs.

He didn't answer.

"Whatever," she muttered.

"How do the Fae mate?" he asked quietly, his mind clicking facts into order as he watched her from his peripheral vision.

She turned to look at him, amusement glimmering in her unique eyes. "Same as most species. Bite, sex, forever." Her voice went husky. "Only demons have a mark."

He'd wondered about the Fae. "Can it be forced?" There were rumors that Kurjans could force a mating with rape, but he didn't know of any other immortals who'd done so. He could be wrong, though.

"I don't know. We've had plenty of arranged matings in our history, so I don't think fate or love have to be involved," she said thoughtfully. Her feet dropped to the ground, and she looked out at the softly falling rain. "The elders wouldn't have created the ten of us if it wasn't possible."

He kept his gaze on the road. That was quite a destiny—and a heavy burden. "You've always known of this so called plan for your life?" It made a chilling sense.

"Yes." She plucked at a string on her pants. "Our duty has always been clear."

That's what he'd thought. "Niall said he's your mate."

She nodded. "You knew that. I told you."

"What do you intend to do?" His chest heated.

She sighed. "I don't know. I've put him off, but I'm twenty-five, and that's the prescribed age. Maybe our scientists are right, and this matchmaking is necessary." Her words were stark, and she wrapped her arms around her waist. "I want to do the right thing, and my people mean everything to me. But something has held me back from committing."

He looked over at her, giving her his full attention. He could ensure that the Fae bloodline would continue with some demon-vampire mix in there. The idea of her mating somebody else felt like a blade through his chest. "If I mate you, your obligation to Niall won't be a problem."

Chapter 27

Mercy awoke with a start and a pain in her neck from leaning her head against the truck window for hours. It was still dark—maybe around two or three in the morning? She straightened. "Where are we?"

"Safe house." Logan released her seat belt and pulled her across the seat to step out of the truck with her held safely against his broad chest.

Cool air brushed her, and she blinked, looking up. A small cabin sat in front of a winding river surrounded by what smelled like pine trees. The single-floor dwelling had a low, pitched roof with broad overhanging eaves. The ribbons of windows, central chimney and strong horizontal lines reminded her of somebody. "It looks like a house by that famous guy."

"Frank Lloyd Wright," Logan said. "I kept his style in mind when designing this."

She liked the layers in Logan Kyllwood. It wasn't so bad being carried against his hard torso, either.

An owl hooted in the far distance, and a coyote answered. Stars blinked high and bright in the sky, finally clear of clouds.

He walked over rough terrain to deposit her on a wide deck that appeared to wrap around the entire cabin. "Go inside while I retrieve the guns and money from the glove box." Without waiting for her reply, he turned and strode back to the truck.

She hugged herself, trying to wake up. Dreams of Logan and mating had plagued her the entire journey. Why had he made that comment about mating? Turning, she nudged the door open and moved into the dark interior. Her body felt as if she'd been touched with a live wire from being shut up in the truck with him for so long.

He moved past her, grabbing a lantern from a table near the door and igniting it, his movements economical and sure. The mellow light revealed a comfortable space with oversize furniture and a rocky fireplace next to a kitchen complete with sparkling appliances and granite counters. Wide windows bracketed a sliding glass door that led out to a river bathed in moonlight. She drank in the beauty.

Logan moved to the fireplace and quickly had a crackling fire warming the room. "Are you hungry?"

She shook her head and moved toward the fire. "No." They'd stopped for burgers hours ago, and the chocolate shake had done her in.

"Okay." He pointed toward the two doorways, his impressive body looking big and broad in the dim light. "Bedroom and bathroom. I'll go start the generator and scout the area. Get ready for bed."

Bed. With Logan. Her stomach did that funny flip-flop thing it only did for him. But the constant ordering around had to stop. Or perhaps he was just as tired as she was, and he was conserving words. Demons didn't seem to need as much sleep as most people—or maybe there just hadn't been enough time for him to sleep. "Okay." She stumbled toward the bathroom.

She freshened up and then found a worn black T-shirt in a drawer. The thin material hung past her thighs and smelled slightly of Logan. Then she sat on the overlarge bed, looking toward the window facing the river, shivering slightly.

The stubborn part of her considered making a break for it with the truck and trying to find her people, but she was just so damn tired. And she had no clue where she was or in which direction to run. And…she wasn't sure she wanted to escape. While mating Logan was a crazy idea, at the very least, she wanted to end things amicably with him. Except for the over-the-top bossiness he exhibited once in a while, he was pretty likable.

Mating Niall would lead to a life of certainty, duty, safety, and probably some fun.

Mating Logan would lead to a life of excitement, uncertainty, danger, and probably some battles.

Neither idea made her particularly comfortable, but only one of them truly intrigued her. Yet Logan seemed determined to complete the ritual of the Seven, and only disaster could result. Either he wouldn't live through the ritual, like ninety percent of the immortals who tried it, or he would survive and destroy the entire universe.

And he would not listen to her about it.

How could she even consider mating a male who wouldn't listen to her? The more she thought about it, the more irritated she became. Dumb immortal males. All of the Seven were hybrids, she realized. Maybe combining demon and vampire DNA led to decreased intelligence. She snorted.

"What's funny?" He moved into the room and kicked off his boots, placing his weapons on the lone pine dresser.

There was no doubt he wouldn't appreciate her humor. "Nothing. We really should talk."

He scrubbed a hand through his thick hair, his eyes so dark they were nearly black. His hands went to his belt and he unbuckled it, the sound unnaturally loud in the quiet night. "Fine, but not about the Seven, war, or mating. I need sleep before tackling any of those."

She opened her mouth and then closed it. The last thing she had the energy for right now was an argument. "Fine." Moving past him, she pulled the heavy covers away from pristine white sheets and slid inside. She sighed. The thread count had to be only six hundred.

He snorted. "You are spoiled." Logan ditched his clothing and moved in next to her, drawing her against his body. "It'll take a while for the cabin to warm up."

She gave in to temptation and snuggled right into his side, feeling safe. "I know it's impossible, but you make me feel protected," she said sleepily, not caring what she revealed with her words.

He stiffened and then relaxed against her, his warmth providing a cocoon. "We should talk about that tomorrow."

"Okay." She murmured something else and then dropped into sleep, knowing that no matter what, Logan Kyllwood would keep her safe for the night.

She'd deal with tomorrow...tomorrow.

* * * *

Logan awoke with a fairy sprawled across him, her long hair draped over his right shoulder, the smell of gardenias surrounding him. He blinked into the early dawn hour, coming back to reality quickly. His dick pulsed against her warm core, and his balls ached like he'd been punched repeatedly in a full-out assault.

God. She was going to kill him. It wasn't a joke any longer.

She mumbled against his neck and shifted her weight, brushing across his cock.

Electricity zapped down his spine and burned his balls. He groaned.

She partially lifted her torso, and her hard nipples scraped his chest. He fisted his fingers into the mattress, and the sheet ripped.

She blinked, her eyes a soft yellow. "Oh."

Yeah. Oh. He kept perfectly still, fighting every instinct he had to roll her over and plunge into all of that wet heat. The control cost him; sweat beaded on his forehead.

She tilted her face. "Hmm." Then the minx rolled her hips.

Even with his eyes open, stars exploded behind them. "Mercy." Jesus, her name did *not* fit her. "You need to get off me."

"Don't want to." Her thighs dropped to bracket his, and she rubbed against him. "Not at all."

He closed his eyes for patience. For help. For a fucking miracle.

Her hands smoothed over his chest, and she made a sound of pure pleasure. "I know you want me."

His dick pulsed against her as if it had a mind of its own, trying to get in. Her panties were definitely wet, an invitation to pure heaven. He opened his eyes. "Yes. Last chance. Get off."

Challenge filled her eyes. "Nope."

"I warned you," he said softly, sounding like he'd sucked on glass all night.

"Yep." She whipped the shirt off over her head, smacking his ear during the process. "I'm all warned. Just keep the marking to yourself."

The pain flashing from his palm did not agree with her.

At the moment, he didn't care. Growling, he rolled them over and kissed her, going as hard and deep as he could. She moaned and wrapped her arms around his neck, arching against his cock. He wrenched his head away, sucking in air, trying for control.

"No." She reached for his boxers, brought up her foot, and used her toes to shove them to his knees. "Don't want slow. We've had foreplay ever since we met, and I'm ready now. No more waiting and no more interruptions."

His control snapped.

Grabbing the sides of her panties, he ripped them off her. Then he kicked his legs free and poised himself at her entrance. His dick had never been this hard. Ever. One time wasn't going to be enough. "Are you sure?" He had to ask, even though it killed him.

"Yes." She dug her nails into his chest. "Now, Logan."

He pushed gingerly inside her, his arms vibrating as he held himself back. Her body fought him, even though she was wet and hot. God, she was tight. And small. Way too small.

She caressed her way down his flanks, urging him on.

"I don't want to hurt you," he murmured, pushing in another inch and then waiting, his body ready to explode.

"You won't," she moaned, widening her legs.

He looked into her eyes and pushed harder. When her pupils widened, he stopped and allowed her to adjust to his size.

"You are big," she snorted, amusement adding to the hunger glimmering in the soft yellow of her eyes. She panted as she visibly tried to relax her body and take him in. "Just go for it."

If he went for it, he'd rip her apart. "No. We'll do this my way." He should've given her a couple of orgasms first, but here they were. And he would not hurt her.

She clamped both hands on his ass and squeezed.

He growled, his fangs dropping low.

She arched her body up, but he went at his own speed, pausing any time her breath caught. She got wetter and hotter around him, loosening just a fraction, until finally she'd taken every last inch of him.

Thank God.

Once he was home, he took a moment, grabbing onto control. Like a lifeline. It was nearly impossible. He wanted to claim her, mark her so she'd always be his.

Her nails scraped up his spine and back down. "Logan," she said, drawing out his name.

He rocked his hips, sliding out of her and then back in, going deeper each time but keeping his pace slow.

"More," she whispered, leaning up and licking beneath his jaw.

Finally, he gave her what she wanted. Grasping her hips, he held her in place, and let himself go. Hard and fast, he pounded into her, knocking the wooden headboard against the wall.

Pleasure filled her face, and she lifted her hips to match him.

He drove deeper into her, feeling a change inside himself. A dark and mysterious filling of a void he hadn't realized existed. He planted his right hand on the pillow next to her head, seeking relief from the demand of the mark. With each hard thrust, he pulled her further into a soul he'd forgotten he had.

Her heart beat against his, and he could hear its rhythm as if it were his own.

Her eyes widened. Her body stiffened. The orgasm took her, zinging against him, and clamping her sex around him with a strength that stole his breath.

His fangs sharpened, and he struck her neck, going on instinct. The taste of her filled his mouth as her body gyrated around him, keeping him inside her, her muscles contracting around him with their own demand.

He hung on to the precipice for a second and then fell right over, his climax shaking through him with a force beyond that of nature. His fangs retracted, and he licked her wound closed. His body was satiated except for the weeping agony on his palm. To be inside her and not mark her was a pain beyond description.

She went limp beneath him, breathing out wildly, her heartbeat audible in the room.

He ground against her one more time, then stopped, looking down at her flushed face. One thought struck him faster than a lightning strike. Oh, he was never letting her go.

Chapter 28

Mercy hummed softly as she stirred powdered eggs in a pan, the tune oddly fast-paced. She'd figured sex with Logan would be exciting, but that one word didn't come close to the right description. Her body was tingly and a mite sore, and they'd only had one time. What could the hybrid do with an entire night?

She shivered.

It was a darn good thing immortals didn't have to worry about diseases or unwanted pregnancies, because she hadn't thought twice about anything but how good he made her feel. In fact, she wanted him again. Right now.

She stared out the window while she stirred, her body thrumming and her heart pumping a little too fast. It was a peaceful day, and she tried to draw that sensation into herself. The cabin was made for comfort, and the view was spectacular. The river rushed outside as the snow pack melted, churning white and throwing up spray. Pine trees on the other side led to a series of mountains, each taller than the last. The sky was overcast and the air misty, but inside it was warm and toasty.

Logan had gone outside to scout and gather more firewood. She suspected he was giving her some time and space after their wild morning, and frankly, she could use it.

She couldn't let him die in the ritual of the Seven. But even when she regained her ability to teleport, he could stop her from taking him away. If she called in reinforcements, he'd just fight them and win and be angry with her again. The guy wasn't leaving her many options. Okay. She was trying really hard to think of one option. Just one.

He stalked in the front door, the phone to his ear. "All right. Give me a minute." Clicking off, he opened the table by the door and drew out a laptop, his gaze seeking hers. "We have a problem."

She moved toward him as he opened it and brought up a video of President Dawn. Mercy's knees wobbled, but she stood next to him as he pressed the Play button.

"Good evening. My name is President Alyssa Dawn of the Fae people." Alyssa wore a smart gray suit with her hair back in an intricate twist. "Our people like to stay out of world politics, but we've discovered an atrocity so terrible that it must be shared."

Mercy bit her lip. "Tell me this isn't on the web."

"No." Logan paused the recording. "It was sent via direct lines to leaders of the Realm, demon, shifter, witch, dragon, Kurjan, and Cyst peoples. Just the leaders." He pressed PLAY again.

The president cleared her throat. "There are seven immortals among you—demon-vampire hybrids—who have perverted the laws of this world, all worlds, to make themselves impenetrable. They sacrificed seven gifted, Enhanced females in a ritual of blood and bone to do this, and they need to be made accountable. They are: Ronan Kayrs, Quade Kayrs, Garrett Kayrs, Benjamin Reese, Adare O'Cearbhaill, Ivar Kjeidsen, and Logan Kyllwood."

"Ah, shit," Logan muttered. His phone buzzed, and he ignored it.

The president continued, "These males have kidnapped one of our people, Mercy O'Malley." A picture of Mercy came up on the screen.

"Fuck," Logan muttered.

The president came back into focus. "I am sending photographs of these males along with all research we've conducted as to their whereabouts, allies, and holdings. I am also attaching proof of my claims. Good day to you." The screen froze.

The smell of smoke caught Mercy's attention. Crap. She turned and ran for the eggs, but Logan beat her there.

He grabbed a towel and flapped it against the flames, putting them out. Then he winced. "You said you could cook."

Yeah, she'd lied. She shook her head, her stomach swirling. "What happens now?"

His phone buzzed again. With a sigh, he lifted it to his ear and listened. He stiffened. Then his expression hardened. Finally, he just nodded. "Understood." He slid the phone back into his pocket. "So. How'd you like to meet my family?"

* * * *

After Logan's question, time seemed to speed up. Mercy had enough of a reprieve to tie up her hair and throw her clothing back on before a helicopter arrived and several armed soldiers, the big, tough kind, flew them to a sprawling lodge overlooking a lake somewhere in the mountains.

They landed and were squired inside the lodge quicker than she could blink.

They were shown into what appeared to be a conference room, complete with wide onyx table and several chairs. Blank computer screens covered all four walls.

Garrett partially stood when they entered.

Logan escorted her to the chair next to Garrett and sat on her other side, effectively flanking her between two massive male bodies, both giving off heat and energy. "She stays between us," he said tersely.

Garrett nodded, his gray eyes calm and yet still sizzling.

Mercy swallowed. "Where are we?"

The door opened, and three males strode into the room. Three very tall and impressive males with shockingly hard bodies and inscrutable expressions. Power blasted through the oxygen.

"You're at Realm headquarters," the male in the middle said. "I'm Dage Kayrs." Oh. The king. He had black hair with a streak of gray at the temple, but he didn't look a day over thirty. The King of the Realm was one of the most respected and feared rulers in the history of, well, everybody. Power all but cascaded from him.

Mercy met his silver gaze directly. "Mercy O'Malley. Fae."

The male to the king's right was Zane Kyllwood. She'd read a dossier on him, and he looked so much like Logan that she would've known him, anyway. Even his eyes were the same pissed off green she'd seen on Logan several times. "King Kyllwood," she murmured.

His eyebrow went up, but he silently took a seat as Dage did the same. "Zane will be fine—I was never formally named king, just the ruler. One king in the Realm and in the room is enough."

The third male flanked Dage Kayrs, his eyes a deep gold and his jaw solid rock. A familiar jaw. "Talen Kayrs," he said by way of introduction.

Yeah. He and Garrett looked so much alike they could be brothers. Or father and son, obviously.

So much power and testosterone and pure maleness swirled around the room that Mercy felt dizzy. Or maybe it was the undercurrent of raw anger that pricked her skin and threatened her ability to breathe normally.

"Well. I'll start." The king placed large hands on the table, his voice pleasant and very peaceful.

Mercy relaxed a little. It was nice to be around a calming influence for once.

The king leaned forward. "What the holy fuck of a fuckup of a disaster have you assholes gotten into?" Dage yelled, his booming voice echoing off every wall to clash back in the middle and ripple out again.

Mercy snorted. Shocked, she clapped her hand to her mouth as both Logan and Garrett swung toward her. "Sorry." A giggle escaped. Then another one. Soon she was laughing hysterically, trying to apologize, tears streaming down her face. The males stared at her with various expressions of disbelief, and she hiccupped, trying to stop. "Um, sorry." She sucked in air.

"Fairy?" Zane asked calmly, as if that explained everything.

The king nodded, blue rims appearing around his silver eyes. Not many people probably laughed at the King of the Realm when he was shouting in their direction.

Mercy held up a hand and tried to regain control. "I'm not crazy. *We're* not crazy. Honest."

"Uh huh," Garrett muttered under his breath.

Mercy regained her composure. "So, well. You all obviously have both Realm and family business to discuss, so perhaps I should take my leave." She began to stand.

"Sit. Back. Down." Logan enunciated each word with such chilling effect that she did exactly that.

Garrett didn't move, but Zane looked at his brother, assessment in his green gaze.

The king looked her over, and she swore he saw right to her soul. "Perhaps you should excuse us for a moment."

"No," Logan said, his chin down.

Surprise flashed across Dage's face, and he cocked his head, studying the soldier. "I do believe that's the first time you've ever contradicted me, Logan Kyllwood." The king's tone hinted that it might be the last.

Mercy shivered, and the spit in her mouth dried up.

Logan didn't twitch. Nor did he look the least bit concerned. Man, he was a badass. "I do believe it is," he agreed.

Talen Kayrs rested his jaw on his fist as he looked at Logan as if he'd started speaking in tongues. Even so, a glimmer of what hopefully was amusement lurked in his golden eyes. "*I* do believe fists are about to start swinging, and in that case, the lady should leave," he said helpfully.

Zane cleared his throat. "Let's start with the lady. Have you been kidnapped, Miss O'Malley?"

She blinked. What the hell should she say? Of course, she'd been kidnapped. Yet loyalty to Logan prevailed. She didn't want to get him into trouble with the Realm or his family. "No," she said.

Dage frowned. "You're a terrible liar."

Oh, she didn't want him to have the wrong idea about her. She sighed. "I'm not that bad. This is such a tense situation. I mean, there are so many undercurrents, you know?" Her voice rose, and she just couldn't stop talking. "Brother to brother, father-son, uncle, the king, the ruler, soldiers, and so on. Plus, the vampires and demons were in a war not too long ago, right? So this is a whole lot of tension." She wound down, her stomach cramping. "My point is that usually I can lie much better than this." There. She'd said it.

Logan took her hand, planted it on his muscled thigh, and squeezed.

She subsided.

The king pinched the bridge of his nose as if his head was about to explode.

"How much of what we've heard is true?" Talen asked softly, his gaze on his son.

Garrett met the gaze evenly. "Sixty percent."

Mercy blinked. That was quite the quick response. She did owe the Realm a warning. "If the Seven finishes the last ritual, the Fae nation will have no choice but to declare war."

The king didn't so much as blink. "Thank you for the heads-up."

"You're very welcome," she responded. Logan squeezed harder, and she hid a wince.

"Who are Ronan and Quade Kayrs?" Dage asked quietly.

Garrett scrubbed a hand through his shaggy hair. "Your great-uncles—brother to your great-grandfather, Jacer Kayrs. And they're both still alive. At least Ronan is. We don't know for sure about Quade."

Dage's left eyebrow rose. "It's odd I know nothing about them. Very odd." His puzzlement swelled through the room with a hint of the anger he'd already shown.

Mercy swallowed. She really needed to contact her people. "Listen. The Seven, who Logan will tell you all about, did not kill Enhanced women to create the shields that become their torsos. They did kill seven Cyst members, who had killed Enhanced women, in order to pervert the laws of physics and create a situation that will end the world as we know it." She glanced at Logan. "Can I go now?"

Silence met her from every direction.

"Yes," the king said. "Soldiers will escort you to safe quarters, while the rest of us have a little chat."

Excellent. She did not want to be present for that talk. Nope. Not at all.

"She stays here," Logan said evenly, definitely the calmest force in the room.

The king's chin lowered. "Why is that?" he growled.

Logan held his hand up, palm out, showing the mark. The mating mark.

Dage's gaze cleared, Talen's eyes widened, and Zane leaned forward. "Bro," he said quietly.

"Well. I guess she stays," Dage agreed quietly.

Wonderful. Now she was totally outnumbered. She opened her mouth to argue, and Logan squeezed again. Her small huff brought a smile to the king's face. Great. Now he was amused.

She was so going to kick Logan's butt after this.

Chapter 29

Logan kicked back in his brother's sprawling house in front of the lake, a beer in his hand, and an ache in his head. Mercy was in the guest shower, having all but run from him once they'd finished with the questioning session of the century. He and Zane had retired to the family room to start drinking.

One of Logan's architectural masterpieces in building blocks was on a table in the corner. He'd built it with Hope last time he'd been in town. The thought that his brother had kept it warmed him.

Zane sucked down half his bottle. "So. The marking."

Logan's beer cooled his throat, if nothing else. "Yeah."

"Want to talk about it?"

"No." He took another drink.

Zane grinned. "Fair enough." He twirled his bottle around in his thick hands. "Are you really going to do the Seven ritual?" His gaze remained on the bottle.

Logan shifted his weight on the overstuffed chair. "You going to order me not to?" Technically, he worked for the demon nation, and Zane was the boss.

Zane met his gaze. "I turned you into an adult when you were twelve years old. I can't change that now."

Logan sighed. His brother had to give up the guilt. "We were both kids, and we did what we had to do." They'd become soldiers—the best. And his brother had trained him to survive. "It's in the past, and we lived through it."

"I don't want to lose you." Vulnerability, so rare to see in Zane, flashed for the quickest of seconds.

"I don't want to be lost." Logan forced a grin. "I can't figure a way around the ritual. The Fae are right to be concerned, but at some point, Ulric's world is going to burst, and he's going to be back in this one. I know that is true—the Kurjans will make it so. I can't let all Enhanced females, including your mate, die."

"It's unthinkable," Zane muttered.

It truly was. "This is something I need to do. I'll make it through—I always do."

Zane rubbed his chin. "True." He shrugged wide shoulders. "I feel like I should try and talk you out of it, but I've always known, somehow, that you had another calling." He cocked his head to the side. "You and Sam."

Logan's ears pricked up. Family really was what mattered. He'd die to protect Zane's mate. In a second. "Do you know what Sam's destiny is?"

"No. Was hoping you did," Zane said, bending sideways to open a minifridge behind him and take out two more bottles. He tossed one Logan's way.

Logan caught it and unscrewed the top. Worry coursed through him, and he covered it with calmness. Letting Zane get all worked up wouldn't help anybody. "Nope. But I think it's time we went in and got him. He's given me the 'kiss' signal twice, but if he hasn't gathered enough intel by now, he deserves to be yanked out."

Zane snorted. "Agreed. I have every computer expert in the Realm on it right now. We'll have a location soon."

The constant muscle ache at the base of Logan's neck released a fraction. It felt right being in this room with his oldest brother, figuring things out. Why had he thought to do it any other way? "Good. It was hell not telling you."

"Well, now your big secret is out." Zane held up his beer. "No more fucking secrets."

Logan clanked bottles with him, finally feeling settled for the first time since finding out about the Seven. His brothers were his blood, and he needed them covering his back, even at a distance. "No more secrets." Then he perked up. "Hey. It's really great to see Hope doing so well."

A wide grin split Zane's hard face. "She's special, that's for sure.."

"Agreed," Logan said softly. The happiness flooding through him took him away from the constant tension and danger for a moment. This was what mattered. Family and the future. He'd do what he had to do in order to keep it all safe. That meant becoming one of the Seven. "You're a good brother, Zane."

"A good brother would probably stop you from doing what you plan," Zane murmured. "You might have a mate to think about."

Logan had known his brother wouldn't be able to leave it alone. "She really is a pain in the ass."

"The best ones usually are." Zane chuckled. "Ask Mom."

Logan laughed. Their mother liked to rob banks in her spare time, and she'd drugged her mate a few times before mating him—once to steal his motorcycle. After a lifetime of being a widow, she was finally happy with her enforcer. "I think Mom would really like Mercy." Hell. They'd probably rob banks—just the bad ones—together. He frowned.

"I'm sure she would," Zane said quietly. "She's in Sweden now but could be home quickly."

Logan shook his head. That was one complication he didn't need right now. "After the ritual, I'll see her." She was a good mom, and she loved her boys, which meant she'd try to stop him from undergoing an initiation that would probably kill him. Her willingness to cross the line into sheer lunacy to protect family made Mercy look like a sane person. That was saying something.

The front door shut loudly, and footsteps pattered closer. "Uncle Logan!" Hope launched herself at him from across the room.

He caught her, putting her next to him and tickling her ribs. "How's my favorite niece?"

"I'm your only niece." She giggled and kicked, slapping at his hands. "I'm good. Hit my head but it's all better now. Where's the fairy?"

Logan stopped and kissed her on the top of the head. "Who told you there was a fairy here?"

Hope rubbed the intricate blue prophet mark on her neck. Her blue eyes sparkled. "Um, nobody?" Her brown hair was mussed up, but it looked like it had been in a braid at one point.

Logan kept his body relaxed. "It's okay if the universe is speaking to you, baby doll." He hated that fact with every fiber of his body, as did his brother, but if it was happening, they couldn't let the girl hide it from them.

She clapped her hands on his scruffy jaw. "She's my fairy, Logan."

Logan blinked. What the heck did that mean? "I thought she was mine." He grinned. "Is she? What do you know?"

Hope rolled her eyes, giving a quick glimpse into what she'd look like as a teenager, way too soon. "I can't answer that. Boys are so dumb."

Logan hugged her close. "You have that right, little one. Definitely. How about we make dinner, and then you can meet our fairy?" He leaned in. "Though she prefers to be called Fae."

Hope giggled. "That's silly. She's a fairy." The girl sobered. "Though you should make her just yours...before you become a Seven." Pushing herself up, she turned and jogged toward the kitchen, oblivious to the sudden silence from the two Kyllwood males. "Hurry up. I'm hungry."

Logan caught Zane's concerned look. Shit. The girl shouldn't know a damn thing about the Seven. "You ever think it's all been decided already and that we're just pawns?" he asked.

Zane shook his head, standing. "No. Fate's undecided, and that worries me more." He moved to go after his daughter. "For now, let's get Janie, and your fairy, and have a nice dinner. We can pretend that the world isn't about to change on us again."

Logan finished his beer as he walked, letting the bottle cool the raging ache on his palm.

The marking was becoming more insistent.

* * * *

With the covers over her head and Pax and Libby on either side of her, Hope watched a movie on the tablet. They were being super quiet because they were supposed to be asleep. She got tired more easily than her friends did, but she tried to pretend she didn't. She was the only girl vampire in the world. She should be tough.

Libby was a feline shifter, and already she could jump across the river.

Paxton was a vampire-demon, and he was getting faster and stronger every day, but he wanted to play his guitar instead of train.

Hope just wanted to fix the world and then maybe buy some new pink lip gloss. The fairy had worn lip gloss, and she was super pretty. The movie finally ended, and the fish found his way home. "It'd be fun to be a fish," she whispered.

Libby giggled, her blond, shoulder-length hair messy. "Fish can't run up trees. That'd be no fun."

Paxton yawned and stretched out his legs, pulling on the sheet. "I don't know. I'd rather be a wolf."

Libby reached across Hope and smacked his arm. "Lions are better than wolves."

Pax blinked his odd silver-blue eyes. "Okay. A lion, then. Anything is better than being a hybrid like me."

Hope sighed and patted his hand. "Everyone is a hybrid around here. You're cool, Paxton."

He grinned. "Right. So, tell us about the fairy. Is she gonna mate your uncle?"

Hope rubbed her eyes. "I don't know. I tried ta ask the universe and Fate, but I got no answers back." She never got the answers she really wanted. "I'm glad you guys can sleep over." She slid the covers off their heads and handed the tablet to Libby, who was closest to the bedside table.

Paxton pushed his hair out of his face. "Are you still having nightmares about the scary white-haired freaks?"

She blinked. "They're called the Cyst." She wasn't supposed to, but she'd researched them on her tablet using her daddy's personal password. It was *Janie Belle,* her mama's name, and he should probably change it.

Libby sucked in air, her eyes wide in the nightlight. "They really exist?"

"Yeah." Hope yawned. She'd already known they existed. "The file said they were Kurjans." There was only one way to find out.

"No." Pax's jaw snapped shut, and he looked older than seven all of a sudden. "You have to stop meeting Drake in that dreamworld. I got a bad feeling about that place and him."

Hope reached down and patted his hand. "It's okay, Pax." She closed her eyes and counted the kittens in her head.

Soon she was walking down the pink beach, but the wind was a little cold. Frowning, she tried to warm it up. Nope. Still cold. That was new.

Drake moved out from behind a rock, his hands in his pockets and his eyes sparkling. His hair was getting longer, and she liked it. "Hey. How's your head?"

"Fine." She grinned. He'd been so nice when she'd been knocked out. "I met a fairy."

His eyebrows lifted just like Talen's did. "A real one?"

"Yep." She rocked back on her heels, showing off a little. "She's super nice. I like her a lot."

Drake kicked pink sand toward the ocean. "That's cool. I've never met a fairy."

Most people hadn't. She cleared her throat. "Um, Drake? Do you know the Cyst?"

He turned toward her. "Yes. Why?"

The last one she'd dreamed about had angry yellow eyes and a scar through his eyebrow. He'd been snarling, and he'd looked super scary. "Because they're bad and they want to hurt me."

He grasped her hand, looking way down, even though they were the same age. "I'm never gonna let anybody hurt you."

Her heart warmed. "Even if the Cyst try?" *She had to know.*

He nodded solemnly. "Yes, but they won't try. They're our priests, Hope. A lot of people don't like them because they're scary looking, but they're lonely and lost. I want to save them."

Sometimes there was good in people that was hard to see. If somebody didn't know her daddy, they might think he was a bad guy when he was angry. Zane Kyllwood could look really scary if somebody wasn't nice to Hope's mama. But she wasn't sure about the Cyst. Maybe it would be her job someday to save Drake from them.

She was sure about Drake, though. "Do you think we'll always be friends?" *Just because her mama and daddy had always stayed friends after the dreamworld didn't mean that she and Drake would.*

"Yes." *He started walking, still holding her hand.* "Otherwise, why would we be here?"

That was a good question. "Have you told anybody about this place?" *she asked, watching the pink sand cover her bare feet.*

"No. Grown-ups wouldn't understand." *His hand was a lot bigger than hers.*

She nodded. "I know. I don't want them to make us stop coming here." *If they could. She wasn't sure. Either way, she didn't want to worry her mama.*

Something jostled her. "I hafta go. Bye."

She woke up, and Pax was shaking her. She smacked him in the chin. "Stop it."

His eyes were more silver than blue in the soft light. "No. You can't meet that Kurjan anymore. It's not safe, and you know it."

"How did you know I was meeting him?" she asked, rubbing her nose.

"I just do," Pax said quietly. "When you're asleep, I can feel an energy."

She blew hair out of her eyes. Right now, she lived in two worlds, and they both called to her. "You don't understand," she said.

His eyes were sadder than usual. "I know, but I can't let you get hurt. You and Libby are all I have, Hope."

That wasn't true. He had a daddy and other friends and the whole Realm. But she took his hand, surprised to find that it was bigger than Drake's even though he wasn't tall. "I don't understand it yet, but you and me and Libby have a job to do someday," she whispered. And Drake. He was a part of it, too. "We'll save everybody. Trust me, Paxton. I'm gonna be safe."

Pax snuggled back down, keeping her hand. "I do trust you." His eyes flashed blue through the silver. "I think that's my job." He closed his eyes and was asleep in a minute.

His job? What did that mean?

Chapter 30

There were two bedrooms in the guesthouse Logan led Mercy to after a wonderful dinner with his family. It was fascinating to watch him with his niece, and by the time he locked the doors of the guesthouse, Mercy had almost forgotten her irritation with him.

Almost.

He set an alarm, punching in a code he blocked with his body. Then he turned. "I need a shower. Just a reminder—you're in the middle of Realm headquarters territory."

Yeah, she'd figured that out, even though she had no clue where they were. Somewhere in the Pacific Northwest of the USA, if she had to guess. "I know."

He ignored her snappy voice. "Every door and window is wired. If you open even one, sensors will go wild all over the subdivision. Lights will flash, and the loudest sound you can imagine will blare from the center of the kitchen. Soldiers will come running from every direction, but I'll get to you before they do." He paused, meeting her gaze directly. "You do not want that."

Her mouth gaped open. He'd been a bossy jackwad with her, and then he'd been unbelievably adorable with his family, and now he was being an uptight jerk?

She just glared.

He nodded. "We'll talk when I get out." He paused in the midst of turning. "Unless you'd like to join me. You're more than welcome." Pivoting, he headed inside what appeared to be the master bedroom.

She crossed her arms, looking over the comfortable room with the sliding glass door leading to the lake. It would serve him right if she triggered the alarm with him buckass naked. The place was very nice, though. Why wasn't he staying with his family?

Oh. Because of her. Because the Realm knew the Fae had plans for Hope Kayrs-Kyllwood. Yeah. She wouldn't let a Fae stay in the same house as Hope, either.

The sound of the shower filtered through the irritation in her head. All right. So he was ticked she'd told the king everything she had. Or maybe he was just fed up with the whole situation. She could understand that. Her people had made a big mess of things for his family.

A tingle wound through her left arm.

She caught her breath, stretching out her arm, fluttering her fingers. Another tingle. Energy bubbled inside her, slowly, like a soda being shaken up.

Her head went back, and she breathed deep, letting the universe fill her. She imagined her apartment in Scotland and tried to gather the energy to teleport. Sparks flew along her arm and then sputtered out. She sighed. The ability was coming back, though. Soon she'd be able to go.

Triumph and an odd sadness filtered through her. Once she left, she and Logan would be on opposite sides again. Her people were determined to stop his ritual, because it was the right thing to do. Without question, she cared about him. But she couldn't let the universe be torn apart—not again. Even if he was right that the Kurjans would figure out a way to release Ulric, her people had time to stop them. Hopefully.

Energy tickled through her legs.

Soon. She'd never been hit with a blaster before, so she hadn't been sure how long it'd take to regain her power.

She bit her lip. Her irritation slipped away. For the moment, before she could leave, she and Logan were still lovers. One more night. Just one to take with her and hold forever. Before he hated her.

She recalled the invitation he'd extended. Why not? One more time? Her clothes were already hitting the floor by the time she reached the steamy bathroom and slid into the shower, where his head was ducked beneath the stream. His back was broad and smooth and so sexy. It was unthinkable for his bones to be fused together into a shield.

He partially turned, his eyes hot. "This is a surprise." His deep voice echoed off the surrounding dark tiles.

"You invited me." She stepped closer, her breasts becoming heavy and full.

His gaze raked her, and the proof of his arousal was obvious. "I'm in a pissy mood, Mercy."

The warning words did nothing but propel her toward him. This was their last night together, and she wanted it. He was the most complex male she could imagine, and even if it was just one more time, she wanted to make him hers. To imagine they could have what Zane and Janie had.

Belonging to Logan would be a wondrous challenge brimming with heat and love and protection. It wasn't her path to follow, but for tonight, she could pretend.

She reached for him, trying to wrap her hand around his cock.

He grasped her wrist, freeing himself, and pressed her against the tiles, body to body. "I thought we were going to fight," he said, holding her in place.

She looked up at his fierce face. "I'd rather fuck." Fighting seemed a waste of time when she was about to leave.

"You always take me by surprise." He ducked his head and kissed her, his tongue sweeping into her mouth with a sense of possession that stole her breath.

She kissed him back and tugged her hand free, exploring the ridges of his abdomen. So tight and ripped. "You like surprises?"

"Not usually, but that's changing." He nipped the shell of her ear and lifted her with both hands on her waist to give him better access to her neck.

She threw her head back and let him explore, his mouth devastating as it moved beneath her jawline and down to her collarbone. Her thighs naturally clamped against his rib cage, and his hands dropped to her butt. She bit him right above the heart, sinking her teeth in far enough that he'd wear her mark for at least a day.

Marking him filled her with a longing that bordered on sadness.

She shook her head, her already wet hair slapping across his chest. He planted his hand, the one with the marking, flat on the tile as if in pain. "Does it hurt?" she whispered, sliding down so she could feel him against her.

"Yes." He kept her aloft with just one hand across her buttocks. His easy strength turned her on even more. How could she possibly let him go?

"You were very gentle last time," she murmured, rubbing against him.

His hand flexed against her. "You're small."

"I know." She leaned in and bit him again, smiling at his hoarse groan. "I don't want gentle, Logan. I want all of you." Just once.

His free hand wrapped around her neck, and the brand burned against her skin. "Careful what you wish for." Then he kissed her again, both hands controlling her, his body blocking the spray of water.

Desire flushed through her and then deepened, sharpening into a need that was more of a craving. Everything about him felt so damn good. He palmed her breasts, tweaking both nipples, before moving down her body, touching every inch. With unerring accuracy, he found her clit.

She arched into his hand, her breath gasping, her body yearning.

"This is mine." He set her down on the narrow bench and dropped to his knees, spreading her thighs wide and leaning in.

She grabbed his shoulders for balance. One flick of his tongue, and she detonated. The orgasm rippled through her with a shocking edge, making her sob his name as he continued to lick her. When she was finished, he turned his head, and pain slashed into her thigh from his fangs.

She cried out as the pain turned to pleasure. He'd marked her, too.

For weeks, she'd have a reminder of this night.

He stood and lifted her, kissing her deep, his lips firm and ferocious. Then he turned her around.

Her heart stuttered, and need filled her, harsher than before. He planted her hands on the bench and tugged her legs back, palming her sex from behind. Pleasure cut through her, and she dropped her head.

"Fuck, you're beautiful," he muttered, pressing into her from behind.

This time he didn't pause. Sure and strong, with firm control, he powered into her one inch at a time. Her body strained but took him in, the pain and pleasure melding together until the only thing that mattered was him. Finally, he shoved all the way in, taking her completely.

Tremors cascaded along her thighs. She closed her eyes, overwhelmed and loving every second of it. His hand slammed the tile near her head, and she reached up, curling her fingers over his knuckles and between his much larger fingers to his palm. The marking burned her fingertips, sending a thrill down to where they were joined.

His other hand manacled her hip, and he pulled out only to power back inside her again. Nerves flared and sparked, so delicious that she kept her eyes closed to enjoy every single sensation.

She tilted her hips, taking more of him, feeling every inch of him fill her.

"God, you feel good," he said, his mouth near her ear, his voice a low groan.

She shivered, feeling both taken and powerful in that she could affect such a primal being. Her hold tightened on his hand, even as the temptation to draw it to her flesh grew stronger. She wanted that marking.

It was hers.

He thrust harder, and pleasure pummeled her. The slap of flesh on flesh filled the steamy shower, his breathing growing as ragged as hers. His fangs struck into her neck faster than any whip. She cried out, throwing her head back, hitting him with her hair.

He drank from her, his body pounding into hers. Hard and fast and sure, he took her over.

He was everything she could ever want. He released her hip and angled his hand down, pressing his finger on her clit. Contractions vibrated inside her, bursting out in a thousand directions.

She stiffened and cried out his name, her voice echoing through the steam. The climax destroyed her, taking away all thought as she came apart. Her sex clamped down on him with each wave, and he followed her, growling against her neck as he came.

She breathed out a sigh of pure pleasure.

His fangs retracted, and he licked her neck clean. Then he lifted her body to turn her. Both hands cupped her face as he moved in for the sweetest kiss she could imagine. His firm lips took hers, her face safely bracketed in his palms. The marking heated and flared against her jawline, and her breath caught.

He nibbled on her bottom lip. "You feel it, too."

She nodded, leaning into him. The marking wouldn't take since he wasn't inside her, but the warmth of it shot inside her and straight to her heart.

Or maybe that was him.

He released her, his thumb rubbing across her cheekbone. "You ready for bed?"

Numbly, her body still rioting, she nodded.

"Want to sleep?"

She could get lost in the otherworldly color of his spectacular green eyes. Slowly, she shook her head.

Those eyes glittered with a hunger he did nothing to hide. "Neither do I."

Chapter 31

After a truly inspiring night, Logan finished eating scrambled eggs for breakfast—that he'd cooked. Mercy had given it another shot and had almost burned down the kitchen.

The woman really should stay as far away from a stove as possible. He grinned, his heart lighter than it had been in days. They'd reached an understanding the previous night—maybe not spoken, but it had been there in every touch. She was his, and she knew it. Somehow they'd work out the problems between the Seven and the Fae.

She was in the bathroom doing something with her hair, although he liked it long and free. Had he told her that? Probably not.

The front door opened, and Garrett strode inside with Zane on his heels.

Logan grinned. "So. We start the next war yet?"

Zane rolled his eyes. "It's too early to tell. Dage and I are meeting with world leaders in shifter territories in about an hour. We'll smooth things over the best we can, but the witches are seriously pissed. You might have to testify to their council."

Logan stood and put his dishes in the sink. "No problem."

Garrett eyed the burned towel on the counter but didn't comment.

Zane looked around. "We found Sam. You and Garrett are going to have to handle the extraction while I try to avoid war. You up to it?"

Adrenaline ripped through his veins. "Hell, yeah." He'd wanted to go in for Sam since the first moment his brother was taken. "Any word on Ivar?"

"No," Garrett said, his gray eyes somber. "We have no trace of the Viking. Not a one."

Fuck. That wasn't good. Logan narrowed his gaze on Zane. "You can't teleport all three of us. That'll leave you weakened when you meet with the leaders."

Zane shrugged. "Not mentally. Dage is already in place with security, so I'll be fine. I'm your only option unless you want to fly to Scotland."

Logan shook his head. The twelve-hour flight would take too long. He had to get to Sam, and now.

Garrett handed over a sheet of paper. "There's a Fae compound right outside of Edinburgh. Here are the schematics. I think Sam is in the dungeon."

Logan memorized the layout, and then shoved the paper in his back pocket.

Mercy came in from the other room and stopped short at seeing the other males.

Logan held out a hand, and she hesitated before moving to take it. "Zane is going to teleport us to Scotland." He'd secure Mercy at the safe house before going for Sam.

Garrett nodded. "I have allies meeting at the safe apartment. We're a go."

Mercy blanched. "Why?"

Logan studied her. They were past the time for lies. "We found Sam, and we're going in to get him. I'll try not to hurt anybody too badly." Especially since there weren't many Fae left.

She paled and studied the three of them. "All four of us via teleportation?"

"Yep." Logan hauled her against his side, sliding an arm over Garrett's wide shoulders.

Zane bunched his legs and leaped forward in a tackle, taking them down and into nothingness.

Logan grimaced in the darkness. Being teleported with two others made the ride more painful than usual, and the time spent hurtling through space and darkness went on for too long. Finally, they landed in the center of the apartment.

Mercy pushed away from him. "You're not very good at this, Zane." She held a hand to her stomach and took several deep breaths.

The thought hit Logan that when they mated, they'd gain each other's gifts. He'd develop the ability to teleport, and she'd learn how to stop somebody from doing so. Would she also learn how to attack minds? Most mates couldn't, but who knew about the Fae? They had unexpected skills.

Garrett moved to the door and opened it, allowing two soldiers to step inside. "For protection."

Logan threw him a grateful look. He needed to keep his focus, and he would've worried about Mercy's safety while he infiltrated the Fae's property.

Zane sucked in air and hugged Garrett. "Be careful."

"You, too," Garrett said, hugging him back.

Zane turned and clapped Logan on the shoulder. "Bring Sam home, and be careful. No mercy."

Logan stepped in and hugged his brother. "I'll call you the second he's secure. Love you, bro."

"Love you, too," Zane whispered, zipping out of sight.

Logan turned and moved to open the wall of weapons, instantly pulling on a vest and tack gear. He tossed a gun to Garrett, who flipped it around a couple of times and then nodded.

Mercy edged away from the soldiers. "Four of you soldiers aren't enough." She held up a hand before he could say anything. "No, I don't know where Sam is being held. But wherever it is, four isn't enough—not against the Fae defenses."

Logan strapped a gun to his thigh. "Just Garrett and I are going." The female really had no clue of what they'd done before peace had finally been achieved. The two of them had worked together for years at this point, their skills a deadly combination of training and talent. "The other two soldiers are here for your safety." Not only would they protect her from any enemy, they'd keep her contained in case she decided to contact the Fae.

Her chin lifted. "You don't trust me." Odd, but she sounded more curious than hurt by that.

He wanted to trust her, he really did. "These are your people, sweetheart. I'm just taking the decision out of your hands." If her people ever questioned her, she could honestly say that he'd locked her down.

She eyed the soldiers and looked back at him. "You don't think I could take these two?"

Amusement ticked his lips into a smile. "No." They were Realm soldiers—pure vampire and deadly as hell. In fact, this babysitting job was probably way beneath them, but Garrett had some pull. Neither male even reacted to her words, their gazes already scouting the apartment for threats or weak points.

She tapped her foot against the wooden floor in a way that was way too cute.

Logan finished suiting up and moved to her, kissing her full on the mouth in front of everyone. "I'm getting my brother, then we're figuring out our future," he whispered against her lips.

Her eyes widened, and she tried to back away, but he held her tight. Then her eyes softened. "Logan, be careful."

Sweet words from a sweet female. He kissed her again and moved for the door, his mind already on the battle to come.

* * * *

"Why are there so many random stone walls in Scotland?" Logan asked, his back pressed to one as he crouched in the high grass.

"Dunno." Garrett's pose was similar as he looked up at the sky. "At least it isn't raining. Nice night, really."

It was. The sky in Scotland was as stunning as in Idaho. Clear and pure. The sound of the evening pressed in around them, creatures stirring and chirping. They were outside of town, in the middle of nowhere, with an impressive stone keep behind them. Had been a small castle at some point in history, probably.

Logan shook out his arms and controlled his heart rate, waiting for the signal to go. Apparently the Realm boys were having problems getting the satellite into position. He drew in a deep breath of the heather-scented air and glanced at his best friend. "You feel any different after the ritual?"

Garrett, always thoughtful, took a moment before answering. "Yeah. Besides the obvious change that my torso is now a shield to keep my organs safe, I feel...connected to something bigger. A pulse of energy. And I can sense the other Seven members in a way I've never felt. I assume it's similar to the connection between blood brothers or even mates."

Logan weighed his words. "We haven't talked about it, but if I don't survive the ritual—"

"You'll survive." Garrett's jaw snapped shut, and he looked into the deep forest.

"I know," Logan said, giving his friend the words he wanted to hear. "But just in case, I need you to cover Zane and Sam for me. Zane will blame himself, and Sam will go nuts trying to figure out a way to change time or the past or reality. You have to force them to go on."

"Nobody is going anywhere," Garrett said tersely. "You'll survive the ritual. I can't do this without you."

The words hit Logan square in the chest. There was nobody he trusted in this life more than Garrett Kayrs. "You're a good brother. I also need you to protect Mercy." He cleared his throat. The idea burned like acid through him, but if he passed on, was there any chance Garrett could mate her? "She'd be a good mate."

Garrett snorted. "She's as crazy as your mother, which is one of the reasons you're falling for her. You mate her. You know she's yours."

Some of the Kayrs males had an odd gift of dreaming of their mates before meeting them. Had Garrett dreamed of Mercy? If so, then Logan's fate was death. "Have you dreamed of her?"

"Nope."

Relief sizzled through Logan. That didn't mean he'd survive, but at least his failure wasn't foretold. Curiosity grabbed him. "Have you dreamed of your mate?" They'd never talked about it.

Garrett pressed his earbud, and then settled back down. "Yes. I think she's human." He sounded perplexed by that. "Sometimes I get glimpses of her, or maybe just a sense of her. I've tried to draw her but can't quite get her features right."

Interesting. Man, Logan had to survive the ritual just to see Garrett go down for a female at some point. Of course, it could be centuries from now.

A low male voice crackled through the ear comms. "Satellite in place. Guards in two-on-two formation with only two teams visible on exterior."

The Fae were too few in number. "Fae or Cyst?" Logan asked quietly.

"Fae," the male replied. "No Cyst in vicinity that we can see. Sending satellite imagery of heat signatures inside now."

Garrett's phone buzzed nearly silently, and he drew it out to show Logan. There were about ten people inside, all with higher heat signatures than the cold-blooded Cyst. Several were in prone positions, no doubt sleeping. In the lowest level a large form was secured to a chair with another form standing close and one at the door. The closest form threw a punch, hitting the secured male.

Anger grabbed Logan, and he tapped his ear. "Any security system in place?"

"Not that we've found," the male said.

Logan tensed and stood. "Let's breach between patrols." He wouldn't even need to put anybody down. "Go in the front door but watch out for the weird burst of air they seem to have for security."

Garrett released his weapon from its thigh strap. "The Fae are too few in number to be fucking with us."

Logan shook his head. "They don't understand the need to be all in or out with allies. There should be three forces of Cyst protecting this place since they're allies."

"Probably don't trust the Cyst completely," Garrett noted, pivoting around the wall.

Logan followed. "Try not to kill anybody, if possible." He didn't want Mercy too pissed at him.

His earbud crackled. "Breach now. You have four minutes until the next patrol goes by the front door."

"Copy that," Garrett said, ducking and running full bore for the wide wooden door. He opened it, and Logan edged to the side as a powerful burst of air exploded between them.

Logan went in low and fast, going left.

Garrett followed him and shut the door.

Quiet filled the darkened three-story gathering room. Nice architecture—great elements. Garrett held out the phone with the live feed and turned to follow a narrow hallway that led to a rough wooden door with a guard on the other side.

Logan gave a hand motion, and Garrett nodded, slipping the phone in his pocket. Taking a deep breath, he wrenched open the door.

Logan was on the soldier before he could turn, smashing him face-first into the wall and then wrapping an arm around his neck. The guy put up a decent struggle, but with his oxygen cut off, he went limp within a minute. Logan settled him on the stairs and frisked him, finding immortal-style guns and knives.

"Damn it," he muttered. "Keep an eye out for a silver gun with red markings on the side." They needed to get their hands on a blaster.

"Copy that." Garrett took out the phone to check the live feed. "We're still good."

Terrible. The security was just horrendous. If Mercy was there, she'd be vulnerable to attack in a way the Fae just hadn't contemplated. While their weapons were superior, their training sucked. He shook his head, leading the way down the rough stone steps.

The satellite feed showed the occupants in the same place as earlier.

Garrett poised himself and kicked the door in.

Logan rushed inside and tackled the closest soldier. This one punched up, making Logan see stars. Finally. Somebody with training. He struck hard and fast for the larynx, partially turning to see Garrett fighting with Niall. Shit.

The air shimmered.

Logan flipped his soldier over, yanking a gun out of his waist. Red markings. Excellent. Rolling, he turned and fired at Niall before he could finish teleporting. The Fae king flew back into a wall and slumped down, out cold.

Pain ripped into Logan's shoulder as the soldier stabbed a blade into him.

Growling, he yanked it out and plunged it into the guy's eye. The Fae shrieked in pain and slumped unconscious. "You'll heal." Logan pushed off him and faced his brother as Garrett rose to his feet.

Sam was tied to a chair, his face and chest bare and bloody. He smiled, and blood dribbled from his mouth. "I didn't call for you."

Garrett moved to release the restraints, jerking his head at Niall. "What about him?"

Logan tucked the blaster at his waist. "Let's bring him along." He winced. "We need a place to question him, though." He couldn't let Mercy see him torture her king. It just wasn't right.

Chapter 32

Mercy paced the kitchen, her body humming with energy. If she were a battery, she'd be at ninety percent. She could probably teleport now. Yet waiting until she was fully charged was much smarter.

Yeah, right. She wanted to make sure Logan was all right before she left. How ridiculous was that, considering he was going to hate her? Or at least be furious. Even so, she couldn't leave yet. They should've been back hours ago. Where the hell were they?

The two Realm soldiers flanked the front door, one of them leaving every once in a while to conduct a perimeter search. They didn't talk or engage with her in any way—obviously just there to do a job. She briefly considered challenging one of them, but since they were twice her size and she wanted to wait until Logan arrived before leaving, it seemed silly.

The door finally opened, and Garrett moved inside, helping Sam Kyllwood. Sam had bruises all over his face as well as some cuts, but they seemed to be healing. He limped, wincing each time his left foot touched the floor.

He grinned. "Hey, Mercy. Had a nice time with your people."

She gasped and rushed forward to help him. "They tortured you?" Her people were more evolved than that, damn it.

"Well, they tried." Sam freed himself and moved to sit gingerly on the sofa. Pain and interesting vibrations came from him. Healing cells in action?

Mercy looked toward the door, fear seizing her. "Where's Logan?"

Garrett cleared his throat. "About that." He nodded to the soldiers, and both took their leave.

It was that easy? Maybe she should've just nodded at the silent guards. Her heart thumped. Hard. "Is Logan okay?" Panic started to sizzle through her veins.

"Fine," Logan answered as he moved through the door, a male over his shoulder. He dumped the guy on the floor.

Mercy jumped back, her eyes widening. Her blood froze. "Niall?" Her eyes widening, she slowly lifted her head to look at Logan. What in the world was the hybrid thinking? "You kidnapped our king?"

Logan kicked the door shut and drew a blaster from his back pocket. "Shot him, too. Let's see how he likes it."

Mercy blinked. Logan was still pissed they'd tased her? Crap. Now Niall couldn't teleport. Man, he'd be furious.

Niall groaned.

She dropped to her knees, noting a myriad of cuts along his neck. And bruises. On his face, down his neck, and going lower. "You beat him?" she whispered, her voice shaking.

"Needed information," Logan said, leaning down and grabbing Niall's arm to haul him up and onto the sofa next to Sam. His careless strength seemed frightening for the first time since she'd met him.

She shook her head, trying to grasp a thought as she stood. Two tortured males on the sofa. "What the hell is wrong with all of you?" she yelled. For the love of Pete. They were the good guys. All of them. Sure, they disagreed on serious matters, but still. "Torture?"

Niall opened his eyes, revealing the blue and brown. He looked around and settled his gaze on her. "You are all right?"

Gulping, she nodded. "You?"

He winced, placing a hand on his ribs. "I will be fine."

Logan watched her carefully. "Your people have aligned themselves with the Cyst, and there are plans in place to interrupt a Seven ritual if necessary. Plans that will lead to betrayal and death."

A surprising disappointment filtered through her at how quickly Niall had given up information. Then raw anger followed, and she glared at Logan. "You *cannot* torture our king." Did the Realm not fear them at all? "While we're new to this plane and your ways of fighting, we can destroy you with our use of dimensional travel. It is time you respected that, demon."

His expression didn't change. "Sit down, *mate*."

Burning hot coals of anger came to life inside her. The possessive tone of his voice would've thrilled her hours ago. Now, with her king bruised and bleeding in front of her, the reality of their positions hit her harder than a hammer to the head. Her loyalties were being shredded by opposing forces. "I am not your mate."

"You will be."

The breath heated in her throat while more fire spread through her abdomen.

Niall watched their exchange, his eyes darkening. He turned his attention to Garrett. "Prince Kayrs. This is an act of war involving the entire Realm. I doubt you have clearance for such an affront."

Garrett leaned back against the wall by the fireplace, his expression revealing nothing.

Logan moved closer to Mercy. "We'll happily exchange Niall for Ivar."

Niall blanched. "I already told you I left him in one of many hell dimensions. He's dead. Long dead and buried."

Garrett caught Logan's eye and gave a barely perceptible shake of the head.

Mercy stilled. Was it possible the Seven could sense each other? Feel if one had died? It kind of made sense. "Ivar had the ability to teleport?" she asked.

"Yes," Logan answered, moving even closer. His heat washed over her.

"Then he might've used that ability to jump dimensions," she said, wanting to kick Niall for doing such a thing. "He could be anywhere."

Garrett sighed. "I don't have the ability to teleport but was able to do so during the ritual. It was horrific."

Mercy's chest hurt. Bad. "Your only chance of finding him is if one of you, one of the Seven, senses him." Even then, the Seven couldn't dimension-hop like the Fae. "I might be able to help."

"No." Niall straightened and wiped blood off his forehead. "As your king, I order you to stand down. As your mate, I declare this farce is over."

Logan growled, the possessive sound spreading heat throughout her entire body.

"Now, Mercy," Niall ordered, the color returning to his face.

Energy flitted beneath her skin, while a shockingly deep sadness pierced her chest. She'd always done her duty, and she couldn't let anybody harm the king of the Fae. Even if her heart was involved. "I'm sorry, Logan," she said, pivoting quickly and diving for Niall.

Logan's roar of protest followed her as she disappeared into the darkness, her body finally set free.

* * * *

"No!" Logan jumped after Mercy, hit his head on the sofa, and bounced back to land on his ass.

She was gone.

He shoved to his feet and ran for the door. Somehow, Garrett put his body in the way, and the sound of them colliding was louder than thunder. Garrett grabbed his arms. "Stop for a second. Where are you going?"

"Back to the holding." Logan shoved him out of the way.

"They won't be there," Sam said wearily, giving up the tough act now that the Fae were gone.

Logan partially turned. "You don't know that."

"I do." His brother leaned his head back and shut his eyes, tingles pulsing from him as he healed. "The keep you infiltrated was temporary, just a place to house me. I'd bet anything they've already vacated it."

Shit, shit, shit. The sense of betrayal clawing through him was almost as sharp as the anger. "I thought she would've chosen me," he muttered. His entire body ached like he'd been beaten with baseball bats.

Garrett slapped an arm around his shoulders and drew him back into the living room. "She didn't *not* choose you. She saved her king. You would've done the same."

Her king who claimed to be her mate.

When had she regained the ability to teleport? She hadn't said a word. Had she been able to leave the night before, when they were in the shower having the best sex of his life? "She lied to me," he said.

"Probably," Garrett said cheerfully. He drew out his phone to make a quick call, ordering the Realm computer experts to trace the occupants from the holding they'd just infiltrated. "We'll have their location shortly."

"It doesn't matter where those soldiers go once they wake up. I'm assuming you knocked a few out." Sam grunted. "They won't lead you to wherever Mercy just took Niall. Even the Fae aren't that trusting."

Logan curled his fingers into fists. He needed to hit somebody, and right now. "Where are they, then?"

Sam opened his eyes, revealing his secondary eye color of electric bronze, only visible in extreme situations. His pain must be worse than he was letting on. "Wherever the president is. She's at a secure location, and that's the reasonable place for Mercy to take their king."

Logan studied his brother, checking out his injuries without being too obvious. "Any clue where that might be?"

"No." A gap along Sam's collarbone slowly mended.

"Hey," Logan said, his voice gentling, his tension mellowing. "I'm glad you're okay. I was worried."

Sam's lips twitched. "It sucks not being able to teleport. Bastards hit me with one of those tasers right off the bat. My strength is about half back, though."

"Did you get any information?" Garrett asked, dropping into the large chair by the fireplace.

Sam nodded. "Of course. They really do think we're going to rip the universe apart if we finish your ritual, Logan."

They might be right. "Do they understand that the Kurjans will make it happen, regardless? That the Seven will be the only way to save Enhanced women?"

Sam blanched. "They do."

Silence ticked around the room for a moment. Ah, shit. Logan shook his head. "They're willing to sacrifice Enhanced women if necessary." All of the mates, so many humans, even the people to come. Anger swelled through him.

Sam nodded. "Yes." He rubbed a bruise along his left hand. "But keep in mind, they think *everyone* will die otherwise. So it's a bad choice among even worse ones."

"Are they right?" Garrett asked softly.

Sam shrugged. "Their science isn't much better than ours." Frustration creased his forehead. "We've teleported for centuries, never quite understanding how. The Fae are further along, but a lot of their research has been lost. It's the humans who've sought knowledge. We'll have to turn to them."

Logan leaned back against the wall and stretched his back. Frustration felt like ants crawling just beneath his skin. "Ivar was working on that before he disappeared. We need to get him back."

"We will," Sam said.

Logan rolled his neck. "Sam? Maybe it's time you told us your function here."

Sam's split lip came back together. "You sound like the Fae. They really had some questions."

"Yet they know more about your role than I do," Logan said evenly, pushing off from the wall. If his brother was in even more danger than before, he fucking wanted to know about it.

Garrett watched the brothers quietly, just waiting.

Sam eyed Logan. "You don't even know your full role yet."

Well. That was true and a mite insulting. "Sam?" Logan tensed. He couldn't hit his brother while Sam was injured, but the guy did heal fast. "What's your function?"

Sam stood and ripped the worn and bloody T-shirt over his head to reveal bruised ribs and unhealed cuts across his torso.

Fury boiled in Logan that his brother had been hurt so. He took a step forward.

Sam held up a hand. "I'm fine. Needed to get information from them, and Niall liked to talk while cutting."

Niall had done this? Fuck. Logan should've beaten him up a lot more. There was barely any blood on his blade. "I'll kill him."

"Meh." Sam lifted a shoulder and turned around.

Logan sucked in air at the intricate, deep-blue marking across his brother's entire back. It looked almost like one of the prophecy marks, but it was bigger and more detailed. Logan stepped closer to study it. Even with bruises and cuts marring the design, he could make out seven numerals, three different key designs, and finally a lock in the center. "What the heck?" he whispered.

Garrett stood and moved closer to study the design. "When did it appear?"

Sam looked over his shoulder. "Five years ago, in the middle of the night, along with a dream of Fate." He shook his head. "Hurt like evil agony, and I can't stand that bitch."

His people had called her worse through the years. If she really existed.

Logan watched as a wound across Sam's spine began to heal. Tingles popped in the air. "So you're, what? The historian of this disaster?"

Sam snorted. "I wish. No. I'm the keeper of the chamber."

Garrett cut Logan a look, and Logan shrugged.

Sam turned back around and sat. "There's a sacred circle where the killing of Ulric has to happen. I protect the place, and only I know where it is."

Logan lifted his chin. Something told him the sacred circle wasn't in this dimension. "Okay. So that's why the Fae tortured you? That's what they wanted to know? The location?"

He nodded. "Yes. That's also why I stayed with them to seek information."

Logan rubbed his chest. The Realm guys should've called with more intel on Mercy by now. He tried to concentrate. His brother was in danger, for sure. "You stayed to find out if they had any inkling where it is?"

"Right. The place was lost when the universe split last time—when the Fae lost most of their people." Sam's eyes burned a deep green again. "They have no idea where it is now."

Logan's phone buzzed, and he yanked it free of his pocket. "Kyllwood."

"Hey, Lo. It's Benny." Loud traffic sounded through the line. "We had an impromptu meeting and decided we needed to get the show on the road here before your Fae buddies figure out a way to stop us—especially since they're aligning with those bastard Cyst dickheads. Adare is working on the location now. How do you feel about undergoing the ritual tomorrow? Becoming one of the Seven?"

Logan's head lifted. "I'm ready."

"Good. You're a decent bloke, Kyllwood. I sure hope you don't die." Benny clicked off.

"Me, too," Logan muttered into the dead phone.

Chapter 33

Mercy landed lightly at their hidden headquarters on an island off the Scottish mainland and let Niall fall from her grasp. He bounced twice on the floor.

"Good. You're here." President Dawn looked up from her seat behind her desk, a wide, hand-cut marble work of art. Her light eyebrows rose. "King? What in the world happened to you?" She stood and moved around the desk, her high heels making no sound on the priceless Persian rug.

Niall stood and dusted off his pants. "Had a run-in with a Kyllwood and a Kayrs." He looked at Mercy. "Thank you for the ride."

She pressed her hands to her hips, finally letting her anger free. At him, at Logan, at the entire universe. She'd just betrayed Logan Kyllwood, and no doubt that was a mistake most people didn't make twice. "You're lucky my ability came back in time. How could you have me tased?"

"That was my idea," the president said. "We weren't quite sure about your plan—you do disobey orders regularly."

That might be true, but come on. A taser? "It took longer than I thought to regain my ability." Now wasn't the time to yell at them. She needed them to listen to her. The Seven might be right about the Kurjans' ability to release Ulric and rip apart the prison world. The Fae needed to work with the Seven. "Do you trust me now?" she demanded.

Niall glanced at the roaring fire shining bright from the marble fireplace. "Yes. President Dawn, I was tased, and Mercy saved me. She brought me here and away from the Seven, who surely want me dead." He looked down at his stained clothing. "I'll go get changed." He flexed his hands. "And healed."

Mercy bit her tongue. If Logan had wanted Niall dead, the king would be dead. Now wasn't the time to argue that point, however.

"What did you learn from Sam Kyllwood?" the president asked.

"Not much. I took pictures of his back, but the design is the same as those of Keepers from the past." Niall prodded the bruises on his neck that looked like finger marks. Logan's fingers. "He wouldn't give up the location of the sacred circle. No matter what I did to him."

Mercy shuddered. "Do you really want to get into a torture contest with Realm soldiers?"

"I wouldn't mind." The door opened, and the largest male she'd ever seen walked in. He stood nearly seven feet tall and had purplish-green eyes, startling white skin, and blood-red lips. One strip of white hair went from the middle of his forehead in a braid down his thick back.

Icicles pricked beneath Mercy's skin. She swallowed. Aye, she'd figured out her people had aligned with them. That was her next bone of contention with Niall and the president. But this? "You've brought the Cyst here?" It was one thing to align themselves with the soldiers, and quite another to trust them.

"Of course," the Cyst soldier said. He wore an all-black uniform with silver medals across his left breast. "I'm General Xeno." He half bowed. "We will help you take down the Seven. More blood will be spilled, more bones broken, that I promise you."

Mercy whirled on the president. "What are you thinking?" Her voice shook.

The president narrowed her gaze. "I'm doing my job." She smoothed out her expression and focused on the general. "Our intel shows the Seven regrouping—somewhere in the cliffs of Oregon. We should have a definite location soon. I have battle plans to share."

Mercy hitched in air. "You don't mean—"

Niall grasped her arm. "Excuse us. I'd like a word with my mate. I'll return after a quick shower." Nodding at the general, he all but dragged Mercy from the room.

She was too stunned to stop him. The president was actually going to help the Cyst go after the Seven, during the ritual. She'd suspected it, but hearing the plan confirmed made her want to vomit. The danger for Logan had increased. How could she save him?

They traveled down the castle tunnels to Niall's quarters, and he shoved her inside.

She stumbled and righted herself. How was she going to rescue Logan? She had to convince Niall to work with her. Maybe he could talk the president into abandoning her insane plan. "This is crazy, Niall."

He locked the heavy oak door.

Her palms grew sweaty and she wiped them on her jeans. "The Cyst want to burst the final prison bubble and you know it. If we give them passage into other dimensions, they might succeed." How could Niall not see that?

"I know." His gaze raked her in that way he'd started a few years back. "But if we're going to chase Logan Kyllwood into the abyss, we need firepower. Grunts we can use and discard."

Was it possible to find the Seven during the ritual? Was Niall that good? "You think you can discard Cyst soldiers?" she whispered, her brain misfiring until her skull ached. The arrogance in that one statement showed how her people would lose this war. "We've aligned ourselves with a species whose main goal is to tear those remaining prison worlds apart."

Niall drew air in through his straight nose and then exhaled, flexing the muscles in his chest. Sometimes she forgot how big he was. "We need them right now. Then we'll handle them."

There was no way to handle the Cyst. She shook her head, disbelief choking her. "We believe in science and exploration. Not war."

"Right. That's why we have the most superior weapons and defenses in the world." Niall drew his shirt over his head, revealing motley bruising and cuts, as well as finely honed muscle.

Even so, his chest wasn't as big as Logan's, by any means.

Feeling she was being ripped in different directions, she tried to center herself. She couldn't let them kill Logan, but she believed in protecting the two bound worlds. What should she do? "Have you even tried to investigate the Cyst? Or the Kurjans?" They were the same people, right? Same species?

He nodded. "Of course. We've studied them and had spies in place for a while. They're spending incredible resources trying to find a way to release Ulric."

"Which is why they want us. Our knowledge," she said.

"Of course."

So they were double-crossing each other. Wonderful. "How close are they to success?" she asked.

His eyebrows drew down. "Close. They're actually quite brilliant. But if we take out the Seven, we'll have time to devote to sabotaging the efforts of the Cyst. This is a multistep plan. The best ones always are."

Actually, the best plans were simple, and his stank. The Fae couldn't beat the Kurjans, and they would have no other allies if the Seven were destroyed. The Realm would be furious if the Cyst took out the Seven, so they'd never help the Fae. She straightened her shoulders. Finally. A clear answer for this problem. Not a good one, but at least a clear way to go. "You're following the wrong path, Niall."

His hands went to his black pants, and she averted her gaze. "My paths are clear," he said quietly.

Why wouldn't he get out of the way? Awareness clacked down her spine. "Ah, I'll go to my quarters. It's not quite dawn yet, and I could use some sleep." She didn't move because he stood between her and the door.

"I think you should stay here." His voice deepened, and the sound of his pants swooshing to the floor pierced the silence. "You asked for time, and I've given you that. But our people come first. We're mating now."

Her people had always come first for her, but the universe often had a bigger plan, and all people belonged to it. Finally. She could see that now. Right now, the Fae couldn't beat the Cyst, and Ulric would be set free. The Seven was their only chance. It might not be a good one, but it was all they had right now.

He sighed. "You've fallen for the demon."

She lifted her gaze to meet his eyes. Her heart belonged to Logan Kyllwood. There was no way around that, and her duty to her people was to help them survive, which Logan would do. "Yes." Pure and simple, she belonged with the demon. Sometimes it really was that simple.

"That's unfortunate." Niall still didn't move out of the way.

She settled her stance, feeling a thousand years old. After having experienced passion with Logan, she couldn't think of any other male. She probably never would be able to do so. "I think you're a decent guy, Niall." When his expression didn't alter, she continued. "The kingship was thrust upon you at an early age, and you've done an admirable job with it. But this breeding plan to repopulate the Fae isn't right. It doesn't serve our people—only freedom does."

"Freedom for one of the purest Fae to breed with a demon-vampire hybrid?" Niall chuckled, the sound dark. "We might be at war with them someday soon, and you want to add your incredible gifts to theirs?"

"Life isn't always about war," she protested.

"Sure it is." He looked strong and fit, standing there just in his boxers.

What was it with her and immortal males in their underwear? It was an odd trend, to be sure. She shook her head, trying to focus. "No. I agree that completing the Seven is dangerous, but we both know it's inevitable. As is the release of Ulric. So killing someone to prevent that final event is stupid."

His chin lifted, showing more bruises beneath his jaw. Logan must've spent his time teaching Niall a lesson. "What's the alternative?"

"Figure out how to save the universe. We have resources that could be put to better use than destroying people."

He leaned back. "Make love, not war?"

Her face heated at his sarcasm, as well as the reminder of her time with Logan. "I won't let you kill him." The words burst out of her before she could stop them.

"You can't stop me," Niall said quietly. "Oh, you're good, but I'm better. Much."

It was true. Niall could jump dimensions far easier than most Fae, maybe all of them. And if Logan underwent the ritual, he'd be weakened in the other dimensions, especially since he couldn't teleport yet. The learning curve might kill him, even without Niall's help. "Why won't you listen to me?" she asked, her heart bleeding for the losses to come.

"Because you're not thinking with your head." He moved away from the door, striding toward her. "It was a mistake not to mate you earlier, and I'll probably pay for it many times over." Reaching her, he pushed a strand of hair off her shoulder.

She took a step back at the intimate gesture. "My answer is no."

"I didn't ask you a question." He kept his stance sure. "I regret not being able to spend time with you this last year as I'd hoped, but the year is up."

How could she get through to him? He was handsome and smart. Driven. Even though they disagreed, he was acting on his convictions. "Don't you want to fall in love? Build a life with somebody, even if it turns out to be a short one?" If there wasn't much time, she wanted to be happy during it. Logan's hard face and bright eyes flashed through her mind. He didn't smile enough.

She could get him to smile more. "Don't you deserve happiness, Niall?"

"Yes." He slid his hand into her hair and cupped her head. "I want you. Have for years." He was warm, but not nearly as warm as Logan Kyllwood. "Now you're going to do your duty. I promise it won't be unpleasant."

The wrong man was holding her.

"My duty isn't with you." She moved to break away, and he tightened his hold. Her heart raced with a sick panic. "Let go."

He yanked her toward him and covered her mouth, his kiss brutal. She struggled, fighting his hold, her mind frozen with the thought that this couldn't be happening. He shoved his tongue into her mouth, and her jaw ached from the pressure. She pushed him with both hands. The jerk pulled her closer and tackled her to the floor.

She kicked out, trying to draw on the energy around her to teleport.

"You can't," he snapped, pulling away, his body pinning her. "Your demon isn't the only one who can stop a teleporting." Niall's face turned a raw red, his eyes an angry, deep yellow. "Didn't know that, did you?"

"No," she gasped, shaking her head to avoid his.

Logan's face swam in front of her eyes, and she calmed. She closed her eyes, breathed deep, then arched up. Kicking, she hit Niall in the hips and threw him over her head.

Then she rolled, coming up by the door. "Guess those self-defense lessons were a good idea after all," she snapped.

He stood, fury crossing his face. Then he lunged.

She teleported before he reached her, grabbing the universe with both hands and sailing through it. Landing right back in the Seven's safe house, she rolled and jumped to her feet where Logan, Sam, and Garrett watched her, all having leapt to fighting stances.

She grabbed her chest and panted, trying to draw in enough air to be able to speak clearly. "Logan. We have to mate. Now."

Chapter 34

Relief and fury slammed into Logan so quickly he froze in place. Mercy was safe, and she was right in front of him. He didn't trust himself to touch her at the moment. Oh, they were going to get some things straight, and right now.

She rubbed her mouth and looked around, her eyes wide. Her white shirt was disheveled, but her light jeans looked all right. Was her mouth swollen?

Logan moved then, taking her hands. The rioting in his head finally abated now that she was safe and close enough to keep that way. He didn't want to tase her, but this teleporting away from him would stop now. "What happened?"

"Nothing. Argument with Niall," she said, her pulse way too fast in her wrist.

Logan settled and calmed his face while the anger continued to flow inside him with the force of a volcano about to erupt. "He hurt you?"

"No." Her bottom lip was red. Had Niall forced a kiss on her? Logan ran his fingertip over her heated mouth. "Right now. Tell me what happened." He wasn't letting her go until she did. If he didn't know the problem, he couldn't fix it.

She huffed out a breath. "He's doing his duty, Logan. I don't agree with it, but his motives are pure." Her body was still shaking as she came down from the adrenaline rush. When Logan didn't release her, she sighed. "Fine. Niall said we were going to mate, grabbed me, and kissed me. I threw him over my head and teleported here."

An instant fury grabbed Logan around the throat, but he kept his hold gentle and his expression calm. She was fragile, and he wouldn't allow himself to frighten her. "You threw him over your head?" How did that make sense?

She shuffled her feet, and her gaze dropped to his chest. "He may have knocked me down first."

A low growl rumbled up from Logan's chest, and he squelched it. The female was scared enough, and he had to remain calm for her. "Are you harmed?" If there was one bruise on her, Niall would feel a thousand.

"No." She looked back up to meet Logan's gaze. Her pupils were still a little wide, but her skin had regained some color. She vibrated a little in place, but her pulse was finally slowing to a normal rate. "I've been training when I could find the time, and I did the feet-to-the-hip move to toss him over my head after he kissed me."

"Good job with throwing him." It was shocking Logan could sound so calm, although his tone had gone demon hoarse. When he found Niall, he'd make sure the king never again could use his mouth. For anything.

She pressed her small hands against his abs, her touch soothing even though he still wanted to hit something—or somebody. "Niall wouldn't have gone through with it, Logan. He's feeling pressure to fulfill this destiny we've been charged with since birth. Oh, I'm mad at him, but he just made a big mistake. Probably already feels bad."

Not as bad as he was going to feel. Possessiveness battled with protectiveness inside Logan until they melded together with one common goal. Make Mercy his. Period. "Why did you change your mind?" Logan had to ask, though the why didn't matter. "About your duty?"

"The elders' plan to repopulate isn't the only way to protect my people. We don't have to follow some arbitrary breeding chart." She swallowed. "Besides, when it comes to the Seven, I think you're right. The Kurjans will set Ulric free, and the bubbles will both burst. Could kill us all, but the Seven are our only chance to deal with Ulric." She sighed and dropped her head for a moment. "We'll have to figure out how to counterbalance the change in dimensions, but one thing at a time."

Not exactly a declaration of love, but he'd take what he could get right now.

"And, I didn't want to mate Niall." She bit her lip but didn't say anything else. Her gaze cut away and uncertainty filtered across her angled cheekbones.

His anger cooled and his center calmed. It was a good start. Hopefully they'd have centuries together, and she'd learn to express those feelings she wanted to hide to protect herself. That was his job now. "I'm glad," Logan said softly.

She exhaled slowly, visibly relaxing. "Okay. So finally we're on the same page here. We need to mate."

The idea roared the blood through Logan's body, but he forced his mind to take over. Oh, the sweetheart. She was more frightened than she let on. He tightened his hold on her delicate hands. "You don't have to mate me to be safe. I can kill him for you." In fact, he should've already done so.

"No." She planted both hands on her face and then dropped them. "Listen to me. You need to mate before you go through the ritual. Niall is planning something, and he's the best at teleporting. He probably has abilities I haven't even realized, and you'll need even a small amount of my teleporting skills to even have a chance."

His chin lifted and his chest warmed. She wanted to protect him. It was sweet but unnecessary. One Fae king who, so far, had only dared to attack a female wasn't a threat to him. "I can handle Niall and anything he's got."

"Your arrogance is not your most appealing quality." She rolled her eyes, panic still widening her pupils. "You have to listen to me. God, you're stubborn. Just mate me, damn it."

He wasn't being clear. "Oh, I am mating you, baby. But it isn't because I need your skills. It's because you're my fucking mate." A fact he'd known with absolute certainty the second she'd teleported away from him.

She blinked and faltered. Her hands wiped down her jeans. "Now wait a minute."

"But first we're going to have a nice chat about you just teleporting out of here a couple of hours ago." He wasn't happy with her, and he had no problem letting her know that one simple fact now that he'd reassured her. It was time she took him seriously. She couldn't just go zipping around with people who wanted to hurt her.

"Now, listen—" she started, her head snapping back.

"No. You listen." He lowered his chin. "We've been dancing around this for too long. It's a done deal, Mercy. You know it, I know it, and it's time to stop fucking around."

She tapped her foot. "I'm the one who showed up here saying we should mate."

Her temper was prodding his, and he struggled to remain reasonable. "I know, but mating comes with some understanding. One, for sure, is that you stay in the same damn dimension as I am." His growl went low and hot. She'd purposely rescued an asshole who wanted to hurt her. That could never happen again. "I will do everything in my power to help your people, but your loyalty is to me. Period."

Sam cleared his throat from near the counter. "Do you two, ah, want some privacy?"

Logan had forgotten the others were even in the room. "Yes. We do." He dipped his nose toward his errant mate's. "Can you teleport us to my cabin? The one by the river?"

She swallowed, her throat moving. "Yes. I can picture it, but if you gave me the location, it'd be easier."

"Priest River, Idaho," he said. They needed privacy for the rest of this discussion. He'd allowed her too much freedom, and she'd teleported away from him and into danger.

"We'll be in contact," Garrett said quietly.

Logan nodded, slipping his phone into Mercy's back pocket, his fingers sliding along her pert backside. Arousal flared inside him from the one little touch. It was a good thing the Fae could transport metal and other objects. Then he looked at Garrett, determined to focus. "Call me when the Seven are prepared for the ritual. Tell them I'm ready." He grasped Mercy's arms.

She looked like she was going to argue, caught sight of the other two males, and then closed her eyes.

The world spun away, darkness surrounding him with the softest of touches. A second later, he stood near the fireplace in his secluded cabin, the sound of thunder rolling high overhead. It was the most comfortable teleporting experience he'd ever had.

She released his arms and took several steps away. Rain poured down outside in the darkness. Yet another nighttime in another time zone. "I think we're going to have to get some things straight, Logan Kyllwood."

"Agreed," he said, the predator inside him stretching wide awake. The rain battered against the solid cabin he'd built, providing a cocoon of intimacy tinged with a dangerous tension.

She faltered. "Um, okay. So. We're mating because we like each other and you need to teleport."

God, she was cute. "Actually, I don't like you very much right now, and I'll gain the skill to teleport on my own at some point." Most demons didn't teleport until they'd lived a hundred years or so. He crossed his arms. "What else?"

"What do you mean you don't like me?" Her eyes opened wide, and her jaw assumed such a stubborn line that he wanted to take a bite.

The woman could be dense. "Do you have any clue why I'd be irritated?" He had to suck down said irritation to keep his voice level.

"No." She tapped her foot again, a sure sign of impatience.

God help him. She'd drive him crazy through the centuries. The female had to acknowledge just a couple of simple facts before he lost his damn mind. He clenched his jaw and spoke through gritted teeth. "You do not teleport out with the enemy. With somebody I just beat up. With somebody who might harm you. Ever."

"Oh, you do not tell me what to do." Her head jerked, and all of that glorious hair tumbled around. "Ever."

"That's not how this is going to work," he said, rather gently if he did say so. When it came to her safety, his will was absolute. He'd rather not have to fight her as well as her enemies, but if she required that, so be it. His phone buzzed behind her backside.

Without looking, she yanked it from her pocket and chucked it at him. He caught it midair, the edge of violence pricking his temper. Oh, she was pushing him too far now. He pressed the screen. "What?"

"Tomorrow. Seven in the morning. I'm sending coordinates," Benny said. "Say your good-byes." The phone went silent.

Fuck, Benny was nuts. Logan settled the phone in his pocket. "So."

"So." She visually shook herself, loosening up. "You can be a bossy jackass tomorrow. We'd better get to the mating."

Chapter 35

Tingles raced down Mercy's body as she pretty much offered herself to the sexiest male she'd ever imagined. She'd told Niall the truth about falling for Logan. The demon had intrigued her from the first picture she'd studied, and the moment he'd finally touched her, she'd felt whole. But now, she had to protect him the same way he'd already saved her—whether he liked it or not.

He watched her like a predator, his eyes a molten green in the darkened room. "I'd love to take the night, but we're not mating." His voice had gone demon low.

"What?" Her head bobbed with the exclamation. Was it really possible the immortal was that stubborn and arrogant? "Have you suffered a head injury?" He made less sense than marshmallow pudding.

"Probably," he muttered. "We'll mate after the Seven ritual, Mercy. Not before."

"But the whole purpose of mating is to save your ass," she snapped, fury bubbling through her like an evil champagne.

He tucked his thumbs in his faded jeans, an implacable force in a rioting world. "Ah, baby. The purpose of mating is forever. You and me. Fun and sex and fights and family. That happens *after* I survive the ritual."

His sweet words rocked her, even through her anger. "You'll be stronger if we mate," she said.

"You won't." Even across the room, his energy pulsed. Strong and powerful. Primal. Drawing her in a way she could barely comprehend. "Mating a demon takes a toll on a female. And if I don't survive the ritual…"

He didn't want to leave her a widow. A mate without a mate for eternity. Just when she wanted to kick him in the head, he had to go and say something endearing.

But this wouldn't do. "Oh, Logan," she murmured. She could almost feel sorry for the guy. If he had any idea how many hours, days, or even weeks she had spent studying him. Truly fascinated by everything about him. His relationships with family, with friends, with foes. His fighting ability and what drove him.

Even what made him.

She knew what lurked at the core of him. The predator he only let loose in times of war to protect his family. A demon-vampire hybrid was the most dangerous creature in a world brimming with deadly beings, and even he, with his calm intelligence, couldn't overcome his true nature.

Not if they were truly meant to be mates.

He tilted his head toward the bedroom. "We do have this night."

A shiver took her, dancing along her spine. An entire night with Logan Kyllwood in a big bed. Very tempting. But she wanted more than a night of great sex. She was going to save him even if it killed them both. There was one way to do it, and it wasn't pretty. Even so, her blood started to burn with anticipation. "No."

His eyebrows shot up. "No?"

"No." She licked her lips. "I'm at a crossroads, Logan. If I mate you and give you powers, you might be able to save the world. Or I could mate Niall and follow his path. Either way, the universe is both threatened and possibly saved. But I'm finished wondering, and I'm finished waiting. It happens tonight."

His indulgent smile barely masked the anger her words created. But it was there glowing in his eternal eyes and undulating in his hard-cut muscles. "You're mating me. On my terms and in my time."

"Well." She threw challenge into her eyes and settled into her plan, no matter the cost. How well did she really understand the demon? She was about to find out. So she gathered as much power from the atmosphere as she could seize, going for the jugular. "I guess it's Niall, then." The air shimmered, and she forced herself into a teleport.

"No!" Logan lunged, grasping her ankles in the nick of time, his grip unbreakable.

But she'd expected him and only jumped outside and across the rushing river, within eyesight of the cabin. His hold on her would've prevented her from going any farther, so she didn't try. They landed in the wet weeds and rolled, rain beating down on them.

She came up onto her feet, already panting, warning ticking through her. Wet weeds dropped from her shirt to the dirt. Water slid over her face and into her hair, not cooling her determination in the slightest.

"What the fuck are you doing?" He rose to his full height, his bellow startling wildlife into flight through the darkness.

She gulped, her jeans and shoes covered in wet grass. "Teleporting to Niall. You've given me no choice." Her knees wobbled, but she met his gaze directly. It was the only way this could possibly work. She couldn't back down. If she showed one ounce of fear, one tiny sliver of doubt, he'd go into protector mode.

She wanted the predator.

He grabbed her hand and turned toward the river, his gaze seeking. The moon glowed slightly through the cloud cover, barely diminishing the darkness. "There are a series of rocks that cross the water nearby."

She jerked away and shoved wet hair off her face. The rain chilled her skin down to her bones. "I am not going with you."

The muscles in his back, clearly defined beneath the wet cotton, bunched and knotted. "Stop this, Mercy. Now."

It was too late. Way too late. "No." Waiting until he turned to face her again, she kicked up with her full strength, striking him beneath the chin. Her one signature move. The sharp crack of his head going back nearly made her rethink her strategy.

Then his chin lowered, and his eyes glowed. Really glowed. His human façade disappeared, leaving only the primal creature at his core.

She turned and ran.

Even though this had been her plan, instinct took over, and she fled as fast as she could. Through weeds, over branches and bushes, she ran as if the devil pursued her.

Because he did.

No predator on Earth—or any other dimension—would allow prey to attack and then flee. It went against their very nature. She knew Logan would have no choice but to pursue her. With his neck hurting and his anger scorching. But what he'd do with her if he caught her was all Logan. A furious demon-vampire hybrid that she'd challenged in the most fundamental of ways. She quickened her pace.

She panted and tried to quiet her breathing. She tripped over a rock and went flying through the rain, her arms windmilling. Somehow, he was in front of her, catching her before her face impacted an ancient cedar tree. Protecting her, even now.

Her momentum made him swing her around, and he set her down, his mouth dragging across hers. "I know what you're doing, and it isn't going to work." Even so, his hand fisted in her hair, and he jerked her head back. Tingles exploded along her scalp, and her nipples pebbled so fast and hard they hurt. "You want to play? I'll play. But you're not going to like the results," he rumbled.

Desire slammed to her core. Edged with a craving she hadn't expected and barely understood. She twisted and caught his knee with her foot, forcing him back. He released her, and she turned to run again. Because he let her.

A trail wound around rocks and branches, barely there, soaked by the rain. She followed it, her head down. The river rushed to one side, and the forest sprawled to the other. Dark laughter and hard footsteps pounded behind her.

Sexy trembles skittered down her back. She was smaller and more agile than he was, and she had challenged the beast. The taste of danger sweetened the rainy air around her. She beelined between a sharp outcropping of rocks, keeping close to the river.

The night smelled of him. Cedar and pine and spicy intent.

She sensed him before she saw him, right on her heels. Yelping, she turned and leaped over a downed tree, barreling into the forest. She ducked and dodged, lifting a branch and letting it snap behind her. It hit him with a crack, and she laughed, wild and free.

"You'll pay for that," he said, his voice riding the storm.

She turned again and caught sight of him—a hunter stalking prey. How did such a robust demon move with such grace? Her plan to slow down and let him catch her burned away with the need to test him. Truly challenge him. Just how good was he?

The game slid away. This was real. Fundamentally so. If he wanted her, really wanted her, he'd have to catch her.

The trail dipped, and she followed it, running full-out. Her heart pounded so hard it drowned out any sounds behind her. She couldn't sense exactly where he was any longer. He was close—she could feel him. But where? In which direction?

She grasped the edge of a rock and boomeranged around it, trying to give herself more speed. Shelter. She needed to duck and hide, at least to regain her breath. Had she thought this out well enough?

What would he do when he caught her?

If he caught her.

A series of rock ledges led down to the river. If she could cross, she could get free. Or wait. She could teleport. The thought hadn't occurred to her because she'd needed him to catch her for this plan to work.

But now? Forget the plan. Now she wanted to win. Wanted to show him she could. At an even more primal level, she needed to know that he could catch her. That he was that good. She took a deep breath, drew in moisture-laden air, and started to teleport midstride.

Something hit her from behind. Strong arms anchored around her waist, and he lifted her straight off her feet, halting her dimensional jump cold. The universe receded and her power sputtered out.

"Cheaters never win." He took her down to the grass, placing her on her back none too gently.

She struggled with his hands, angry he'd captured her so easily the second she'd tried to leave. Had he just been playing with her the entire time? The damn male wasn't even out of breath.

He dropped to his knees, straddling her and yanking her torso up toward him. Then his mouth devoured hers.

Chapter 36

Logan fought the beast inside him, straddling his female, having caught her. "You shouldn't have challenged me." His hands curled over her slim shoulders.

Her smile was pure sass. "You call that a challenge?"

His gaze tracked over the light flush across her face, the hard nipples beneath her wet shirt, and the tremors cascading through her slim thighs. The scent of her arousal, sweet and pure, dropped his fangs to his lip.

He retracted them. "Yeah. I call that a challenge."

Her eyes glittered, one blue and one green. "So who won?"

That was the question, wasn't it? The marking on his palm burned hotter than before, the *K* in the center hungry for her flesh. She belonged to him. Always would. She deserved an answer. "I won, Mercy. Will every time. Feel free to make me prove it."

"So prove it." Her wild red hair spread out on the wet grass, darkening in the rain.

He ripped her shirt in half, enjoying her sharp gasp. Arousal clamped on him with sharp claws. The rain washed over her smooth skin, turning her bra translucent. A flick of his fingers, and he tore it in two.

God, she was beautiful. Headstrong and too ready to leap into danger, but stunning as she did it. The wildness in her called to him as much as her serious side. But one would get her killed, and that he wouldn't allow. She already held his heart, perhaps his soul. For the remainder of his life, no matter how long he had, it would be Mercy he craved.

He palmed her breasts, her pretty pink nipples brushing his flesh. She arched into his hold, her lips curving in a half smile.

Then she dug her nails into his shirt, biting past the cotton to his skin. The slight pain drove him higher.

Defiance clearly in her eyes, she gathered the energy around them. Challenging him.

He felt the universe tug on her, and he pushed it back, keeping her in place. "I fully intend to survive the ritual tomorrow, but if the worst happens, I'd rather not spend our last night together teaching you a lesson." His voice dropped to a hoarse growl.

"Teach me, Logan," she whispered, not bothering to hide her sarcasm.

The reins on his control jerked hard. Keeping her gaze, he grasped her waist and pulled her up, tearing her jeans off her before tossing her onto her stomach.

Her surprised shriek ended on a chuckle. She was laughing?

The twin globes of her ass showed clearly through the panties he mercilessly destroyed.

She tried to turn back over, but he planted a hand across her ass, hard, holding her in place. The smack echoed through the rain. Her inhale was sharp, and her legs quivered. She threw her head back, and her hair nearly hit him in the face. The smell of gardenias unleashed the demon inside him.

He traced her ass, finally moving between her legs to palm her sex. She was wet and slightly swollen. All Mercy. Ready. The blood pounded between his ears, roaring through his head. Lightning cracked across the forest, and thunder followed with a bellow. He flipped her to her back and pulled her to her feet. "We're returning to the cabin."

"No." She stepped into him, caressing his straining cock through his jeans. In the rain, fully nude with her long hair hanging down her back, she was magical. Perfect. His.

A growl rumbled up from his chest, and his arms shook as he fought for control.

She licked her lips and reached for his shirt with her free hand while stroking him with the other. "I like it out here."

He ducked his head as she pulled off the shirt. Rain sluiced over him, failing to cool him in the slightest.

She dropped to her knees, humming, and he was lost. Her hands were aggressive and rough as she pulled his jeans down, and he kicked them away along with his boots. Then her mouth was on him.

His eyes rolled back, and he planted one hand on the top of her head to keep from falling on his ass. She licked him from base to tip, humming, like a cat with cream. His legs quivered. Electricity torpedoed down his spine to explode in his balls.

Hunger tortured him, turning him inside out. He twisted her hair in his hand and forced her to stand, even though she gave a sigh of disappointment. He kissed her, tethering her in place, tasting the rain on her mouth.

It was too late for the cabin.

With his mouth locked on hers, he laid her down, covering her with his body, careful to keep his weight on his forearms. Then he shoved inside her with one hard push.

She cried out and arched against him, her thighs slapping his and her body gyrating.

He paused, panting, rain dripping from his hair to her forehead.

Her eyes wide, she slid her wet hands over his shoulders as her body trembled around his. "Logan," she whispered. The way she said his name. Every time. He kissed her gently, letting her body accept him.

She moved restlessly, rubbing her clit against him.

Watching her expression, his body rioting, he slid out and then back in. She moaned and clutched her nails into his chest, scraping down to his abs.

Marking him.

She leaned up and bit him. Hard. The bite went through his skin, straight to his heart. She lay back, smiling. "It isn't fair that female Fae don't have fangs."

"You have enough weapons," he said, pulling out and shoving back in.

"I want more." She licked a spot of his blood off her lip. "This matters, Logan. We do. Waiting is a mistake. I want every minute." The defiance fled her expression, and pure sweetness remained. "Please."

His body settled. Fully embedded in her, surrounded by her, he'd give her anything. And she knew it.

He brushed the hair from her face. "Are you sure?"

"Yes." She blinked rain out of her eyes. "Are you?"

He was. Everything inside him wanted to be whole. So he pulled out and powered back inside her, going deep, going hard. The storm increased in force around them, and branches flew past them. He couldn't stop. Her moans pushed him on.

Finally, her eyelids flew open and she cried out, arching against him as waves of pleasure pummeled her entire body. They took him, rushing around him, giving him more pleasure than he could've ever imagined. With a soft sigh, she relaxed onto the wet grass, her eyes glimmering. Then sharpening. Then widening.

The beast inside him finally broke its chains. He was still hard inside her. "You're mine, Mercy."

* * * *

Logan framed her face with his hands and kissed her, going deep, taking everything she had. He was everywhere. In her, around her, over her.

Yet it wasn't enough. "More," she whispered, her hands frantic over his shoulders, learning every dip and valley.

"Yes." He withdrew and easily flipped her over onto her hands and knees.

The rain splattered down her back.

A wicked flash of heat pulsed through her. His hands were rough as he grabbed her hips, pausing for just a breath before hammering inside her. She rocked forward, and he twisted a hand in her hair.

Movement was impossible. He held her trapped, locked in place against his powerful body. So easily, he stole her control. A desperate ache, edged with sharp demand, pounded through her entire body. A need so great she couldn't define it.

"You're perfect, Mercy." His mouth was at her ear, his breath hot. He held her hip and her hair, thrusting deeper, harder each time. She rocked against him, helpless in his hold, taking all of him. Her heart pounded crazily as he slammed into her.

She climbed higher, needing more, her body tightening like a bow. Her lungs constricted as the climax took her. Her body spasmed around him, and she cried out his name.

His fangs pierced into her neck, going deep, slicing with a pain that went far beyond the physical.

Tears filled her eyes even as the pleasure burst through her. A flash of heat burned from her left shoulder blade to her spine. The marking. Placed deliberately close to her heart.

His hips jerked as he came hard inside her.

The storm raged on.

His fangs remained for several heartbeats, leaving permanent indents in her skin. They retracted slowly, scraping up, reminding her who'd claimed her. Finally, he licked the wounds closed. Then he released her hair and caressed her back, smoothing rain over the burn. The pain slowly subsided.

She shivered, suddenly overcome. What in the world had she just done? Talk about jumping into the fire feet first. This was more than she'd imagined.

He withdrew from her body, and she gave an involuntary moan of protest. But she couldn't move.

His chuckle was dark as he lifted her into his arms, his movements graceful and sure. She might never move again. Closing her eyes, she rested her cheek against his chest, listening to the even beat of his heart, feeling protected and safe. He moved rapidly through the rain and through the raging river, not bothering to find the rock path.

Mother Nature was no match for him.

They were back inside the cabin before she knew it. He settled her into the bed with a soft kiss on the forehead. "I'll be back in a minute. Need to secure the area." Then he was gone.

She curled onto her side, suddenly chilled. Energy popped through her blood, changing her somehow on a cellular level. Probably deeper than cellular. She hadn't spent much time researching the physical reactions to a mating. Tiredness swamped her, but she struggled to keep her eyes open.

The rain pattered against the window, lulling her into calmness. She'd mated Logan Kyllwood. The enormity of that fact pressed on her like the strongest gravity in any dimension. It had been the best way to deal with the Seven situation and the danger of the Cyst. And she liked him. Wanted him. Felt more than she'd expected for him. She wasn't up to examining *how* much more right now.

But how well did she really know him? What she knew, she truly did like.

Though there was something about him she couldn't define. Something dark—even more primal than she'd thought. She'd been right to challenge him, but in the end, it was an honest plea that had earned his marking. Logan didn't play games, and he was impossible to manipulate now that he knew her.

He wanted her bare and honest.

She swallowed, trying to warm up in the chilly sheets. Her hair was still wet.

He came into the room, moving silently, lifting the covers and sliding in. One arm went around her and pulled her into his side, while he lay on his back. "We're secure," he said quietly.

His big body warmed her instantly, and she cuddled closer. "Do you feel different?"

He caressed her hair. "Yes. Energized and aware."

She yawned. In just a few hours, he'd undergo the ritual. What if he didn't survive? He had to. She placed a hand over his heart, reassured by its strong beat. A part of her wanted to ask him not to undergo the ritual. But she knew him better than that. This world was a safer place with him in it. "Are you sorry?" She had pushed him into the storm.

"No." His hold tightened. "Just worried about the ritual and how to keep you safe."

She'd been keeping herself safe her entire life. "That's not your job." He had to join the Seven. It would be more than enough.

He turned them both, spooning around her with a heat that seeped into her bones. "Your safety is my most important job. I want to take you to demon headquarters tomorrow before I meet with the Seven. You're covered."

"No. I want to go to the ritual," she said sleepily.

"Absolutely not." The firmness in his voice stopped her midyawn. "It's way too dangerous. Nobody but the Seven can be there."

She was a teleporting Fae. "I'm going with you, Logan."

His arm wrapped around her waist, holding her flush against him. The marking on her shoulder pulsed. "I said no."

She blinked, her voice deserting her for several moments. Finally, she swallowed. "I wasn't asking your permission. Why are you being so bossy?"

"I warned you, Mercy. There's no halfway with me. You mated me with your eyes wide open, and I've never hidden a thing from you." His voice was calm but held a certainty that was as sexy as it was annoying. "While I'm undergoing the ritual, you'll stay safely away from me as well as the Fae. We'll deal with them together once I'm back."

Huh. He had another think coming. That was for sure.

He nipped her ear, sending awareness through her body. "Don't cross me, mate. Not over this."

Yep. Without question, things were about to become very interesting. "You mated me with your eyes wide open, too," she reminded him, her voice sleepy and her mind fighting to make her point. But he was just so warm and strong behind her. "Don't make me regret this." Now she was getting grumpy.

The hand at her throat, lifting her chin, surprised her into opening her eyes to see the storm outside the window. His hard body bracketed her from behind.

"Regrets or not, it's done, mate." His easy hold was impossible for her to break, reminding her once again of his strength. "Tell me you understand me so we can get some sleep." His hold tightened, not hurting but showing he'd stay there all night until she gave him the words.

"Fine," she huffed out, sleep dragging her under. "I understand you." What she'd do with that knowledge was up to her.

Chapter 37

Logan finished cooking the rest of the powdered eggs and called Mercy in from the other room. He needed to get this place stocked up better. Dawn had barely broken over the mountains, and yet he was restless. It was as if the ritual itself was calling to him like prickling needles just beneath his skin. What had he been thinking to mate Mercy before the ritual?

He glanced at the bedroom door to make sure she wasn't standing there. Then, just out of curiosity, he tried to teleport.

Nope. He grinned at himself. It must be too early to get the skill, but who knew. Maybe during the ritual it would give him some slight advantage. Garrett had teleported during it, so Logan probably could, too. "Mercy? Food's ready." He needed to get her to demon headquarters fairly soon.

His phone dinged, and he pressed a button to see his brother's face on the screen. "Zane. You're up early." He took a big drink of coffee—the instant kind—and grimaced at the sour taste. "How was the meeting?"

Irritation sizzled in Zane's eyes. "Not great. The witches and shifter nations have issued *habeas corpus* orders for the members of the Seven to appear in front of them, including you."

Ah. Latin. A lost language. The last thing he needed was to have a bunch of witches pissed off at him, considering his mother had recently mated a witch enforcer. This situation was causing problems on so many levels he was starting to lose count. His temples started to pound again. "What are the positions of the demon nation and the Realm overall?" Everyone belonged to the Realm as a member, but individual nations had their own laws as well.

"The demon nation hasn't publicly decided, meaning I haven't spoken out about it," Zane said, lines fanning out from his mouth. Had the guy slept lately? "As for the Realm, you've put Dage in a world of hurt. He has to listen to the witch and shifter nations, but the Seven is comprised of his family members as well as you. His diplomacy skills are being put to the test."

Logan grimaced. "We'll have to deal with the orders once I'm done."

Zane stiffened. "It's today?"

"Yeah." Logan and his brother already hugged and said their good-byes. Just in case. With so much turmoil, he couldn't ask the demon nation to take in Mercy, so that plan no longer worked. Especially since the Fae claimed she'd been kidnapped. "I may have kidnapped and beaten up the king of the Fae. Just to keep you informed."

Zane's chin dropped. "Damn it, Logan. Are you trying to make my life impossible?"

"Nope," he said cheerfully.

"Did you kill him?"

Logan's chest heated. "Unfortunately, no. I let him go, which turns out was a mistake." The male would pay for bruising Mercy.

Zane pressed his index finger right above his eye as if a headache was about to kill him. "Call me when it's over. And bro?" He focused again. "Survive this." The call ended.

Logan sat back. Yeah. He had to survive this.

The main reason why suddenly stood in the doorway to the kitchen. He looked her over, possessiveness whipping through his veins with shocking strength.

She'd taken his dark blue sweater to wear as a dress and secured it with his belt, wrapped around her waist twice. "I don't have shoes." Her legs were long, smooth, and bare to her adorable feet.

He frowned. The woman wouldn't need shoes if she did as he asked. He couldn't take her to demon headquarters now, and the thought of trusting her to keep herself safe opened a pit in his stomach. For once, she had to listen to him. "I'm hoping you'll stay here today." He'd try cajoling before ordering. Maybe that would work.

She'd piled her dark red hair atop her head, and without makeup, looked around eighteen. Her skin was smooth and her lips a natural pink. But those eyes. One green, one blue, both stunning. But dark circles marred them. "I have to teleport you."

He crooked his finger for her to approach the table.

She did so, and when she arrived, he hooked an arm around her waist and tumbled her onto his lap. Right where she belonged. His world centered. "How are you feeling?" He'd been rough with her the previous night, and mating a demon took a toll on a female, or so he'd heard.

"Tired." She caressed the side of his neck. "Why aren't you?"

He was too worked up about the ritual. "Mating a demon is difficult. Apparently mating a Fae is a walk in the park." He grinned at her frown. "Life isn't fair, baby."

"No kidding," she muttered. "I've been thinking. When you're in the ritual, if you're moving between dimensions like Garrett did, you might be able to find Ivar."

He'd been thinking the same thing. "Garrett says he can sense the other Seven members, so I figured I'd be able to sense the Viking if I end up going through dimensions like Garrett did. The other members of the Seven all had different experiences from each other, so who knows." But he sure as hell was going to try. The Viking needed to be brought home.

She snuggled closer, worried thoughts chasing each other across her face. The clip released, and her hair cascaded down around her shoulders. "You must know you'll run into trouble. My people have been preparing for this, and I don't believe I've been told the entire plan."

He smoothed his hand down her hair. "It'll be over before they know it."

She knocked her head back, hitting his chin. "No, Logan. You don't get it. Everything in this world is connected. The Fae are tuned in. The very second you start the ritual, they'll know it." Her sigh was full of frustration. "Naïveté and arrogance will get you killed."

She was sweet to worry, but he'd been through worse. Several times, actually. "I'll be careful."

"They'll be armed," she retorted.

He kissed the tip of her nose, wanting nothing more than to take her back to bed. "Promise me you'll stay safe today. That you'll teleport back here and spend the day resting from the mating." They would have plenty to worry about after he survived, but one thing at a time. "I need your promise, mate."

She blinked twice and then her body softened against his. "All right. This once, I'll promise to do nothing. Briefly."

He kissed her, memorizing the feel of her mouth against his. Soft and sweet. Once he returned, they'd have an eternity to figure each other out. But everything inside him knew she was his. Meant for him. "I won't let anything hurt you ever again," he vowed, giving all that he had.

"You need to focus today," she said, placing her hand over his heart. "The universe is inside you as well as all around you. *Everything* is connected. Work within yourself and not against any force. Trust me."

"I do." He looked at the dismal eggs. "Let's eat, and then I'll give you the coordinates." God, he hoped he survived this.

* * * *

Mercy landed barefoot in the darkened cave with Logan by her side. It was even easier to teleport him this time. Soon he'd have the skill himself, and then what? Did he really think he could lock her in a castle somewhere while he fought all of the big bads? She might not be a soldier, but she'd never hide while others did all the fighting for her.

For now, he needed to focus, so she just smiled. Her cheeks hurt from it.

Garrett waited for them dressed in a light T-shirt and ripped jeans. "We've created the circle way down beneath the surface of the cavern. Adare is sure it's the place meant for you."

Logan nodded, his eyes clear and his jaw determined.

Garrett looked at her, paused, and then lifted his chin. "I'll meet you down there. He'll be okay, Mercy. I'm sure of it." The worry in his eyes said otherwise, but Mercy kept her fake smile in place and just nodded. Garrett turned and strode into the darkness of the cave, and his footsteps slowly faded.

Logan turned her to him. "I'll have Adare bring me home as soon as possible." His grin flashed white teeth in the darkness. "Or who knows? After the ritual, maybe I'll be able to teleport myself."

"Don't," she warned, her smile coming more naturally this time. "At first, you can't control it very well. You might end up in the middle of the ocean." She'd done it once. Hence her dislike of sharks.

"I can't wait to hear all of your stories," he rumbled, his knuckles brushing her cheek. "Stay safe today."

"You stay safe." She rose to her toes and kissed him, wanting to teleport him anywhere but here. Instead, she dropped back down and put her hand over his heart. She loved feeling it beat. So strong and steady and all hers. "See you soon."

He studied her, his gaze serious. Then he nodded. "Teleport, baby."

She stepped back, filled her eyes with this last glimpse of him, and drew on the energy around her to transport herself.

Right outside an alley in New York City. She dodged into a store, slammed a pair of brown boots on her feet, hit the dressing room, and teleported right back outside the cave, making a mental note to send the store a check the following week. Then reality hit her. Sighing, she teleported again, this time to an outfitter's store. A human-made gun would be useless, but she lifted several knives before disappearing.

She landed near a tree covered in snow, and the chill instantly pierced her sweater. The boots kept her feet toasty, though. She counted to sixty and then strode around a series of rocks and into the cave where Logan had just been, tucking the knives into her clothing. If he thought she was deserting him right now, he truly was crazy.

But, man, the three jumps had already tired her. She shook out aching muscles and continued on. Following the darkness, she found a path winding down. The walls were a dull brown with veins of silver probably worth a fortune.

Interesting. She'd have to send a mining team back here. Her heart lifted.

Warmth filtered around her, instantly drying her sweater. The air clogged with gravity and sulfur. But she continued circling down, and the walls started to shimmer from lack of oxygen and too much heat. Her lungs protested, feeling like they were on fire.

Sweat slid down her torso and past her breasts.

Her skin itched and contracted, hurting like an open wound.

Lava bubbled off the side of the trail. A shield of some sort, an alteration of physical laws, kept her from burning up completely. Curiosity filled her as she forced herself to keep descending into the earth.

Finally, she reached a small cavern with no exit. Going on instinct, she reached the far wall and placed her hand upon it. A current coursed through her. She closed her eyes. Logan was on the other side of that wall.

She settled herself and tried to take a normal breath.

Waiting.

Chapter 38

This was definitely the craziest thing he'd ever done. Logan stood in the center of a cavern that seemed too hot to survive, with the remaining members of the Seven standing at the four points of the compass, their shirts off and sweat coating their chests. Torches illuminated the walls around them.

An unnatural power, something ancient and undefinable, roared through the chamber. Time and space spun away, shifting and shimmering in the air. The laws of physics no longer existed, and neither did he. For a moment.

His body heated and then chilled, shocking him.

Garrett stepped closer to the middle, and Logan lowered his chin, trusting his best friend.

"We share blood," Garrett said, his voice low and hoarse. "These are the words spoken for each ritual. When the bonding starts, it hurts like hell, man."

Those weren't the words. Logan forced a grin, but his jaw cracked.

Garrett continued. "Send your mind elsewhere. You'll see things you've never imagined. Creatures that want to eat you. The stream of time. The unknown." He shuddered and wavered. "Look for Ivar, and look for Quade."

Logan nodded, his vocal chords burned away. The small circle around him began to lighten and glow a fierce red. Was it actual fire? Lava? His boots bubbled and burned away, leaving his feet in agony.

A haze surrounded him, decreasing his vision. He *was* pain.

Smells and sounds attacked him. Unfamiliar and terrifying. Where was he? He couldn't see. His skin folded, and the cells inside his body popped like balloons attacked with an ice pick. He panicked and leaped for his best friend, but his feet remained in place. His muscles didn't move.

There was no way to freedom.

At the thought, Mercy's face flashed through his mind. He calmed, gathered his control. He was a Kyllwood, and he'd survive this.

A blade flashed. Squinting, he tried to see it. Garrett held a sharp silver knife, lifted it, and swiped the blade across his left palm. Blood, sweet and pure, scented the air.

Pain cut hard and deep through Logan's palm, and he looked down to see an identical cut. Garrett stepped even closer, and his boots burned off, but he held up his hand with the palm dripping blood to the earth. An offering of sorts. Logan's arm moved on its own, palm up, and he caught Garrett's blood on it.

Garrett's eyes closed and he said something, but the void ripped the words away.

The earth rumbled and roared, quaking. Garrett moved away, and Ronan took his place, slicing his hand and creating an identical cut, somehow, on Logan. They repeated the ritual, and then Benny and Adare took their turns. Finally, blood from all four mingled with Logan's on his palm.

He tipped his head and drank without thought. Raw nails cut down his throat, the feeling true agony. How could this be good?

The blood on his hand bubbled, turning black, digging into the cuts. He gasped and dropped to his knees. Blades pierced his ribs from inside, heating them until they glowed beneath his skin. Unimaginable pain, too deep to be called pain, overtook him.

He opened his mouth to scream, but there was no sound. Then he flew away, ripped out of this reality with the force of the wind.

His body continued to burn, but he left it, only feeling echoes of the pain. A force shot him from one place to the next too fast for him to catch his breath. Hot places, cold, painful, pleasurable. Different gravities and different atmospheres. At first he was too stunned to react, and then thought returned.

The Viking. He had to find the Viking.

Could he stop this wild ride? Remembering Mercy's words, he drew on the forces inside himself. "Stop!" he bellowed.

Instantly, he dropped out of cool air into a blast of heat, smashing into a series of rocks that pierced his legs. Gasping in pain, he sat up, covered in blood. But his actual body was back in that chamber. Sure as shit didn't feel like it. This hurt.

Planting his damaged palm on a rock, he pushed himself to his feet. The atmosphere pushed back, heavier than he was.

"Damn it to fuck," growled a mangled voice.

He jumped around to see a massive male covered in bruises and cuts storm toward him, fury across his face. His familiar face. "Quade Kayrs," Logan whispered, his voice unrecognizable.

Quade reached him, grabbing his burned arms and shaking him. "What the fuck are you doing here?"

Logan's vision fuzzed, and he shook his head. "Ritual."

Quade breathed. "Yes. But you should not be here." He looked up as the sky cracked, opening to an abyss. "This place is about to explode. Get out. Now."

Logan shook his head, trying to remain standing. His legs felt like they were gone. "Ivar. The Viking. Is he here?"

Quade blinked, his eyes so dark they'd turned black. "Viking? A thousand years ago. He didn't make it back?"

"No. Just last week. He's been gone a few days." Logan swallowed, and dust coated his throat. He coughed.

Quade shook him. "Ivar was here a millennia ago. Time is different here. Faster." The sky cracked again in several places like a shattered eggshell. "Go. Get out." Without waiting for an answer, he shoved Logan off the cliff.

Logan yelled, swung his arms, and plunged through a swirling mass of energy.

He landed in a place worse than the last, where icicles pointed at him from every direction. One pierced his foot, and he snarled, looking around. White and quiet and frozen. The chill carved into his skin with a pain too sharp to withstand. He knew the way out. Instinctively, he knew how to jump back to the chamber and end this.

But the Viking was near. *The Seven.* Logan closed his eyes and imagined the Seven. Warriors bonded in blood and bone. Even from this distance, he could feel their bond. Seven portals opened in the ice, all dark, all leading somewhere more painful than this. He imagined Ivar's face, sensed his spirit.

Gathering his strength, Logan leaped through the center portal. Into hell.

* * * *

Mercy felt the moment when Logan's essence left this plane. A sense of being ripped down the middle assaulted her, and she took several deep breaths to banish the pain. He was in agony, and she could feel it. The fresh Kyllwood marking on her skin beat with the force of a heart hammering. Logan's heart. In exact harmony with hers.

She didn't know where he'd gone, but she had to find him.

Lifting her arms, embracing the universe, she leaped out of this dimension and into the next, forcing herself to stop quickly.

The air was pure, the gravity light, the smells delicious. She opened her eyes to a grassy meadow surrounded by bubbling brooks. It was one of her favorite dimensions, and oddly enough, a jumping point into more worlds than she could count. Niall had beaten her there.

He turned as a portal closed behind him.

She blinked. "Who just went through?" While many of the Fae could hop dimensions, only a few of them could control the where and when. Why was Niall right there?

He strode toward her through the soft grass, his bruises healed, his body strong again. "The Seven are conducting their ritual right now. It has already sent vibrations through a million universes. Probably more."

"I know," she said quietly. "It's too late to stop it. We have no choice but to work with the Seven." They had an unnatural strength, and she'd have to figure out how to use that to protect the world. At this point, there was no alternative. God, she hoped Logan survived. Was he hurting too badly? Her chest heated, and she calmed herself. There had to be a way to help him.

Niall lifted his head, exhaling deeply. Fury crackled from him, disturbing the calm atmosphere. "You mated him?" His voice was high and loud.

The scent of Logan was all over her. "I did. You and I were never meant to be." She frowned. "But we have known each other a long time, Niall. Few of us have survived through the years, and we're both Fae. We both want what's best for our people." She wanted to punch him in the face again for his attack, but her people came first. "Help me stop this war."

"It's too late." Red suffused his face.

"What have you done?" she asked, her stomach quivering. Was Logan in even more danger than she'd thought?

Niall grabbed a weapon from his back pocket. "I've won. Like always."

"Wait." She held up her hands. If he tased her, she'd be stuck here for days. While they'd never been intimate, and he'd pretty much turned into an asshole last time, they were still of the same people. This was her king. "Niall. What are you doing?"

"I gave you an order, and you disobeyed it. That's treason." He aimed the gun.

Her temper blew. "You're overstepping your authority." Her voice shook, she was so angry. "You're nothing more than a figurehead.

The president is our leader. She is the one who put you in place, and she's the one I answer to."

"Not anymore. I rule our people." The ambition he'd always shown had turned darker. More intense. "My path is the right one. The Seven must be stopped for good."

"I won't let you hurt Logan," she said, her head reeling.

Niall shook his head. "How could you choose him? I'm your king."

"Someday you'll fall in love, and you'll understand," she said, trying to be gentle when all she wanted to do was kick him again.

"You're not in love." Niall aimed at her. "You're just looking for excitement like you always have. Jumping in headfirst, and this time with the enemy. You've chosen the wrong path, that of a traitor."

She didn't know the right path, but she had to pick a side. Heck. She'd chosen a side the second she'd mated Logan. Her legs bunched, and she gathered energy. The second Niall fired, she backflipped into the air and dove into another dimension.

He followed her, breathing down her neck. She caught her breath and jumped again, leading him on a chase through too many dimensions to count.

She was good, but she'd already jumped three times that day, once when carrying Logan. The guy weighed a ton, even when the universe took over.

But she had to find him. She jumped from dimension to dimension, trying to find familiar ones, until she felt an energy. A new one. Logan. Closing her eyes, she concentrated with all her strength and trusted the marking to help her find him.

She went through several more dimensions with Niall right on her ass. She couldn't outrun him.

He brought her down in an unfamiliar dimension. This one was filled with odd, froglike creatures on a pink carpet of what felt like velvet. She rolled and came up swinging, punching the gun out of his hand. It flew through the air to land on a frog. The reptile squealed and turned from green to red, rising on its hind legs and expanding to the size of a full-grown elephant.

Shit. Closing her eyes, Mercy leaped through another portal, having no clue where she was going.

Niall followed right behind her, and her limbs started to tire. Never in her life had she jumped this many times at once, and her heart rate began to slow alarmingly. Her blood was sluggish in her veins. Her muscles went lax.

Logan's smiling face filled her mind. So good and strong. She could find him. While jumping, she concentrated on the marking pounding against her flesh. *His* marking.

Going on instinct, using all that she had left, she jumped one more time.

Chapter 39

Logan plunged, falling fast and slamming into a sparkling diamond of a rock that threw him back in the air. This time he landed on his feet, bouncing slightly. The surface was covered with the odd rocks, while trees rose high and tall around him, their branches a deep crimson and covered in spikes. Thank God he hadn't landed on one of them.

A blast of energy filled the air, and a rush of wind hit him. He dropped to his belly out of instinct. Fire swept across the land, burning the trees, scalding his back, then disappearing.

Quiet reigned again. Until something roared in the distance, the sound so raw that chills rippled down his spine.

He had to get out of there.

His body ached, the pain a part of him now. Heaviness attacked his limbs. Exhaustion would soon take him. Yet he rolled to his side and looked at the trees.

A gap between two of them caught his attention. He glanced warily around for more fire, stood, and ran toward the gap. His legs moved in slow motion like a nightmare he'd had once about playing baseball and not being able to run the bases. He lowered his head and forged on, growling with the effort.

Finally, he bounced off the last mushy diamond and landed on hard-packed dirt. A spike caught his arm and ripped through flesh.

He ignored the newest pain and ducked to avoid more spikes.

A cave lay ahead. Energy ticked from it—faint and intermittent.

His back flashed hot and deep along every rib of his shield. "Ivar?" His senses tried to tune in to the energy, but the air was changing around him. Shit. Just as the blast of fire hit again, he dove headfirst into the cave, striking his forehead on a rock. A solid one. Flashes of light pierced the backs of his eyes.

The flames followed him in, burning the bottoms of his bare feet. Then they receded. Again.

He grunted and rolled to his side. A figure lay prone in the corner, curled around one of the diamond rocks. Logan tried to stand, but his legs wobbled. So he crawled, reaching the figure and pulling him over onto his back. Hope filled him, finally piercing the pain. His chest heaved. "Ivar?"

The Viking blinked, his face and body covered in burns and scars. One of his eyes was missing, as was his left hand. "Who?" He coughed, and blood bubbled from his mouth. Then he passed out again.

Logan dug deep and made himself stand, clasping Ivar's arm and pulling him up. "I knew I could find you." The agony of ducking a shoulder and lifting Ivar over it nearly dropped him to the ground again, but he staggered out of the cave, forcing his legs to keep moving. He'd found Ivar. Triumph sang through the agony in his head.

He bounced across the diamonds, letting them take his weight. Portal. They needed a portal.

One opened, and his heart leapt.

Then figures came through. First a Fae soldier, one he recognized from his attack on their headquarters. Then a Cyst dropped next to him. The Fae threw a sword to the Cyst.

Logan shook his head to focus. The Cyst was huge. At least seven feet tall with deep purple eyes. Fuck. He looked frantically around for another portal, but none opened. Could the Fae control that? Gingerly, he set Ivar down on the ground, hopefully flat enough that the fire couldn't get him.

Logan had nothing left. He'd never lost a fight in his life, but this might be the first.

By the smile on the Cyst's face, he knew it. "Logan Kyllwood. This will be a pleasure." He twirled the enormous sword as if it were a child's toy. "You know we make these special to decapitate the Seven?"

Yeah. Logan had heard. Though his torso was now solid and impenetrable, he was still vulnerable beneath his chin. His head could still be taken off with the right weapon. The Cyst had that weapon. "If you kill me, somebody will take my place."

"Maybe. Or not." The guy's medals showed he was a general with the Kurjans.

Logan studied him. "Xeno." Yeah, he'd seen a dossier. "The Kayrs family would like a word with you." Rumor had it Xeno had killed members of their family. "Why don't you go visit them?" His vision was graying and turning red at the corners.

"I plan to." Xeno took a fighting stance as the Fae soldier circled around Logan.

Where the hell was the portal? Any portal? Logan dug into the universe, trying to find an escape. His legs were about to give out, and then he wouldn't be able to protect Ivar.

The air swirled and a portal opened behind the Cyst general. Logan caught his breath. There was a chance.

Until Mercy and Niall dropped from the portal onto a diamond and bounced several times. She stopped moving, her eyes wide, her gaze seeking him. In his sweater and a pair of scratched brown boots, she looked small and fragile.

Everything in him, in the universe around him, went still. Even the pain disappeared.

A fury, way beyond any rage, quaked through him with a force that shot steel into his very bones. "What the hell are you doing here?" he yelled.

* * * *

The heat pouring from her mate was more intense than the oppressive air around her. She gulped and jumped away from Niall onto a weird sparkly and oddly bouncy rock. Logan stood with his legs braced and his body rigid. A male lay prone on the ground behind him. He'd found the Viking.

Logan glared at Niall. "I tased you."

Mercy coughed out the heated air. "We have defenses against our weapons. There's a taser that can reinstate the ability to teleport faster than waiting for nature to take its course." Though she'd heard it hurt like hell. Like having shock therapy.

Niall jumped to her rock while a Cyst soldier leaped between them and Logan.

She balanced on the mushy surface, feeling as if she was trapped on a heated bouncy ball. This was a strange freaking world. Jocko, a Fae soldier, drew a gun out of his back pocket. Crap. Another taser to stop teleporting. She gulped. "Let's all get out of here. Negotiate a truce," she said, hoping against hope.

Xeno turned and swung with the sword, aiming for her neck.

She yelped and dropped to the rock, bouncing up too quickly. The blade caught her boot and tore the leather. Logan roared and charged, hitting Xeno midcenter and crashing them both to skid across the rocks like skipping stones.

Niall lunged for her, and she rolled to the side, kicking her feet down and bouncing into the air to backflip toward the passed-out Viking.

Logan and Xeno rolled end over end, both throwing punches so quickly they could barely be seen. They hit a circular rock and flew in opposite directions. Soon blood covered the diamond rocks, and the combatants were slipping and sliding, somehow bouncing as well.

Logan landed near Jocko and grabbed him by the neck, using him as a shield. "Mate? Come here."

She tried to move his way, but Niall jumped in front of her.

"Get out of the way, or I end him," Logan snarled, his fangs dropping low, holding the Fae soldier a foot off the ground by the neck. Jocko struggled, his feet kicking, his face turning an unhealthy red.

"Do it," Niall said, angling his body to block Mercy.

Logan struck the back of Jocko's neck with his fangs, his fingers shoving beneath the Fae's chin at the same moment. Blood spurted, and Jocko's head bounced, landing several rocks away.

Mercy's stomach heaved.

Logan threw the body at Xeno, who blocked with a swipe of his massive arm, sending the corpse toward the burned crimson trees. It landed with a thump and twitched once before going still.

Bile rose in Mercy's throat, and she swallowed it down.

Logan partially turned, blood on his fangs, his shirt torn to reveal solid muscle. "Get away from her, Niall." The raw threat in his voice heated the already boiling air.

Mercy yanked two of the knives out of her boots. She tossed one at Logan, who caught it easily. Then she circled Niall. Why hadn't she spent more time learning to fight with weapons? He shook out his hands, dropping into a fighting stance, his muscles knotting.

Xeno bellowed and ran at Logan, sword out. Logan pivoted and flew into motion at Xeno, his arm up with the blade. They collided with enough force to send a ripple through all of the sparkly rocks. Mercy locked her knees to keep her balance, nearly falling on her face.

She kept her knife at the ready. "I don't want to hurt you."

Niall dropped to a crouch and then stood, withdrawing a weapon from his boot. He shot before she could blink, and the taser tore into her, electrocuting and burning her nerves. She gasped and absorbed the pain, dropping to her knees. Then she lifted her head, even though her neck muscles had gone soft. "You have *got* to be kidding me." Drool slid out of her mouth. The asshole had another taser?

Her energy sputtered out. She was stuck here.

Logan and Xeno fought fiercely, sword to knife, parrying across the strange rocks and colliding to punch and kick, spraying blood all over the diamonds.

They moved nearer.

Mercy gathered her strength and rushed Niall with the knife. He blocked her, smashing down and knocking it from her hand. Her strength was gone. The taser had loosened her limbs. She could barely remain upright, but she faced him, trying to gather enough power to punch him in the nose.

Still fighting with Xeno and drawing nearer, Logan yelled her name.

A rush of air burst over her skin. She paused.

"Drop!" Logan bellowed.

She obeyed instantly, hitting the diamond rock and bouncing. Xeno rolled toward her just as Niall dove down, manacled them both, and dragged them painfully through space.

The last thing she heard was Logan roaring her name before darkness took her completely.

Chapter 40

Logan dove for the Viking and shut his eyes, trying desperately to open a portal. The fire burned over his back. The rock opened up and they fell through, landing in the center of the circle back on Earth.

His heart thudded and his body felt like it had been through a cement mixer. He groaned.

Strong hands grabbed him, and Garrett leaned close, his eyes worried. Sweat coated his face. "You alive?"

"Barely." Logan didn't protest as Garrett hauled him up, rushing him out of the chamber while Adare threw Ivar over his shoulder and followed.

The air cooled up the trail, and finally they stood outside in the snow. It was fucking heavenly. Logan looked at the members of the Seven. His brothers and the warriors who would save the world. God, he hurt. But he shook his head. "I have to get to Mercy." Niall had her, and he was with the Cyst. God, he had to hurry. "Need to breach Fae headquarters again in Scotland."

Garrett nodded. "Then that's what we'll do."

Adare grunted under the weight of Ivar, who looked even worse off than he had before. Burned almost beyond recognition. "I have two choppers en route. Need to get this guy to safety."

Logan struggled to contain his panic. Ronan's mate was a doctor, and no doubt Adare needed to get back to his mate as well, even though supposedly he didn't like her. "We'll be in touch as soon as we can."

Benny slapped him on the shoulder. "What do you need from me?"

Logan leaned on Garrett, his mind spinning. "Enough of this shit. Gather up all the Fae you can find. Make them tell you the locations of the others—take them all to demon headquarters." He'd better call Zane and clear the mission from the helicopter. It was time to show the Fae that superior weapons couldn't beat sheer numbers. "I'll take the heat from the Realm."

The choppers came into sight.

Logan straightened. What he wouldn't give to be able to teleport. Of the Seven, only Adare could, and he was barely standing beneath Ivar's weight. The ritual had taken a toll on them all.

His vision went black and then slowly returned. Where was Mercy? Was she okay? He'd bet anything Niall had taken her to their headquarters—with the Cyst general. The fucking Fae didn't know they were dealing with monsters.

"You okay?" Garrett asked.

He nodded. He had to be, to get his mate. Zane or Sam would need to come teleport them. But he'd just done it—traveled through more dimensions than he could count. Something sparked along his legs. He drew energy from the earth itself—just like Mercy had told him to. He felt her energy all around him. Even inside him. They'd mated, and the effect was already changing him. "I think I can teleport there. You at my back?"

"Every time and always." Garrett wiped blood off his palm. "We took Fae headquarters easy enough before."

The choppers landed and they ran through swirling snow to jump inside. Benny and Garrett bracketed Logan on the seat as they quickly took off, waving to Adare in the other helicopter. Ronan and Ivar were already out of sight behind him, flat on the benches, no doubt recuperating.

Benny tossed Logan a headset as he grabbed his own and started barking orders.

Logan took a deep breath. He needed time to heal, but that was impossible. So he took precious moments to contact his brother, knowing he was asking for the biggest favor of all time. If this went south, and it probably would, he'd just plunged the demon nation back into war.

One the Realm might not join.

They reached his cabin in record time, and he and Garrett jumped out, giving Benny a salute. The crazy male nodded and zipped out of sight, arguing with the pilot over who should fly.

"Bad news," Garrett said, ripping the headset off. "The Realm satellites are busy watching the shifter nations. There's been movement, and we can't focus the satellites on Scotland."

"Movement by the shifters?" What a disaster. Logan strode toward his cabin with his left leg numb. "They won't declare war."

"Hope not," Garrett said, striding up the steps. "We'll have to go in blind to get her."

Wouldn't be the first time. Logan paused on the deck and turned to face his best friend. Garrett was too loyal sometimes. Logan had never teleported before and could plant them on the moon. "This is too much. I can go in alone."

"Shut up." Garrett brushed past him, pausing to look at the rushing river. "Just don't drop us on a bear or anything."

Logan tried to heal the cuts on his arm, but they remained open and bleeding. It was a damn good thing his torso was fused and shielded. At least his organs were safe. "All I can say is that she'd better be there."

Garrett's gray eyes sobered. "Having a mate seems to be a lot of work."

"I'm sure you'll find out soon enough." Logan tried to force his leg to feel, but the numbness remained.

"Not a chance." Garrett scrubbed his hands down his shirt and over the scorch marks from the heated chamber. "We'll have to suit up in Scotland. I've already called in for supplies." He looked up. "Assuming we make it safely."

Logan paused, even though everything hurt. "Thanks, G." There was a lot more he wanted to say, a thank-you for friendship and brotherhood, a promise of loyalty always, but the words stuck in his throat.

"No problem." Garrett eyed him. "Same here."

Good enough. Their first interaction had been to punch each other so hard and fast that they'd demolished a cabin in the middle of nowhere, blowing out a wall. They'd soon become friends, then brothers-in-law, and finally brothers.

Logan clapped him on the arm. "You ready?"

"Fuck no." Garrett settled into a fighting stance, obviously expecting trouble.

Logan exhaled, and his torso felt heavier than usual. Was he just tired, or was this a result of the bonding? He shook off his thoughts and shut his eyes, drawing on the power around him and focusing on the hills of Scotland.

Pain zipped up his legs and over his abdomen. The deck disappeared, and they were flying, landing in the middle of a lake. Shit. He tightened his hold on Garrett and tried again, landing three other places before finally falling on his face outside of Edinburgh Castle.

Garrett landed on his knees and hauled them both to their feet. "Only you could find a nudist colony in Antarctica." He shivered. "From what I saw, it was way too cold to be naked."

Logan's head spun, but he stayed on his feet. His heart pounded, and the marking on his palm burned. He could feel her energy, and he thought it had drawn him right here and now. She'd directed him here somehow. He rose to his full height. "She's close."

"Good." Garrett pulled him past a crowd looking at them like they'd dropped out of nowhere, which they had. "Let's suit up and get your girl."

* * * *

Mercy landed in the president's office, her body hurting so badly she didn't have the energy to groan. She'd reached out to Logan with all her senses.

Had he caught her message? Was he coming after her?

She dropped into a guest chair, the smell of burned everything all over her. Then her eyes focused. "What the hell?" The president was tied to her chair, fury in her dual-colored eyes, a gag in her mouth.

Niall stood and looked around, his eyes wide.

Xeno punched him in the face and he went down, out cold. One punch. Just one. Mercy shook her head. The general smiled with yellowed teeth. "You've failed to stop the ritual."

The president struggled against her bindings, making grunting noises.

"She wouldn't shut up," came a voice from the door.

Mercy partially turned, her head aching, to see another Cyst soldier standing there. His gaze ran over her ripped and torn clothing, and his eyes burned hot.

She shivered.

"Status?" Xeno asked, sliding his sword into a scabbard at his waist.

"We've tased them all, starting with their president," the soldier said, standing straighter. "None of the fairies can teleport from here. We're rounding them up worldwide as we speak."

Mercy looked for a way out, but her body felt like a wet noodle. Where was Logan? Had he escaped the horrible fire? She wanted to cry, but there wasn't time. She had to get herself under control and rescue her president.

"Good." Xeno dismissed the soldier with a wave of his broad hand. "Stand guard outside the door." He brushed soot off his dark uniform, frowning at the blood still coating his arms. Then he went to the president and removed the gag. "I apologize for the rough treatment."

She pulled against the restraints tying her arms to the chair. "Release me. Right now."

"No," Xeno said, leaning in to smell her. "I give the orders."

The president's eyes widened, but her jaw firmed. "Back away, mutt." She eyed Mercy, barely raising an eyebrow.

Mercy shook her head. No, she couldn't teleport. But she tilted her head toward Niall, who still hadn't moved. She nudged him with her foot, as subtly as she could. He didn't even twitch.

The president's face cleared.

The door opened, and a tall male with red-tipped black hair strode inside. His skin was pasty-white, his eyes greenish-purple, and his lips blood-red. "Xeno. Did you take care of Kyllwood?"

"Unfortunately, no." Xeno pointed at Mercy. "I did bring his mate, however."

She shivered but kept her face stoic, facing the Kurjan. Should she know him? He obviously wasn't afraid of Xeno. "We're supposed to be allies," she said.

"You're no longer useful to us." The Kurjan looked over at the president. "Though you're not mated. Yet."

The president lowered her chin and glared.

Mercy straightened. "Who are you?"

The male looked at her. "My name is Dayne, and I rule the Kurjan nation. We allied with you to stop the Seven, and since you failed to do that, you have nothing we need." He glanced back at the president. "Except potential mates. Your abilities would be useful to us."

Irritation clawed through the fear. "What is up with all the breeding plans?" She let anger fill her face and then kicked Niall in an effort to wake him the hell up. "I assure you that we're not interested."

"Your opinion means little to me." Dayne looked down at Niall. "That the king?"

Xeno nodded.

"He's the one who teleported you?" Dayne asked.

"Yes," Xeno said. "Brought me back, and I knocked him out. He's irritating and whiny."

"Interesting." Dayne pulled a taser from the back of his waist, aimed, and hit Niall in the leg. Niall's body jerked several times, and blood dripped from his ear. "Bet you forgot to tase him."

Xeno lifted one white eyebrow. "You know, I did forget." He looked at Mercy and smiled, his fangs glistening. "Though apparently others did not."

Bollocks. Now Niall couldn't get the president out of there. Mercy had dropped her knife in the blast of fire. She looked around for a weapon. Anything she could use to get free. The fireplace poker looked heavy. She could ram it through Xeno's throat. Maybe?

Something exploded in front of headquarters, shaking the entire castle. The chandelier swung wildly, and Mercy's heart jumped hard. Was Logan there?

Shouts and screams of pain filled the silence along with gunfire and several more explosions.

"Lord? You should take your leave," Xeno said grimly, drawing his sword.

Two Cyst soldiers rushed inside and slammed the door, taking up defensive positions, guns in hand and swords at their waists.

Dayne nodded. "Let's go. Bring her." He waved carelessly at the president and strode for the back door, shoving it open to reveal a Blackhawk waiting on the wide lawn. The second he appeared outside, it lit up, revealing two pilots already in place and ready to fly.

Xeno looked at his soldiers. "No quarter. Kill anyone who challenges you." He turned toward the president and ripped her bindings apart.

Mercy launched herself at the fireplace poker and swung it at his head as hard as she could. "Run!" she yelled at the president, hitting him again and trying to shove it through his throat.

The president scrambled for a letter opener, slicing it toward Xeno.

Mercy yanked the poker free and struck him again, simultaneously kicking at his balls. "President Dawn, please go," she screamed, trying to hold Xeno off. "You have to survive." The president was needed to lead their people, and she had to get her ass out of there. "Go. Please."

The president faltered, then nodded, turning and running outside and away from the helicopter.

Xeno roared, his fangs dropping. He shoved Mercy in the shoulder, and she careened across the office to collide with the fireplace. Pain exploded down her side, and she fell to her butt. He ran outside after the president.

Mercy's stomach heaved, but she forced herself to stand, facing the two Cyst soldiers.

The sound of a heavy boot hitting the door came right before the wood cracked in two. Logan Kyllwood burst inside and took one soldier down while Garrett followed in pursuit of the other. They were fast and brutal in their attack.

The helicopter rose outside.

Mercy remained still, unable to move. The immortals fought hard, but soon the Cyst soldiers were dead.

Logan rose, bloody and battered, his eyes a furious hue. "Hello, mate."

Chapter 41

Logan helped Mercy into the private plane, his temper nowhere close to being appeased. "You flying?" he asked Garrett.

Garrett glanced from Mercy to Logan. "Yep. I'll be up with the pilot." He tapped his ear comm. "The Fae have been rounded up and are being flown to demon headquarters in a Realm 747. We should beat them there by an hour or so." Then he made himself scarce.

Logan shut the door and nudged his mate into a seat. Every bone in his body hurt, but that pain was nothing compared to the raging ache in his temples. "You have one minute to explain to me how you ended up in a fucking hell world when I told you to return to my cabin."

The plane rushed down the runway and he took the seat next to her before he fell on his ass. His strength was nowhere near back. But as her gardenia scent filled his head, his blood started to pump faster. He allowed her to remain silent until they had ascended and the plane leveled off. Then he waited.

She crossed her arms and looked straight ahead, at a flat-screen television big enough to be viewed from all six leather seats.

"We need to talk," he murmured, feeling his legs starting to heal. Finally.

"No." Her mulish response failed to amuse him this time.

He reached for her, lifting her with one hand to straddle him. She planted both hands on his chest and pushed, trying to jump off his lap. "Settle," he ordered, keeping her in place until she stopped struggling. Now they could talk. He relaxed a fraction—and thus didn't see the punch to the neck coming until she landed it.

Pain charged up into his head, and his temper roared. He grasped her biceps and partially lifted her, drawing her within an inch of his face. "Do that again."

She blinked, her eyes flashing yellow and then back to the blue and green. Her nostrils flared. "No."

"Smart choice." Apparently they needed to start with the basics. "No hitting, no kicking, and no fucking teleporting into hell dimensions."

She lifted her chin. "Don't be stupid enough to get hit or kicked." She leaned the final inch, her nose almost touching his. "And if I have to teleport into hell dimensions to be of use, then that's what I'll damn well do."

Her words struck him. She'd said something similar before, and he thought he'd been clear with her. Awareness competed with the fury in him. "Sweetheart? You are more than enough just being you. You matter—without having a so-called use."

She blinked. Then leaned back and away from him. Vulnerability shimmered for the briefest of seconds in her eyes. "I, but…" Her voice trailed off.

He could picture her as a little girl among those ten kids, needing to have a function. How could she not see her value lay in her kind heart and big brain? Not to mention her sense of loyalty and fairness. He'd need several lifetimes to prove her worth to her, and that was fine with him. But first, he had to keep her alive. "You're more than enough for both your people and me, Mercy."

A slight pink filled her cheeks.

He tried to find a gentle way to explain the rest. "You're my mate. That means your safety comes above all else—and that's nonnegotiable." There. That was fucking gentle.

Her fine brows slanted down. "I disagree."

He smiled, and by the widening of her eyes, it wasn't a pleasant sight. Good. He was starting to feel unpleasant again. "How so?" he asked softly, his blood pounding.

She swallowed. "Well, if you're in danger, then I am, too."

Sweet. Very sweet. "Wrong."

Her mouth opened and closed. Her frown deepened. "Right."

Okay. They could go back and forth all day. The feel of her thighs against his and her core right above his suddenly aching cock was making polite discussion impossible. "I'm a soldier, you're not. I'm trained, you're not." He kissed her hard on the mouth. "I fight, you don't."

"Me Tarzan, you Jane," she muttered.

He barked out a laugh. How could she make him laugh when he was still pissed off? "God, I love you."

Her chin dropped to her chest, surprise lightening her expression. It was completely unguarded for the first time. "You do?"

His heart rolled right over and gave up. "Yes. Completely. All of you."

She smiled, delight on her entire face. "I love you, too."

Yeah, he'd figured. She had come after him into a hell dimension.

She hopped happily on his lap. "Well then. I guess that gives me the power."

Ah, she was cute. And about to learn different. He stood, his hands on her ass, and headed for the bedroom in the rear of the plane. "You think so?" he asked mildly.

* * * *

Mercy wanted to purr. He loved her. Actually loved her. The pleasure blooming inside her was only slightly dimmed by a warning in the back of her head. Should she have joked about power? They crossed into the bedroom, which held an ultralarge bed and not much else. He shut and locked the door, still holding her aloft. She nipped his chin, enjoying the salty taste of his skin.

"You going to show me who's boss?" Why the heck wouldn't her mouth just be quiet?

"Yes." He didn't smile.

A quiver started in her abdomen and spread out, lighting her nerves. Her breath caught, and her body hummed. "Um."

"Too late for um." He set her down and tore off his shirt, revealing that wickedly strong chest. His front looked the same—big and powerful and badass.

She motioned for him to turn. "Let me see."

He paused, and then turned around, revealing the intricate darkness of the shield that made up his back. It took her breath away.

As did he. He turned back around, his hands already going for her. "I want my sweater back." The raveled fabric joined his shirt somewhere on the floor, leaving her naked.

Cool air brushed across her bare skin. Her nipples sharpened.

His inhale was quick and hot. "I can teleport now." He reached out and ran a finger down the center of her chest. "Know what that means?"

The blood rushed inside her head. She palmed the ridges of his abs. "You're gifted?"

"I can catch you if you run." He twisted a hand in her hair, spiraling sparks of erotic pain all the way down her spine. "And you don't want to run again. Tell me you get me."

She didn't want to give in, but she definitely wanted to have him. And since the guy loved her, she should probably reassure him. Nobody had loved her before, that she could remember. "All right. I won't rush into danger unless necessary." See? She could totally be reasonable.

He moved in, fast and sure, lifting her and swinging her around. Her stomach hit his thighs before she realized he'd put her over his knee.

"Are you kidding me?" She kicked out, more surprised than anything else.

His hand landed with a hard smack that vibrated through her entire lower body, making her even wetter than before. "What in the hell are you doing?" she groaned, not nearly as forcefully as she wanted.

He twirled her, setting her to straddle him. "Anything I want to. Are you understanding?"

Her hair flopped into her face, and she tossed her head, trapped by his gaze. She'd always been excellent at figuring out puzzles. Her tingling butt and throbbing sex made it hard to concentrate, but she tried. "You're saying you're bigger and stronger and more dangerous."

"And?" Okay. A whole lot of arrogant, too.

She curled her nails into his shoulders, loving the feel of his warm skin. "And that your main goal, for some inexplicable reason, is to keep me safe."

"Yes. How am I going to do that?" His lips were so firm and kissable—even when in a straight and rather bossy line.

She sighed. "Any way you have to. I get it. Safety first."

He twirled her again, she landed on her stomach, he slapped her ass, and put her back into position facing him. The demon was truly economical with his movements. "Lose the smart-ass attitude," he ordered.

She laughed, unable to help herself. He truly didn't want anything from her other than for her to be safe and with him. For the first time in way too long to remember, she didn't have to prove herself. She also had no doubt he'd do whatever he had to do to keep her safe. Logan Kyllwood didn't bluff. Pushing him would be a mistake. "I'll stay safe, Logan." Unless he was in dire danger and needed her. Then she'd do what was necessary. She smiled.

His eyes glittered as if he saw right through her.

Butterflies winged along her nerves. He did see her. All of her. She'd run circles around people for so long, it was intriguing to be loved by him. "I'm not the obedient type," she said, wanting to be honest.

"No shit," he retorted, his hands caressing her flanks, gliding over each rib to her hips. "I'm not the bossy type."

That was so untrue it was laughable. She bit her lip, amusement mingling with arousal. "Uh huh."

"So on the rare occasion when I give an order, you obey it." He nibbled along her jawline to nip at her ear. "Got it?"

She sighed, leaning into him.

He pulled back, his gaze on her, his face serious even with lust glittering in his eyes. "Tell me you get me."

She saw him then. All of him. "You're enough on your own, too." Since he'd reminded her, it was fair she did the same.

"What?" His hands tightened on her hips.

"This shield thing you have going on. Protecting me, protecting your family, protecting the Realm. You matter just as much as everyone else." She smoothed over a bruise on his rib cage. "I love you for you." And she owed him a promise, even if he'd given her no choice in it. "I'll be safe. But you have to be safe, too."

"It's a deal." His gaze warm, he stood and set her down before kicking off his jeans. Then he covered her, his erection hot and full against her.

She lifted her knees, wanting him. All of him. So she grasped him, stroked once, and pressed him to her opening. "Don't make me wait."

He shoved inside her all the way to the hilt, shocking her with a fine pain edged by swamping pleasure. He began to move, and she dug her fingers into his shoulders, holding on tight. He kissed her, his tongue taking control as quickly as his body did.

This time, he wasn't holding anything back.

Fast, deep, and hard.

He looked down at her, powering himself into her, his features tight with hunger. Nothing else existed except right here and right now. The marking on her back warmed, spreading tingles throughout her entire torso and straight to her heart. He pinned her in place with his glittering gaze as much as he did with his warrior's body.

Her heart burst with a fierce warmth. He was the most amazing male in the universe, and he was hers. Intense and beautiful—protective and possessive.

"You're mine, Mercy O'Malley," he said, proving it.

She could only nod, holding on with all she had. Wrapping her legs around his waist, she tried to take even more of him. Lightning zapped through her, and she broke without warning. She came hard, her body shaking, her heart thundering.

Before she could catch her breath, he grabbed her butt and tilted her, giving him deeper access.

How was it even possible? She cried out as he took her higher, giving her no choice but to climb the pinnacle again. "Logan," she moaned. "Too much. I can't."

"You will." His fangs flashed, and he scraped them along her neck. The feeling was so wickedly decadent, so inherently dangerous, that a quaking started deep inside her. Again.

Then they pierced her, right where her neck met her shoulder.

He rode her hard, and that quaking turned into a full-out tidal wave. She cried out his name, shutting her eyes, trusting him to protect her. Only then did he let himself go, thrusting one last time inside her, so deep she thought she would die, then going still, shuddering with his release.

She wrapped her arms around his shoulders and held on with the small amount of strength she had left. Then, with him still inside her, she dropped right off to sleep.

Chapter 42

Realm headquarters was stationed about five miles from demon headquarters at a private lake in Idaho. Mercy paced a small waiting room in the main lodge after Logan had kissed her and left her, promising to be back shortly. She'd already showered, and Logan had found clothing for her. Gray pencil skirt, white shirt, and yellow wedges. Just her style.

Two soldiers were stationed outside the doorway, and added to the six others she'd noticed in the lodge, she figured she was damn well protected.

And not going anywhere.

She thought back to every interaction she'd had with Logan. He was always between her and danger. And when Garrett was around, she was always positioned between them. Protected by the most dangerous warriors in history.

Damn if that didn't make her feel a little bit special.

The room held a sofa, two overstuffed chairs, a coffee table and a stunning oil painting of a mountain range. The door opened, and President Alyssa Dawn strode in.

Mercy rushed to her, enveloping the woman in a hug. "I'm so glad you're alive."

The president patted her back. "Of course. I owe you my life."

Mercy released her, heat flying into her face. The president wasn't an overtly affectionate person, although she was a hell of a leader. "What now?"

"I don't know." The blonde straightened her shoulders. She wore a blue suit, complete with dangerous red high heels, her hair up in a pearl clip.

"Well, they found us nice clothing," Mercy mused. "So they can't be planning on killing us." Or rather, the president. No way would Logan leave Mercy if she were in any danger. "I have to think that the Realm nations want to ally themselves with us." Man, she hoped so.

"Where is our king?" the president asked.

As if on cue, the door opened, and Logan shoved Niall inside. "Your king has an announcement," he said, taking up the entire doorway.

Niall wore a perfectly cut blue suit, but his hair was mussed and his lip was split. He inched gingerly into the room as if every movement hurt. "I have decided that the monarchy will return to a figurehead type of position, and I would like to devote myself to research."

Mercy's chin dropped and she gave Logan a look.

"What?" he asked, looking devastating in faded jeans and a green button-down shirt that brought out the myriad of colors in his eyes and stretched intriguingly across his large chest.

She tapped her foot, trying to find anger. Nope. Just amusement and a lot of gooey love.

"He put his mouth on you," Logan said, his gaze completely lacking in amusement. "The bastard, excuse my language, President, is lucky he's still breathing. Right, Niall?" He slapped the king on the back, and Niall leaned over, coughing.

The president's red lips twitched. "Agreed."

"Excellent." Logan shoved Niall across the room. "Soldiers will be here to escort you back to your people in a few moments. We have them put up, quite safely and comfortably, at demon headquarters." He smiled. "Ladies? If you would please come with me."

Mercy allowed the president to go first and then followed, noting that Logan waited until she passed to shut the door, covering her back.

A soldier in front of the president led the way to the same conference room as before. King Dage Kayrs and King Zane Kyllwood sat on one side, while she and the president sat on the other. Logan stood right behind her chair, his warmth comforting.

Dage began. "When you aligned yourselves with the Kurjans and their Cyst faction, you essentially declared war on the Realm."

Mercy bit her lip.

The president remained quiet and cool, folding her hands on the table and looking as if she was out for a nice brunch. Amusement and pride filtered through Mercy. The Fae were just as tough as the rest of these immortals.

Zane nodded. "Then you released the long-held secret about the Seven, thus putting the entire universe in jeopardy."

Mercy watched them. They were calm and collected this time, and the atmosphere in the room was mellow. No tension.

Dage exhaled. "Your weapons are impressive, as are your defenses and ability to travel inter-dimensionally." For the first time, the King of the Realm smiled. She could hear hearts melting for miles. "I have to admit, before I met you, Mercy, I was starting to think fairies were as mythical as unicorns."

Mercy's eyebrows went up, and she shared a look with the president.

Dage frowned. "You don't mean to tell me..."

Mercy nodded. "Yep. I've seen them myself. Horns and all." Not in this dimension, of course.

"Huh." Zane looked over her head at his brother. "Did you see any unicorns?"

"Nope." Logan rested a hand on her shoulder, and she leaned back toward him. "I saw evil."

Dage's eyes darkened to a deeper silver. "Something to worry about another day. For today, President Dawn, we'd like to offer a treaty to the Fae nation. You become a member of the Realm and we exchange knowledge. You teach us how to make your weapons, and we'll train your soldiers."

The president smiled. "The Fae nation accepts." She turned to Mercy. "Thank goodness. Your loyalties can remain undivided." She winked.

Mercy stared. Had the president just actually winked? Talk about miracles. She placed her hand over Logan's on her shoulder, covering about half of it. "No matter what happened here today, my loyalties are undivided. They belong to Logan. Always."

The sound of his indrawn breath filled the air.

Zane smiled. "Welcome to the family, Mercy O'Malley."

Her heart filled with warmth and gushed over. She was family. She had brothers. Tears pricked her eyes, startling her. "Thank you." Her voice grew husky.

"One more thing," Dage said, shifting his weight. "A favor, if you will. Would both of you submit to blood tests?"

Zane barked out laughter, as did Logan behind her.

She turned to study her mate's handsome face. "What?"

He leaned down and kissed her. "The queen is a geneticist, and she is determined to learn all about immortal blood and maybe cure some human diseases in the process. It's much easier to just give her the blood. The woman will chase you with a needle if necessary."

Mercy turned back to Dage, who winced. "She really will. I'd count it as a personal favor if you'd stop by the lab before you leave today," the king said.

"Leave?" Mercy repeated.

"Yes," Logan said quietly from behind her. "While the Realm and Fae nations are apparently on the same page, the Seven has some work to do with the shifter and witch nations. We'll be back within the week, when Mom gets here for a celebration of our mating." His fingers firmed on her shoulders. "We'll go over a few guidelines first."

Guidelines? Mercy straightened. "I know the difference between a salad fork and a fish fork, Logan." How insulting, and unlike him. Was his mother a high-society snob?

He chuckled. "No. Not that kind of guideline. More like the guideline that if my mother asks you to rob a bank with her, you refuse. It's all I ask."

She blinked. "Your mother robs banks?"

"Yes," all three males in the room sighed simultaneously, their voices long-suffering.

Mercy smiled. Yeah. She could rob a bank or two. Why not?

"No." Logan tugged her out of the chair with a nod at the other males. "If you'll excuse us, I'd like to check in with Sam before we head out. You all can hammer out the details without us." He ushered her out of the room, taking her hand in his much larger one.

She tripped alongside him, glad to be out of the meeting. "I want to keep my job as chief investor for the Fae nation," she said. In fact, she had too much cash in their portfolio that wasn't generating a return.

"Sure." He cut her a smile. "Any chance you'll invest some of my holdings?"

"Definitely." She hopped twice. "What do you have?"

He shrugged. "I'll give you the account numbers, and you can go to town. I usually have the Realm experts invest for me, but you can take over any or all of it."

That trust warmed her as much as his love. They walked out of the lodge into a calm spring day. "You know? I'd like to learn to fight." How much fun could they have grappling on mats?

"Oh, you're going to learn to fight. Without question." He nodded to a couple of soldiers as they walked along a sidewalk in what appeared to be a normal high-end lakefront subdivision. If normal meant vampires, demons, and other immortals with unimaginable defenses. "We'll start training next week, once your powers are back and we're both healed."

She admired a planting of bright yellow tulips in front of a log-and-stone mansion. "You said I can't fight."

"No. I said you'll always be protected. Part of protection is making sure you can handle yourself if anything should ever go really wrong." He turned up the walkway of the next home, which had pink, purple, and white tulips growing in every direction.

He pushed open the door and escorted her inside.

"Hey." Sam Kyllwood looked up from reading a stack of papers while Hope played at his feet, running miniature cars over his boots. He stood, swung the girl in the air, and moved to hug his brother. "It's good to see you."

Logan hugged him back and took Hope to swing her around. "It's good to be seen. What's the word from the Seven?"

"The Viking doesn't remember much of anything, including any of us," Sam said. "But he did remember seeing Quade in a hell world, and now the rest of the members are determined to get him out of there."

Logan winced. "I agree. It was bad, Sam. I saw Quade and his world, and I can't even describe it. The horror of it. Is Ivar beginning to heal?"

"Not Ivar any longer," Sam said. "Said Ivar is dead, and he's Vike. Short for Viking?"

Mercy's heart hurt for the male. To be trapped in hell dimensions where one minute was an eternity was unfathomable. "We'll see him soon, Logan. Tonight." All of the Seven except for Quade in one place at one time. Would the universe feel a change?

"Any luck with your project, Sam?" Logan smacked a kiss on Hope's forehead and set her down.

She snorted and moved to Mercy, taking her hand. "Uncle Sam is looking for the sacred circle. That's his project."

Logan swung and cut a look at Sam. Sam shrugged. "I didn't tell her."

Hope sighed and drew Mercy further into the room. Her bright blue eyes sparkled with intelligence. "I know stuff I shouldn't. They worry. It's a thing."

Mercy chuckled, entranced by the young beauty. "Males do worry."

"They hafta do something, Auntie Mercy," Hope said, pulling her toward the sofa. "Worrying is better than smashing walls."

Mercy faltered. Aunt Mercy. She was an aunt to this precious little girl. She had brothers. And family. She wasn't alone. It was so much. It was everything. Her entire essence smiled. "I have two best friends named Sandy and Trina. You'll like them." She didn't have family to offer, but Sandy and Trina were pretty wonderful.

Logan somehow moved behind her and wrapped his arms around her waist. "Sandy and Trina are at demon headquarters, and we'll make sure they're invited to the party when we get back. You're more than enough all on your own, baby. I'm never going to let you forget that."

Hope giggled and went back to playing with her cars. "She's not a baby."

"She's mine," Logan said, kissing beneath Mercy's ear and sending shivers down her neck.

Hope looked up. "Then what are you going to call your real baby?"

Logan stiffened. "My real baby? Are we having a real baby?"

Mercy looked up at his face. He was deadly serious. Wait a minute? A baby? She focused on the brunette imp. "Are we, I mean—"

Hope snorted. "Not now. He won't be here for a while."

He. They were having a he. Someday. Mercy smiled. "Logan," she breathed. "Did you ever think life would end up like this?"

"I really did." His breath brushed the top of her head. "I knew someday, if I did my best, Fate would give me Mercy."

Read on for an excerpt from Rebecca Zanetti's next Dark Protectors novel, *ALPHA'S PROMISE*, available soon!

Across the windy cemetery, beyond the rows of gravestones, a man leaned against a pine tree and watched her. Even at that distance, the deep blue of his eyes cut through the day. He stood over six feet tall, his chest broad, his legs long. His gaze was so direct it felt almost physical, and it caught her off guard.

Dr. Promise Williams shivered and broke eye contact to focus in front of her.

Meager sunlight glinted off the coffin as it was lowered into the wet earth. The clouds had finally parted and stopped dropping rain on the mourners. She closed her umbrella and tucked it into her overlarge bag, noting the wet grass all over her smart boots.

"It was a nice service. Earlier, I mean," Dr. Mark Brookes said from her side, wiping his thick glasses on a handkerchief. He wore a tailored black suit with a striped blue tie, his eyes earnest and his thinning hair wet from the earlier rain.

Promise nodded, her stomach aching. The group standing around was mainly silent with a couple of soft sobs piercing the quiet. She knew all of them. Six professors, a dean, and two grad students. The earlier service had been packed with students, more faculty, and even the local press. This part of the day was reserved for family.

Dr. Victory Rashad hadn't had any family. Other than the faculty, of course.

The wind picked up, brushing across Promise's face. She shivered. Who did she have? If she died tomorrow, who would attend the burial part of her service? Reflexively, she looked toward the pine tree.

The man was gone.

Not a surprise. No doubt he'd just been checking out the assembled group to see what was going on. His focus hadn't been solely on her. She shook her head and tried to dispel the dread she'd been feeling since the police had found Dr. Rashad. The woman had been missing for nearly three days before her body was discovered—torn apart.

Who would do such a thing?

The gears of the lowering device stopped. "Well." Mark held out an arm, and Promise naturally slipped her glove into his elbow. "Would you like to get something to eat?" He turned and escorted her over the uneven ground to their vehicles parked on the silent road.

"Thanks, but I'd rather go home." She'd once attended an Irish wake where the family members drank into the next day, toasting the dead with stories. Tons and tons of stories, and all told with love. What was it about her world that lent itself to quiet services and maybe one toast? "Thank you, though."

Mark paused at her car and waited for her to unlock the door. "I hadn't realized you and Victory were close."

"We weren't," Promise said quietly, opening the door. Victory had joined the physics department at the university midsemester, and they'd only said hello at department meetings. That was it. Maybe a lunch or two in the cafeteria, but she didn't remember the details. "Are any of us close to anybody?"

Mark scratched his chin. "I am. Two brothers, both married with kids. In fact, Mike is having a barbeque this Sunday. I've been meaning to ask you."

"I should probably work." The idea of a happy family was too painful to think about right now. What was wrong with her?

"Okay." He waited until she sat before leaning over the open door. "Two dates, and now I'm not sure what's going on." His intelligent brown eyes studied her, while the too-musky scent of his cologne wafted in her face. "I'm thirty-five and don't have time for games, Promise. Are we going out again or not?"

She forced a smile. "No." He was a nice man, but she'd rather work with supersymmetry or cosmological inflation than spend time with him. Of course, who wouldn't? "I think we're better off as friends."

"Well. I do appreciate your honesty." His tone indicated that he did not, in fact, appreciate the truth. He straightened. "I'll see you Monday." He shut her door with extra force.

Cripes. Maybe the truth had been a mistake. She started the engine and pulled away from the curb, winding through the cemetery and wondering about Dr. Rashad. The police hadn't indicated any movement on the case, but she felt as if she should do something. Perhaps she'd call on Monday and ask for a status update.

She sped up slightly, and her doors locked. Her shoulders relaxed slightly. It had to be a coincidence that Dr. Fissure, a colleague from Great Britain, was also missing. She'd collaborated with him on a paper several years before.

The wind picked up, and rain splattered against the windshield again. Several roads spread out in different directions through the sprawling cemetery. She hadn't paid close attention when she'd driven in. How stupid of her. So she took the first left, allowing her mind to wander as she drove among the peaceful dead. She flicked on the wipers and turned down another road.

Suddenly, her passenger door was wrenched open, the sound of the damaged lock protesting loudly.

A man thrust himself into the passenger seat and slammed the door.

She reacted in slow motion. How was this happening? Her eyes widened, and she turned her head to fully face him. How had he broken the door lock of her new car? That quickly, she recognized him from his position at the pine tree earlier. "You were watching me."

"I was." His voice was low and mangled, gritty to the point of being hoarse. Those blue eyes were even darker inside the vehicle.

Adrenaline flooded her, and she finally reacted, slamming on the brakes and reaching for her door. Her seat belt constricted her, but she fought it, silent in her bid to escape him. He manacled one incredibly strong hand around her arm and yanked her back into place. "Drive."

Her shoulders collided with her seat back, and she opened her mouth to scream.

He pressed a gun into her rib cage.

Her scream sputtered into a whisper. She looked frantically around, but the road ahead and behind her was empty.

"I said drive," he repeated, no inflection in his hoarse tone.

She swallowed, and fear finally engulfed her. The sound she made was so much of a whimper that she winced. "My purse is on the floor. Take whatever you want and get out." Her voice shook almost harder than her hands on the steering wheel.

"I have what I want. Drive." The gun and his hold on it remained level. He took up more than his own seat, his arms and torso solid muscle. His face was hard and angled—cut in a way that almost looked unreal.

His words chilled her. How could she get free of him? She pressed the gas pedal again and drove among fresh graves, spotting the exit farther ahead. Her heart increased its force, and her ribs ached. "What do you want from me?" She held her breath.

"Just your brain," he said, the sound weary.

She jerked, turning her head to him again. "To eat?" she gasped.

He blinked. Once and then again. "No, not to eat." His perplexed reaction drew his cheeks up and his darker brows down. "Geez. To eat? Why would I eat your brain? That's just gross. Ick."

Her kidnapper had just said *ick* and looked at her as if she was insane. She eyed him with her peripheral vision so she could better describe him. At least six feet six, long, dark blond hair with brown streaks, handsome face. Kind of rugged but also sharp, with what appeared to be burn marks down his neck. Wait a minute. Her brain? Heat spiraled through her chest. "Did you want Victory Rashad's brain, too?"

"Yes."

Oh God. He was going to kill her. Panic took her again, and she slammed her foot on the gas pedal.

"Wait," he said, grasping her arm. "I won't hurt you. I'm here to help you."

Affirmative. Yes. The guy with the gun was here to help her. She ducked her head and floored the gas pedal, bumping out of the cemetery and speeding along the quiet road.

"Slow down," he hissed, his hold tightening enough to bruise.

She zipped around a corner and into traffic, driving as fast as she could.

He swore and grabbed for the key, which wasn't in the dash. She'd used the button. She swerved around a minivan and finally saw a police cruiser up ahead. Slapping at him, knowing if he got her out of the car she was dead, she took her chances with the gun.

Yelling, she slammed into the rear of the police cruiser.

Everything stopped for a second and then sped up. The crash was thunderous. Her passenger bellowed and flew through the window. The airbags deployed right into her face and propelled her back into the seat.

Pain smashed through her skull. She blinked, her ears ringing.

A police officer ran up and opened her door. "What in the hell?" he muttered, blood on his chin.

She gasped and shoved the airbag down. "Where is he?" she coughed, her eyesight blurry. Her assailant was sprawled on the pavement, blood on his face as rain pelted down. The other officer leaned over him, talking into a radio at his shoulder.

Then her would-be kidnapper jerked awake and leaped to his feet. Blood covered his face and his neck, while his left arm hung at an unnatural angle. He stood several inches taller than the officer. "Promise!" he bellowed.

She gasped. How did he know her name?

The cop tried to grab him, but he shoved the officer into the side of the car. Before the officer next to Promise could draw his gun, the kidnapper turned and ran into an alley.

The police officers quickly pursued him.

She panted, her mind buzzing, her body aching. He'd known her name. It wasn't a random kidnapping.

The police officers soon returned, both shaking their heads.

Oh God. He was gone.

About the Author

New York Times and *USA Today* bestselling author **Rebecca Zanetti** has worked as an art curator, Senate aide, lawyer, college professor, and a hearing examiner—only to culminate it all in stories about alpha males and the women who claim them. She writes contemporary romances, dark paranormal romances, and romantic suspense novels.

Growing up amid the glorious backdrops and winter wonderlands of the Pacific Northwest has given Rebecca fantastic scenery and adventures to weave into her stories. She resides in the wild north with her husband, children, and extended family who inspire her every day—or at the very least, give her plenty of characters to write about.

Please visit Rebecca at: www.rebeccazanetti.com

Facebook: www.facebook.com/RebeccaZanetti.Books

Twitter: www.twitter.com/RebeccaZanetti

Printed in the United States
by Baker & Taylor Publisher Services